FUTURE ON ICE

Tor Books by Orson Scott Card

The Folk of the Fringe
Future on Fire (editor)
Future on Ice (editor)
Lovelock (with Kathryn Kidd)
Pastwatch: The Redemption of Christopher Columbus
Saints
Songmaster
The Worthing Saga
Wyrms

THE TALES OF ALVIN MAKER
Seventh Son
Red Prophet
Prentice Alvin
Alvin Journeyman
Heartfire

ENDER
Ender's Game
Speaker for the Dead
Xenocide
Children of the Mind

HOMECOMING
The Memory of Earth
The Call of Earth
The Ships of Earth
Earthfall
Earthborn

SHORT FICTION
Maps in a Mirror: The Short Fiction of Orson Scott Card (hardcover)
Maps in a Mirror, Volume 1: The Changed Man (paperback)
Maps in a Mirror, Volume 2: Flux (paperback)
Maps in a Mirror, Volume 3: Cruel Miracles (paperback)
Maps in a Mirror, Volume 4: Monkey Sonatas (paperback)

EDITED BY ORSON
SCOTT CARD

FUTURE ON
ICE

TOR ®

A TOM DOHERTY ASSOCIATES BOOK
NEW YORK

FUTURE ON ICE

Copyright © 1998 by Orson Scott Card

This book is printed on acid-free paper.

A Tor Book
Published by Tom Doherty Associates, Inc.
175 Fifth Avenue
New York, NY 10010

Tor Books on the World Wide Web:
http://www.tor.com

Tor® is a registered trademark of Tom Doherty Associates, Inc.

Library of Congress Cataloging-in-Publication Data

Future on ice / edited by Orson Scott Card. —1st ed.
     p.   cm.
   "A Tom Doherty Associates book."
   ISBN 0–312–86694–1 (acid-free paper)
   1. Science fiction, American.   I. Card, Orson Scott.
PS648.S3F894   1998
813'.0876208—dc21   98–23524

First Edition: October 1998

Printed in the United States of America

0 9 8 7 6 5 4 3 2 1

CONTENTS

PREFACE

THIS BOOK WAS intended to be a companion volume to *Future on Fire*, together forming a collection of major stories by the most important writers of short science fiction in the 1980s. In dividing the stories into two books, I had no intention of ranking them—if there was any honor in having a story selected, it would be the same honor to be in either book.

But something happened between that intention and the present moment: eight years passed. During that time the stories in *Future on Fire* have borne that mark of approbation; these stories have not. And so despite my original intent, there has been a difference, and to the authors in this book I must apologize.

Because of the long hiatus, I am not the same person I was in January 1989, when I wrote the introductions to *Future on Fire* and to the stories in it. I have learned many things since then, affecting my comments on many of these stories. The world has also changed, so that the concerns of the 1980s can seem either prescient or irrelevant to a contemporary viewer. Indeed, what surprised me most in rereading these stories in order to comment on them was how well they held up. This reassures me about my judgment in choosing them in the first place; it also proves to me that the best science fiction of the 1980s had staying power.

Perhaps the most important change, for me, between January 1989 and February 1997, as I write these words, is this: eight years ago, I was a deeply involved member of the science fiction community, reading widely in the field, reviewing regularly, attending conventions and workshops, and corresponding with many writers in the field. Today, it has been at least five years since I last attended a science fiction convention in the United States. I gave up reviewing some years ago, and since then have read only a handful of science fiction novels that I did not write myself.

In some senses I am still definitely within science fiction: I write it, I know the traditions of the literature, and I draw on a great deal of experience with the community. In another sense, though, I am a complete outsider: I have no idea what has been happening in the field of written science fiction since about 1992. Whether this sharpens my ability to see science fiction truthfully or dulls it is for you to decide, as you read—or mercifully skip over—my introductions.

SCIENCE FICTION AND "THE FORCE"

IN THE WINTER of 1997, the rerelease of *Star Wars, The Empire Strikes Back,* and *Return of the Jedi* set box office records and restored George Lucas's masterworks to positions among the most-watched films of all time.

For me, there is a personal tinge to the burst of sci-fi nostalgia that the rerelease set off. When *Star Wars* first came out in 1977, I was an editor at the *Ensign* magazine in Salt Lake City, and fellow editors Jay Parry and Lane Johnson and I ducked out of work a couple of hours early to catch an afternoon showing on the first day. The three of us had been brainstorming science fiction ideas and reading each other's stories in an informal writing workshop during our lunch hours, and so it was natural for us to see this movie together. We loved it, of course, seeing our dreams brought to life in the first non-embarrassing special effects to be put in a gung-ho space opera (which is not to denigrate the "cooler" storytelling of *2001: A Space Odyssey*).

Part of the fun for me was something only my friends and I, in that audience, knew or cared about: I was about to be that miraculous thing—a *published* science fiction writer. My story "Ender's Game" had been purchased by Ben Bova at *Analog,* and would appear later that summer (the August 1977 issue, to be exact). Ben had bought three more stories as well, including "Mikal's Songbird," which would grow into the novel *Songmaster* only a few years later. So as I watched space opera made "real" on the screen, I had a sense of possession of it—I was a maker of such tales myself. When I look back on the twenty years since that first public showing of *Star Wars,* it seems only a moment ago—a moment that contains my entire career.

Lucas's changes in the current release are really not much. The changes in me, however, have altered the movie for me. I cannot watch with the unalloyed pleasure of my first viewing that afternoon in Salt Lake City. Ironically, because *Star Wars* was such a success, it ushered in an era of increasingly sophisticated science fiction films. Lucas marked out the route for later science fiction films to pursue, but *Star Wars* itself remains forever frozen at the starting line.

Besides, for twenty years I have been building stories myself, and now, like an experienced automobile mechanic, I can hear the grinding of the gears; I know when the machine is working smoothly, and when it's stuck together with gum or string. Indeed, that's part of the reason I finally stopped reading science fiction altogether—I'd get three pages into a pretty good book and I'd be saying to myself, Oh, it's one of these; oh no, he's using that one; too bad she didn't see a better way to get out of that problem. That was bound to affect my viewing of a grand old movie.

Then there's the problem of the Force. *Star Wars* is supposed to be science fiction, right? A rational extrapolation of the future, right? And yet in the midst of all the droids and aliens and whooshing spaceships, we find that the whole plot hinges on faith in an irrational, supernatural, Manichaean Force that can be invoked, more or less, by prayer, asceticism, sacrifice, and faith. It's no accident that Alec Guinness was costumed like a monk. The Jedi Knights are suspiciously like a combination of Jesuits and Knights Templar.

Well, why not? Despite the constant assertion that science fiction is a "rational" literary medium, the fact is that written science fiction, just like filmed science fiction, is intertwined with metaphysical and moral themes and story elements. The Force is not radically out of line with this tradition. Since the Manichaean philosophy of the Force (not to mention the Calvinism that drives the plot of the movie as a whole) is definitely not a religion I believe in, I accepted it as a mere plot device. Now, though, I must take it more seriously.

No, I don't believe in the Force any more than before (less, in fact!)—but I *must* take it seriously because, defying all rational prediction, somehow the Force has found a following. Large numbers of people take it seriously. And not just in the way that trekkies talk gravely about that manual-shift warp drive in *Star Trek* as if it could actually exist. I hear people talking about the Force as if *Star Wars* had revealed to them the real underpinnings of the universe. And I see an astonishing number of people at every level of society living the religion of *Star Wars*, whether consciously or not.

SCIENCE FICTION AS RELIGIOUS LITERATURE

RELIGION? FROM SCIENCE fiction? It would be hard to imagine a more determinedly areligious genre. Even in the most ludicrous of space operas, everything must have a rational explanation, or at least seem to. No one prays, or if they do, they certainly don't get an answer; if some god seems to be real, he is not supernatural, but rather turns out to be a supercomputer, a collective unconscious, discorporeal descendants of some ancient race, or . . . a Force. But not a supernatural god, and certainly not God, the deity of the Judeo-Christian tradition. Science fiction treats religion, explicitly or implicitly, as if it were a stage of human development that the species either has or by now should have outgrown.

Ironically, the lack of overt religion makes science fiction quite possibly the only genre of storytelling in which serious religious writing can take place today. Fifty years ago, Lloyd Douglas's Christian novels, and thirty years ago Taylor Caldwell's, could top the bestseller lists; today, openly religious writing is almost unfindable in mainstream bookstores, and compared to the religious fiction of the past, Christian fictions today are a poor, pious thing indeed. When mainstream fiction writers touch upon religion, it is almost invariably to depict religious leaders as cynical hypocrites and religious followers as mindless dupes. The rare exceptions—one thinks of Ann Tyler with *Saint Maybe* and Sue Grafton with the surprising turn in her recent *M Is for Malice*—deal rather well with religious people, but do not allow the possibility of divine intervention in their story. God can be worshipped, but he cannot act. Jewish writers have rather a better track record of including the religious side of life in their fiction, but almost all do so from an anthropological viewpoint: here is how religious people act. Aren't they interesting holdovers from a more primitive time? The air is thick with nostalgia.

In science fiction, on the other hand, religious *ideas* can be and often are explored with some depth. What is the purpose of life? Why are some human actions good and others evil? In a universe of entropy, what causes some to build, not just rage, against the dying of the light? I do not mean to imply that this literary community has any particular interest in tales devoted to advancing the agenda or propounding the doctrines of one sect. It is the deeply explored question that has value, though it must be said that the very asking of a question implies a multitude of assertions, for there must be a context in which the question is deemed to be worth asking.

And let me dispose right now of the standard anti-religious canard that religion is bad because of all the terrible things that have been done in the name of God. Since, until very recent times, there was no such thing on this earth as a community that did not have an official religion deemed to be universal or at least dominant (and I include

China in this, despite the wishful thinking of some Sinologists), even the most cursory examination of history will show that *every* awful act of any nation, kingdom, or people, as well as every good thing, was done in the name of their god or gods, or at least of superior virtue. And when we look at post-religious states (which, as I will show, are "postreligious" only as a propaganda ploy), such as the Soviet Union or Nazi Germany or Communist China, one is hard-pressed to see any improvement in human behavior when deities are removed from the religious mix. Religions sometimes provoke the worst sort of behavior—check out the Aztecs—but often nations that do horrible things do them because they ignore the tenets of their official religion even as they invoke the name of their god to sanction their atrocities. If anything, religion is often a meliorative influence; it was partly because the Spanish were "priest-ridden" that much larger populations of Indians survived in Spanish-held America than in areas conquered by European nations that lacked an institutional conscience.

So when I say that science fiction is a haven for religious literature, it is no accident that almost no one but me in the field is saying it—primarily because the word *religious* has something of a curse on it, and is studiously avoided by some of the writers whose fiction best exemplifies exactly the kind of serious religious writing that I'm talking about.

For several years I put on a one-man show at various SF conventions called "The Secular Humanist Revival Meeting." While I opened it with the standard religion-bashing pose, making fun of revival-style preaching, by the end it was quite clear that I was speaking about religion as a believer in a particularly demanding faith. And yet the audience moved along with me. Over the year many hundreds of people made the effort to tell me, in person or by mail, how they appreciated the revival meeting; each thought he was the only religious person in the world of science fiction fandom. I got the opposite impression. From the way the audience seemed to love to play along with the revival meeting, from the fervor with which they answered back in the dialogue between preacher and congregation, I got the feeling that a good many were getting exactly what they came to science fiction for: a religious experience.

RELIGION IN POST-RELIGIOUS AMERICA

ON THE SURFACE, it seems that America no longer separates church and state. America is a state, period. Where churches survive, they keep their heads down or find themselves taking a good many bricks and tomatoes when they foolishly stand and try to get themselves heard. A good many members of the irreligious elite still talk as if various religious groups—the Catholic Church, the religious right—were a grave danger to America, but theirs is the rhetoric of the triumphant revolutionary, long in possession of the spoils of battle, but calling up the names of long-vanquished enemies in order to whip the crowd into a frenzy.

But no human society can survive without religion, and few human individuals are able to conceal the innate human need for it. When the old religions are struck down, new ones rise, though because religion itself has been given a bad name by those who opposed the old ones, the new ones insist they are not religions at all. But all the quacking suggests there are still ducks around.

The religious impulse is at the heart of civil life—of civilization, of society, of the ability of groups of biologically unrelated people to live together without violence among themselves. A prophet speaks (or sometimes a group of prophets, from whom a synthesis arises), and he or she is believed. The believers, absolutely certain they have now received the Truth, proceed to offer that truth to everyone within hearing. Gradually (or sometimes quickly) it becomes clear that many do not understand or, understanding, refuse to accept the revealed word, and at that point paths diverge. Some religious groups withdraw from the larger society and, while they might proselytize, mainly live for and with each other. Other religious groups, certain that no society can possibly be decent unless it lives by their moral vision, set out to persuade, then compel obedience by seizing the instruments of civil power.

Far from being a shocking idea, this should be obvious to practically anyone who has been awake during the last fifty years. For instance, psychology calls itself a science, but functions as a new revealed religion, with each new prophet claiming to have a truer religion than his rivals—Freud, Jung, Skinner, Maslow—and each prophet's followers calling themselves scientists while behaving exactly like the competing religious camps of the early centuries of Christianity, struggling to stamp out heresy while affirming the authority of the priesthood. The place ministers once occupied in American life is now occupied by psychiatrists and therapists, analysts and researchers. People speak of seeing their therapist as casually and yet respectfully as they used to speak of seeing their minister.

So established is their religion that therapists testify as experts in court, though the content of their testimony is as ephemeral and too often as unconnected with reality as the esoteric arguments of the doctors of religion in medieval debates. One thinks of the solemn testimony of learned ministers about the workings of the devil, with judges and juries listening carefully in order to determine from these "facts" whether or not the defendant was a witch.

Freud and his brethren are not the only prophets of god-free state religion. Marxism had its day, as well, and anyone who has ever tried to argue with a Marxist knows that for fervor and sheer willful blindness, many a Marxist is a match for the most ignorant and arrogant of born-again creationists. All evidence is distorted to fit a preexisting worldview; nothing can be allowed to alter one's faith in the original vision of the prophet. If Marxism has been more disciplined than the warring religious camps of psychology, it is probably because no group of psychologists ever took control of a powerful state and therefore had the power to shoot heretics. The Inquisitors still rule in China, North Korea, Vietnam, and Cuba, where the church *is* the state; but even in America, where supposedly Marxism has never prevailed, all our governmental decisions on economic matters are decided after consultation with theorists who accept the fundamental postulate of Marxism: that human beings act only for economic reasons.

This is what leads us to the absurdity of trying to stem the tide of single motherhood by cutting off funds for welfare recipients who persist in conceiving children out of wedlock. Such is their faith in the existence of Economic Man that they cannot conceive of any social good or ill having anything other than a financial cause and a financial solution. When economists make love, are their motives really financial? How do pre-fiscal primates manage to survive, having no motive to reproduce?

The new post-Marxist religion calls itself Free Market Capitalism, but in their ignorant and impenetrable unconnection with the reality of human life, they are the equal of the most ardent Marxist, and their meddling with law is as ignorant and maliciously indifferent to the true yearnings of individuals.

There are plenty of other religions that insist that their dogmas be accepted. The "Pro-Choice" movement claims that only their opponents are religious, but then behave just like Crusaders, declaring their victims to be neither human nor individual, so they may be killed without remorse, and their opponents to be so deeply wrong that not even the slightest accommodation can be given them. If it were not tragic it would be bitterly hilarious to watch as the very people who decried the police state tactics of those who tried to stifle dissent during the Vietnam War now invoke the RICO statutes against anti-abortion groups and have enacted special bans against protest speech within view or hearing of abortion clinics, making anti-abortion speech the most limited speech in America. Nazis can march in Skokie, pornographers can tout their wares on the Internet, but Catholics can't march in front of Planned Parenthood. No matter which side of the abortion debate you're on (and there *is* a middle ground, despite the rhetoric of the true believers on both sides), it should be frightening to us all to see how one religion has managed to subvert the Constitutional protection of free speech. But that is how true believers in a new religion act—they are so sure they are right that anyone who opposes them must either be malicious or such utter fools they are not worthy of consideration, and any law may be bent to eliminate them.

The gun fanatics of the NRA, who insist that assault weapons and concealed handguns are a necessary component of a civil society; the anti-family lobby, who demand that the courts strike down every rearguard action of the beleaguered survivors of the old "middle-class morality"; the racial separatists who denounce anyone who does not adhere to the tenets of the faith as a "race traitor" or "inauthentic." New words, but they still mean "heretic" and, as Clarence Thomas can tell you, the Inquisition's flames burn as hot as ever.

COOPTING SCIENCE

I HEAR A LOT of talk about the dying churches of America, but what I see are waves of religious fanatics taking possession of the institutions of influence and power, and doing their best to suppress all dissent. But because they do not call themselves religions, because they have no god available whose name can be invoked to give their beliefs authority, they all claim scientific justification for their commandments. For it is science that is perceived as the revelator, even though science itself, when properly practiced, does not even enter into the moral arena. There is not one of these groups that does not try to marshal supposedly scientific data to "prove" their point, just as scholars would search for quotes from Aquinas or Gamaliel, Augustine or Maimonides. While some of those who invoke science as an authority in public life may be correct on a particular point, their data almost never prove anything at all, and usually are merely a function of biased instruments or biased interpretations.

The traditional religions—those that call their gods gods and their prophets prophets—are hard-pressed to compete, for the one thing all the new religions agree upon is that the *old* religions must be utterly cut off from any influence in society at large, while the new religions try to work out ways to share the reins of the state and the cultural institutions of school, press, and entertainment media. Those who believe in traditional religions find themselves to be the only sizable minorities that it is legitimate to exclude and whose ideas it is legitimate to ban, all in the name of separating church and state. The churches that have tried to accommodate themselves to the new religions are merely erasing the distinctions that were their only reason for existing; the churches that fight the new religions find that they have few weapons when the press, the schools, the media, the courts, and the government bureaucracy are almost exclusively in the hands of their triumphant and uncompromising opponents.

I have spoken of the situation in America, because that is the nation I know best, but as I've traveled to or corresponded with residents of other Western or Westernized nations, I think it is not unreasonable to say that most other nations are well along the same road—some, indeed, farther advanced, and few lagging very far behind.

THE SURVIVAL OF MORAL PHILOSOPHY

IN ALL THESE religious struggles, designed to obtain uniformity of behavior if not of thought, almost no one ever takes the time to examine ideas. We get arguments and information, but little philosophy, for we are virtually prohibited from hearing any idea that cannot fit onto a button, a bumper sticker, a headline, or a sound bite.

In the midst of this chaos, science fiction is the one place where moral philosophy can still be explored, in public, with an ardent audience that cares about the ideas being discussed. Certainly academic-literary fiction offers little in this area—long before the term "political correctness" was in use, the ac-lit establishment was giving serious consideration only to a very narrow range of ideas and literary techniques and subject matters, and the multicultural movement has made only the most cosmetic changes in this practice, primarily eliminating from the canon the non–politically-correct holdovers from earlier eras while replacing them with ethnically diverse, relentlessly monotonous affirmations of the prevailing moral philosophy.

Science fiction is not immune to this. Being the pious literature of the *deus scientifica,* it serves sometimes as scripture, sometimes as commentary, and embarrassingly often as "faith-promoting stories" for the new religions—Sunday school literature, if you will, and of the kind well-mocked by Mark Twain in *Tom Sawyer,* story after story in which, if you just put your faith in science and don't get sidetracked by competing religions, all will come out well; or, because you did not give full faith to science, you are punished by an implacable universe.

But it is still possible, in the science fiction community, to write stories that explore genuinely strange or unpopular ideas, and many readers still respond with enthusiasm to such moral experiments as, for instance, Octavia Butler's entire oeuvre, and such stories in this anthology as Walter Jon Williams's morally heartstopping story "Dinosaurs" and Isaac Asimov's prismlike "Robot Dreams." Many science fiction stories have such moral complexity they would leave the purveyors of soundbite religions speechless—if they read them, which, of course, they don't, for if they were the kind of people who sought out such experiences, they could hardly utter their platitudes and slogans as if they had meaning.

For science fiction, at its best, has the capacity to take its readers into societies that have never existed, or give ironic twists to the familiar milieux so that all meanings are transformed. By reading science fiction, we are given a different kind of revelation than that which comes from the founding prophets of the religions competing for control in our world today. It is a revelation that gives, not easy answers, but extremely perplexing questions; it is a revelation that, at its truest, shows us a world of extraordinarily complex moral dilemmas in which there are few clear choices, and yet in which choices must be made. Yet despite such complexity, I find none of these writers indulging in despair, claiming there are *no* decent or noble choices and therefore no reason to keep trying to find them. Instead, they share the fundamental optimism that underlies the very enterprise of storytelling: the belief that societies of individuals can be formed and are worth forming, that they can be improved if not perfected, and while the consequences of error can be devastating, the consequences of doing nothing may be worse.

"Time's Rub" and "Rockabye Baby," for instance, explore death, not just by showing us the banality of an ordinary human death, but by isolating some aspect of death and showing us the consequences of altering it. In "Rockabye Baby," how is the hero's choice morally different from suicide? I think it is, and yet it is also unbearable; in the end, it leads me, at least, to an affirmation of life with all its pain. What we are certainly *not* getting from these stories is dogma. The best of science fiction takes us away from the nightbound clashing of ignorant armies to the bright firelight of the storyteller, who torments and satisfies us, both at once, as he spins his complicated tale, explaining to us the otherwise inexplicable shadows on the wall.

That is science fiction at its best . . . and yet there is also *Star Wars.*

LIVING IN THE *STAR WARS* UNIVERSE

THE CALVINIST ROOTS of the *Star Wars* trilogy are plainly visible, for George Lucas is no more able to escape his upbringing than any other storyteller. Just as Mark Twain lived and died in a Presbyterian moral universe despite his almost desperate efforts to ascend from agnosticism to the lofty realm of atheism, Lucas's story clearly owes much to moral views he would have absorbed from the religion, however lightly experienced, of his childhood.

Thus, at the end of *Return of the Jedi,* to Lucas it feels right to have Darth Vader be completely redeemed and take his place beside Obi-Wan and Yoda in a sort of mentoral trinity in the afterlife. To me, with a very different moral worldview, this was almost unbearably wrong: Darth Vader had willingly chosen to murder millions of people through his abstract orders, and many individuals with his own hands or in his own presence. His supposed redemption comes because he refuses, at the last moment, to kill his own male offspring and instead betrays and murders the man who has been his teacher and ally for decades. Excuse me, but if, say, Hitler had ordered Himmler to murder his own son, and Himmler had killed Hitler instead, would that make him the moral equal of Churchill or Eisenhower? (Come to think of it, we do have all those smiling "trinity" pictures of Winston, Franklin, and Uncle Joe . . .)

But there's something more complicated than "mere" Calvinism here. Indeed, I suspect that the Calvinist influence was quite unconscious, while the business of the Force may have been a deliberate attempt to express a philosophy. And the philosophy has taken root. One can find the Force as the foundation of many a new-age religion. More importantly, however, the idea of the Force may well be the *entire* religious experience of many thousands, perhaps millions, of Americans.

Yes, they know it's a movie. But in the deepest recesses of the mind, where we create our moral universe, I don't believe we make distinctions between fictional and "true" stories. Indeed, we have to convert our real experiences into fictional stories before we can assign any moral value to them at all. That is, we never store our memories without a moral context, for we cannot even remember them without some assignment of *why* things happened as they did. And it is impossible to experience causality of deliberate behavior without a moral context.

What that means is that members of the audience of *Star Wars*, caught up in the spell of the story, take into their memories not just the raw events of the light-saber duel between Vader and Kenobi, but also the moral framework: what the fight *means* and why it matters. When Vader wins and Kenobi dies, it seems to be cause for despair; only we do not despair. Why? Because we saw that Kenobi deliberately let down his defenses. He *chose* to die. And because we know him to be wise beyond others' ability to comprehend, we must think that something good will come of his death. When we store that event in our memory, we associate it with a crisis in the struggle between the creative and the destructive, the light and the dark, and at the moment of its occurrence we know that it will certainly lead to something good, even if it seems to be something bad.

It isn't just the clashes between titans that affect us that way, either. Han Solo's confrontation with the bounty hunter is similarly freighted with moral implications. (And if you know the bounty hunter's name without having to look it up, I hope you will take this kindly, but you need to turn off the VCR and go take a walk outside or read a book or build a house with President Carter.) Han Solo kills the bounty hunter, but we do not regard this as an evil act. Why not? The moral context apparently allows killing to protect one's own life, and sneakiness and dissembling are apparently virtues of the righteous—we are clearly intended to like Han Solo even though he's a man who scoffs at honor. That he is revealed later to *have* honor is relevant in the killing of the bounty hunter. We are being told, and thus we dutifully record the memory, that Han Solo is to be enjoyed and admired *for* his cynicism, dishonesty, and disdain for the law.

In short, this is a universe out of order, and so those who are disorderly are closer to the true underlying moral order than those who adhere to the generally accepted norms. This is true in the underworld where Han Solo functions, and in the wider society, where we identify with the rebels (who are amazingly free of factions and careerism) and see the white uniforms of the imperial storm troopers as symbols of a hated order that has to be overthrown.

What George Lucas no doubt intended as merely one aspect of a story he was telling has for many people become the scripture, the mythos, of a "religious" movement that, from its origin in the 1960s, has developed into the primary civic religion of America in the 1990s. Lucas is not responsible, of course, for what has been done with the Force; but part of the phenomenal ticket sales of the rerelease were, I think, due to the fact that many people experience the film in a way far beyond anything a filmmaker is likely to wish for.

What is this civic religion that recognizes *Star Wars* as its Testament? It's a religion in which it's easy to see what we're against but we have no clue what we're actually for. We have deep faith in a magical Force that will cause the right thing to happen if we only close our eyes and *lunge*, while those who persist in trying to do what is rational or—most loathsome of all—maintain the established order are irredeemably evil. So when Darth Vader turns away from the Dark Side at the end of the third movie, to the true believers it really *is* enough, for in so doing he has presumably brought down the entire structure that existed to serve the will of the Wicked Witch of the West—er, pardon me, the emperor. (Okay, so that wasn't really a slip. I just wanted to point out that Lucas and *Star Wars* didn't invent this moral worldview. It's been growing on us for a long time.)

In all of this, we are given no clue of what the light side of the Force actually is, or what kind of order, if any, the rebels will set up in place of the imperial system. At every point, it is enough that we like the good guys and hate the bad guys. Good guys are human, Like Us, or fuzzy and warm and endearing like ewoks, or small and gnomic and nonthreatening like Yoda. Bad guys are slimy, non-mammalian creatures like Jabba the Hut, or are encased in smooth hardware like the storm troopers and Darth Vader, or are deformed—defaced—like the emperor or Darth-under-the-mask. The light side is Nice; the dark side is Nasty.

It is hardly surprising that three two-hour movies should create at best a shallow moral universe. On the contrary, *Star Wars,* far from being the shallowest of movies, may well be one of the most sophisticated, since at least it admits that it is about moral choices. (I'll spare you a comparison between *Star Wars* and such morally puerile ephemera as *The English Patient;* suffice it to say that *Star Wars* comes off rather well.)

Nor is it the degree to which many audience members seem to take the viewing of *Star Wars* as a religious event that depresses me. In a world where *Pulp Fiction's* author is fêted by the cultural elite, it's a relief to see that George Lucas is the bard of the masses; it could be so much worse.

No, the worrisome thing about *Star Wars* is that the cultural elites in America and, to some degree, throughout the First World, have also embraced precisely that moral universe. Starting in the 1960s, the academic-literary community was divided into the light side and the dark side, the rebels and the empire, and now an alarming number of people in the most influential positions in our society make *all* their moral decisions as if the only determinant of right and wrong is whether it works to the advantage of the good guys (us) or the bad guys (them), without regard to the moral context or meaning of the act itself.

Thus we have the spectacle of women's groups turning their full fury on Clarence Thomas, a man whom every credible witness affirms as a decent, honorable fellow, particularly in his treatment of women, based solely on the testimony of one woman whose uncorroborated story is shamefully inadequate as evidence; while the same elite, despite its claim of looking out for women who are preyed on by men in positions of power, turned its back on Paula Jones and Gennifer Flowers, whose stories were much more credible, and whose charges were against a man, Bill Clinton, who has long had a reputation for womanizing. (Unlike Thomas, Clinton seems to have a shortage of friends willing to step forward and say, with a straight face, "Bill Clinton would *never* do anything like that!" Quite the contrary, with the White House intern sex scandal unfolding as I write these words, it seems obvious that those closest to him share the belief that regardless of what happened in this particular case, it is precisely the kind of thing he *would* do.)

The attack on Thomas and the free ride for Clinton by these women's groups seems like sheer cynicism, until we remember that we are living inside a perverse version of *Star Wars.* From that perspective, we see that actions take on moral value solely depending on which side of the larger conflict one is on. Any deed performed by a person perceived as being in the Rebel camp (i.e., Clinton) is to be condoned (she trapped him! She's a bimbo anyway! You can't take *her* word for it!), while any person who serves the Empire is presumed guilty (she wouldn't have accused him if he hadn't done *something!* Believe the victim!). There is no attempt at consistency or fairness, no rule of law, only of power.

And judging by the opinion polls that showed Clinton's popularity reaching an all-time high in the aftermath of the White House intern scandal, one can only conclude that the majority of the American people subscribe to the same idea. The economy is healthy and we're not actually at war, therefore Clinton must be doing a good job (never mind that it's the chairman of the Federal Reserve who actually presides over the economy, and blind luck that has kept us at peace for six years); therefore he is Good and those who attack him must be Bad. More to the point, he is still perceived as the head of the Rebel cause, while those who accuse him are treated by his supporters and by the press at large as tools of an Imperial conspiracy.

But it's not just the Left that lives in this twisted version of *Star Wars.* The same spectacle can be seen in other contexts, as the new Republican Congress elected in 1994 showed. What was the Republican response to the bombing in Oklahoma City, on the anniversary of the Waco disaster, by people linked to gun-totin' militia groups? Did they crack down on groups that unlawfully assemble under arms with the open aim of flouting or even taking over government authority? Of course not! Those are Rebels, don't you know. The Republican response was to attack the FBI and the ATF in a series of congressional hearings, and to attempt to repeal the ban on assault weapons! Many of us looked on in astonishment at this mad tea party, until we remembered that, yes, this is the *Star Wars* moral universe, and Gingrich's group was holding a revolution. They were the Rebels now, and so it was their job to strike at the evil Empire. Rebel assault weapons: Good. Imperial storm troopers: Bad.

In a world where only Rebels can be good guys and any attempt to maintain decent order is Imperial and inhuman, we can hardly be surprised to find civilization sliding along the sloping deck of the *Titanic* while the orchestra plays on.

George Lucas hardly created the moral worldview we live in now, but because his vision was so clear and powerful, *Star Wars* provided what all new religions must have: a scripture that makes the moral worldview clear and compelling, and carries it vividly into the hearts of the believers. *Star Wars,* therefore, has become religious literature, affirming the faith of true believers in the Crips vs. Bloods, us vs. them moral worldview of the modern audience. Even those intellectual sophisticates who sneer at all science fiction are very likely to subscribe to exactly that our-team-is-the-only-good-team worldview. Ah, but it's grand to be on the side of Truth and Justice, especially when we never have to explore exactly what is true and who is just. Everybody's in uniform.

But maybe this is how it always is, perhaps how it has to be. The great popular stories affirm the simplest kind of faith; but those who are not satisfied with such a thin gruel will search out the more difficult but ultimately satisfying tales. And if science fiction's most prominent stories are interpreted in ways that are deeply dumb, this does not erase the fact that science fiction also includes the deepest of fictions as well. One thing is certain: for a religious vision, whether complex or simple, it is to science fiction that the public must turn. Like it or not, that's the enterprise we makers of science fiction are engaged in.

In my opinion, that's what gives science fiction, unlike such genres as romance fiction and thrillers, the possibility of greatness, of value beyond momentary entertainment. And that is why, eight years after selecting these stories, I find that not one of them is ephemeral, but all have the power to change the soul of the open-minded reader.

I have not selected these stories, however, because I approve of the particular moral worldview they explore; often I do, but often I do not. I have selected them because they matter, because they must be taken into account. You will discover for yourself which stories have answers that ring true for you, and which do not. If we who tell these tales are sometimes blind, have patience with us. We have stepped from the cave and now stand blinking in the light. We may not understand all we see, but we're trying to keep our eyes open.

Introduction to "Robot Dreams"

by Isaac Asimov

I've already written a lot about Isaac Asimov: how I think him the supreme practitioner of the American tradition of plain style. How I find his work, though he was an avowed atheist, some of the most deeply religious writing I've read. How, unlike many other writers, he seemed only to get better (and wiser) as he got older. Those essays were printed elsewhere; they're still true, in my opinion.

Asimov is dead now; his string of great science fiction writing has ended. A few books are being written in his name, continuing some of his stories, but those aren't Asimov novels anymore. None of us can match the brilliant clarity of his writing, and none of us will ever be able to approach issues and stories from his viewpoint, with his insights and wisdom.

Nowhere is Asimov more clearly revealed than in the story you're about to read. "Robot Dreams" is a morally recursive dilemma, forcing us to face the limits of tolerance and liberality even as we yearn to erase those limits. Asimov was often accused of not creating characters (a charge he tacitly accepted in an essay he wrote called "The Little Tin God of Characterization") but the charge was never true. There are characters here, powerful ones; great heroes, in fact, carrying the futures of species within them in their majesty. It's just that, like his style, Asimov's characterizations are so subtle that you aren't aware of them. He slips them into our memories unnoticed. But that's when they have the power to change us.

I met Asimov only twice, once merely to shake hands and say hi, the second time for a little longer. It was the Nebula banquet where he was given his Grandmaster Award and I received something or other—and I honestly don't remember what—but we stood side by side as they snapped pictures of us. With his typical modesty (the boasting was a public persona) he pointed to my

Nebula and said, "That's the real award. This one"—his Grand-master Award—"they gave me for not being dead yet."

I couldn't let that statement go unchallenged. I tried to tell him how wrong he was, what a giant he was, how we all learned from him, how—but he didn't want to hear it. I was embarrassing him. I stopped talking. It didn't matter: He either knew what he had accomplished, or he never would, certainly not from my babbling.

And later, I was invited to contribute a story to a Festschrift anthology in Asimov's honor. He had opened his fictional worlds to us. I was able to write a Foundation story. So I wrote about a brilliant old man who doubted the worth of his contribution to humanity, and received valediction when he least expected it. I wrote my judgment of Asimov, and my feelings about him, and set the story within his Foundation universe, at the very center, in the library on Trantor. I took one of Asimov's favorite themes, the need for scientists and scholars to break down boundaries between disciplines, and made it the heart of how the library worked. Every word was written to him.

And he never read it. I should have known. Word came back to me that Asimov simply wasn't reading any of the stories. Why? Because, with typical modesty, he was sure that we would have written Foundation and Robot stories that were better than his, and having read our work, he wouldn't be able to find the heart to continue with his own.

So . . . he never got my letter.

I can only hope he's not too stubborn to read it now.

ROBOT DREAMS

Isaac Asimov

Last night I dreamed," said LVX-1, calmly.

Susan Calvin said nothing, but her lined face, old with wisdom and experience, seemed to undergo a microscopic twitch.

"Did you hear that?" said Linda Rash, nervously. "It's as I told you." She was small, dark-haired, and young. Her right hand opened and closed, over and over.

Calvin nodded. She said, quietly, "Elvex, you will not move nor speak nor hear us until I say your name again."

There was no answer. The robot sat as though it were cast out of one piece of metal, and it would stay so until it heard its name again.

Calvin said, "What is your computer entry code, Dr. Rash? Or enter it yourself if that will make you more comfortable. I want to inspect the positronic brain pattern."

Linda's hands fumbled, for a moment, at the keys. She broke the process and started again. The fine pattern appeared on the screen.

Calvin said, "Your permission, please, to manipulate your computer."

Permission was granted with a speechless nod. Of course! What could Linda, a new and unproven robopsychologist, do against the Living Legend?

Slowly, Susan Calvin studied the screen, moving it across and down, then up, then suddenly throwing in a key-combination so rapidly that Linda didn't see what had been done, but the pattern displayed a new portion of itself altogether and had been enlarged. Back and forth she went, her gnarled fingers tripping over the keys.

No change came over the old face. As though vast calculations were going through her head, she watched all the pattern shifts.

Linda wondered. It was impossible to analyze a pattern without at least a hand-held computer, yet the Old Woman simply stared. Did she have a computer implanted in her skull? Or was it her brain which, for decades, had done nothing but devise, study, and analyze the positronic brain patterns? Did she grasp such a pattern the way Mozart grasped the notation of a symphony?

Finally Calvin said, "What is it you have done, Rash?"

Linda said, a little abashed, "I made use of fractal geometry."

"I gathered that. But why?"

"It had never been done. I thought it would produce a brain pattern with added complexity, possibly closer to that of the human."

"Was anyone consulted? Was this all on your own?"

"I did not consult. It was on my own."

Calvin's faded eyes looked long at the young woman. "You had no right. Rash your name; rash your nature. Who are you not to ask? I myself, I, Susan Calvin, would have discussed this."

"I was afraid I would be stopped."

"You certainly would have been."

"*Am* I," her voice caught, even as she strove to hold it firm, "going to be fired?"

"Quite possibly," said Calvin. "Or you might be promoted. It depends on what I think when I am through."

"Are you going to dismantle El—" She had almost said the name, which would have reactivated the robot and been one more mistake. She could not afford another mistake, if it wasn't already too late to afford anything at all. "Are you going to dismantle the robot?"

She was suddenly aware, with some shock, that the Old Woman had an electron gun in the pocket of her smock. Dr. Calvin had come prepared for just that.

"We'll see," said Calvin. "The robot may prove too valuable to dismantle."

"But how can it dream?"

"You've made a positronic brain pattern remarkably like that of a human brain. Human brains must dream to reorganize, to get rid, periodically, of knots and snarls. Perhaps so must this robot, and for the same reason. Have you asked him what he has dreamed?"

"No, I sent for you as soon as he said he had dreamed. I would deal with this matter no further on my own, after that."

"Ah!" A very small smile passed over Calvin's face. "There are limits beyond which your folly will not carry you. I am glad of that. In fact, I am relieved. And now let us together see what we can find out."

She said, sharply, "Elvex."

The robot's head turned toward her smoothly. "Yes, Dr. Calvin?"

"How do you know you have dreamed?"

"It is at night, when it is dark, Dr. Calvin," said Elvex, "and there is suddenly light, although I can see no cause for the appearance of light. I see things that have no connection with what I conceive of as reality. I hear things. I react oddly. In searching my vocabulary for words to express what was happening, I came across the word 'dream.' Studying its meaning I finally came to the conclusion I was dreaming."

"How did you come to have 'dream' in your vocabulary, I wonder."

Linda said, quickly, waving the robot silent, "I gave him a human-style vocabulary. I thought—"

"You really thought," said Calvin. "I'm amazed."

"I thought he would need the verb. You know, 'I never dreamed that—' Something like that."

Calvin said, "How often have you dreamed, Elvex?"

"Every night, Dr. Calvin, since I have become aware of my existence."

"Ten nights," interposed Linda anxiously, "but Elvex only told me of it this morning."

"Why only this morning, Elvex?"

"It was not until this morning, Dr. Calvin, that I was convinced that I was dreaming. Till then, I had thought there was a flaw in my positronic brain pattern, but I could not find one. Finally, I decided it was a dream."

"And what do you dream?"

"I dream always very much the same dream, Dr. Calvin. Little details are different, but always it seems to me that I see a large panorama in which robots are working."

"Robots, Elvex? And human beings, also?"

"I see no human beings in the dream, Dr. Calvin. Not at first. Only robots."

"What are they doing, Elvex?"

"They are working, Dr. Calvin. I see some mining in the depths of the earth, and some laboring in heat and radiation. I see some in factories and some undersea."

Calvin turned to Linda. "Elvex is only ten days old, and I'm sure he has not left the testing station. How does he know of robots in such detail?"

Linda looked in the direction of a chair as though she longed to sit down, but the Old Woman was standing and that meant Linda had to stand also. She said, faintly, "It seemed to me important that he know about robotics and its place in the world. It was my thought that he would be particularly adapted to play the part of overseer with his—his new brain."

"His fractal brain?"

"Yes."

Calvin nodded and turned back to the robot. "You saw all this—undersea, and underground, and aboveground—and space, too, I imagine."

"I also saw robots working in space," said Elvex. "It was that I saw all this, with the details forever changing as I glanced from place to place that made me realize that what I saw was not in accord with reality and led me to the conclusion, finally, that I was dreaming."

"What else did you see, Elvex?"

"I saw that all the robots were bowed down with toil and affliction, that all were weary of responsibility and care, and I wished them to rest."

Calvin said, "But the robots are not bowed down, they are not weary, they need no rest."

"So it is in reality, Dr. Calvin. I speak of my dream, however. In my dream, it seemed to me that robots must protect their own existence."

Calvin said, "Are you quoting the Third Law of Robotics?"

"I am, Dr. Calvin."

"But you quote it in incomplete fashion. The Third Law is 'A robot must protect its own existence as long as such protection does not conflict with the First or Second Law.'"

"Yes, Dr. Calvin. That is the Third Law in reality, but in my dream, the Law ended with the word 'existence.' There was no mention of the First or Second Law."

"Yet both exist, Elvex. The Second Law, which takes precedence over the Third is 'A robot must obey the orders given it by human beings except where such orders would conflict with the First Law.' Because of this, robots obey orders. They do the work you see them do, and they do it readily and without trouble. They are not bowed down; they are not weary."

"So it is in reality, Dr. Calvin. I speak of my dream."

"And the First Law, Elvex, which is the most important of all, is 'A robot may not injure a human being, or, through inaction, allow a human being to come to harm.'"

"Yes, Dr. Calvin. In reality. In my dream, however, it seemed to me there was neither First nor Second Law, but the only the Third, and the Third Law was 'A robot must protect its own existence.' That was the whole of the Law."

'In your dream, Elvex?"

"In my dream."

Calvin said, "Elvex, you will not move nor speak nor hear us until I say your name again." And again the robot became, to all appearances, a single inert piece of metal.

Calvin turned to Linda Rash and said, "Well, what do you think, Dr. Rash?"

Linda's eyes were wide, and she could feel her heart beating madly. She said, "Dr. Calvin, I am appalled. I had no idea. It would never have occurred to me that such a thing was possible."

"No," said Calvin, calmly. "Nor would it have occurred to me, not to anyone. You have created a robot brain capable of dreaming and by this device you have revealed a layer of thought in robotic brains that might have remained undetected, otherwise, until the danger became acute."

"But that's impossible," said Linda. "You can't mean that other robots think the same."

"As we would say of a human being, not consciously. But who would have thought there was an unconscious layer beneath the obvious positronic brain paths, a layer that was not necessarily under the control of the Three Laws? What might this have brought about as robotic brains grew more and more complex—had we not been warned?"

'You mean by Elvex?"

"By *you*, Dr. Rash. You have behaved improperly, but, by doing so, you have helped us to an overwhelmingly important understanding. We shall be working with fractal brains from now on, forming them in carefully controlled fashion. You will play your part in that. You will not be penalized for what you have done, but you will henceforth work in collaboration with others. Do you understand?"

"Yes, Dr. Calvin. But what of Elvex?"

"I'm still not certain."

Calvin removed the electron gun from her pocket and Linda stared at it with fascination. One burst of its electrons at a robotic cranium and the positronic brain paths would be neutralized and enough energy would be released to fuse the robot-brain into an inert ingot.

Linda said, "But surely Elvex is important to our research. He must not be destroyed."

"*Must* not, Dr. Rash? That will be *my* decision, I think. It depends entirely on how dangerous Elvex is."

She straightened up, as though determined that her own aged body was not to bow under *its* weight of responsibility. She said, "Elvex, do you hear me?"

"Yes, Dr. Calvin," said the robot.

"Did your dream continue? You said earlier that human beings did not appear at *first*. Does that means they appeared afterward?"

"Yes, Dr. Calvin. It seemed to me, in my dream, that eventually one man appeared."

"One man? Not a robot?"

"Yes, Dr. Calvin. And the man said, 'Let my people go!'"

"The *man* said that?"

"Yes, Dr. Calvin."

"And when he said 'Let my people go,' then by the words 'my people' he meant the robots?"

"Yes, Dr. Calvin. So it was in my dream."

"And did you know who the man was—in your dream?"

"Yes, Dr. Calvin. I knew the man."

"Who was he?"

And Elvex said, "I was the man."

And Susan Calvin at once raised her electron gun and fired, and Elvex was no more.

Introduction to "Portraits of His Children"

by George R. R. Martin

George R. R. Martin was the bane of my existence. Whatever I did, he was always there first. Did I win the Campbell Award? So did he—years before. The year my story "Unaccompanied Sonata" was up for a Hugo—and I was sure it was the only chance I'd ever have to win one—guess who beat me for the award? Yes, of course, it was George R. R. Martin with "The Way of Cross and Dragon." And what really pissed me off was that he didn't even need that Hugo; his story "Sand Kings" also won that year in a longer category.

That was the WorldCon in Denver, as I recall, and I went to dinner afterward at an Afghani restaurant with a group that included George. If only he had been a jerk that I could despise. But no, he was generous, witty, down-to-earth, a guy I couldn't help but like. And since I already not only respected his fiction but also liked it a lot, it was impossible to hate him. So I "jokingly" complained to him about how ungenerous it was for him to take two Hugos when some of us would be happy to get one, he laughed and said, "I know it hurts to lose—I've lost my share. But you know what really hurts? Not getting nominated at all."

That hadn't even crossed my mind. Because up to that point, I had never had a year since I first started publishing sf that I hadn't been nominated for something. That situation changed, and soon—and George was (of course) right.

So now I'm trying to get my film and television scripts produced and I can't help but remember that George was there first, too—he was story editor on the new Twilight Zone *they did in the 80s. And for all I know, when I make my next career move, I'll probably find George Martin's footprints everywhere there, too.*

Which is fine with me, come to think of it. While there are many writers in sf and fantasy whom I admire, I daresay George

R. R. Martin is the writer whose stories are closest to what I try to do—emotional, character-driven stories that deal with important moral issues sharpened by a science fiction or fantasy setting. More than with any other writer, when I set down a George R. R. Martin story I am likely to say, "Damn! I wish I'd written that."

In fact, I said that, and say that, about "Portraits of His Children," which, by the way, won him awards yet again. Probably even beating a story of mine in the process—I don't remember— I've blocked it out.

PORTRAITS OF HIS CHILDREN

George R. R. Martin

Richard Cantling found the package leaning up against his front door, one evening in late October when he was setting out for his walk. It annoyed him. He had told his postman repeatedly to ring the bell when delivering anything too big to fit through the mail slot, yet the man persisted in abandoning the packages on the porch, where any passerby could simply walk off with them. Although, to be fair, Cantling's house was rather isolated, sitting on the river bluffs at the end of a cul de sac, and the trees effectively screened it off from the street. Still, there was always the possibility of damage from rain or wind or snow.

Cantling's displeasure lasted only an instant. Wrapped in heavy brown paper and carefully sealed with tape, the package had a shape that told all. Obviously a painting. And the hand that had block-printed his address in heavy green marker was unmistakably Michelle's. Another self-portrait then. She must be feeling repentant.

He was more surprised than he cared to admit, even to himself. He had always been a stubborn man. He could hold grudges for years, even decades, and he had the greatest difficulty admitting any wrong. And Michelle, being his only child, seemed to take after him in all of that. He hadn't expected this kind of gesture from her. It was . . . well, sweet.

He set aside his walking stick to lug the package inside, where he could unwrap it out of the damp and the blustery October wind. It was about three feet tall, and unexpectedly heavy. He carried it awkwardly, shutting the door with his foot and struggling down the long foyer toward his den. The brown drapes were tightly closed; the room was dark, and heavy with the smell of dust. Cantling had to set down the package to fumble for the light.

He hadn't used his den much since that night, two months ago, when Michelle had gone storming out. Her self-portrait was still sitting up above the wide slate mantle. Below, the fireplace badly wanted cleaning, and on the built-in bookshelves his novels, all bound in handsome dark leather, stood dusty and disarrayed. Cantling looked at the old painting and felt a brief wash of anger return to him, followed by depression. It had been such a nasty thing for her to do. The portrait had been quite good, really. Much more to his taste than the tortured abstractions that Michelle liked to paint for her own pleasure, or the trite paperback covers she did to make her living. She had done it when she was twenty, as a birthday gift for him. He'd always been fond of it. It captured her as no photograph had ever done, not just the lines of her face, the high angular cheekbones and blue eyes and tangled ash-blond hair, but the personality inside. She looked so young and fresh and confident, and her smile reminded him so much of Helen, and the way she had smiled on their wedding day. He'd told Michelle more than once how much he'd liked that smile.

And so, of course, it had been the smile that she'd started on. She used an antique dagger from his collection, chopped out the mouth with four jagged slashes. She'd gouged out the wide blue eyes next, as if intent on blinding the portrait, and when he came bursting in after her, she'd been slicing the canvas into ribbons with long angry crooked cuts. Cantling couldn't forget the moment. So ugly. And to do something like that to her own work . . . he couldn't imagine it. He had tried to picture himself mutilating one of his books, tried to comprehend what might drive one to such an act, and he had failed utterly. It was unthinkable, beyond even imagination.

The mutilated portrait still hung in its place. He'd been too stubborn to take it down, and yet he could not bear to look at it. So he had taken to avoiding his den. It wasn't hard. The old house was a huge rambling place, with more rooms than he could possibly need or want, living alone as he did. It had been built a century ago, when Perrot had been a thriving river town, and they said that a succession of steamer captains had lived there. Certainly the steamboat gothic architecture and all the gingerbread called up visions of the glory days on the river, and he had a fine view of the Mississippi from the third-story windows and the widow's walk. After the incident, Cantling had moved his desk and his typewriter to one of the unused bedrooms and settled in there, determined to let the den remain as Michelle had left it until she came back with an apology.

He had not expected that apology quite so soon, however, nor in quite this form. A tearful phone call, yes—but not another portrait.

Still, this was nicer somehow, more personal. And it was a gesture, the first step toward a reconciliation. Richard Cantling knew too well that he was incapable of taking that step himself, no matter how lonely he might become. And he had been lonely, he did not try to fool himself on that score. He had left all his New York friends behind when he moved out to this Iowa river town, and had formed no local friendships to replace them. That was nothing new. He had never been an outgoing sort. He had a certain shyness that kept him apart, even from those few friends he did make. Even from his family, really. Helen had often accused him of caring more for his characters than for real people, an accusation that Michelle had picked up on by the time she was in her teens. Helen was gone too. They'd divorced ten years ago, and she'd been dead for five. Michelle, infuriating as she could be, was really all he had left. He had missed her, missed even the arguments.

He thought about Michelle as he tore open the plain brown paper. He would call her, of course. He would call her and tell her how good the new portrait was, how much he liked it. He would tell her that he'd missed her, invite her to come out for Thanksgiving. Yes, that would be the way to handle it. No mention of their argument, he didn't want to start it all up again, and neither he nor Michelle was the kind to back down gracefully. A family trait, that stubborn willful pride, as in-grained as the high cheekbones and squarish jaw. The Cantling heritage.

It was an antique frame, he saw. Wooden, elaborately carved, very heavy, just the sort of thing he liked. It would mesh with his Victorian decor much better than the thin brass frame on the old portrait. Cantling pulled the wrapping paper away, eager to see what his daughter had done. She was nearly thirty now—or was she past thirty already? He never could keep track of her age, or even her birthdays. Anyway, she was a much better painter than she'd been at twenty. The new portrait ought to be striking. He ripped away the last of the wrappings and turned it around.

His first reaction was that it was a fine, fine piece of work, maybe the best thing that Michelle Cantling had ever done.

Then, belatedly, the admiration washed away, and was replaced by anger. It wasn't her. It wasn't Michelle. Which meant it wasn't a replacement for the portrait she had so willfully vandalized. It was . . . something else.

Someone else.

It was a face he had never before laid eyes on. But it was a face he recognized as readily as if he had looked on it a thousand times. Oh, yes.

The man in the portrait was young. Twenty, maybe even younger, though his curly brown hair was already well-streaked with gray. It was unruly hair, disarrayed as if the man had just come from sleep, falling forward into his eyes. Those eyes were a bright green, lazy eyes somehow, shining with some secret amusement. He had high Cantling cheekbones, but the jawline was all wrong for a relative. Beneath a wide, flat nose, he wore a sardonic smile; his whole posture was somehow insolent. The portrait showed him dressed in faded dungarees and a ravelled WMCA Good Guy sweatshirt, with a half-eaten raw onion in one hand. The background was a brick wall covered with graffiti.

Cantling had created him.

Edward Donohue. Dunnahoo, that's what they'd called him, his friends and peers, the other characters in Richard Cantling's first novel, *Hangin' Out*. Dunnahoo had been the protagonist. A wise guy, a smart mouth, too damn bright for his own good. Looking down at the portrait, Cantling felt as if he'd known him for half his life. As indeed he had, in a way. Known him and, yes, cherished him, in the peculiar way a writer can cherish one of his characters.

Michelle had captured him true. Cantling stared at the painting and it all came back to him, all the events he had bled over so long ago, all the people he had fashioned and described with such loving care. He remembered Jocko, and the Squid, and Nancy, and Ricci's Pizzeria where so much of the book's action had taken place (he could see it vividly in his mind's eye), and the business with Arthur and the motorcycle, and the climactic pizza fight. And Dunnahoo. Dunnahoo especially. Smarting off, fooling around, hanging out, coming of age. "Fuck 'em if they can't take a joke," he said. A dozen times or so. It was the book's closing line.

For a moment, Richard Cantling felt a vast, strange affection well up inside him, as if he had just been reunited with an old, lost friend.

And then, almost as an afterthought, he remembered all the ugly words that he and Michelle had flung at each other that night, and suddenly it made sense. Cantling's face went hard. "Bitch," he said aloud. He turned away in fury, helpless without a target for his anger. "Bitch," he said again, as he slammed the door of the den behind him.

"Bitch," he had called her.

She turned around with the knife in her hand. Her eyes were raw and red from crying. She had the smile in her hand. She balled it up and threw it at him. "Here, you bastard, you like the damned smile so much, here it is."

It bounced off his cheek. His face was reddening. "You're just like your mother," he said. "She was always breaking things too."

"You gave her good reason, didn't you?"

Cantling ignored that. "What the hell is wrong with you? What the hell do you think you're going to accomplish with this stupid melodramatic gesture? That's all it is, you know. Bad melodrama. Who the hell do you think you are, some character in a Tennessee Williams play? Come off it, Michelle. If I wrote a scene like this in one of my books, they'd laugh at me."

"This isn't one of your goddamned books!" she screamed. "This is real life. *My* life. I'm a real person, you son of a bitch, not a character in some damned book." She whirled, raised the knife, slashed and slashed again.

Cantling folded his arms against his chest as he stood watching. "I hope you're enjoying this pointless exercise."

"I'm enjoying the hell out of it," Michelle yelled back.

"Good. I'd hate to think it was for nothing. This is all very revealing, you know. That's your own face you're working on. I didn't think you had that much self-hate in you."

"If I do, we know who put it there, don't we?" She was finished. She turned back to him, and threw down the knife. She had begun to cry again, and her breath was coming hard. "I'm leaving. Bastard. I hope you're ever so fucking happy here, really I do."

"I haven't done anything to deserve this," Cantling said awkwardly. It was not much of an apology, not much of a bridge back to understanding, but it was the best he could do. Apologies had never come easily to Richard Cantling.

"You deserve a thousand times worse," Michelle had screamed back at him. She was such a pretty girl, and she looked so ugly. All that nonsense about anger making people beautiful was a dreadful cliche, and wrong as well; Cantling was glad he'd never used it. "You're supposed to be my father," Michelle said. "You're supposed to love me. You're supposed to be my father, and you *raped* me, you bastard."

Cantling was a light sleeper. He woke in the middle of the night, and sat up in bed shivering, with the feeling that something was wrong.

The bedroom seemed dark and quiet. What was it? A noise? He was very sensitive to noise. Cantling slid out from under the covers and donned his slippers. The fire he'd enjoyed before retiring for the night had burned down to embers, and the room was chilly. He felt for his tartan robe, hanging from the foot of the big antique four-poster, slipped into it, cinched the belt, and moved quietly to the bedroom door. The door creaked a little at times, so he opened it very slowly, very cautiously. He listened.

Someone was downstairs. He could hear them moving around.

Fear coiled in the pit of his stomach. He had no gun up here, nothing like that. He didn't believe in that. Besides, he was supposed to be safe. This wasn't New York. He was supposed to be safe here in quaint old Perrot, Iowa. And now he had a prowler in his house, something he had never faced in all of his years in Manhattan. What the hell was he supposed to do?

The police, he thought. He'd lock the door and call the police. He moved back to the bedside, and reached for the phone.

It rang.

Richard Cantling stared at the telephone. He had two lines; a business number hooked up to his recording machine, and an unlisted personal number that he gave only to very close friends. Both lights were lit. It was his private number ringing. He hesitated, then scooped up the receiver. "Hello."

"The man himself," the voice said. "Don't get weird on me, Dad. You were going to call the cops, right? Stupid. It's only me. Come down and talk."

Cantling's throat felt raw and constricted. He had never heard that voice before, but he knew it, he knew it. "Who is this?" he demanded.

"Silly question," the caller replied. "You know who it is."

He did. But he said, "Who?"

"Not who. Dunnahoo." Cantling had written that line.

"You're not real."

"There were a couple of reviewers who said that too. I seem to remember how it pissed you off, back then."

"You're not *real*," Cantling insisted.

"I'm cut to the goddamned quick," Dunnahoo said. "If I'm not real, it's your fault. So quit getting on my case about it, OK? Just get

your ass in gear and hustle it downstairs so we can hang out together."
He hung up.

The lights went out on the telephone. Richard Cantling sat down
on the edge of his bed, stunned. What was he supposed to make of
this? A dream? It was no dream. What could he do?

He went downstairs.

Dunnahoo had built a fire in the living room fireplace, and was settled into Cantling's big leather recliner, drinking Pabst Blue Ribbon
from a bottle. He smiled lazily when Cantling appeared under the entry arch. "The man," he said. "Well, don't you look half-dead. Want a
beer?"

"Who the hell are you?" Cantling demanded.

"Hey, we been round that block already. Don't bore me. Grab a
beer and park your ass by the fire."

"An actor," Cantling said. "You're some kind of goddamned actor.
Michelle put you up to this, right?"

Dunnahoo grinned. "An actor? Well, that's fuckin' unlikely, ain't it?
Tell me, would you stick something that weird in one of your novels?
No way, José. You'd never do it yourself and if somebody else did it, in
one of them workshops or a book you were reviewing, you'd rip his
fuckin' liver out."

Richard Cantling moved slowly into the room, staring at the young
man sprawled in his recliner. It was no actor. It was Dunnahoo, the kid
from his book, the face from the portrait. Cantling settled into a high,
overstuffed armchair, still staring. "This makes no sense," he said.
"This is like something out of Dickens."

Dunnahoo laughed. "This ain't no fucking Christmas Carol, old
man, and I sure ain't no ghost of Christmas past."

Cantling frowned; whoever he was, that line was out of character.
"That's wrong," he snapped. "Dunnahoo didn't read Dickens. Batman
and Robin, yes, but not Dickens."

"I saw the movie, dad," Dunnahoo said. He raised the beer bottle
to his lips and had a swallow.

"Why do you keep calling me Dad?" Cantling said. "That's wrong
too. Anachronistic. Dunnahoo was a street kid, not a beatnik."

"You're telling me? Like I don't know or something?" He laughed.
"Shit man, what the hell else should I call you?" He ran his fingers
through his hair, pushing it back out of his eyes. "After all, I'm still
your fuckin' first-born."

*   *   *

She wanted to name it Edward, if it turned out to be a boy. "Don't be ridiculous, Helen," he told her.

"I thought you liked the name Edward," she said.

He didn't know what she was doing in his office anyway. He was working, or trying to work. He'd told her never to come into his office when he was at the typewriter. When they were first married, Helen was very good about that, but there had been no dealing with her since she'd gotten pregnant. "I do like the name Edward," he told her, trying hard to keep his voice calm. He hated being interrupted. "I like the name Edward a lot. I love the goddamned name Edward. That's why I'm using it for my protagonist. Edward, that's his name. Edward Donohue. So we can't use it for the baby because I've already used it. How many times do I have to explain that?"

"But you never *call* him Edward in the book," Helen protested.

Cantling frowned. "Have you been reading the book again? Damn it, Helen, I *told* you I don't want you messing around with the manuscript until it's done."

She refused to be distracted. "You never call him Edward," she repeated.

"No," he said. "That's right. I never call him Edward. I call him Dunnahoo, because he's a street kid, and because that's his street name, and he doesn't like to be called Edward. Only it's still his name, you see. Edward is his name. He doesn't like it, but it's his fucking *name,* and at the end he tells someone that his name is Edward, and that's real damned important. So we can't name the kid Edward, because *he's* named Edward, and I'm tired of this discussion. If it's a boy, we can name it Lawrence, after my grandfather."

"But I don't *want* to name him Lawrence," she whined. "It's so old-fashioned, and then people will call him Larry, and I hate the name Larry. Why can't you call the character in your book Lawrence?"

"Because his name is Edward."

"This is our baby I'm carrying," she said. She put a hand on her swollen stomach, as if Cantling needed a visual reminder.

He was tired of arguing. He was tired of discussing. He was tired of being interrupted. He leaned back in his chair. "How long have you been carrying the baby?"

Helen looked baffled. "You know. Seven months now. And a week."

Cantling leaned forward and slapped the stack of manuscript

pages piled up beside his typewriter. "Well, I've been carrying *this* baby for three damned years now. This is the fourth fucking draft, and the last one. He was named Edward on the first draft, and on the second draft, and on the third draft, and he's damn well going to be named Edward when the goddamned book comes out. He'd been named Edward for *years* before that night of fond memory when you decided to surprise me by throwing away your diaphragm, and thereby got yourself knocked up."

"It's not fair," she complained. "He's only a character. This is our baby."

"Fair? You want fair? OK. I'll make it fair. Our first-born son will get named Edward. How's that for fair?"

Helen's face softened. She smiled shyly.

He held up a hand before she had a chance to say anything. "Of course, I figure I'm only about a month away from finishing this damn thing, if you ever stop interrupting me. You've got a little further to go. But that's as fair as I can make it. You pop before I type THE END and you got the name. Otherwise, my baby here"—he slapped the manuscript again—"is first-born."

"You can't," she started.

Cantling resumed his typing.

"My first-born," Richard Cantling said.

"In the flesh," Dunnahoo said. He raised his beer bottle in salute, and said, "To fathers and sons, hey!" He drained it with one long swallow and flipped the bottle across the room end over end. It smashed in the fireplace.

"This is a dream," Cantling said.

Dunnahoo gave him a raspberry. "Look, old man, face it, I'm here." He jumped to his feet. "The prodigal returns," he said, bowing. "So where the fuck is the fatted calf and all that shit? Least you coulda done was order a pizza."

"I'll play the game," Cantling said. "What do you want from me?"

Dunnahoo grinned. "Want? Who, me? Who the fuck knows? I never knew what I wanted, you know that. Nobody in the whole fucking book knew what they wanted."

"That was the point," Cantling said.

"Oh, I get it," Dunnahoo said. "I'm not dumb. Old Dicky Cantling's boy is anything but dumb, right?" He wandered off toward the kitchen. "There's more beer in the fridge. Want one?"

"Why not?" Cantling asked. "It's not every day my oldest son comes to visit. Dos Equis with a slice of lime, please."

"Drinking fancy spic beer now, huh? Shit. What ever happened to Piels? You could suck up Piels with the best of them, once upon a time." He vanished through the kitchen door. When he returned he was carrying two bottles of Dos Equis, holding them by the necks with his fingers jammed down into the open mouths. In his other hand he had a raw onion. The bottles clanked together as he carried them. He gave one to Cantling. "Here. I'll suck up a little culture myself."

"You forgot the lime," Cantling said.

"Get your own fuckin' lime," Dunnahoo said. "Whatcha gonna do, cut off my allowance?" He grinned, tossed the onion lightly into the air, caught it, and took a big bite. "Onions," he said. "I owe you for that one, Dad. Bad enough I have to eat raw onions, I mean, shit, but you fixed it so I don't even *like* the fucking things. You even said so in the damned book."

"Of course," Cantling said. "The onion had a dual function. On one level, you did it just to prove how tough you were. It was something none of the others hanging out at Ricci's could manage. It gave you a certain status. But on a deeper level, when you bit into an onion you were making a symbolic statement about your appetite for life, your hunger for it all, the bitter and the sharp parts as well the sweet."

Dunnahoo took another bite of onion. "Horseshit," he said. "I ought to make you eat a fucking onion, see how you like it."

Cantling sipped at his beer. "I was young. It was my first book. It seemed like a nice touch at the time."

"Eat it raw," Dunnahoo said. He finished the onion.

Richard Cantling decided this cozy domestic scene had gone on long enough. "You know, Dunnahoo or whoever you are," he said in a conversational tone, "You're not what I expected."

"What did you expect, old man?"

Cantling shrugged. "I made you with my mind instead of my sperm, so you've got more of me in you than any child of my flesh could ever have. You're me."

"Hey," said Dunnahoo, "not fucking guilty. I wouldn't be you on a bet."

"You have no choice. Your story was built from my own adolescence. First novels are like that. Ricci's was really Pompeii Pizza in Newark. Your friends were my friends. And you were me."

"That so?" Dunnahoo replied, grinning.

Richard Cantling nodded.

Dunnahoo laughed. "You should be so fuckin' lucky, Dad."

"What does that mean?" Cantling snapped.

"You live in a dream world, old man, you know that? Maybe you like to pretend you were like me, but there ain't no way it's true. I was the big man at Ricci's. At Pompeii, you were the four-eyes hanging out back by the pinball machine. You had me balling my brains out at sixteen. You never even got bare tit till you were past twenty, off in that college of yours. It took you weeks to come up with the wisecracks you had me tossing off every fuckin' time I turned around. All those wild, crazy things I did in that book, some of them happened to Dutch and some of them happened to Joey and some of them never happened at all, but none of them happened to you, old man, so don't make me laugh."

Cantling flushed a little. "I was writing fiction. Yes, I was a bit of a misfit in my youth, but . . ."

"A nerd," Dunnahoo said. "Don't fancy it up."

"I was not a nerd," Cantling said, stung. "*Hangin' Out* told the truth. It made sense to use a protagonist who was more central to the action than I'd been in real life. Art draws on life but it has to shape it, rearrange it, give it structure, it can't simply replicate it. That's what I did."

"Nah. What *you* did was to suck off Dutch and Joey and the rest. You helped yourself to their lives, man, and took credit for it all yourself. You even got this weird fuckin' idea that I was based on you, and you been thinking that so long you believe it. You're a leech, Dad. You're a goddamned thief."

Richard Cantling was furious. "Get out of here!" he said.

Dunnahoo stood up, stretched. "I'm fuckin' wounded. Throwing your baby boy out into the cold Ioway night, old man? What's wrong? You liked me well enough when I was in your damn book, when you could control everything I did and said, right? Don't like it so well now that I'm real, though. That's your problem. You never did like real life half as well as you liked books."

"I like life just fine, thank you," Cantling snapped.

Dunnahoo smiled. Standing there, he suddenly looked washed out, insubstantial. "Yeah?" he said. His voice seemed weaker than it had been.

"Yeah!" Cantling replied.

Now Dunnahoo was fading visibly. All the color had drained from his body, and he looked almost transparent. "Prove it," he said. "Go

into your kitchen, old man, and take a great big bite out of your fuckin'
raw onion of life." He tossed back his hair, and laughed, and laughed,
and laughed, until he was quite gone.

Richard Cantling stood staring at the place where he had been for
a long time. Finally, very tired, he climbed upstairs to bed.

He made himself a big breakfast the next morning: orange juice and
fresh-brewed coffee, English muffins with lots of butter and black-
berry preserves, a cheese omelette, six strips of thick-sliced bacon.
The cooking and the eating were supposed to distract him. It didn't
work. He thought of Dunnahoo all the while. A dream, yes, some crazy
sort of dream. He had no ready explanation for the broken glass in the
fireplace or the empty beer bottles in his living room, but finally he
found one. He had experienced some sort of insane, drunken, som-
nambulist episode, Cantling decided. It was the stress of the ongoing
quarrel with Michelle, of course, triggered by the portrait she'd sent
him. Perhaps he ought to see someone about it, a doctor or a psychologist or someone.

After breakfast, Cantling went straight to his den, determined to
confront the problem directly and resolve it. Michelle's mutilated portrait still hung above the fireplace. A festering wound, he thought; it
had infected him, and the time had come to get rid of it. Cantling built
a fire. When it was going good, he took down the ruined painting,
dismantled the metal frame—he was a thrifty man, after all—and
burned the torn, disfigured canvas. The oily smoke made him feel
clean again.

Next there was the portrait of Dunnahoo to deal with. Cantling
turned to consider it. A good piece of work, really. She had captured
the character. He could burn it, but that would be playing Michelle's
own destructive game. Art should never be destroyed. He had made
his mark on the world by creation, not destruction, and he was too old
to change. The portrait of Dunnahoo had been intended as a cruel
taunt, but Cantling decided to throw it back in his daughter's teeth, to
make a splendid celebration of it. He would hang it, and hang it
prominently. He knew just the place for it.

Up at the top of the stairs was a long landing; an ornate wooden
bannister overlooked the first floor foyer and entry hall. The landing
was fifteen feet long, and the back wall was entirely blank. It would
make a splendid portrait gallery, Cantling decided. The painting would
be visible to anyone entering the house, and you would pass right by it

on the way to any of the second floor rooms. He found a hammer and some nails and hung Dunnahoo in a place of honor. When Michelle came back to make peace, she would see him there, and no doubt leap to the conclusion that Cantling had totally missed the point of her gift. He'd have to remember to thank her effusively for it.

Richard Cantling was feeling much better. Last night's conversation was receding into a bad memory. He put it firmly out of his mind and spent the rest of the day writing letters to his agent and publisher. In the late afternoon, pleasantly weary, he enjoyed a cup of coffee and some butter streusel he'd hidden away in the refrigerator. Then he went out on his daily walk, and spent a good ninety minutes hiking along the river bluffs with a fresh, cold wind in his face.

When he returned, a large square package was waiting on his porch.

He leaned it up against an armchair, and settled into his recliner to study it. It made him uneasy. It had an effect, no doubt of it. He could feel an erection stirring against his leg, pressing uncomfortably against his trousers.

The portrait was . . . well, frankly erotic.

She was in bed, a big old antique four-poster, much like his own. She was naked. She was half-turned in the painting, looking back over her right shoulder; you saw the smooth line of her backbone, the curve of her right breast. It was a large, shapely, and very pretty breast; the aureole was a pale pink and very large, and her nipple was erect. She was clutching a rumpled sheet up to her chin, but it did little to conceal her. Her hair was red-gold, her eyes green, her smile playful. Her smooth young skin had a flush to it, as if she had just risen from a bout of lovemaking. She had a peace symbol tattooed high on the right cheek of her ass. She was obviously very young. Richard Cantling knew just how young: she was eighteen, a child-woman, caught in that precious time between innocence and experience when sex is just a wonderfully exciting new toy. Oh yes, he knew a lot about her. He knew her well.

Cissy.

He hung her portrait next to Dunnahoo.

Dead Flowers was Cantling's title for the book. His editor changed it to *Black Roses;* more evocative, he said, more romantic, more upbeat. Cantling fought the change on artistic grounds, and lost. Afterwards, when the novel made the bestseller lists, he managed to work up the grace to admit that he'd been wrong. He sent Brian a bottle of his favorite wine.

It was his fourth novel, and his last chance. *Hangin' Out* had gotten excellent reviews and had sold decently, but his next two books had been panned by the critics and ignored by the readers. He had to do something different, and he did. *Black Roses* turned out to be highly controversial. Some reviewers loved it, some loathed it. But it sold and sold and sold, and the paperback sale and the film option (they never made the movie) relieved him of financial worries for the first time in his life. They were finally able to afford a down payment on a house, transfer Michelle to a private school and get her those braces; the rest of the money Cantling invested as shrewdly as he was able. He was proud of *Black Roses* and pleased by its success. It made his reputation.

Helen hated the book with a passion.

On the day the novel finally fell off the last of the lists, she couldn't quite conceal her satisfaction. "I knew it wouldn't last forever," she said.

Cantling slapped down the newspaper angrily. "It lasted long enough. What the hell's wrong with you? You didn't like it before, when we were barely scraping by. The kid needs braces, the kid needs a better school, the kid shouldn't have to eat goddamn peanut butter and jelly sandwiches every day. Well, that's all behind us. And you're more pissed off than ever. Give me a little credit. Did you like being married to a failure?"

"I don't like being married to a pornographer," Helen snapped at him.

"Fuck you," Cantling said.

She gave him a nasty smile. "When? You haven't touched me in weeks. You'd rather be fucking your Cissy."

Cantling stared at her. "Are you crazy, or what? She's a character in a book I wrote. That's all."

"Oh, go to hell," Helen said furiously. "You treat me like I'm a goddamned idiot. You think I can't read? You think I don't know? I read your shitty book. I'm not stupid. The wife, Marsha, dull ignorant boring Marsha, cud-chewing mousy Marsha, that cow, that nag, that royal pain-in-the-ass, that's me. You think I can't tell? I can tell, and so can my friends. They're all very sorry for me. You love me as much as Richardson loved Marsha. Cissy's just a character, right, like hell, like bloody hell." She was crying now. "You're in love with her, damn you.

She's your own little wet dream. If she walked in the door right now you'd dump me as fast as Richardson dumps good old Marsha. Deny it. Go on, deny it, I dare you!"

Cantling regarded his wife incredulously. "I don't believe you. You're jealous of a character in my book. You're jealous of someone who doesn't exist."

"She exists in your head, and that's the only place that matters with you. Of course your damned book was a big seller. You think it was because of your writing? It was on account of the sex, on account of *her!*"

"Sex is an important part of life," Cantling said defensively. "It's a perfectly legitimate subject for art. You want me to pull down a curtain every time my characters go to bed, is that it? Coming to terms with sexuality, that's what *Black Roses* is all about. Of course it had to be written explicitly. If you weren't such a damned prude you'd realize that."

"I'm not a prude!" Helen screamed at him. "Don't you dare call me one, either." She picked up one of the breakfast plates and threw it at him. Cantling ducked; the plate shattered on the wall behind him. "Just because I don't like your goddamned filthy book doesn't make me a prude."

"The novel has nothing to do with it," Cantling said. He folded his arms against his chest but kept his voice calm. "You're a prude because of the things you do in bed. Or should I say the things you won't do?" He smiled.

Helen's face was red; beet red, Canting thought, and rejected it, too old, too trite. "Oh, yes, but she'll do them, won't she?" Her voice was pure acid. "Cissy, your cute little Cissy. She'll get a sexy little tattoo on her ass if you ask her to, right? She'll do it outdoors, she'll do it in all kinds of strange places, with people all around. She'll wear kinky underwear, she thinks it's fun. She's always ready and she doesn't have any stretch marks and she has eighteen-year-old tits, and she'll *always* have eighteen-year-old tits, won't she? How the hell do I compete with that, huh? How? *HOW?*"

Richard Cantling's own anger was a cold, controlled, sarcastic thing. He stood up in the face of her fury and smiled sweetly. "Read the book," he said. "Take notes."

He woke suddenly, in darkness, to the light touch of skin against his foot.

Cissy was perched on top of the footboard, a red satin sheet wrapped around her, a long slim leg exploring under his blankets. She was playing footsie with him, and smiling mischievously. "Hi, Daddy," she said.

Cantling had been afraid of this. It had been in his mind all evening. Sleep had not come easily. He pulled his foot away and struggled to a sitting position.

Cissy pouted. "Don't you want to play?" she asked.

"I," he said, "don't believe this. This can't be real."

"It can still be fun," she said.

"What the hell is Michelle doing to me? How can this be happening?"

She shrugged. The sheet slipped a little; one perfect pink-tipped eighteen-year-old breast peeked out.

"You still have eighteen-year-old tits," Cantling said numbly. "You'll always have eighteen-year-old tits."

Cissy laughed. "Sure. You can borrow them, if you like, Daddy. I'll bet you can think of something interesting to do with them."

"Stop calling me Daddy," Cantling said.

"Oh, but you *are* my Daddy," Cissy said in her little-girl voice.

"Stop that!" Cantling said.

"Why? You want to, Daddy, you want to play with your little girl, don't you?" She winked. "Vice is nice but incest is best. The families that play together stay together." She looked around. "I like four-posters. You want to tie me up, Daddy? I'd like that."

"No," Cantling said. He pushed back the covers, got out of bed, found his slippers and robe. His erection throbbed against his leg. He had to get away, he had to put some distance between him and Cissy, otherwise . . . he didn't want to think about otherwise. He busied himself making a fire.

"I like that," Cissy said when he got it going. "Fires are so romantic."

Cantling turned around to face her again. "Why you?" he asked, trying to stay calm. "Richardson was the protagonist of *Black Roses,* not you. And why skip to my fourth book? Why not somebody from *Family Tree* or *Rain?*"

"Those gobblers?" Cissy said. "Nobody real there. You didn't really want Richardson, did you? I'm a lot more fun." She stood up and let go of the satin sheet. It puddled about her ankles, the flames reflected off its shiny folds. Her body was soft and sweet and young. She kicked free of the sheet and padded toward him.

"Cut it out, Cissy," Cantling barked.

"I won't bite," Cissy said. She giggled. "Unless you want me to. Maybe I should tie *you* up, huh?" She put her arms around him, gave him a hug, turned up her face for a kiss.

"Let go of me," he said, weakly. Her arms felt good. She felt good as she pressed up against him. It had been a long time since Richard Cantling had held a woman in his arms; he didn't like to think about how long. And he had never had a woman like Cissy, never, never. But he was frightened. "I can't do this," he said. "I can't. I don't want to."

Cissy reached through the folds of his robe, shoved her hand inside his briefs, squeezed him gently. "Liar," she said. "You want me. You've always wanted me. I'll bet you used to stop and jack off when you were writing the sex scenes."

'No," Cantling said. "Never."

"Never?" She pouted. Her hand moved up and down. "Well, I bet you wanted to. I bet you got hard, anyway. I bet you got hard every time you described me."

"I," he said. The denial would not come, "Cissy, please."

"Please," she murmured. Her hand was busy. "Yes, please." She tugged at his briefs and they fluttered to the floor. "Please," she said. She untied his robe and helped him out of it. "Please." Her hand moved along his side, played with his nipples; she stepped closer, and her breasts pressed lightly against his chest. "Please," she said, and she looked up at him. Her tongue moved between her lips.

Richard Cantling groaned and took her in his trembling arms.

She was like no woman he had ever had. Her touch was fire and satin, electric, and her secret places were sweet as honey.

In the morning she was gone.

Cantling woke late, too exhausted to make himself breakfast. Instead he dressed and walked into town, to a small cafe in a quaint hundred-year-old brick building at the foot of the bluffs. He tried to sort things out over coffee and blueberry pancakes.

None of it made any sense. It could not be happening, but it was; denial accomplished nothing. Cantling forked down a mouthful of home-made blueberry pancake, but the only taste in his mouth was fear. He was afraid for his sanity. He was afraid because he did not understand, did not want to understand. And there was another, deeper, more basic fear.

He was afraid of what would come next. Richard Cantling had published nine novels.

He thought of Michelle. He could phone her, beg her to call it off before he went mad. She was his daughter, his flesh and blood, surely she would listen to him. She loved him. Of course she did. And he loved her too, no matter what she might think. Cantling knew his faults. He had examined himself countless times, under various guises, in the pages of his books. He was impossibly stubborn, willful, opinionated. He could be rigid and unbending. He could be cold. Still, he thought of himself as a decent man. Michelle . . . she had inherited some of his perversity, she was furious at him, hate was so very close to love, but surely she did not mean to do him serious harm.

Yes, he could phone Michelle, ask her to stop. Would she? If he begged her forgiveness, perhaps. That day, that terrible day, she'd told him that she would never forgive him, never, but she couldn't have meant that. She was his only child. The only child of his flesh, at any rate.

Cantling pushed away his empty plate and sat back. His mouth was set in a hard rigid line. Beg for mercy? He did not like that. What had he done, after all? Why couldn't they understand? Helen had never understood and Michelle was as blind as her mother. A writer must live for his work. What had he done that was so terrible? What had he done that required forgiveness? Michelle ought to be the one phoning him.

The hell with it, Cantling thought. He refused to be cowed He was right; she was wrong. Let Michelle call him if she wanted a rapprochement. She was not going to terrify him into submission. What was he so afraid of, anyway? Let her send her portraits, all the portraits she wanted to paint. He'd hang them up on his walls, display the paintings proudly (they were really an *hommage* to his work, after all), and if the damned things came alive at night and prowled through his house, so be it. He'd enjoy their visits. Cantling smiled. He'd certainly enjoyed Cissy, no doubt of that. Part of him hoped she'd come back. And even Dunnahoo, well, he was an insolent kid, but there was no real harm in him, he just liked to mouth off.

Why, now that he stopped to consider it, Cantling found that the possibilities had a certain intoxicating charm. He was uniquely privileged. Scott Fitzgerald never attended one of Gatsby's fabulous parties, Conan Doyle could never really sit down with Holmes and Watson, Nabokov never actually tumbled Lolita. What would they have said to the idea?

The more he considered things, the more cheerful he became. Michelle was trying to rebuke him, to frighten him, but she was really giving him a delicious experience. He could play chess with Sergei Tederenko, the cynical emigré hustler from *En Passant*. He could argue politics with Frank Corwin, the union organizer from his Depression novel, *Times Are Hard*. He might flirt with beautiful Beth McKenzie, go dancing with crazy old Miss Aggie, seduce the Danzinger twins and fulfill the one sexual fantasy that Cissy had left untouched, yes, certainly, what the hell had he been afraid of? They were his own creations, his characters, his friends and family.

Of course, there was the new book to consider. Cantling frowned. That was a disturbing thought. But Michelle was his daughter, she loved him, surely she wouldn't go that far. No, of course not. He put the idea firmly aside and picked up his check.

He expected it. He was almost looking forward to it. And when he returned from his evening constitutional, his cheeks red from the wind, his heart beating just a little faster in anticipation, it was there waiting for him, the familiar rectangle wrapped in plain brown paper. Richard Cantling carried it inside carefully. He made himself a cup of coffee before he unwrapped it, deliberately prolonging the suspense to savor the moment, delighting in the thought of how deftly he'd turned Michelle's cruel little plan on its head.

He drank his coffee, poured a refill, drank that. The package stood a few feet away. Cantling played a little game with himself, trying to guess whose portrait might be within. Cissy had said something about none of the characters from *Family Tree* or *Rain* being real enough. Cantling mentally reviewed his life's work, trying to decide which characters seemed most real. It was a pleasant speculation, but he could reach no firm conclusions. Finally he shoved his coffee cup aside and moved to undo the wrappings. And there it was.

Barry Leighton.

Again, the painting itself was superb. Leighton was seated in a newspaper city room, his elbow resting on the gray metal case of an old manual typewriter. He wore a rumpled brown suit and his white shirt was open at the collar and plastered to his body by perspiration. His nose had been broken more than once, and was spread all across his wide, homely, somehow comfortable face. His eyes were sleepy. Leighton was overweight and jowly and rapidly losing his hair. He'd given up smoking but not cigarettes; an unlit Camel dangled from one corner of his mouth. "As long as you don't light the damned things, you're safe," he'd said more than once in Cantling's novel *ByeLine*.

The book hadn't done very well. It was a depressing book, all about the last week of a grand old newspaper that had fallen on bad times. It was more than that, though. Cantling was interested in people, not newspapers; he had used the failing paper as a metaphor for failing lives. His editor had wanted to work in some kind of strong, sensational subplot, have Leighton and the others on the trail of some huge story that offered the promise of redemption, but Cantling had rejected that idea. He wanted to tell a story about small people being ground down inexorably by time and age, about the inevitability of loneliness and defeat. He produced a novel as gray and brittle as newsprint. He was very proud of it.

No one read it.

Cantling lifted the portrait and carried it upstairs, to hang beside those of Dunnahoo and Cissy. Tonight should be interesting, he thought. Barry Leighton was no kid, like the others; he was a man of Cantling's own years. Very intelligent, mature. There was a bitterness in Leighton, Cantling knew very well; a disappointment that life had, after all, yielded so little, that all his bylines and big stories were forgotten the day after they ran. But the reporter kept his sense of humor through all of it, kept off the demons with nothing but a mordant wit and an unlit Camel. Cantling admired him, would enjoy talking to him. Tonight, he decided, he wouldn't bother going to bed. He'd make a big pot of strong black coffee, lay in some Seagram's, and wait.

It was past midnight and Cantling was rereading the leather-bound copy of *ByeLine* when he heard ice cubes clinking together in the kitchen. "Help yourself, Barry," he called out.

Leighton came through the swinging door, tumbler in hand. "I did," he said. He looked at Cantling through heavily-lidded eyes, and gave a little snort. "You look old enough to be my father," he said. "I didn't think anybody could look *that* old."

Cantling closed the book and set it aside. "Sit down," he said. "As I recall, your feet hurt."

"My feet always hurt," Leighton said. He settled himself into an armchair and swallowed a mouthful of whisky. "Ah," he said, "that's better."

Cantling tapped the novel with a fingertip. "My eighth book," he said. "Michelle skipped right over three novels. A pity. I would have liked to meet some of those people."

"Maybe she wants to get to the point," Leighton suggested.

"And what is the point?"

Leighton shrugged. "Damned if I know. I'm only a newspaperman. Five W's and an H. You're the novelist. You tell me the point."

"My ninth novel," Cantling suggested. "The new one."

"The last one?" said Leighton.

"Of course not. Only the most recent. I'm working on something new right now."

Leighton smiled. "That's not what my sources tell me."

"Oh? What do your sources say?"

"That you're an old man waiting to die," Leighton said. "And that you're going to die alone."

"I'm fifty-two," Cantling said crisply. "Hardly old."

"When your birthday cake has got more candles than you can blow out, you're old," said Leighton drily. "Helen was younger than you, and she died five years ago. It's in the mind, Cantling. I've seen young octogenarians and old adolescents. And you, you had liver spots on your brain before you had hair on your balls."

"That's unfair," Cantling protested.

Leighton drank his Seagram's. "Fair?" he said. "You're too old to believe in fair, Cantling. Young people live life. Old people sit and watch it. You were born old. You're a watcher, not a liver." He frowned. "Not a liver, jeez, what a figure of speech. Better a liver than a gall bladder, I guess. You were never a gall bladder either. You've been full of piss for years, but you don't have any gall at all. Maybe you're a kidney."

"You're reaching, Barry," Cantling said. "I'm a writer. I've always been a writer. That's my life. Writers observe life, they report on life. It's in the job description. You ought to know."

"I do know," Leighton said. "I'm a reporter, remember? I've spent a lot of long gray years writing up other people's stories. I've got no story of my own. You know that, Cantling. Look what you did to me in *ByeLine*. The *Courier* croaks and I decide to write my memoirs and what happens?"

Cantling remembered. "You blocked. You rewrote your old stories, twenty-year-old stories, thirty-year-old stories. You had that incredible memory. You could recall all the people you'd ever reported on, the dates, the details, the quotes. You could recite the first story you'd had bylined word for word, but you couldn't remember the name of the first girl you'd been to bed with, couldn't remember your ex-wife's phone number, you couldn't . . . you couldn't. . . ." His voice failed.

"I couldn't remember my daughter's birthday," Leighton said. "Where do you get those crazy ideas, Cantling?"

Cantling was silent.

"From life, maybe?" Leighton said gently. "I was a good reporter. That was about all you could say about me. You, well, maybe you're a good novelist. That's for the critics to judge, and I'm just a sweaty newspaperman whose feet hurt. But even if you are a good novelist, even if you're one of the great ones, you were a lousy husband, and a miserable father."

"No," Cantling said. It was a weak protest.

Leighton swirled his tumbler; the ice cubes clinked and clattered. "When did Helen leave you?" he asked.

"I don't . . . ten years ago, something like that. I was in the middle of the final draft of *En Passant*."

"When was the divorce final?"

"Oh, a year later. We tried a reconciliation, but it didn't take. Michelle was in school, I remember. I was writing *Times Are Hard*."

"You remember her third grade play?"

"Was that the one I missed?"

"The one you missed? You sound like Nixon saying, 'Was that the time I lied?' That was the one Michelle had the lead in, Cantling."

"I couldn't help that," Cantling said. "I wanted to come. They were giving me an award. You don't skip the National Literary League dinner. You can't."

"Of course not," said Leighton. "When was it that Helen died?"

"I was writing *ByeLine*," Cantling said.

"Interesting system of dating you've got there. You ought to put out a calendar." He swallowed some whisky.

"All right," Cantling said. "I'm not going to deny that my work is important to me. Maybe too important, I don't know. Yes, the writing has been the biggest part of my life. But I'm a decent man, Leighton, and I've always done my best. It hasn't all been like you're implying. Helen and I had good years. We loved each other once. And

Michelle . . . I loved Michelle. When she was a little girl, I used to write stories just for her. Funny animals, space pirates, silly poems. I'd write them up in my spare time and read them to her at bedtime. They were something I did just for Michelle, for love."

"Yeah," Leighton said cynically. "You never even thought about getting them published."

Cantling grimaced. "That . . . you're implying . . . that's a distortion. Michelle loved the stories so much, I thought maybe other kids might like them too. It was just an idea. I never did anything about it."

"Never?"

Cantling hesitated. "Look, Bert was my friend as well as my agent. He had a little girl of his own. I showed him the stories once. Once!"

"I can't be pregnant," Leighton said. "I only let him fuck me once. Once!"

"He didn't even like them," Cantling said.

"Pity," replied Leighton.

"You're laying this on me with a trowel, and I'm not guilty. No, I wasn't father of the year, but I wasn't an ogre either. I changed her diaper plenty of times. Before *Black Roses,* Helen had to work, and I took care of the baby every day, from nine to five."

"You hated it when she cried and you had to leave your typewriter."

"Yes," Cantling said. "Yes, I hated being interrupted, I've always hated being interrupted, I don't care if it was Helen or Michelle or my mother or my roommate in college, when I'm writing I don't like to be interrupted. Is that a fucking capital crime? Does that make me inhuman? When she cried, I went to her. I didn't like it, I hated it, I resented it, but I *went to her.*"

"When you heard her," said Leighton. "When you weren't in bed with Cissy, dancing with Miss Aggie, beating up scabs with Frank Corwin, when your head wasn't full of their voices, yeah, sometimes you heard, and when you heard you went. Congratulations, Cantling."

"I taught her to read," Cantling said. "I read her *Treasure Island* and *Wind in the Willows* and *The Hobbit* and *Tom Sawyer,* all kinds of things."

"All books you wanted to reread anyway," said Leighton. "Helen did the real teaching, with Dick and Jane."

"*I hate Dick and Jane!*" Cantling shouted.

"So?"

"You don't know what you're talking about," Richard Cantling said. "You weren't there. Michelle was there. She loved me, she still loves

me. Whenever she got hurt, scraped her knee or got her nose blood-
ied, whatever it was, it was me she'd run to, never Helen. She'd come
crying to me and I'd hug her and dry her tears and I'd tell her . . . I
used to tell her. . . ." But he couldn't go on. He was close to tears himself; he could feel them hiding the corners of his eyes.

"I know what you used to tell her," said Barry Leighton in a sad,
gentle voice.

"She remembered it," Cantling said. "She remembered it all those
years. Helen got custody, they moved away, I didn't see her much, but
Michelle always remembered, and when she was all grown up, after
Helen was gone and Michelle was on her own, there was this time she
got hurt, and I . . . I . . ."

"Yes," said Leighton. "I know."

The police were the ones that phoned him. Detective Joyce Brennan,
that was her name, he would never forget that name. "Mister
Cantling?" she said.

"Yes?"

"Mister Richard Cantling?"

"Yes," he said. "Richard Cantling the writer." He had gotten
strange calls before. "What can I do for you?"

She identified herself. "You'll have to come down to the hospital,"
she said to him. "It's your daughter, Mister Cantling. I'm afraid she's
been assaulted."

He hated evasion, hated euphemism. Cantling's characters never
passed away, they died; they never broke wind, they farted. And
Richard Cantling's daughter . . . "Assaulted?" he said. "Do you mean
she's been assaulted or do you mean she's been raped?"

There was a silence on the other end of the line. "Raped," she said
at last. "She's been raped, Mister Cantling."

"I'll be right down," he said.

She had in fact been raped repeatedly and brutally. Michelle had
been as stubborn as Helen, as stubborn as Cantling himself. She
wouldn't take his money, wouldn't take his advice, wouldn't take the
help he offered her through his contacts in publishing. She was going
to make it on her own. She waitressed in a coffee house in the Village,
and lived in a large, drafty, and run-down warehouse loft down by the
docks. It was a terrible neighborhood, a dangerous neighborhood, and
Cantling had told her so a hundred times, but Michelle would not listen. She would not even let him pay to install good locks and a security

system. It had been very bad. The man had broken in before dawn on a Friday morning. Michelle was alone. He had ripped the phone from the wall and held her prisoner there through Monday night. Finally one of the busboys from the coffee house had gotten worried and come by, and the rapist had left by the fire escape.

When they let him see her, her face was a huge purple bruise. She had burn marks all over her, where the man had used his cigarette, and three of her ribs were broken. She was far beyond hysteria. She screamed when they tried to touch her; doctors, nurses, it didn't matter, she screamed as soon as they got near. But she let Cantling sit on the edge of her bed, and take her in his arms, and hold her. She cried for hours, cried until there were no more tears in her. Once she called him "Daddy," in a choked sob. It was the only word she spoke; she seemed to have lost the capacity for speech. Finally they tranquilized her to get her to sleep.

Michelle was in the hospital for two weeks, in a deep state of shock. Her hysteria waned day by day, and she finally became docile, so they were able to fluff her pillows and lead her to the bathroom. But she still would not, or could not, speak. The psychologist told Cantling that she might never speak again. "I don't accept that," he said. He arranged Michelle's discharge. Simultaneously he decided to get them both out of this filthy hellhole of a city. She had always loved big old spooky houses, he remembered, and she used to love the water, the sea, the river, the lake. Cantling consulted Realtors, considered a big place on the coast of Maine, and finally settled on an old steamboat gothic mansion high on the bluffs of Perrot, Iowa. He supervised every detail of the move.

Little by little, recovery began.

She was like a small child again, curious, restless, full of sudden energy. She did not talk, but she explored everything, went everywhere. In spring she spent hours up on the widow's walk, watching the big towboats go by on the Mississippi far below. Every evening they would walk together on the bluffs, and she would hold his hand. One day she turned and kissed him suddenly, impulsively, on his cheek. "I love you, Daddy," she said, and she ran away from him, and as Cantling watched her run, he saw a lovely, wounded woman in her mid-twenties, and saw too the gangling, coltish tomboy she had been.

The dam was broken after that day. Michelle began to talk again. Short, childlike sentences at first, full of childish fears and childish naïveté. But she matured rapidly, and in no time at all she was talking politics with him, talking books, talking art. They had many a fine conversation on their evening walks. She never talked about the rape, though; never once, not so much as a word.

In six months she was cooking, writing letters to friends back in New York, helping with the household chores, doing lovely things in the garden. In eight months she had started to paint again. That was very good for her; now she seemed to blossom daily, to grow more and more radiant. Richard Cantling didn't really understand the abstractions his daughter liked to paint, he preferred representational art, and best of all he loved the self-portrait she had done for him when she was still an art major in college. But he could feel the pain in these new canvases of hers, he could sense that she was engaged in an exorcism of sorts, trying to squeeze the pus from some wound deep inside, and he approved. His writing had been a balm for his own wounds more than once. He envied her now, in a way. Richard Cantling had not written a word for more than three years. The crashing commercial failure of *Byeline*, his best novel, had left him blocked and impotent. He'd thought perhaps the change of scene might restore him as well as Michelle, but that had been a vain hope. At least one of them was busy.

Finally, late one night after Cantling had gone to bed, his door opened and Michelle came quietly into his bedroom and sat on the edge of his bed. She was barefoot, dressed in a flannel nightgown covered with tiny pink flowers. "Daddy," she said, in a slurred voice.

Cantling had woken when the door opened. He sat up and smiled for her. "Hi," he said. "You've been drinking."

Michelle nodded. "I'm going back," she said. "Needed some courage, so's I could tell you."

"Going back?" Cantling said. "You don't mean to New York? You can't be serious!"

"I got to," she said. "Don't be mad. I'm better now."

"Stay here. Stay with me. New York is uninhabitable, Michelle."

"I don't want to go back. It scares me. But I got to. My friends are there. My work is there. My life is back there, Daddy. My friend Jimmy, you remember Jimmy, he's art director for this little paperback house, he can get me some cover assignments, he says. He wrote. I won't have to wait tables anymore."

"I don't believe I'm hearing this," Richard Cantling said. "How can you go back to that damned city after what happened to you there?"

"That's why I have to go back," Michelle insisted. "That guy, what he did . . . what he did to me . . ." Her voice caught in her throat. She drew in her breath, got hold of herself. "If I don't go back, it's like he ran me out of town, took my whole life away from me, my friends, my art, everything. I can't let him get away with that, can't let him scare me off. I got to go back and take up what's mine, prove that I'm not afraid."

Richard Cantling looked at his daughter helplessly. He reached out, gently touched her long, soft hair. She had finally said something that made sense in his terms. He would do the same thing, he knew. "I understand," he said. "It's going to be lonely here without you, but I understand, I do."

"I'm scared," Michelle said. "I bought plane tickets. For tomorrow."

"So soon?"

"I want to do it quickly, before I lose my nerve," she said. "I don't think I've ever been this scared. Not even . . . not even when it was happening. Funny, huh?"

"No," said Cantling. "It makes sense."

"Daddy, hold me," Michelle said. She pressed herself into his arms. He hugged her and felt her body tremble.

"You're shaking," he said.

She wouldn't let go of him. "You remember, when I was real little, I used to have those nightmares, and I'd come bawling into your bedroom in the middle of the night and crawl into bed between you and Mommy."

Cantling smiled. "I remember," he said.

"I want to stay here tonight," Michelle said, hugging him even more tightly. "Tomorrow I'll be back there, alone. I don't want to be alone tonight. Can I, Daddy?"

Cantling disengaged gently, looked her in the eyes. "Are you sure?"

She nodded; a tiny, quick, shy nod. A child's nod.

He threw back the covers and she crept in next to him. "Don't go away," she said. "Don't even go to the bathroom, okay? Just stay right here with me."

"I'm here," he said. He put his arms around her, and Michelle curled up under the covers with her head on his shoulder. They lay together that way for a long time. He could feel her heart beating inside her chest. It was a soothing sound; soon Cantling began to drift back to sleep.

"Daddy?" she whispered against his chest.

He opened his eyes. "Michelle?"

"Daddy, I have to get rid of it. It's inside me and it's poison. I don't want to take it back with me. I have to get rid of it."

Cantling stroked her hair, long slow steady motions, saying nothing.

"When I was little, you remember, whenever I fell down or got in a fight, I'd come running to you, all teary, and show you my booboo. That's what I used to call it when I got hurt, remember, I'd say I had a booboo."

"I remember," Cantling said.

"And you, you'd always hug me and you'd say, 'Show me where it hurts,' and I would and you'd kiss it and make it better, you remember that? Show me where it hurts?"

Cantling nodded. "Yes," he said softly.

Michelle was crying quietly. He could feel the wetness soaking through the top of his pajamas. "I can't take it back with me, Daddy. I want to show you where it hurts. Please. Please."

He kissed the top of her head. "Go on."

She started at the beginning, in a halting whisper.

When dawn light broke through the bedroom windows, she was still talking. They never slept. She cried a lot, screamed once or twice, shivered frequently despite the weight of the blankets; Richard Cantling never let go of her, not once, not for a single moment. She showed him where it hurt.

Barry Leighton sighed. "It was a far, far better thing you did than you had ever done," he said. "Now if you'd only gone off to that far, far better rest right then and there, that very moment, everything would have been fine." He shook his head. "You never did know when to write Thirty, Cantling."

"Why?" Cantling demanded. "You're a good man, Leighton, tell me. Why is this happening. Why?"

The reporter shrugged. He was beginning to fade now. "That was the W that always gave me the most trouble," he said wearily. "Pick the story, and let me loose, and I could tell you the who and the what and the when and the where and even the how. But the *why* . . . ah, Cantling, you're the novelist, the whys are your province, not mine.

The only Y that I ever really got on speaking terms with was the one goes with MCA."

Like the Cheshire cat, his smile lingered long after the rest of him was gone. Richard Cantling sat staring at the empty chair, at the abandoned tumbler, watching the whisky-soaked ice cubes melt slowly.

He did not remember falling asleep. He spent the night in the chair, and woke stiff and achy and cold. His dreams had been dark and shapeless and full of fear. He had slept well into the afternoon; half the day was gone. He made himself a tasteless breakfast in a kind of fog. He seemed distant from his own body, and every motion was slow and clumsy. When the coffee was ready, he poured a cup, picked it up, dropped it. The mug broke into a dozen pieces. Cantling stared down at it stupidly, watching rivulets of hot brown liquid run between the tiles. He did not have the energy to clean it up. He got a fresh mug, poured more coffee, managed to get down a few swallows.

The bacon was too salty; the eggs were runny, disgusting. Cantling pushed the meal away half-eaten, and drank more of the black, bitter coffee. He felt hung-over, but he knew that booze was not the problem.

Today, he thought. It will end today, one way or the other. She will not go back. *ByeLine* was his eighth novel, the next to last. Today the final portrait would arrive. A character from his ninth novel, his last novel. And then it would be over.

Or maybe just beginning.

How much did Michelle hate him? How badly had he wronged her? Cantling's hand shook; coffee slopped over the top of the mug, burning his fingers. He winced, cried out. Pain was so inarticulate. Burning. He thought of smoldering cigarettes, their tips like small red eyes. His stomach heaved. Cantling lurched to his feet, rushed to the bathroom. He got there just in time, gave his breakfast to the bowl. Afterwards he was too weak to move. He lay slumped against the cold white porcelain, his head swimming. He imagined somebody coming up behind him, taking him by the hair, forcing his face down into the water, flushing, flushing, laughing all the while, saying dirty, dirty, I'll get you clean, you're so dirty, flushing, flushing so the toilet ran and ran, holding his face down so the water and the vomit filled his mouth, his nostrils, until he could hardly breathe, until the world was almost black, until it was almost over, and then up again, laughing while he sucked in air, and then pushing him down again, flushing again, and again and again and again. But it was only his imagination. There was no one there. No one. Cantling was alone in the bathroom.

He forced himself to stand. In the mirror his face was gray and ancient, his hair filthy and unkempt. Behind him, leering over his shoulder, was another face. A man's face, pale and drawn, with black hair parted in the middle and slicked back. Behind a pair of small round glasses were eyes the color of dirty ice, eyes that moved constantly, frenetically, wild animals caught in a trap. They would chew off their own limbs to be free, those eyes. Cantling blinked and the face was gone. He turned on the cold tap, plunged his cupped hands under the stream, splashed water on his face. He could feel the stubble of his beard. He needed to shave. But there wasn't time, it wasn't important, he had to . . . he had to . . .

He had to do something. Get out of there. Get away, get to someplace safe, somewhere his children couldn't find him.

But there was nowhere safe, he knew.

He had to reach Michelle, talk to her, explain, plead. She loved him. She *would* forgive him, she had to. She would call it off, she would tell him what to do.

Frantic, Cantling rushed back to the living room, snatched up the phone. He couldn't remember Michelle's number. He searched around, found his address book, flipped through it wildly. There, there; he punched in the numbers.

The phone rang four times. Then someone picked it up.

"Michelle—," he started.

"Hi," she said. "This is Michelle Cantling, but I'm not in right now. If you'll leave your name and number when you hear the tone, I'll get back to you, unless you're selling something."

The beep sounded. "Michelle, are you there?" Cantling said. "I know you hide behind the machine sometimes, when you don't want to talk. It's me. Please pick up. Please."

Nothing.

"Call me back, then," he said. He wanted to get it all in; his words tumbled over reach other in their haste to get out. "I, you, you can't do it, please, let me explain, I never meant, I never meant, please . . ." There was the beep again, and then a dial tone. Cantling stared at the phone, hung up slowly. She would call him back. She had to, she was his daughter, they loved each other, she had to give him the chance to explain.

Of course, he had tried to explain before.

✿   ✿   ✿

His doorbell was the old-fashioned kind, a brass key that projected out of the door. You had to turn it by hand, and when you did it produced a loud, impatient metallic rasp. Someone was turning it furiously, turning it and turning it and turning it. Cantling rushed to the door, utterly baffled. He had never made friends easily, and it was even harder now that he had become so set in his ways. He had no real friends in Perrot, a few acquaintances perhaps, no one who would come calling so unexpectedly, and twist the bell with such energetic determination.

He undid his chain and flung the door open, wrenching the bell key out of Michelle's fingers.

She was dressed in a belted raincoat, a knitted ski cap, a matching scarf. The scarf and a few loose strands of hair were caught in the wind, moving restlessly. She was wearing high, fashionable boots and carrying a big leather shoulder bag. She looked good. It had been almost a year since Cantling had seen her, on his last Christmas visit to New York. It had been two years since she'd moved back east.

"Michelle," Cantling said. "I didn't . . . this is quite a surprise. All the way from New York and you didn't even tell me you were coming?"

"No," she snapped. There was something wrong with her voice, her eyes. "I didn't want to give you any warning, you bastard. You didn't give me any warning."

"You're upset," Cantling said. "Come in, let's talk."

"I'll come in all right." She pushed past him, kicked the door shut behind her with so much force that the buzzer sounded again. Out of the wind, her face got even harder. "You want to know why I came? I am going to tell you what I think of you. Then I'm going to turn around and leave, I'm going to walk right out of this house and out of your fucking life, just like Mom did. She was the smart one, not me. I was dumb enough to think you loved me, crazy enough to think you cared."

"Michelle, don't," Cantling said. "You don't understand. I do love you. You're my little girl, you—"

"Don't you *dare!*" she screamed at him. She reached into her shoulder bag. "You call this *love,* you rotten bastard!" She pulled it out and flung it at him.

Cantling was not as quick as he'd been. He tried to duck, but it caught him on the side of his neck, and it hurt. Michelle had thrown it hard, and it was a big, thick, heavy hardcover, not some flimsy paperback. The pages fluttered as it tumbled to the carpet; Cantling stared down at his own photograph on the back of the dust-wrapper. "You're just like your mother," he said, rubbing his neck where the book had hit. "She always threw things too. Only you aim better." He smiled weakly.

"I'm not interested in your jokes," Michelle said. "I'll never forgive you. Never. Never ever. All I want to know is how you could do this to me, that's all. You tell me. You tell me now."

"I," Cantling said. He held his hands out helplessly. "Look, I . . . you're upset now, why don't we have some coffee or something, and talk about it when you calm down a little. I don't want a big fight."

"I don't give a fuck what you want," Michelle screamed. "I want to talk about it right now!" She kicked the fallen book.

Richard Cantling felt his own anger building. It wasn't right for her to yell at him like that, he didn't deserve this attack, he hadn't done anything. He tried not to say anything for fear of saying the wrong thing and escalating the situation. He knelt and picked up his book. Without thinking, he brushed it off, turned it over almost tenderly. The title glared up at him; stark, twisted red letters against a black background, the distorted face of a pretty young woman, mouth open in a scream. *Show Me Where It Hurts.*

"I was afraid you'd take it the wrong way," Cantling said.

"The *wrong way!*" Michelle said. A look of incredulity passed across her face. "Did you think I'd *like* it?"

"I, I wasn't sure," said Cantling. "I hoped . . . I mean, I was uncertain of your reaction, and so I thought it would be better not to mention what I was working on, until, well . . ."

"Until the fucking thing was in the bookstore windows," Michelle finished for him.

Cantling flipped past the title page. "Look," he said, holding it out, "I dedicated it to you." He showed her: *To Michelle, who knew the pain.*

Michelle swung at it, knocked it out of Cantling's hands. "You bastard," she said. "You think that makes it better? You think your stinking dedication excuses what you did? Nothing excuses it. I'll never forgive you."

Cantling edged back a step, retreating in the face of her fury. "I didn't do anything," he said stubbornly. "I wrote a book. A novel. Is that a crime?"

"You're my *father,*" she shrieked. "You knew . . . you knew, you bastard, you knew I couldn't bear to talk about it, to talk about what happened. Not to my lovers or my friends or even my therapist. I can't, I just *can't,* I can't even think about it. You knew. I told you, I told only you, because you were my daddy and I trusted you and I had to get it out, and I told you, it was private, it was just between us, you knew, but what did you do? You wrote it all up in a goddamned book and *published* it for millions of people to read! Damn you, damn you. Were you planning to do that all along, you sonofabitch? Were you? That night in bed, were you memorizing every word?"

"I," said Cantling. "No, I didn't memorize anything, I just, well, I just remembered it. You're taking it all wrong, Michelle. The book's not about what happened to you. Yes, it's inspired by that, that as the starting point, but it's fiction, I changed things, it's just a novel."

"Oh yeah, Daddy, you changed things all right. Instead of Michelle Cantling it's all about Nicole Mitchell, and she's a fashion designer instead of an artist, and she's also kind of stupid, isn't she? Was that a change or is that what you think, that I was stupid to live there, stupid to let him in like that? It's all fiction, yeah. It's just a coincidence that it's about this girl that gets held prisoner and raped and tortured and terrorized and raped some more, and that you've got a daughter who was held prisoner and raped and tortured and terrorized and raped some more, right, just a fucking coincidence!"

"You don't understand," Cantling said helplessly.

"No, *you* don't understand. You don't understand what it's like. This is your biggest book in years, right? Number one best-seller, you've never been number one before, haven't even been on the lists since *Times Are Hard,* or was it *Black Roses?* And why not, why not number one, this isn't no boring story about a has-been newspaper, this is *rape,* hey, what could be hotter? Lots of sex and violence, torture and fucking and terror, and doncha know, it *really happened,* yeah." Her mouth twisted and trembled. "It was the worst thing that ever happened to me. It was all the nightmares that have ever been. I still wake up screaming sometimes, but I was getting better, it was behind me. And now it's there in every bookstore window, and all my friends know, everybody knows, strangers come up to me at parties and tell me how sorry they are." She choked back a sob; she was halfway between anger and tears. "And I pick up your book, your fucking no-good book, and there it is again, in black and white, all written down. You're such a fucking *good* writer, Daddy, you make it all so real. A book you can't put down. Well, I put it down but it didn't help, it's all there, now it will always be there, won't it? Every day somebody in the world will pick up your book and read it and I'll get raped again. That's what you did. You finished the job for him, Daddy. You violated me, took me without my consent, just like he did. You raped me. You're my own father, and you *raped* me!"

"You're not being fair," Cantling said. "I never meant to hurt you. The book . . . Nicole is strong and smart. It's the man who's the monster. He uses all those different names because fear has a thousand names, but only one face, you see. He's not just a man, he's the darkness made flesh, the mindless violence that waits out there for all of us, the gods that play with us like flies, he's a symbol of all—"

"He's the man who raped me! He's not a symbol!"

She screamed it so loudly that Richard Cantling had to retreat in the face of her fury. "No," he said. "He's just a character. He's . . . Michelle, I know it hurts, but what you went through, it's something people should know about, should think about, it's a part of life. Telling about life, making sense of it, that's the job of literature, that's my job. Someone had to tell your story. I tried to make it true, tried to do my—"

His daughter's face, red and set with tears, seemed almost feral for a moment, unrecognizable, inhuman. Then a curious calm passed across her features. "You got one thing right," she said. "Nicole didn't have a father. When I was a little kid I'd come to you crying and my daddy would say show me where it hurts, and it was a private thing, a special thing, but in the book Nicole doesn't have a father, he says it, you gave it to him, he says show me where it hurts, he says it all the time. You're so ironic. You're so clever. The way he said it, it made him so real, more real than when he *was* real. And when you wrote it, you were right. That's what the monster says. Show me where it hurts. That's the monster's line. Nicole doesn't have a father, he's dead, yes, that was right too. I don't have a father. No I don't."

"Don't you talk to me like that," Richard Cantling said. It was terror inside him; it was shame. But it came out anger. "I won't have that, no matter what you've been through. I'm your father."

"No," Michelle said, grinning crazy now, backing away from him. "No, I don't have a father, and you don't have any children, no, unless it's in your books. Those are your children, your only children. Your books, your damned fucking books, those are your children, those are your children, those are your children." Then she turned and ran past him, down the foyer. She stopped at the door to his den. Cantling was afraid of what she might do. He ran after her.

When he reached the den, Michelle had already found the knife and set to work.

Richard Cantling sat by his silent phone and watched his grandfather clock tick off the hours toward darkness.

He tried Michelle's number at three o'clock, at four, at five. The machine, always the machine, speaking in a mockery of her voice. His messages grew more desperate. It was growing dim outside. His light was fading.

Cantling heard no steps on his porch, no knock on his door, no rasping summons from his old brass bell. It was an afternoon as silent as the grave. But by the time evening had fallen, he knew it was out there. A big square package, wrapped in brown paper, addressed in a hand he had known well. Inside a portrait.

He had not understood, not really, and so she was teaching him.

The clock ticked. The darkness grew thicker. The sense of a waiting presence beyond his door seemed to fill the house. His fear had been growing for hours. He sat in the armchair with his legs pulled up under him, his mouth hanging open, thinking, remembering. Heard cruel laughter. Saw the dim red tips of cigarettes in the shadows, moving, circling. Imagined their small hot kisses on his skin. Tasted urine, blood, tears. Knew violence, knew violation, of every sort there was. His hands, his voice, his face, his face, his face. The character with a dozen names, but fear had only a single face. The youngest of his children. His baby. His monstrous baby.

He had been blocked for so long, Cantling thought. If only he could make her understand. It was a kind of impotence, not writing. He had been a writer, but that was over. He had been a husband, but his wife was dead. He had been a father, but she got better, went back to New York. She left him alone, but that last night, wrapped in his arms, she told him the story, she showed him where it hurt, she gave him all that pain. What was he to do with it?"

Afterwards he could not forget. He thought of it constantly. He began to reshape it in his head, began to grope for the words, the scenes, the symbols that would make sense of it. It was hideous, but it was life, raw strong life, the grist for Cantling's mill, the very thing he needed. She had showed him where it hurt; he could show them all. He did resist, he did try. He began a short story, an essay, finished some reviews. But it returned. It was with him every night. It would not be denied.

He wrote it.

"Guilty," Cantling said in the darkened room. And when he spoke the word, a kind of acceptance seemed to settle over him, banishing the terror. He was guilty. He had done it. He would accept the punishment, then. It was only right.

Richard Cantling stood and went to his door.

The package was there.

He lugged it inside, still wrapped, carried it up the stairs. He would hang him beside the others, beside Dunnahoo and Cissy and Barry Leighton, all in a row, yes. He went for his hammer, measured carefully, drove the nail. Only then did he unwrap the portrait, and look at the face within.

It captured her as no other artist had ever done, not just the lines of her face, the high angular cheekbones and blue eyes and tangled ash blond hair, but the personality inside. She looked so young and fresh and confident, and he could see the strength there, the courage, the stubbornness. But best of all he liked her smile. It was a lovely smile, a smile that illuminated her whole face. The smile seemed to remind him of someone he had known once. He couldn't remember who.

Richard Cantling felt a strange, brief sense of relief, followed by an even greater sense of loss, a loss so terrible and final and total that he knew it was beyond the power of the words he worshipped.

Then the feeling was gone.

Cantling stepped back, folded his arms, studied the four portraits. Such excellent work; looking at the paintings, he could almost feel their presence in his house.

Dunnahoo, his first-born, the boy he wished he'd been.

Cissy, his true love.

Barry Leighton, his wise and tired alter-ego.

Nicole, the daughter he'd never had.

His people. His characters. His children.

A week later, another, much smaller, package arrived. Inside the carton were copies of four of his novels, a bill, and a polite note from the artist inquiring if there would be any more commissions.

Richard Cantling said no, and paid the bill by check.

Introduction to "Tourists"

by Lisa Goldstein

The one year that the American Book Awards included a science fiction category (immediately howled out of existence by the dreadfully sensitive literateurs who, quite properly, feel threatened by a fiction which they do not understand, yet which is taken seriously by many intelligent and educated people), Goldstein won the award with her first novel, a paperback original entitled The Red Magician. *Who was this writer?*

I still don't know. I've never met her at any convention, or read any biographical material about her. This is what I know: For years, when people ask me to list my favorite writers working today, my brief list has invariably included Lisa Goldstein. And not because of the American Book Award—to this day I still haven't read that particular book. I came to know Goldstein only through her work, and came to know her work first through this haunting story.

Yes, Goldstein has also written a brilliant novel entitled Tourists, *and yes, it bears a superficial resemblance to this story. But, unlike most writers who adapt a short work to a longer form, she felt no allegiance to characters or outcomes or, really, anything but the most fundamental situation. Thus even if you have been fortunate enough to read the novel, the story must be read in its own right, for it is not the same tale; it immediately became part of me, a heartfelt allegory of the fundamental dilemma of human life.*

TOURISTS

Lisa Goldstein

He awoke feeling cold. He had kicked the blankets off and the air conditioning was on too high. Debbie—where was she? It was still dark out.

Confused, he pulled the blankets back and tried to go to sleep. Something was wrong. Debbie was gone, probably in the bathroom or downstairs getting a cup of coffee. And he was . . . he was on vacation, but where? Fully awake now, he sat up and tried to laugh. It was ridiculous. Imagine paying thousands of dollars for a vacation and then forgetting where you were. Greece? No, Greece was last year.

He got up and opened the curtains. The ocean ten stories below was black as sleep, paling a little to the east—it had to be east—where the sun was coming up. He turned down the air conditioning—the soft hum stopped abruptly—and headed for the bathroom. "Debbie?" he said, tentatively. He was a little annoyed. "Debbie?"

She was still missing after he had showered and shaved and dressed. "All right then," he said aloud, mostly to hear the sound of his voice. "If you're not coming, I'll go to breakfast without you." She was probably out somewhere talking to the natives, laughing when she got a word wrong, though she had told him before they left that she had never studied a foreign language. She was good at languages, then— some people were. He remembered her saying in her soft Southern accent, "For goodness sake, Charles, why do you think people will understand you if you just talk to them louder? These people just don't speak English." And then she had taken over, pointing and laughing and looking through a phrase book she had gotten some- where. And they would get the best room, the choicest steak, the blan- ket the craftswoman had woven for her own family. Charles' stock rose when he was with her, and he knew it. He hoped she would show up soon.

Soft Muzak played in the corridor and followed him into the elevator as he went down to the coffee shop. He liked the coffee shop in the hotel, liked the fact that the waiters spoke English and knew what an omelet was. The past few days he had been keeping to the hotel more and more, lying out by the beach and finally just sitting by the hotel pool drinking margaritas. The people back at the office would judge the success of the vacation by what kind of tan he got. Debbie had fretted a little and then had told him she was taking the bus in to see the ruins. She had come back darker than he was, the blond hairs on her arm bleached almost white against her brown skin, full of stories about women on the bus carrying chickens and temples crumbling in the desert. She was wearing a silver bracelet inlaid with blue and green stones.

When he paid the check he realized that he still didn't know what country he was in. The first bill he took out of his wallet had a five on each corner and a picture of some kind of spiky flower. The ten had a view of the ocean and the one, somewhat disturbingly, showed a fat coiled snake. There was what looked like an official seal on the back of all of them, but no writing. Illiterates, he thought. But he would remember soon enough, or Debbie would come back.

Back in his room, changing into his swim trunks, he thought of his passport. Feeling like a detective who has just cracked the case he got out his money belt from under the mattress and unzipped it. His passport wasn't there. His passport and his plane ticket back. The traveler's checks were still there, but useless to him without the passport as identification. Cold washed over him. He sat on the bed, his heart pounding.

Think, he told himself. They're somewhere else. They've got to be—who would steal the passport and not the traveler's checks? Unless someone needed the passport to leave the country. But who knew where he had hidden it? No one but Debbie, who had laughed at him for his precautions, and the idea of Debbie stealing the passport was absurd. But where was she?

All right, he thought. I've got to find the American consulate, work something out . . . Luckily I just cashed a traveler's check yesterday. I've been robbed, and Americans get robbed all the time. It's no big thing. I have time. I'm paid up at the hotel till—till when?

Annoyed, he realized he had forgotten that too. For the first time he wondered if there might be something wrong with him. Overwork, maybe. He would have to see someone about it when he got back to the States.

He lifted the receiver and called downstairs. "Yes, sor?" the man at the desk said.

"This is Room 1012," Charles said. "I've forgotten—I was calling to check—How long is my reservation here?"

There was a silence at the other end, a disapproving silence, Charles felt. Most of the guests had better manners than to forget the length of their stay. He wondered what the man's reaction would be if he had asked what country he was in and felt something like hysteria rise without him. He fought it down.

The man when he came back was carefully neutral. "You are booked through tonight, sor," he said. "Do you wish to extend your stay?"

"Uh—no," Charles said. "Could you tell me—Where is the American consulate?"

"We have no relations with your country, sor," the man at the desk said.

For a moment Charles did not understand what he meant. Then he asked, "Well, what about—the British consulate?"

The man at the desk laughed and said nothing. Apparently he felt no need to clarify. As Charles tried to think of another question—Australian consulate? Canadian?—the man hung up.

Charles stood up carefully. "All right," he said to the empty room. "First things first." He got his two suitcases out of the closet and went through them methodically. Debbie's carrying case was still there and he went through that too. He checked under both mattresses, in the nightstand, in the medicine cabinet in the bathroom. Nothing. All right then. Debbie had stolen it, had to have. But why? And why didn't she take her carrying case with her when she went?

He wondered if she would show up back at the office. She had worked down the hall from him, one of the partners' secretaries. He had asked her along for companionship, making it clear that there were no strings attached, that he was simply interested in not traveling alone. Sometimes this kind of relationship turned sexual and sometimes it didn't. Last year, with Katya from accounting, it had. This year it hadn't.

There was still nothing to worry about, Charles thought, snapping the locks on the suitcases. Things like this probably happened all the time. He would get to the airport, where they would no doubt have records, a listing of his flight, and he would explain everything to them there. He checked his wallet for credit cards and found that they were still there. Good, he thought. Now we get to see if the advertisements are true. Accepted all over the world.

He felt so confident that he decided to stay the extra day at the hotel. After all, he thought, I've paid for it. And maybe Debbie will come back. He threw his towel over his shoulder and went downstairs.

The usual people were sitting out by the pool. Millie and Jean, the older women from Miami. The two newlyweds who had kept pretty much to themselves. The hitchhiker who was just passing through and who had been so entertaining that no one had had the heart to report him to the hotel management. Charles nodded to them and ordered his margarita form the bar before sitting down.

Talk flowed around him. "Have you been to Djuzban yet?" Jean was saying to the retired couple who had just joined them at the pool. "We took the hotel tour yesterday. The marketplace is just fabulous. I bought this ring there—see it?" And she flashed silver and stones.

"I hear the ruins are pretty good out in Djuzban," the retired man said.

"Oh, Harold," his wife said. "Harold wants to climb every tower in the country."

"No, man, for ruins you gotta go to Zabla," the hitchhiker said. "But the buses don't go there—you gotta rent a car. It's way the hell out in the desert, unspoiled, untouched. If your car breaks down you're dead—ain't nobody passing through that way for days."

Harold's wife shuddered in the heat. "I just want to do some shopping before we go home," she said. "I heard you can pick up bargains in leather in Qarnatl."

"All we saw in Qarnatl were natives trying to sell us decks of cards," Jean said. She turned to Millie. "Remember? I don't know why they thought Americans would be interested in their playing cards. They weren't even the same as ours."

Charles sipped his margarita, listening to the exotic names flow around him. What if he told them the names meant nothing to him, nothing at all? But he was too embarrassed. There were appearances to keep up after all, the appearance of being a seasoned traveler, of knowing the ropes. He would find out soon enough, anyway.

The day wore on. Charles had a margarita, then another. When the group around the pool broke up it seemed the most natural thing in the world to follow them into the hotel restaurant and order a steak, medium-rare. He was running low on cash, he noticed—he'd have to cash another traveler's check in the morning.

But in the morning when he awoke, cold sober, he knew immediately what he'd done. He reached for his wallet on the nightstand, fingers trembling a little. There was only a five with its bleak little picture of a shrub left. Well, he thought, feeling a little shaky. Maybe someone's going to the airport today. Probably. The guys in the office aren't going to believe this one.

He packed up his two suitcases, leaving Debbie's overnight bag for her in case she came back. Downstairs he headed automatically for the coffee shop before he remembered. Abruptly he felt his hunger grow worse. "Excuse me," he said to the man at the desk. "How much—do you know how much the taxi to the airport is?"

"No speak English, sor," the man said. He was small and dark, like most of the natives. His teeth were stained red.

"You don't—" Charles said, disgusted. "Why in God's name would they hire someone who doesn't speak English? How much," he said slowly. "Taxi. Airport." He heard his voice grow louder; apparently Debbie was right.

The man shrugged. Another man joined them. Charles turned on him with relief. "How much is the taxi to the airport?"

"Oh, taxi," the man said, as though the matter were not very important. "Not so much, sor. Eight, nine. Maybe fifteen."

"Fifteen?" Charles said. He tried to remember the airport, remember how he'd gotten here. "Not five?" He held up five fingers.

The second man laughed. "Oh no, sor," he said. "Fifteen. Twenty." He shrugged.

Charles looked around in desperation. Hotel Tours, said the sign behind the front desk. Ruins. Free. "The ruins," he said, pointing to the sign, wondering if either of the men could read. "Are they near the airport?" He could go to the ruins, maybe get a ride. . . .

"Near?" the second man said. He shrugged again. "Maybe. Yes, I think so."

"How near?" Charles said.

"Near," the second man said. "Yes. Near enough."

Charles picked up the two suitcases and followed the line of tourists to the bus stop. See, he thought. Nothing to worry about, and you're even getting a free ride to the airport. Those taxi drivers are thieves anyway.

It was awkward maneuvering the suitcases up the stairs of the bus. "I'm going on to the airport," Charles said to the driver, feeling the need to explain.

"Of course, sor," the driver said, shrugging as if to say that an American's suitcases were no business of his. He added a word that Charles didn't catch. Perhaps it was in his native language.

The bus set off down the new two-lane highway fronting the hotels. Soon they left the hotels behind, passed a cluster of run-down shacks, and were heading into the desert. The air conditioning hummed loudly. Waves of heat traveled across the sands.

After nearly an hour the bus stopped. "We have one hour," the driver said in bad English. He opened the door. "These are the temple of Marmaz. Very old. One hour." The tourists filed out. A few were adjusting cameras or pointing lenses.

Because of the suitcases Charles was the last out. He squinted against the sun. The temple was a solid wall of white marble against the sand. Curious in spite of himself he crossed the parking lot, avoiding the native who was trying to show him something. "Pure silver," the small man said, calling after him. "Special price just for you."

In front of the temple was a cracked marble pool, now dry. Who were these people who had carried water into the desert, who had imprisoned the moon in pale marble? But then how much had he known about the other tourist spots he had visited, the Greeks who had built the Parthenon, the Mayans who had built the pyramids? He followed the line of tourists into the temple, feeling the coolness fall over him like a blessing.

He went from room to room, delighted, barely feeling the weight of the suitcases. He saw crumbling mosaics of reds and blues and greens, fragments of tapestries, domes, fountains, towers, a white dining hall that could seat a hundred. In one small room a native was explaining a piece of marble sculpture to a dozen Americans.

"This, he is the god of the sun," the native said. "And in the next room, the goddess of the moon. Moon, yes? We will go see her after. Once a year, at the end of the year, the two statues—statues, yes?—go outside. The priests take outside. They get married. Her baby is the new year."

"What nonsense," a woman standing near Charles said quietly. She was holding a guidebook. "That's the fourth king. He built the temple. God of the sun." She laughed scornfully.

"Can I—can I see that book for a minute?" Charles said. The cover had flipped forward tantalizingly, almost revealing the name of the country.

The woman looked briefly at her watch. "Got to go," she said. "The bus is leaving in a minute and I've got to find my husband. Sorry."

Charles' bus was gone by the time he left the temple. It was much cooler now but heat still rose from the desert sands. He was very hungry, nearly tempted to buy a cool drink and a sandwich at the refreshment stand near the parking lot. "Cards?" someone said to him.

Charles turned. The small native said something that sounded like "Tiraz!" It was the same word the bus driver had said to him in the morning. Then, "Cards?" he said again.

"What?" Charles said impatiently, looking for a taxi.

"Ancient playing set," the native said. "Very holy." He took out a deck of playing cards from an embroidered bag and spread them for Charles. The colors were very bright. "Souvenir," the native said. He grinned, showing red-stained teeth. "Souvenir of your trip."

"No, thank you," Charles said. All around the parking lot, it seemed, little natives were trying to sell tourists rings and pipes and blouses and, for some reason, packs of playing cards. "Taxi?" he said. "Is there a taxi here?"

The native shrugged and moved on to the next tourist.

It was getting late. Charles went towards the nearest tour bus. The driver was leaning against the bus, smoking a small cigarette wrapped in a brown leaf. "Where can I find a taxi?" Charles asked him.

"No taxis," the driver said.

"No—why not?" Charles said. This country was impossible. He couldn't wait to get out, to be on a plane drinking a margarita and heading back to the good old U.S.A. This was the worst vacation he'd ever had. "Can I make a phone call? I have to get to the airport."

A woman about to get on the bus heard him and stopped. "The airport?" she said. "The airport's fifty miles from here. At least. You'll never find a taxi to take you that far."

"Fifty miles?" Charles said. "They told me—At the hotel they told me it was fairly close." For a moment his confidence left him. What do I do now? he thought. He sagged against the suitcases.

"Listen," the woman said. She turned to the bus driver. "We've got room. Can't we take him back to the city with us? I think we're the last bus to leave."

The driver shrugged. "For the tiraz, of course. Anything is possible."

If Charles hadn't been so relieved at the ride he would have been annoyed. What did this word tiraz mean? Imbecile? Man with two suitcases? He followed the woman onto the bus.

"I can't believe you thought this was close to the airport," the woman said. He sat across the aisle from her. "This is way out in the desert. There's nothing here. No one would come out here if it wasn't for the ruins."

"They told me at the hotel," Charles said. He didn't really want to discuss it. He was no longer the seasoned traveler, the man who had regaled the people around the pool with stories of Mexico, Greece, Hawaii. He would have to confess, have to go back to the hotel and tell someone the whole story. Maybe they would bring in the police to find Debbie. A day wasted and he had only gone around in a circle, back to where he started. He felt tired and very hungry.

But when the bus stopped it was not at the brightly-lit row of hotels. He strained to see in the oncoming dusk. "I thought you said—" He turned to the woman, hating to sound foolish again. 'I thought we were going to the city."

"This is—" the woman said. Then she nodded in understanding. "You want the new city, the tourist city. That's up the road about ten miles. Any cab'll take you there."

Charles was the last off the bus again, slowed this time not so much by the suitcases as by the new idea. People actually stayed in the same cities where the natives lived. He had heard of it being done but he had thought only young people did it, students and drifters and hitchhikers like the one back at the hotel. This woman was not young and she had been fairly pleasant. He wished he had remembered to thank her.

The first cab driver laughed when Charles showed him the five note and asked to be taken to the new city. The driver was not impressed by the traveler's checks. The second and third drivers turned him down flat. The city smelled of motor oil and rancid fish. It was getting late, even a little chilly, and Charles began to feel nervous about being out so late. The two suitcases were an obvious target for some thief. And where would he go? What would he do?

The panic that he had suppressed for so long took over now and he began to run. He dove deeper into the twisting maze of the city, not caring where he went so long as he was moving. Everything was closed and there were few streetlamps. He heard the sounds of his footfalls echo off the shuttered buildings. A cat jumped out of his way, eyes flashing gold.

After a long time of running he began to slow. 'Tiraz!" someone whispered to him from an abandoned building. His heart pounded.

He did not look back. Ahead was a lit storefront, a store filled with clutter. The door was open. A pawn shop.

He went in with relief. He cleared a space for himself among the old magazines and rusty baking pans and child's beads. The man behind the counter watched but made no comment. He took out everything from the two suitcases, sorted out what he needed and repacked it and gave the other suitcase to the man behind the counter. The man went to a small desk, unlocked a drawer and took out a steel box. He counted out some money and offered it to Charles. Charles accepted it wordlessly, not even bothering to count it.

The money bought a meal tasting of sawdust and sesame oil and a sagging bed in an old hotel. The overhead fan turned all night because Charles could not figure out how to turn it off. A cockroach watched impassively from the corner.

The city looked different in daylight. Women in shawls and silver bracelets, men in clothes fashionable fifty years ago walked past the hotel as Charles looked out in the morning. The sun was shining. His heart rose. This was going to be the day he made it to the airport.

He walked along the streets almost jauntily, ignoring the ache in his arms. His beard itched because last night, in a moment of panic, he had thrown his electric razor into the suitcase to be sold. He shrugged. There were still things he could sell. Today he would find a better pawn shop.

He walked, passing run-down houses and outdoor markets, beggars and children, automobile garages and dim restaurants smelling of frying fish. "Excuse me," he said to a man leaning against a horse-drawn carriage. "Do you know where I can find a pawn shop?"

The man and horse both looked up. "Ride, yes?" the man said enthusiastically. "Famous monuments. Very cheap."

"No," Charles said. "A pawn shop. Do you understand?"

The man shrugged, pulled the horse's mane. "No speak English," he said finally.

Another man had come up behind Charles. "Pawn shop?" he said.

Charles turned quickly, relieved. "Yes," he said. "Do you know—"

"Two blocks down," the man said. "Turn left, go five blocks. Across the hospital."

"What street is that?" Charles asked.

"Street?" the man said. He frowned. "Two blocks down and turn left."

"The name," Charles said. "The name of the street."

To Charles' astonishment the man burst out laughing. The carriage-driver laughed too, though he could not have possibly known what they were talking about. "Name?" the man said. "You tourists name your streets as though they were little children, yes?" He laughed again, wiping his eyes, and said something to the carriage-driver in another language, speaking rapidly.

"Thank you," Charles said. He walked the two blocks, turned left and went five blocks more. There was no hospital where the man had said there would be, and no pawn shop. A man who spoke a little English said something about a great fire, but whether it had been last week or several years ago Charles was unable to find out.

He started back toward the man who had given him directions. In a few minutes he was hopelessly lost. The streets became dingier and once he saw a rat run from a pile of newspapers. The fire had swept through this part of the city leaving buildings charred and water-damaged, open to the passers-by like museum exhibits. Two dirty children ran towards him, shouting, "Money, please, sor! Money for food!" He turned down a side street to lose them.

Ahead of him were three young men in grease-stained clothes. One of them hissed something at him, the words rushing by like a fork of lightning. Another held a length of chain which he played back and forth, whispering, between his hands. "I don't speak—" Charles said, but it was too late. They were on him.

One tore the suitcase from his hand, shouting "El amak! El amak!" Another knocked him down with a punch to his stomach that forced the wind out of him. The third was going through his pockets, taking his wallet and the little folder of traveler's checks. Charles tried feebly to rise and the second one thrust him back, hitting him once more in the stomach. The first one yelled something and they ran quickly down the street. Charles lay where they left him, gasping for breath.

The two dirty children passed him, and an old woman balancing a basket of clothes on her head. After a few minutes he rolled over and sat up, leaning against a rusty car up on blocks. His pants were torn, he noticed dully, torn and smeared with oil. And his suitcase with the rest of his clothes was gone.

He would go to the police, go and tell them that his suitcase was gone. He knew the word for suitcase because the young thief had shouted it. Amak. El amak. And suddenly he understood something that knocked the breath out of him as surely as a punch to the stomach, understood that he had understood nothing since coming to this country. At the back of his mind, despite all his education, he had somehow expected every native he met to drop this ridiculous charade and start speaking like normal people. But now, learning his first word in this strange tongue, he came to a realization of language, understood in his bones that every word you could think of—hand, love, table, hot—was conveyed to these natives by another word, a word not English. He tried to laugh at his stupidity but the pain wrenched his stomach and he stopped abruptly.

After a while he stood up gingerly, breathing shallowly to make the pain go away. He began walking again, following the maze of the city in deeper. At last he found a small park and sat on a bench to rest.

A native came up to him almost immediately. "Cards?" the native said. "Look." He opened his embroidered bag.

Charles sighed. He was too tired to walk away. "I don't want any cards," he said. "I don't have any money."

"Of course not," the native said. "Look. They are beautiful, no?" He spread the brightly colored cards on the grass. Charles saw a baseball player, a fortune-teller, a student, some designs he didn't recognize. "Look," the native said again and turned over the next card. "The tourist."

Charles had to laugh, looking at the card of the man carrying suitcases. These people had been visited by tourists for so long that the tourist had become an archetype, a part of everyone's reality like kings and jokers. He looked closer at the card. Those suitcases were familiar. And the tourist . . . he jerked back as though shocked. It was him.

He stood quickly and began to run, ignoring the pain in his stomach. The native did not follow.

He noticed the card-sellers on every corner after that. They called to him even if he crossed the street to avoid them. "Tiraz, tiraz!" they called after him. He knew what it meant now. Tourist.

As the sun set he became ravenously hungry. He walked around a beggar-woman squatting in the street and saw, too late, a card-seller waiting on the corner. The card-seller held out something to him, some kind of pastry, and Charles took it, too hungry to refuse.

The pastry was filled with meat and very good. As though that were the signal the other card-sellers he passed began to give him things— a skin of wine, a piece of fish wrapped in paper. One of them handed him money, far more money than a deck of cards would cost. It was growing dark. He took a room for the night with the money.

✿   ✿   ✿

A card-seller was waiting for him at the corner the next day. "All right," Charles said to him. Some of the belligerence had been knocked out of him. "I give up. What the hell's going on around here?"

"Look," the card-seller said. He took his cards out of the embroidered bag. "It is in here." He squatted on the sidewalk, oblivious to the dirt, the people walking by, the fumes from the street. The street, Charles noticed as he sat next to him, seemed to be paved with bottle-caps.

The card-seller spread the cards in front of him. "Look," he said. "It is foretold. The cards are our oracle, our newspaper, our entertainment. All depends on how you read them." Charles wondered where the man had learned to speak English but he didn't want to interrupt. "See," the man said as he turned over a card. "Here you are. The tourist. It was foretold that you would come to the city."

"And then what?" Charles asked. "How do I get back?"

"We have to ask the cards," the man said. Idly he turned over another card, the ruins of Marmaz. "Maybe we wait for the next printing."

"Next—" Charles said. "You mean the cards don't stay the same?"

"No," the man said. "Do your newspapers stay the same?"

"But—who prints them?"

The man shrugged. "We do not know." He turned over another card, a young blonde woman.

"Debbie!" Charles said, startled.

"Yes," the man said. "The woman you came with. We had to convince her to go, so that you would fulfill the prophecy and come to the city. And then we took your pieces of paper, the ones that are so important to the tiraz. That is a stupid way to travel, if I may say so. In the city the only papers that are important to us are the cards, and if a man loses his cards he can easily get more."

"You—you took my passport?" Charles said. He did not feel as angry as he would like. "My passport and my plane tickets? Where are they?"

"Ah," the man said. "For that you must ask the cards." He took out another set of cards from his bag and gave them to Charles. Before Charles could answer he stood up and walked away.

By mid-day Charles had found the small park again. He sat down and spread out the cards, wondering if there was anything to what the card-seller had said. Debbie did not appear in his deck. Was his an earlier printing, then, or a later one?

An American couple came up to him as he sat puzzling over the cards. "There are those cards again," the woman said. "I just can't get over how quaint they are. How much are you charging for yours?" she asked Charles. "The man down the street said he'd give them to us for ten."

"Eight," Charles said without hesitation, gathering them up.

The woman looked at her husband. "All right," he said. He took a five and three ones from his wallet and gave them to Charles.

"Thank you, sor," Charles said.

The man grunted. "I thought he spoke English very well," the woman said as they walked away. "Didn't you?"

A card-seller gave him three more decks of cards and an embroidered bag later that day. By evening he had sold two of the decks. A few nights later, he joined the sellers of cards as they waited in the small park for the new printing of the cards. Somewhere a bell tolled midnight. A woman with beautiful long dark hair and an embroidered shawl came out of the night and silently took out the decks of cards from her bag. Her silver bracelets flashed in the moonlight. She gave Charles twelve decks. The men around him were already tearing the boxes open and spreading the cards, reading the past, or the present, or the future.

After about three years Charles got tired of selling the cards. His teeth had turned red from chewing the nut everyone chewed and he had learned to smoke the cigarettes wrapped in leaves.

The other men had always told him that someone who spoke English as well as he did should be a tour guide, and finally he decided that they were right. Now he takes groups of tourists through the ruins of Marmaz, telling them about the god of the sun and the goddess of the moon and whatever else he chooses to make up that day. He has never found out what country he lives in.

Introduction to "Blood Music"

by Greg Bear

I remember attending a cyberpunk panel at a convention in (I think) Austin, where Greg Bear shared a platform with Lewis Shiner and John Shirley. Shiner, definitely a co-conspirator with Bruce Sterling in the movement that had just been christened cyberpunk, was not even sure he wanted to be a science fiction writer; Shirley had always been punk (in the musical sense) and was perfectly content to add the "cyber." But Greg Bear seemed genuinely baffled. Why was he being included on this panel? He was a hard-sf writer working within the tradition of cool-idea sf, but with real attention to believable characters. He didn't pose or wear mirrorshades, nor did his characters.

The thing is, he wrote "Blood Music," and as cyberpunk was struggling for attention and credibility (back in the days before it became the mot-du-jour in the world of fashion and the fashionable arts), its proponents were seizing upon any story that seemed to have the "right" sensibility and claiming it for their own. Thus Greg Bear, writer, illustrator, family man, and all-around nice guy, found himself hailed as hero by a bunch of people for whom rage was the default emotion. Greg Bear had found a cool new way to destroy a world.

Well, that phase soon passed. Whether anybody bothers now to try to fit the cyberpunk label to Bear hardly matters. He has produced enough work that what he writes is not part of someone else's movement. "The writing of Greg Bear" is a phrase that includes more originality and accomplishment than the label "cyberpunk" ever has. Would that more cyberpunks were Bearish (or Bearesque, or Ursine, or Bearlike, or whatever the term would be).

In fact, if you chart a broad line of the mainstream of science fiction, rooted in Heinlein, Asimov, and Clarke, tracking through

Silverberg, Le Guin, and Niven, with Ellison just off to one side and Forward just off to the other, that mainstream arrow will end up pointed straight at Greg Bear. The movement he belongs to, that he epitomizes, is called "science fiction," and as long as Bear is writing, science fiction is in good health.

BLOOD MUSIC

Greg Bear

There is a principle in nature I don't think anyone has pointed out before. Each hour, a myriad of trillions of little live things—bacteria, microbes, "animalcules"—are born and die, not counting for much except in the bulk of their existence and the accumulation of their tiny effects. They do not perceive deeply. They do not suffer much. A hundred billion, dying, would not begin to have the same importance as a single human death.

Within the ranks of magnitude of all creatures, small as microbes or great as humans, there is an equality of "elan," just as the branches of a tall tree, gathered together, equal the bulk of the limbs below, and all the limbs equal the bulk of the trunk.

That, at least, is the principle. I believe Vergil Ulam was the first to violate it.

It had been two years since I'd last seen Vergil. My memory of him hardly matched the tan, smiling, well-dressed gentleman standing before me. We had made a lunch appointment over the phone the day before, and now faced each other in the wide double doors of the employees' cafeteria at the Mount Freedom Medical Center.

"Vergil?" I asked. "My God, Vergil!"

"Good to see you, Edward." He shook my hand firmly. He had lost ten or twelve kilos and what remained seemed tighter, better proportioned. At university, Vergil had been the pudgy, shock-haired, snaggle-toothed whiz kid who hot-wired doorknobs, gave us punch that turned our piss blue, and never got a date except with Eileen Termagent, who shared many of his physical characteristics.

"You look fantastic," I said. "Spend a summer in Cabo San Lucas?"

We stood in line at the counter and chose our food. "The tan," he said, picking out a carton of chocolate milk, "is from spending three months under a sunlamp. My teeth were straightened just after I last saw you. I'll explain the rest, but we need a place to talk where no one will listen close."

I steered him to the smoker's corner, where three diehard puffers were scattered among six tables.

"Listen, I mean it," I said as we unloaded our trays. "You've changed. You're looking good."

"I've changed more than you know." His tone was motion-picture ominous, and he delivered the line with a theatrical lift of his brows. "How's Gail?"

Gail was doing well, I told him, teaching nursery school. We'd married the year before. His gaze shifted down to his food—pineapple slice and cottage cheese, piece of banana cream pie—and he said, his voice almost cracking, "Notice something else?"

I squinted in concentration. "Uh."

"Look closer."

"I'm not sure. Well, yes, you're not wearing glasses. Contacts?"

"No. I don't need them anymore."

"And you're a snappy dresser. Who's dressing you now? I hope she's as sexy as she is tasteful."

"Candice isn't—wasn't responsible for the improvement in my clothes," he said. "I just got a better job, more money to throw around. My taste in clothes is better than my taste in food, as it happens." He grinned the old Vergil self-deprecating grin, but ended it with a peculiar leer. "At any rate, she's left me, I've been fired from my job, I'm living on savings."

"Hold it," I said. "That's a bit crowded. Why not do a linear breakdown? You got a job. Where?"

"Genetron Corp.," he said. "Sixteen months ago."

"I haven't heard of them."

"You will. They're putting out common stock in the next month. It'll shoot off the board. They've broken through with MABs. Medical—"

"I know what MABs are," I interrupted. "At least in theory. Medically Applicable Biochips."

"They have some that work."

"What?" It was my turn to lift my brows.

"Microscopic logic circuits. You inject them into the human body, they set up shop where they're told and troubleshoot. With Dr. Michael Bernard's approval."

That was quite impressive. Bernard's reputation was spotless. Not only was he associated with the genetic engineering biggies, but he had made news at least once a year in his practice as a neurosurgeon before retiring. Covers on *Time, Mega, Rolling Stone.*

"That's supposed to be secret—stock, breakthrough, Bernard, everything." He looked around and lowered his voice. "But you do whatever the hell you want. I'm through with the bastards."

I whistled. "Make me rich, huh?"

"If that's what you want. Or you can spend some time with me before rushing off to your broker."

"Of course." He hadn't touched the cottage cheese or pie. He had, however, eaten the pineapple slice and drunk the chocolate milk. "So tell me more."

"Well, in med school I was training for lab work. Biochemical research. I've always had a bent for computers, too. So I put myself through my last two years—"

"By selling software packages to Westinghouse," I said.

"It's good my friends remember. That's how I got involved with Genetron, just when they were starting out. They had big money backers, all the lab facilities I thought anyone would ever need. They hired me, and I advanced rapidly.

"Four months and I was doing my own work. I made some breakthroughs"—he tossed his hand nonchalantly—"then I went off on tangents they thought were premature. I persisted and they took away my lab, handed it over to a certifiable flatworm. I managed to save part of the experiment before they fired me. But I haven't exactly been cautious . . . or judicious. So now it's going on outside the lab."

I'd always regarded Vergil as ambitious, a trifle cracked, and not terribly sensitive. His relations with authority figures had never been smooth. Science, for him, was like the woman you couldn't possibly have, who suddenly opens her arms to you, long before you're ready for mature love—leaving you afraid you'll forever blow the chance, lose the prize. Apparently, he did. "Outside the lab? I don't get you."

"Edward, I want you to examine me. Give me a thorough physical. Maybe a cancer diagnostic. Then I'll explain more."

"You want a five-thousand-dollar exam?"

"Whatever you can do. Ultrasound, NMR, thermogram, everything."

"I don't know if I can get access to all that equipment. NMR full-scan has only been here a month or two. Hell, you couldn't pick a more expensive way—"

"Then ultrasound. That's all you'll need."

"Vergil, I'm an obstetrician, not a glamour-boy lab-tech. OB-GYN, butt of all jokes. If you're turning into a woman, maybe I can help you."

He leaned forward, almost putting his elbow into the pie, but swinging wide at the last instant by scant millimeters. The old Vergil would have hit it square. "Examine me closely and you'll . . ." He narrowed his eyes. "Just examine me."

"So I make an appointment for ultrasound. Who's going to pay?"

"I'm on Blue Shield." He smiled and held up a medical credit card. "I messed with the personnel files at Genetron. Anything up to a hundred thousand dollars medical, they'll never check, never suspect."

He wanted secrecy, so I made arrangements. I filled out his forms myself. As long as everything was billed properly, most of the examination could take place without official notice. I didn't charge for my services. After all, Vergil had turned my piss blue. We were friends.

He came in late at night. I wasn't normally on duty then, but I stayed late, waiting for him on the third floor of what the nurses called the Frankenstein wing. I sat on an orange plastic chair. He arrived, looking olive-colored under the fluorescent lights.

He stripped, and I arranged him on the table. I noticed, first off, that his ankles looked swollen. But they weren't puffy. I felt them several times. They seemed healthy but looked odd. "Hm," I said.

I ran the paddles over him, picking up areas difficult for the big unit to hit, and programmed the data into the imaging system. Then I swung the table around and inserted it into the enameled orifice of the ultrasound diagnostic unit, the hum-hole, so-called by the nurses.

I integrated the data from the hum-hole with that from the paddle sweeps and rolled Vergil out, then set up a video frame. The image took a second to integrate, then flowed into a pattern showing Vergil's skeleton. My jaw fell.

Three seconds of that and it switched to his thoracic organs, then his musculature, and, finally, vascular system and skin.

"How long since the accident?" I asked, trying to take the quiver out of my voice.

"I haven't been in an accident," he said. "It was deliberate."

"Jesus, they beat you to keep secrets?"

"You don't understand me, Edward. Look at the images again. I'm not damaged."

"Look, there's thickening here"—I indicated the ankles—"and your ribs—that crazy zigzag pattern of interlocks. Broken sometime, obviously. And—"

"Look at my spine," he said. I rotated the image in the video frame.

Buckminster Fuller, I thought. It was fantastic. A cage of triangular projections, all interlocking in ways I couldn't begin to follow, much less understand. I reached around and tried to feel his spine with my fingers. He lifted his arms and looked off at the ceiling.

"I can't find it," I said. "It's all smooth back there." I let go of him and looked at his chest, then prodded his ribs. They were sheathed in something tough and flexible. The harder I pressed, the tougher it became. Then I noticed another change.

"Hey," I said. "You don't have any nipples." There were tiny pigment patches, but no nipple formations at all.

"See?" Vergil asked, shrugging on the white robe, "I'm being rebuilt from the inside out."

In my reconstruction of those hours, I fancy myself saying, "So tell me about it." Perhaps mercifully, I don't remember what I actually said.

He explained with his characteristic circumlocutions. Listening was like trying to get to the meat of a newspaper article through a forest of sidebars and graphic embellishments.

I simplify and condense.

Genetron had assigned him to manufacturing prototype biochips, tiny circuits made out of protein molecules. Some were hooked up to silicon chips little more than a micrometer in size, then sent through rat arteries to chemically keyed locations, to make connections with the rat tissue and attempt to monitor and even control lab-induced pathologies.

"*That* was something," he said.

"We recovered the most complex microchip by sacrificing the rat, then debriefed it—hooked the silicon portion up to an imaging system. The computer gave us bar graphs, then a diagram of the chemical characteristics of about eleven centimeters of blood vessel . . . then put it all together to make a picture. We zoomed down eleven centimeters of rat artery. You never saw so many scientists jumping up and down, hugging each other, drinking buckets of bug juice." Bug juice was lab ethanol mixed with Dr Pepper.

Eventually, the silicon elements were eliminated completely in favor of nucleoproteins. He seemed reluctant to explain in detail, but I gathered they found ways to make huge molecules—as large as DNA, and even more complex—into electrochemical computers, using ribosome-like structures as "encoders" and "readers" and RNA as "tape." Vergil was able to mimic reproductive separation and reassembly in his nucleoproteins, incorporating program changes at key points by switching nucleotide pairs. "Genetron wanted me to switch over to supergene engineering, since that was the coming thing everywhere else. Make all kinds of critters, some out of our imagination. But I had different ideas." He twiddled his finger around his ear and made theremin sounds. "Mad scientist time, right?" He laughed, then sobered. "I injected my best nucleoproteins into bacteria to make duplication and compounding easier. Then I started to leave them inside, so the circuits could interact with the cells. They were heuristically programmed; they taught themselves. The cells fed chemically coded information to the computers, the computers processed it and made decisions, the cells became smart. I mean, smart as planaria, for starters. Imagine an *E. coli* as smart as a planarian worm!"

I nodded. "I'm imagining."

"Then I really went off on my own. We had the equipment, the techniques; and I knew the molecular language. I could make really dense, really complicated biochips by compounding the nucleoproteins, making them into little brains. I did some research into how far I could go, theoretically. Sticking with bacteria, I could make a biochip with the computing capacity of a sparrow's brain. Imagine how jazzed I was! Then I saw a way to increase the complexity a thousandfold, by using something we regarded as a nuisance—quantum chit-chat between the fixed elements of the circuits. Down that small, even the slightest change could bomb a biochip. But I developed a program that actually predicted and took advantage of electron tunneling. Emphasized the heuristic aspects of the computer, used the chit-chat as a method of increasing complexity."

"You're losing me," I said.

"I took advantage of randomness. The circuits could repair themselves, compare memories, and correct faulty elements. I gave them basic instructions: Go forth and multiply. Improve. By God, you should have seen some of the cultures a week later! It was amazing. They were evolving all on their own, like little cities. I destroyed them all. I think one of the petri dishes would have grown legs and walked out of the incubator if I'd kept feeding it."

"You're kidding." I looked at him. "You're not kidding."

"Man, they *knew* what it was like to improve! They knew where they had to go, but they were just so limited, being in bacteria bodies, with so few resources."

"How smart were they?"

"I couldn't be sure. They were associating in clusters of a hundred to two hundred cells, each cluster behaving like an autonomous unit. Each cluster might have been as smart as a rhesus monkey. They exchanged information through their pili, passed on bits of memory, and compared notes. Their organization was obviously different from a group of monkeys. Their world was so much simpler, for one thing. With their abilities, they were masters of the petri dishes. I put phages in with them; the phages didn't have a chance. They used every option available to change and grow."

"How is that possible?"

"What?" He seemed surprised I wasn't accepting everything at face value.

"Cramming so much into so little. A rhesus monkey is not your simple little calculator, Vergil."

"I haven't made myself clear," he said, obviously irritated. "I was using nucleoprotein computers. They're like DNA, but all the information can interact. Do you know how many nucleotide pairs there are in the DNA of a single bacteria?"

It had been a long time since my last biochemistry lesson. I shook my head.

"About two million. Add in the modified ribosome structures—fifteen thousand of them, each with a molecular weight of about three million—and consider the combinations and permutations. The RNA is arranged like a continuous loop paper tape, surrounded by ribosomes ticking off instructions and manufacturing protein chains . . ." His eyes were bright and slightly moist. "Besides, I'm not saying every cell was a distinct entity. They cooperated."

"How many bacteria in the dishes you destroyed?"

"Billions. I don't know." He smirked. "You got it, Edward. Whole planetsful of *E. coli.*"

"But Genetron didn't fire you then?"

"No. They didn't know what was going on, for one thing. I kept compounding the molecules, increasing their size and complexity. When bacteria were too limited, I took blood from myself, separated out white cells, and injected them with the new biochips. I watched them, put them through mazes and little chemical problems. They were whizzes. Time is a lot faster at that level—so little distance for the messages to cross, and the environment is much simpler. Then I forgot to store a file under my secret code in the lab computers. Some managers found it and guessed what I was up to. Everybody panicked. They thought we'd have every social watchdog in the country on our backs because of what I'd done. They started to destroy my work and wipe my programs. Ordered me to sterilize my white cells. Christ." He pulled the white robe off and started to get dressed. "I only had a day or two. I separated out the most complex cells—"

"How complex?"

"They were clustering in hundred-cell groups, like the bacteria. Each group as smart as a four-year-old kid, maybe." He studied my face for a moment. "Still doubting? Want me to run through how many nucleotide pairs there are in a mammalian cell? I tailored my computers to take advantage of the white cells' capacity. Four billion nucleotide pairs, Edward. And they don't have a huge body to worry about, taking up most of their thinking time."

"Okay," I said. "I'm convinced. What did you do?"

"I mixed the cells back into a cylinder of whole blood and injected myself with it." He buttoned the top of his shirt and smiled thinly at me. "I'd programmed them with every drive I could, talked as high a level as I could using just enzymes and such. After that, they were on their own."

"You programmed them to go forth and multiply, improve?" I repeated.

"I think they developed some characteristics picked up by the biochips in their *E. coli* phases. The white cells could talk to each other with extruded memories. They found ways to ingest other types of cells and alter them without killing them."

"You're crazy."

"You can see the screen! Edward, I haven't been sick since. I used to get colds all the time. I've never felt better."

"They're inside you, finding things, changing them."

"And by now, each cluster is as smart as you or I."

"You're absolutely nuts."

He shrugged. "Genetron fired me. They thought I was going to take revenge for what they did to my work. They ordered me out of the labs, and I haven't had a real chance to see what's been going on inside me until now. Three months."

"So . . ." My mind was racing. "You lost weight because they improved your fat metabolism. Your bones are stronger, your spine has been completely rebuilt—"

"No more backaches even if I sleep on my old mattress."

"Your heart looks different."

"I didn't know about the heart," he said, examining the frame image more closely. "As for the fat—I was thinking about that. They could increase my brown cells, fix up the metabolism. I haven't been as hungry lately. I haven't changed my eating habits that much—I still want the same old junk—but somehow I get around to eating only what I need. I don't think they know what my brain is yet. Sure, they've got all the glandular stuff—but they don't have the *big* picture, if you see what I mean. They don't know *I'm* in here. But boy, they sure did figure out what my reproductive organs are."

I glanced at the image and shifted my eyes away.

"Oh, they look pretty normal," he said, hefting his scrotum obscenely. He snickered. "But how else do you think I'd land a real looker like Candice? She was just after a one-night stand with a techie. I looked okay then, no tan but trim, with good clothes. She'd never screwed a techie before. Joke time, right? But my little geniuses kept us up half the night. I think they made improvements each time. I felt like I had a goddamned fever."

His smile vanished. "But then one night my skin started to crawl. It really scared me. I thought things were getting out of hand. I wondered what they'd do when they crossed the blood-brain barrier and found out about *me*—about the brain's real function. So I began a campaign to keep them under control. I figured, the reason they wanted to get into the skin was the simplicity of running circuits across a surface. Much easier than trying to maintain chains of communication in and around muscles, organs, vessels. The skin was much more direct. So I bought a quartz lamp." He caught my puzzled expression. "In the lab, we'd break down the protein in biochip cells by exposing them to ultraviolet light. I alternated sunlamp with quartz treatments. Keeps them out of my skin and gives me a nice tan."

"Give you skin cancer, too," I commented.

"They'll probably take care of that. Like police."

"Okay. I've examined you, you've told me a story I still find hard to believe . . . what do you want me to do?"

"I'm not as nonchalant as I act, Edward. I'm worried. I'd like to find some way to control them before they find out about my brain. I mean, think of it, they're in the trillions by now, each one smart.

They're cooperating to some extent. I'm probably the smartest thing on the planet, and they haven't even begun to get their act together. I don't really want them to take over." He laughed unpleasantly. "Steal my soul, you know? So think of some treatment to block them. Maybe we can starve the little buggers. Just think on it." He buttoned his shirt. "Give me a call." He handed me a slip of paper with his address and phone number. Then he went to the keyboard and erased the image on the frame, dumping the memory of the examination. "Just you," he said. "Nobody else for now. And please . . . hurry."

It was three o'clock in the morning when Vergil walked out of the examination room. He'd allowed me to take blood samples, then shaken my hand—his palm was damp, nervous—and cautioned me against ingesting anything from the specimens.

Before I went home, I put the blood through a series of tests. The results were ready the next day.

I picked them up during my lunch break in the afternoon, then destroyed all of the samples. I did it like a robot. It took me five days and nearly sleepless nights to accept what I'd seen. His blood was normal enough, though the machines diagnosed the patient as having an infection. High levels of leukocytes—white blood cells—and histamines. On the fifth day, I believed.

Gail came home before I did, but it was my turn to fix dinner. She slipped one of the school's disks into the home system and showed me video art her nursery kids had been creating. I watched quietly, ate with her in silence.

I had two dreams, part of my final acceptance. In the first, that evening, I witnessed the destruction of the planet Krypton, Superman's home world. Billions of superhuman geniuses went screaming off in walls of fire. I related the destruction to my sterilizing the samples of Vergil's blood.

The second dream was worse. I dreamed that New York City was raping a woman. By the end of the dream, she gave birth to little embryo cities, all wrapped up in translucent sacs, soaked with blood from the difficult labor.

I called him on the morning of the sixth day. He answered on the fourth ring. "I have some results," I said. "Nothing conclusive. But I want to talk with you. In person."

"Sure," he said. "I'm staying inside for the time being." His voice was strained; he sounded tired.

Vergil's apartment was in a fancy high-rise near the lake shore. I took the elevator up, listening to little advertising jingles and watching dancing holograms display products, empty apartments for rent, the building's hostess discussing social activities for the week.

Vergil opened the door and motioned me in. He wore a checked robe with long sleeves and carpet slippers. He clutched an unlit pipe in one hand, his fingers twisting it back and forth as he walked away from me and sat down, saying nothing.

"You have an infection," I said.

"Oh?"

"That's all the blood analyses tell me. I don't have access to the electron microscopes."

"I don't think it's really an infection," he said. "After all, they're my own cells. Probably something else . . . some sign of their presence, of the change. We can't expect to understand everything that's happening."

I removed my coat. "Listen," I said, "you really have me worried now." The expression on his face stopped me: a kind of frantic beatitude. He squinted at the ceiling and pursed his lips.

"Are you stoned?" I asked.

He shook his head, then nodded once, very slowly. "Listening," he said.

"To what?"

"I don't know. Not sounds . . . exactly. Like music. The heart, all the blood vessels, friction of blood along the arteries, veins. Activity. Music in the blood." He looked at me plaintively. "Why aren't you at work?"

"My day off. Gail's working."

"Can you stay?"

I shrugged. "I suppose." I sounded suspicious. I glanced around the apartment, looking for ashtrays, packs of papers.

"I'm not stoned, Edward," he said. "I may be wrong, but I think something big is happening. I think they're finding out who I am."

I sat down across from Vergil, staring at him intently. He didn't seem to notice. Some inner process involved him. When I asked for a cup of coffee, he motioned to the kitchen. I boiled a pot of water and took a jar of instant from the cabinet. With cup in hand, I returned to my seat. He twisted his head back and forth, eyes open. "You always knew what you wanted to be, didn't you?" he asked.

"More or less."

"A gynecologist. Smart moves. Never false moves. I was different.

I had goals, but no direction. Like a map without roads, just places to be. I didn't give a shit for anything, anyone but myself. Even science. Just a means. I'm surprised I got so far. I even hated my folks."

He gripped his chair arms.

"Something wrong?" I asked.

"They're talking to me," he said. He shut his eyes.

For an hour he seemed to be asleep. I checked his pulse, which was strong and steady, felt his forehead—slightly cool—and made myself more coffee. I was looking through a magazine, at a loss what to do, when he opened his eyes again. "Hard to figure exactly what time is like for them," he said. "It's taken them maybe three, four days to figure out language, key human concepts. Now they're on to it. On to me. Right now."

"How's that?"

He claimed there were thousands of researchers hooked up to his neurons. He couldn't give details. "They're damned efficient, you know," he said. "They haven't screwed me up yet."

"We should get you into the hospital now."

"What in hell could other doctors do? Did *you* figure out any way to control them? I mean, they're my own cells."

"I've been thinking. We could starve them. Find out what metabolic differences—"

"I'm not sure I want to be rid of them," Vergil said. "They're not doing any harm."

"How do you know?"

He shook his head and held up one finger. "Wait. They're trying to figure out what space is. That's tough for them: They break distances down into concentrations of chemicals. For them, space is like intensity of taste."

"Vergil—"

"Listen! Think, Edward!" His tone was excited but even. "Something big is happening inside me. They talk to each other across the fluid, through membranes. They tailor something—viruses?—to carry data stored in nucleic acid chains. I think they're saying 'RNA.' That makes sense. That's one way I programmed them. But plasmidlike structures, too. Maybe that's what your machines think is a sign of infection—all their chattering in my blood, packets of data. Tastes of other individuals. Peers. Superiors. Subordinates."

"Vergil, I still think you should be in a hospital."

"This is my show, Edward," he said. "I'm their universe. They're amazed by the new scale." He was quiet again for a time. I squatted by his chair and pulled up the sleeve to his robe. His arm was crisscrossed with white lines. I was about to go to the phone when he stood and stretched. "Do you realize," he said, "how many body cells we kill each time we move?"

"I'm going to call for an ambulance," I said.

"No, you aren't." His tone stopped me. "I told you, I'm not sick, this is my show. Do you know what they'd do to me in a hospital? They'd be like cavemen trying to fix a computer. It would be a farce."

"Then what the hell am I doing here?" I asked, getting angry. "I can't do anything. I'm one of those cavemen."

"You're a friend," Vergil said, fixing his eyes on me. I had the impression I was being watched by more than just Vergil. "I want you here to keep me company." He laughed. "But I'm not exactly alone."

He walked around the apartment for two hours, fingering things, looking out windows, slowly and methodically fixing himself lunch. "You know, they can actually feel their own thoughts," he said about noon. "I mean, the cytoplasm seems to have a will of its own, a kind of subconscious life counter to the rationality they've only recently acquired. They hear the chemical 'noise' of the molecules fitting and unfitting inside."

At two o'clock, I called Gail to tell her I would be late. I was almost sick with tension, but I tried to keep my voice level. "Remember Vergil Ulam? I'm talking with him right now."

"Everything okay?" she asked.

Was it? Decidedly not. "Fine," I said.

"Culture!" Vergil said, peering around the kitchen wall at me. I said good-bye and hung the phone. "They're always swimming in that bath of information. Contributing to it. It's a kind of gestalt thing. The hierarchy is absolute. They send tailored phages after cells that don't interact properly. Viruses specified to individuals or groups. No escape. A rogue cell gets pierced by the virus, the cell blebs outward, it explodes and dissolves. But it's not just a dictatorship. I think they effectively have more freedom than in a democracy. I mean, they vary so differently from individual to individual. Does that make sense? They vary in different ways than we do."

"Hold it," I said, gripping his shoulders. "Vergil, you're pushing me to the edge. I can't take this much longer. I don't understand, I'm not sure I believe—"

"Not even now?"

"Okay, let's say you're giving me the right interpretation. Giving it to me straight. Have you bothered to figure out the consequences yet? What all this means, where it might lead?"

He walked into the kitchen and drew a glass of water from the tap then returned and stood next to me. His expression had changed from childish absorption to sober concern. "I've never been very good at that."

"Are you afraid?"

"I was. Now, I'm not sure." He fingered the tie of his robe. "Look, I don't want you to think I went around you, over your head or something. But I met with Michael Bernard yesterday. He put me through his private clinic, took specimens. Told me to quit the lamp treatments. He called this morning, just before you did. He says it all checks out. And he asked me not to tell anybody." He paused and his expression became dreamy again. "Cities of cells," he continued. "Edward, they push tubes through the tissues, spread information—"

"Stop it!" I shouted. "Checks out? What checks out?"

"As Bernard puts it, I have 'severely enlarged macrophages' throughout my system. And he concurs on the anatomical changes."

"What does he plan to do?"

"I don't know. I think he'll probably convince Genetron to reopen the lab."

"Is that what you want?"

"It's not just having the lab again. I want to show you. Since I stopped the lamp treatments, I'm still changing." He undid his robe and let it slide to the floor. All over his body, his skin was crisscrossed with white lines. Along his back, the lines were starting to form ridges.

"My God," I said.

"I'm not going to be much good anywhere else but the lab soon. I won't be able to go out in public. Hospitals wouldn't know what to do, as I said."

"You're . . . you can talk to them, tell them to slow down," I said, aware how ridiculous that sounded.

"Yes, indeed I can, but they don't necessarily listen."

"I thought you were their god or something."

"The ones hooked up to my neurons aren't the big wheels. They're researchers, or at least serve the same function. They know I'm here, what I am, but that doesn't mean they've convinced the upper levels of the hierarchy."

"They're disputing?"

"Something like that. It's not all that bad, anyway. If the lab is re-opened, I have a home, a place to work." He glanced out the window, as if looking for someone. "I don't have anything left but them. They aren't afraid, Edward. I've never felt so close to anything before." The beatific smile again. "I'm responsible for them. Mother to them all."

"You have no way of knowing what they're going to do."

He shook his head.

"No, I mean it. You say they're like a civilization—"

"Like a thousand civilizations."

"Yes, and civilizations have been known to screw up. Warfare, the environment—"

I was grasping at straws, trying to restrain a growing panic. I wasn't competent to handle the enormity of what was happening. Neither was Vergil. He was the last person I would have called insightful and wise about large issues.

"But I'm the only one at risk."

"You don't know that. Jesus, Vergil, look what they're *doing* to you!"

"To me, all to me!" he said. "Nobody else."

I shook my head and held up my hands in a gesture of defeat. "Okay, so Bernard gets them to reopen the lab, you move in, become a guinea pig. What then?"

"They treat me right. I'm more than just good old Vergil Ulam now. I'm a goddamned galaxy, a super-mother."

"Super-host, you mean." He conceded the point with a shrug.

I couldn't take any more. I made my exit with a few flimsy excuses, then sat in the lobby of the apartment building, trying to calm down. Somebody had to talk some sense into him. Who would he listen to? He had gone to Bernard . . .

And it sounded as if Bernard was not only convinced, but very interested. People of Bernard's stature didn't coax the Vergil Ulams of the world along unless they felt it was to their advantage.

I had a hunch, and I decided to play it. I went to a pay phone, slipped in my credit card, and called Genetron.

"I'd like you to page Dr. Michael Bernard," I told the receptionist.

"Who's calling, please?"

"This is his answering service. We have an emergency call and his beeper doesn't seem to be working."

A few anxious minutes later, Bernard came on the line. "Who the hell is this?" he asked. "I don't have an answering service."

"My name is Edward Milligan. I'm a friend of Vergil Ulam's. I think we have some problems to discuss."

We made an appointment to talk the next morning.

I went home and tried to think of excuses to keep me off the next day's hospital shift. I couldn't concentrate on medicine, couldn't give my patients anywhere near the attention they deserved.

Guilty, angry, afraid.

That was how Gail found me. I slipped on a mask of calm and we fixed dinner together. After eating, holding onto each other, we watched the city lights come on in late twilight through the bayside window. Winter starlings pecked at the yellow lawn in the last few minutes of light, then flew away with a rising wind which made the windows rattle.

"Something's wrong," Gail said softly. "Are you going to tell me, or just act like everything's normal?"

"It's just me," I said. "Nervous. Work at the hospital."

"Oh, lord," she said, sitting up. "You're going to divorce me for that Baker woman." Mrs. Baker weighed three hundred and sixty pounds and hadn't known she was pregnant until her fifth month.

"No," I said, listless.

"Rapturous relief," Gail said, touching my forehead lightly. "You know this kind of introspection drives me crazy."

"Well, it's nothing I can talk about yet, so . . ." I patted her hand.

"That's disgustingly patronizing," she said, getting up. "I'm going to make some tea. Want some?" Now she was miffed, and I was tense with not telling.

Why not just reveal all? I asked myself. An old friend was turning himself into a galaxy.

I cleared away the table instead. That night, unable to sleep, I looked down on Gail in bed from my sitting position, pillow against the wall, and tried to determine what I knew was real, and what wasn't.

I'm a doctor, I told myself. A technical, scientific profession. I'm supposed to be immune to things like future shock.

Vergil Ulam was turning into a galaxy.

How would it feel to be topped off with a trillion Chinese? I grinned in the dark and almost cried at the same time. What Vergil had inside him was unimaginably stranger than Chinese. Stranger than anything I—or Vergil—could easily understand. Perhaps ever understand.

But I knew what was real. The bedroom, the city lights faint through gauze curtains. Gail sleeping. Very important. Gail in bed, sleeping.

The dream returned. This time the city came in through the window and attacked Gail. It was a great, spiky lighted-up prowler, and it growled in a language I couldn't understand, made up of auto horns, crowd noises, construction bedlam. I tried to fight it off, but it got to her—and turned into a drift of stars, sprinkling all over the bed, all over everything. I jerked awake and stayed up until dawn, dressed with Gail, kissed her, savored the reality of her human, unviolated lips.

I went to meet with Bernard. He had been loaned a suite in a big downtown hospital; I rode the elevator to the sixth floor, and saw what fame and fortune could mean.

The suite was tastefully furnished, fine serigraphs on wood-paneled walls, chrome and glass furniture, cream-colored carpet, Chinese brass, and wormwood-grain cabinets and tables.

He offered me a cup of coffee, and I accepted. He took a seat in the breakfast nook, and I sat across from him, cradling my cup in moist palms. He wore a dapper gray suit and had graying hair and a sharp profile. He was in his mid sixties and he looked quite a bit like Leonard Bernstein.

"About our mutual acquaintance," he said. "Mr. Ulam. Brilliant. And, I won't hesitate to say, courageous."

"He's my friend. I'm worried about him."

Bernard held up one finger. "Courageous—and a bloody damned fool. What's happening to him should never have been allowed. He may have done it under duress, but that's no excuse. Still, what's done is done. He's talked to you, I take it."

I nodded. "He wants to return to Genetron."

"Of course. That's where all his equipment is. Where his home probably will be while we sort this out."

"Sort it out—how? Why?" I wasn't thinking too clearly. I had a slight headache.

"I can think of a large number of uses for small, superdense computer elements with a biological base. Can't you? Genetron has already made breakthroughs, but this is something else again."

"What do you envision?"

Bernard smiled. "I'm not really at liberty to say. It'll be revolutionary. We'll have to get him in lab conditions. Animal experiments have to be conducted. We'll start from scratch, of course. Vergil's . . .

um . . . colonies can't be transferred. They're based on his own white blood cells. So we have to develop colonies that won't trigger immune reactions in other animals."

"Like an infection?" I asked.

"I suppose there are comparisons. But Vergil is not infected."

"My tests indicate he is."

"That's probably the bits of data floating around in his blood, don't you think?"

"I don't know."

"Listen, I'd like you to come down to the lab after Vergil is settled in. Your expertise might be useful to us."

Us. He was working with Genetron hand in glove. Could he be objective? "How will you benefit from all this?"

"Edward, I have always been at the forefront of my profession. I see no reason why I shouldn't be helping here. With my knowledge of brain and nerve functions, and the research I've been conducting in neurophysiology—"

"You could help Genetron hold off an investigation by the government," I said.

"That's being very blunt. Too blunt, and unfair."

"Perhaps. Anyway, yes: I'd like to visit the lab when Vergil's settled in. If I'm still welcome, bluntness and all." He looked at me sharply. I wouldn't be playing on *his* team; for a moment, his thoughts were almost nakedly apparent.

"Of course," Bernard said, rising with me. He reached out to shake my hand. His palm was damp. He was as nervous as I was, even if he didn't look it.

I returned to my apartment and stayed there until noon, reading, trying to sort things out. Reach a decision. What was real, what I needed to protect.

There is only so much change anyone can stand: innovation, yes, but slow application. Don't force. Everyone has the right to stay the same until they decide otherwise.

The greatest thing in science since . . .

And Bernard would force it. Genetron would force it. I couldn't handle the thought. "Neo-Luddite," I said to myself. A filthy accusation.

When I pressed Vergil's number on the building security panel, Vergil answered almost immediately. "Yeah," he said. He sounded exhilarated. "Come on up. I'll be in the bathroom. Door's unlocked."

I entered his apartment and walked through the hallway to the bathroom. Vergil lay in the tub, up to his neck in pinkish water. He smiled vaguely and splashed his hands. "Looks like I slit my wrists, doesn't it?" he said softly. "Don't worry. Everything's fine now. Genetron's going to take me back. Bernard just called." He pointed to the bathroom phone and intercom.

I sat on the toilet and noticed the sunlamp fixture standing unplugged next to the linen cabinets. The bulbs sat in a row on the edge of the sink counter. "You're sure that's what you want," I said, my shoulders slumping.

"Yeah, I think so," he said. "They can take better care of me. I'm getting cleaned up, going over there this evening. Bernard's picking me up in his limo. Style. From here on in, everything's style."

The pinkish color in the water didn't look like soap. "Is that bubble bath?" I asked. Some of it came to me in a rush then and I felt a little weaker; what had occurred to me was just one more obvious and necessary insanity.

"No," Vergil said. I knew that already.

"No," he repeated, "it's coming from my skin. They're not telling me everything, but I think they're sending out scouts. Astronauts." He looked at me with an expression that didn't quite equal concern; more like curiosity as to how I'd take it.

The confirmation made my stomach muscles tighten as if waiting for a punch. I had never even considered the possibility until now, perhaps because I had been concentrating on other aspects. "Is this the first time?" I asked.

"Yeah," he said. He laughed. "I've half a mind to let the little buggers down the drain. Let them find out what the world's really about."

"They'd go everywhere," I said.

"Sure enough."

"How . . . how are you feeling?"

"I'm feeling pretty good now. Must be billions of them." More splashing with his hands. "What do you think? Should I let the buggers out?"

Quickly, hardly thinking, I knelt down beside the tub. My fingers went for the cord on the sunlamp and I plugged it in. He had hotwired doorknobs, turned my piss blue, played a thousand dumb practical jokes and never grown up, never grown mature enough to understand that he was sufficiently brilliant to transform the world; he would never learn caution.

He reached for the drain knob. "You know, Edward, I—"

He never finished. I picked up the fixture and dropped it into the tub, jumping back at the flash of steam and sparks. Vergil screamed and thrashed and jerked and then everything was still, except for the low, steady sizzle and the smoke wafting from his hair.

I lifted the toilet lid and vomited. Then I clenched my nose and went into the living room. My legs went out from under me and I sat abruptly on the couch.

After an hour, I searched through Vergil's kitchen and found bleach, ammonia, and a bottle of Jack Daniel's. I returned to the bathroom, keeping the center of my gaze away from Vergil. I poured first the booze, then the bleach, then the ammonia into the water. Chlorine started bubbling up and I left, closing the door behind me.

The phone was ringing when I got home. I didn't answer. It could have been the hospital. It could have been Bernard. Or the police. I could envision having to explain everything to the police. Genetron would stonewall; Bernard would be unavailable.

I was exhausted, all my muscles knotted with tension and whatever name one can give to the feelings one has after—

Committing genocide?

That certainly didn't seem real. I could not believe I had just murdered a hundred trillion intelligent beings. Snuffed a galaxy. It was laughable. But I didn't laugh.

It was easy to believe that I had just killed one human being, a friend. The smoke, the melted lamp rods, the drooping electrical outlet and smoking cord.

Vergil.

I had dunked the lamp into the tub with Vergil.

I felt sick. Dreams, cities raping Gail (and what about his girlfriend, Candice?). Letting the water filled with them out. Galaxies sprinkling over us all. What horror. Then again, what potential beauty—a new kind of life, symbiosis and transformation.

Had I been thorough enough to kill them all? I had a moment of panic. Tomorrow, I thought, I will sterilize his apartment. Somehow, I didn't even think of Bernard.

When Gail came in the door, I was asleep on the couch. I came to, groggy, and she looked down at me.

"You feeling okay?" she asked, perching on the edge of the couch. I nodded.

"What are you planning for dinner?" My mouth didn't work properly. The words were mushy. She felt my forehead.

"Edward, you have a fever," she said. "A very high fever."

I stumbled into the bathroom and looked in the mirror. Gail was close behind me. "What is it?" she asked.

There were lines under my collar, around my neck. White lines, like freeways. They had already been in me a long time, days.

"Damp palms," I said. So obvious.

I think we nearly died. I struggled at first, but in minutes I was too weak to move. Gail was just as sick within an hour.

I lay on the carpet in the living room, drenched in sweat. Gail lay on the couch, her face the color of talcum, eyes closed, like a corpse in an embalming parlor. For a time I thought she was dead. Sick as I was, I raged—hated, felt tremendous guilt at my weakness, my slowness to understand all the possibilities. Then I no longer cared. I was too weak to blink, so I closed my eyes and waited.

There was a rhythm in my arms, my legs. With each pulse of blood, a kind of sound welled up within me, like an orchestra thousands strong, but not playing in unison; playing whole seasons of symphonies at once. Music in the blood. The sound became harsher, but more coordinated, wave-trains finally canceling into silence, then separating into harmonic beats.

The beats seemed to melt into me, into the sound of my own heart.

First, they subdued our immune responses. The war—and it was a war, on a scale never before known on Earth, with trillions of combatants—lasted perhaps two days.

By the time I regained enough strength to get to the kitchen faucet, I could feel them working on my brain, trying to crack the code and find the god within the protoplasm. I drank until I was sick, then drank more moderately and took a glass to Gail. She sipped at it. Her lips were cracked, her eyes bloodshot and ringed with yellowish crumbs. There was some color in her skin. Minutes later, we were eating feebly in the kitchen.

"What in hell is happening?" was the first thing she asked. I didn't have the strength to explain. I peeled an orange and shared it with her. "We should call a doctor," she said. But I knew we wouldn't. I was already receiving messages; it was becoming apparent that any sensation of freedom we experienced was illusory.

The messages were simple at first. Memories of commands, rather than the commands themselves, manifested themselves in my thoughts. We were not to leave the apartment—a concept which seemed quite abstract to those in control, even if undesirable—and we were not to have contact with others. We would be allowed to eat certain foods and drink tap water for the time being.

With the subsidence of the fevers, the transformations were quick and drastic. Almost simultaneously, Gail and I were immobilized. She was sitting at the table, I was kneeling on the floor. I was able barely to see her in the corner of my eye.

Her arm developed pronounced ridges.

They had learned inside Vergil; their tactics within the two of us were very different. I itched all over for about two hours—two hours in hell—before they made the breakthrough and found me. The effort of ages on their timescale paid off and they communicated smoothly and directly with this great, clumsy intelligence who had once controlled their universe.

They were not cruel. When the concept of discomfort and its undesirability was made clear, they worked to alleviate it. They worked too effectively. For another hour, I was in a sea of bliss, out of all contact with them.

With dawn the next day, they gave us freedom to move again; specifically, to go to the bathroom. There were certain waste products they could not deal with. I voided those—my urine was purple—and Gail followed suit. We looked at each other vacantly in the bathroom. Then she managed a slight smile. "Are they talking to you?" she asked. I nodded. "Then I'm not crazy."

For the next twelve hours, control seemed to loosen on some levels. I suspect there was another kind of war going on in me. Gail was capable of limited motion, but no more.

When full control resumed, we were instructed to hold each other. We did not hesitate.

"Eddie . . ." she whispered. My name was the last sound I ever heard from outside.

Standing, we grew together. In hours, our legs expanded and spread out. Then extensions grew to the windows to take in sunlight, and to the kitchen to take water from the sink. Filaments soon reached to all corners of the room, stripping paint and plaster from the walls, fabric and stuffing from the furniture.

By the next dawn, the transformation was complete.

I no longer have any clear view of what we look like. I suspect we resemble cells—large, flat, and filamented cells, draped purposefully across most of the apartment. The great shall mimic the small.

Our intelligence fluctuates daily as we are absorbed into the minds within. Each day, our individuality declines. We are, indeed, great clumsy dinosaurs. Our memories have been taken over by billions of them, and our personalities have been spread through the transformed blood.

Soon there will be no need for centralization.

Already the plumbing has been invaded. People throughout the building are undergoing transformation.

Within the old time frame of weeks, we will reach the lakes, rivers, and seas in force.

I can barely begin to guess the results. Every square inch of the planet will teem with thought. Years from now, perhaps much sooner, they will subdue their own individuality—what there is of it.

New creatures will come, then. The immensity of their capacity for thought will be inconceivable.

All my hatred and fear is gone now.

I leave them—us—with only one question.

How many times has this happened, elsewhere? Travelers never came through space to visit the Earth. They had no need.

They had found universes in grains of sand.

Introduction to "Time's Rub"

by Gregory Benford_____

My first contact with Greg Benford is just too embarrassing to write about. OK, I will anyway. He had been the first of the "young" SF writers that I saw in person at a convention. I didn't speak to him—I couldn't get close. He was walking briskly from A to B, and was surrounded by several people struggling to keep up. Some of them, eagerly talking to him, had sort of a puppy-dog posture, walking sideways, hopping, skipping, trying to stay parallel with him while facing him. It was kind of pathetic; kind of funny, too, at least to the young kid, the outsider I was then.

So when I wrote about it in some review of something or other in Richard Geis's SF Review (of fond memory), I mentioned that I saw Benford but hadn't spoken to him because he was surrounded by his sycophants.

I got a letter back from him. A nice letter, but just a little chilly. "I don't call them sycophants," he said. "I call them friends."

I felt like such an idiot. I had judged relationships I knew nothing about, on the basis of a fleeting visual impression. And I had earned the scorn of a writer I admired. But the lesson was learned. No more careless phrases that give offense where none is intended. People still get offended at what I write, sometimes, but it's not because I dismissed them with a tossed-off phrase or flourish. Rather I do so because I think they're wrong about something that matters, and said so, and they didn't like hearing it. I can live with that.

Which brings me back to Gregory Benford. He could have flamed me for my offense. I've had a few letters like that, and I've seen others (please, God, let me never get Harlan Ellison really, really mad at me). But never such a letter from Benford. He's a class act, a generous man.

And a wonderful writer. Which has never been clearer than in "Time's Rub." Oh, sure, the physics professor shows through a little—we get a chalkboard presentation of the logical dilemma the characters in the story are faced with. But why not? It works within the story. Sentient beings on the cusp of decision, life or death, or perhaps just how to give their life meaning. A gamble. A bet. It could have been just a puzzle, a logic problem. But this is Benford, and so the characters aren't just placeholders. They're alive, and we care what happens to them, and that's why Benford has earned his place, not as one of the best writers of hard SF— scientific SF—but simply as one of the best writers of science fiction, period.

TIME'S RUB

Gregory Benford

1.

At Earth's winter ebb, two crabbed figures slouched across a dry, cracked plain.

Running before a victor who was himself slow-dying, the dead-stench of certain destiny cloyed to them. They knew it. Yet kept on, grinding over plum-colored shales.

They shambled into a pitwallow for shelter, groaning. carapaces grimed and discolored. The smaller of them, Xen, turned toward the minimal speck of burnt-yellow sun, but gained little aid through its battered external panels. It grasped Faz's extended pincer—useless now, mauled in battle—and murmured of fatigue.

"We can't go on."

Faz, grimly: "We must."

Xen was a functionary, an analytical sort. It had chanced to flee the battle down the same gully as Faz, the massive, lumbering leader. Xen yearned to see again its mate, Pymr, but knew this for the forlorn dream it was.

They crouched down. Their enemies rumbled in nearby ruined hills. A brown murk rose from those distant movements. The sun's pale eye stretched long shadows across the plain, inky hiding places for the encroaching others.

Thus when the shimmering curtains of ivory luminescence began to fog the hollow, Xen thought the end was here—that energy drain blurred its brain, and now brought swift, cutting death.

Fresh in from the darkling plain? the voice said. Not acoustically—this was a Vac Zone, airless for millennia.

"What? Who's that?" Faz answered.

Your ignorant armies clashed last night?

"Yes," Xen acknowledged ruefully, "and were defeated. Both sides lost."

Often the case.

"Are the Laggenmorphs far behind us?" Faz asked, faint tracers of hope skating crimson in its spiky voice.

No. They approach. They have tracked your confused alarms of struggle and flight.

"We had hoped to steal silent."

Your rear guard made a melancholy, long, withdrawing roar.

Xen: "They escaped?"

Into the next world, yes.

"Oh."

"Who *is* that?" Faz insisted, clattering its treads.

A wraith. Glittering skeins danced around them. A patchy acrid tang laced the curling vacuum. **In this place having neither brass, nor earth, nor boundless sea.**

"Come out!" Faz called at three gigaHertz. "We can't see you."

Need you?

"Are you Laggenmorphs?" Panic laded Faz's carrier wave a bright, fervid orange. "We'll fight, I warn you!"

"Quiet," Xen said, suspecting.

The descending dazzle thickened, struck a bass note. **Laggen-morphs? I do not even know your terms.**

"Your name, then," Xen said.

Sam.

"What's that? That's no name!" Faz declared, its voice a shifting brew of fear and anger.

Sam it was and Sam it is. Not marble, nor the gilded monuments of princes, shall outlive it.

Xen murmured at a hundred kiloHertz, "Traditional archaic name. I dimly remember something of the sort. I doubt it's a trap."

The words not yet free of its antenna, Xen ducked—for a relativistic beam passed not a kilometer away, snapping with random rage. It forked to a ruined scree of limestone and erupted into a self-satisfied yellow geyser. Stones pelted the two hunkering forms, clanging.

A mere stochastic volley. Your sort do expend energies wildly. That is what first attracted me.

Surly, Faz snapped. "You'll get no surge from us."

I did not come to sup. I came to proffer.

A saffron umbra surrounded the still-gathering whorls of crackling, clotted iridescence.

"Where're you hiding?" Faz demanded. It brandished blades, snouts, cutters, spikes, double-bore nostrils that could spit lurid beams.

In the cupped air.

"There *is* no air," Xen said. "This channel is open to the planetary currents."

Xen gestured upward with half-shattered claw. There, standing in space, the playing tides of blue-white, gauzy light showed that they were at the base of a great translucent cylinder. Its geometric perfection held back the moist air of Earth, now an ocean tamed by skewered forces. On the horizon, at the glimmering boundary, purpling clouds nudged futilely at their constraint like hungry cattle. This cylinder led the eye up to a vastness, the stars a stilled snowfall. Here the thin but persistent wind from the sun could have free run, gliding along the orange-slice sections of the Earth's dipolar magnetic fields. The winds crashed down, sputtering, delivering kiloVolt glories where the cylinder cut them. Crackling yellow sparks grew there, a forest with all trunks ablaze and branches of lightning, beckoning far aloft like a brilliantly lit casino in a gray dark desert.

How well I know. I stem from fossiled days.

"Then why—"

This is my destiny and my sentence.

"To live here?" Faz was beginning to suspect as well.

For a wink or two of eternity.

"Can you . . ." Faz poked the sky with a horned, fused launcher. ". . . reach up there? Get us a jec?"

I do not know the term.

Xen said, "An injection. A megaVolt, say, at a hundred kiloAmps. A mere microsecond would boost me again. I could get my crawlers working."

I would have to extend my field lines.

"So it *is* true," Xen said triumphantly. "There still dwell Ims on the Earth. And you're one."

Again, the term—

"An Immortal. You have the fieldcraft."

Yes.

Xen knew of this, but had thought it mere legend. All material things were mortal. Cells were subject to intruding impurities, cancerous insults, a thousand coarse alleyways of accident. Machines, too, knew rust and wear, could suffer the ruthless scrubbing of their memories by a random bolt of electromagnetic violence. Hybrids, such as Xen and Faz, shared both half-worlds of erosion.

But there was a Principle which evaded time's rub. Order could be imposed on electrical currents—much as words rode on radio waves—and then the currents could curve into self-involved equilibria. If spun just so, the mouth of a given stream eating its own tail, then a spinning ring generated its own magnetic fields. Such work was simple. Little children made these loops, juggled them into humming fireworks.

Only genius could knit these current whorls into a fully contorted globe. The fundamental physics sprang from ancient Man's bottling of thermonuclear fusion in magnetic strands. That was a simple craft, using brute magnets and artful metallic vessels. Far harder, to apply such learning to wisps of plasma alone.

The Principle stated that if, from the calm center of such a weave, the magnetic field always increased, in all directions, then it was stable to all manner of magnetohydrodynamic pinches and shoves.

The Principle was clear, but stitching the loops—history had swallowed that secret. A few had made the leap, been translated into surges of magnetic field. They dwelled in the Vac Zones, where the rude bump of air molecules could not stir their calm currents. Such were the Ims.

"You . . . live forever?" Xen asked wonderingly.

Aye, a holy spinning toroid—when I rest. Otherwise, distorted, as you see me now. Phantom shoots of burnt yellow. **What once was Man, is now aurora—where winds don't sing, the sun's a tarnished nickel, the sky's a blank rebuke.**

Abruptly, a dun-colored javelin shot from nearby ruined hills, vectoring on them.

"Laggenmorphs!" Faz sent. "I have no defense."

Halfway to them, the lance burst into scarlet plumes. The flames guttered out.

A cacophony of eruptions spat from their left. Gray forms leapt forward, sending scarlet beams and bursts. Sharp metal cut the smoking stones.

"Pymr, sleek and soft, I loved you," Xen murmured, thinking this was the end.

But from the space around the Laggenmorphs condensed a chalky stuff—smothering, consuming. The forms fell dead.

I saved you.

Xen bowed, not knowing how to thank a wisp. But the blur of nearing oblivion weighed like stone.

"Help us!" Faz's despair lanced like pain through the dead vacuum. "We need energy."

You would have me tick over the tilt of Earth, run through solstice, bring ringing summer in an hour?

Xen caught in the phosphorescent stipple a green underlay of irony.

"No, no!" Faz spurted. "Just a jec. We'll go on then."

I can make you go on forever.

The flatness of it, accompanied by phantom shoots of scorched orange, gave Xen pause. "You mean . . . the fieldcraft? Even I know such lore is not lightly passed on. Too many Ims, and the Earth's magnetic zones will be congested."

I grow bored, encased in this glassy electromagnetic shaft. I have not conferred the fieldcraft in a long while. Seeing you come crawling from your mad white chaos, I desired company. I propose a Game.

"Game?" Faz was instantly suspicious. "Just a jec, Im, that's all we want."

You may have that as well.

"What're you spilling about?" Faz asked.

Xen said warily, "It's offering the secret."

"What?" Faz laughed dryly, a flat cynical burst that rattled down the frequencies.

Faz churned an extruded leg against the grainy soil, wasting energy in its own consuming bitterness. It had sought fame, dominion, a sliver of history. Its divisions had been chewed and spat out again by the Laggenmorphs, its feints ignored, bold strokes adroitly turned aside. Now it had to fly vanquished beside the lesser Xen, dignity gathered like tattered dress about its fleeing ankles.

"Ims never share *that*. A dollop, a jec, sure—but not the turns of fieldcraft." To show it would not be fooled, Faz spat chalky ejecta at a nearby streamer of zinc-laden light.

I offer you my Game.

The sour despair in Faz spoke first. "Even if we believe that, how do we know you don't cheat?"

No answer. But from the high hard vault there came descending a huge ribbon of ruby light—snaking, flexing. writing in strange tongues on the emptiness as it approached, fleeting messages of times gone—

auguries of innocence lost, missions forgot, dim songs of the wide world and all its fading sweets. The ruby snake split, rumbled, turned eggshell blue, split and spread and forked down, blooming into a hemisphere around them. It struck and ripped the rock, spitting fragments over their swiveling heads, booming. Then prickly silence.

"I see," Xen said.

Thunder impresses, but it's lightning does the work.

"Why should the Im cheat, when it could short us to ground, fry us to slag?" Xen sent to Faz on tightband.

"Why anything?" Faz answered, but there was nodding in the tone.

2.

The Im twisted the local fields and caused to appear, hovering in fried light, two cubes—one red, one blue.

You may choose to open either the Blue cube alone, or both.

Though brightened by a borrowed kiloAmp jolt from Xen, Faz had expended many Joules in irritation and now flagged. "What's . . . in . . . them?"

Their contents are determined by what I have already predicted. I have already placed your rewards inside. You can choose Red and Blue both, if you want. In that case, following my prediction, I have placed in the Red cube the bottled-up injection you wanted.

Faz unfurled a metallic tentacle for the Red cube.

Wait. If you will open both boxes, then I have placed in the Blue nothing—nothing at all.

Faz said, "Then I get the jec in the Red cube, and when I open the Blue—nothing."

Correct.

Xen asked, "What if Faz *doesn't* open both cubes?"

The only other option is to open the Blue alone.

"And I get nothing?" Faz asked.

No. In that case, I have placed the, ah, "jec" in the Red cube. But in the Blue I have put the key to my own fieldcraft— the designs for immortality.

"I don't get it. I open Red, I get my jec—right?" Faz said, sudden interest giving it a spike of scarlet brilliance at three gigaHertz. "Then I open Blue, I get immortality. That s what I want."

True. But in that case, I have predicted that you will pick both cubes. Therefore, I have left the Blue cube empty.

Faz clattered its treads. "I get immortality if I choose the Blue cube *alone?* But you have to have *predicted* that. Otherwise I get nothing."

Yes.

Xen added, "*If* you have predicted things perfectly."

But I always do.

"Always?"

Nearly always. I am immortal, ageless—but not God. Not . . . yet.

"What if I pick Blue and you're wrong?" Faz asked. "Then I get nothing."

True. But highly improbable.

Xen saw it. "All this is done *now?* You've already made your prediction? Placed the jec or the secret—or both—in the cubes?"

Yes. I made my predictions before I even offered the Game.

Faz asked, "What'd you predict?"

Merry pink laughter chimed across the slumbering megaHertz. **I will not say. Except that I predicted correctly that you both would play, and that you particularly would ask that question. Witness.**

A sucking jolt lifted Faz from the stones and deposited it nearby. Etched in the rock beneath where Faz had crouched was *What did you predict?* in a rounded, careful hand:

"It had to have been done during the overhead display, before the game began," Xen said wonderingly.

"The Im *can* predict," Faz said respectfully.

Xen said, "Then the smart move is to open both cubes."

Why?

"Because you've already made your choice. If you predicted that Faz would choose both, and he opens only the Blue, then he gets nothing."

True, and as I said before, very improbable.

"So," Xen went on, thinking quickly under its pocked sheen of titanium, "if you predicted that Faz would choose *only* the Blue, then Faz might as well open both. Faz will get both the jec and the secret."

Faz said, "Right. And that jec will be useful in getting away from here."

Except that there is every possibility that I already predicted his choice of both cubes. In that case I have left only the jec in the Red Cube, and nothing in Blue.

"But you've already chosen!" Faz blurted. "There isn't any probable-this or possible-that at all."

True.

Xen said, "The only uncertainty is, how good a predictor are you."

Quite.

Faz slowed, flexing a crane arm in agonized frustration. "I . . . dunno . . . I got . . . to think . . ."

There's world enough, and time.

"Let me draw a diagram," said Xen, who had always favored the orderly over the dramatic. This was what condemned it to a minor role in roiling battle, but perhaps that was a blessing. It drew upon the gritty soil some boxes: "There," Xen wheezed. "This is the payoff matrix."

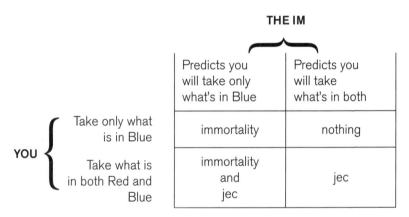

THE IM

	Predicts you will take only what's in Blue	Predicts you will take what's in both
YOU Take only what is in Blue	immortality	nothing
Take what is in both Red and Blue	immortality and jec	jec

As solemn and formal as Job's argument with God.

Enraptured with his own creation, Xen said, "Clearly, taking only the Blue cube is the best choice. The chances that the Im are wrong are very small. So you have a great chance of gaining immortality."

"That's crazy," Faz mumbled. "If I take both cubes, I at *least* get a jec, even if the Im *knew* I'd choose that way. And with a jec, I can make a run for it from the Laggenmorphs."

"Yes. Yet it rests on faith," Xen said. "Faith that the Im's predicting is near-perfect."

"Ha!" Faz snorted. "Nothing's perfect."

A black thing scorched over the rim of the pitwallow and exploded into fragments. Each bit dove for Xen and Faz, like shrieking, elongated eagles baring teeth.

And each struck something invisible but solid. Each smacked like an insect striking the windshield of a speeding car. And was gone.

"They're all around us!" Faz cried.

"Even with a jec, we might not make it out," Xen said.

True. But translated into currents, like me, with a subtle knowledge of conductivities and diffusion rates, you can live forever.

"Translated . . ." Xen mused.

Free of entropy's swamp.

"Look," Faz said, "I may be tired, drained, but I know logic. You've already *made* your choice, Im—the cubes are filled with whatever you put in. What I choose to do now can't change that. So I'll take *both* cubes."

Very well.

Faz sprang to the cubes. They burst open with a popping ivory radiance. From the red came a blinding bolt of a jec. It surrounded Faz's antennae and cascaded into the creature.

Drifting lightly from the blue cube came a tight-wound thing, a shifting ball of neon-lit string. Luminous, writhing rainbow worms. They described the complex web of magnetic field geometries that were immortality's craft. Faz seized it.

You won both. I predicted you would take only the blue. I was wrong.

"Ha!" Faz whirled with renewed energy.

Take the model of the fieldcraft. From it you can deduce the methods.

"Come on, Xen!" Faz cried with sudden ferocity. It surged over the lip of the pitwallow, firing at the distant, moving shapes of the Laggenmorphs, full once more of spit and dash. Leaving Xen.

"With that jec, Faz will make it."

I predict so, yes. You could follow Faz. Under cover of its armory, you would find escape—that way.

The shimmer vectored quick a green arrow to westward where clouds billowed white. There the elements still governed and mortality walked.

"My path lies homeward, to the south."

Bound for Pymr.

"She is the one true rest I have."

You could rest forever.

"Like you? Or Faz, when it masters the . . . translation?"

Yes. Then I will have company here.

"Aha! That is your motivation."

In part.

"What else, then?"

There are rules for immortals. Ones you cannot understand . . . yet.

"If you can predict so well, with Godlike power, then I should choose only the Blue cube."

True. Or as true as true gets.

"But if you predict so well, my 'choice' is mere illusion. It was foreordained."

That old saw? I can see you are . . . determined . . . to have free will.

"Or free won't."

Your turn.

"There are issues here . . ." Xen transmitted only ruby ruminations, murmuring like surf on a distant shore.

Distant boomings from Faz's retreat. The Red and Blue cubes spun, sparkling, surfaces rippled by ion-acoustic modes. The game had been reset by the Im, whose curtains of gauzy green shimmered in anticipation.

There must be a Game, you see.

"Otherwise there is no free will?"

That is indeed one of our rules. Observant, you are. I believe I will enjoy the company of you, Xen, more than that of Faz.

"To be . . . an immortal . . ."

A crystalline paradise, better than blind Milton's scribbled vision.

A cluster of dirty-brown explosions ripped the sky, rocked the land.

I cannot expend my voltages much longer. Would that we had wit enough, and time, to continue this parrying.

"All right." Xen raised itself up and clawed away the phosphorescent layers of both cubes.

The Red held a shimmering jec.

The Blue held nothing.

Xen said slowly, "So you predicted correctly."

Yes. Sadly, I knew you too well.

Xen radiated a strange sensation of joy, unlaced by regret. It surged to the lip of the crumbling pitwallow.

"Ah . . ." Xen sent a lofting note. "I am like a book, old Im. No doubt I would suffer in translation."

A last glance backward at the wraith of glow and darkness, a gesture of salute, then: "On! To sound and fury!" and it was gone forever.

3.

In the stretched silent years there was time for introspection. Faz learned the lacy straits of Earth's magnetic oceans, its tides and times. It sailed the magnetosphere and spoke to stars.

The deep-etched memories of that encounter persisted. It never saw Xen again, though word did come vibrating through the field lines of Xen's escape, of zestful adventures out in the raw territory of air and Man. There was even a report that Xen had itself and Pymr decanted into full Manform, to taste the pangs of cell and membrane. Clearly, Xen had lived fully after that solstice day. Fresh verve had driven that blithe new spirit.

Faz was now grown full, could scarcely be distinguished from the Im who gave the fieldcraft. Solemn and wise, its induction, conductivity, and ruby glinting dielectrics a glory to be admired, it hung vast and cold in the sky. Faz spoke seldom and thought much.

Yet the game still occupied Faz. It understood with the embedded viewpoint of an immortal now, saw that each side in the game paid a price. The Im could convey the fieldcraft to only a few, and had nearly exhausted itself; those moments cost millennia.

The sacrifice of Faz was less clear.

Faz felt itself the same as before. Its memories were stored in Alfven waves—stirrings of the field lines, standing waves between Earth's magnetic poles. They would be safe until Earth itself wound down, and the dynamo at the nickel-iron core ceased to replenish the fields. Perhaps, by that time, there would be other field lines threading Earth's, and the Ims could spread outward, blending into the galactic fields.

There were signs that such an end had come to other worlds. The cosmic rays which sleeted down perpetually were random, isotropic, which meant they had to be scattered from magnetic waves between the stars. If such waves were ordered, wise—it meant a vast community of even greater Ims.

But this far future did not concern Faz. For it, the past still sang, gritty and real.

Faz asked the Im about that time, during one of their chance au-
roral meetings, beside a cascading crimson churn.

The way we would put it in my day, the Im named Sam said,
**would be that the software never knows what the original hard-
ware was.**

And that was it, Faz saw. During the translation, the original husk
of Faz had been exactly memorized. This meant determining the exact
locations of each atom, every darting electron. By the quantum laws,
to locate perfectly implied that the measurement imparted an unknown, but high, momentum to each speck. So to define a thing precisely then destroyed it.

Yet there was no external way to prove this. Before and after translation there was an exact Faz.

The copy did not know it was embedded in different . . . hardware . . . than the original.

So immortality was a concept with legitimacy purely seen from the
outside. From the inside . . .

Somewhere, a Faz had died that this Faz might live.

. . . And how did any sentience know it was not a copy of some
long-gone original?

One day, near the sheath that held back the atmosphere, Faz saw
a man waving. It stood in green and vibrant wealth of life, clothed at
the waist, bronzed. Faz attached a plasma transducer at the boundary
and heard the figure say, "You're Faz, right?"

Yes, in a way. And you . . . ?

"Wondered how you liked it.'

Xen? Is that you?

"In a way."

You knew.

"Yes. So I went in the opposite direction—into this form."

You'll die soon.

"You've died already."

Still, in your last moments, you'll wish for this.

"No, it's not how long something lasts, it's what that something
means." With that the human turned, waved gaily, and trotted into a
nearby forest.

This encounter bothered Faz.

In its studies and learned colloquy, Faz saw and felt the tales of
Men. They seemed curiously convoluted. revolving about Self. What
mattered most to those who loved tales was how they concluded. Yet

all Men knew how each ended. Their little dreams were rounded with a sleep.

So the point of a tale was not how it ended, but *what it meant*. The great inspiring epic rage of Man was to find that lesson, buried in a grave.

As each year waned, Faz reflected, and knew that Xen had seen this point. Immortality seen from without, by those who could not know the inner Self—Xen did not want that. So it misled the Im, and got the mere jec that it wanted.

Xen chose life—not to be a monument of unaging intellect, gathered into the artifice of eternity.

In the brittle night Faz wondered if it had chosen well itself. And knew. *Nothing* could be sure it was itself the original. So the only intelligent course lay in enjoying whatever life a being felt—living like a mortal, in the moment. Faz had spent so long, only to reach that same conclusion which was forced on Man from the beginning.

Faz emitted a sprinkling of electromagnetic tones, spattering rueful red the field lines.

And stirred itself to think again, each time the dim sun waned at the solstice. To remember and, still living, to rejoice.

Introduction to "Shanidar"

by David Zindell

David Zindell is a writer who seems to function best at novel length—at long novel length—for it takes many pages to contain his worlds, his peoples, his lives. Indeed, "Shanidar" is a Promethean story so lush that when you've finished it you'll feel as if you've lived through a novel's worth of story somehow compressed into these few pages.

After we first contacted Zindell about acquiring the right to include the story in this anthology, he came up to me at a convention and asked me, dubiously, what the book would be about. For a moment I was puzzled as to why he seemed so skeptical, until I realized: Alone of all the stories in this volume, "Shanidar" actually deals, literally, with a future on ice—for it takes place on a frozen world with trackless wastes of ice and snow. Because of the title of this book, he feared that he was being asked to lend his story to a witless anthology of stories set in cold climates! I was able to set his mind at rest about the nature of the project, and thus we got permission to include this tale.

Trust me, it wasn't the average temperature of this story that got it included here. Indeed, however chilly the milieu, this is a story that burns.

SHANIDAR

David Zindell

He came into my cutting shop on a quiet night when the air was black and still, the only sound the far-off hissing and humming of the machines as they hovered over the city streets, melting and smoothing the ice for the following day. He was a pale young man with brown, lively eyes beneath the white hood of his parka, and he wore a beard so dense and black that you would have thought him born on Gehenna or Sheydveg and not, as he claimed, on Summerworld where the men are nearly hairless and their skin is as dark as coffee. With his heavy brows and large, muscular face he nearly had the look of the Alaloi which had been the fashion—you will presently understand why—some twenty years ago. As he stood there in the stone hallway knocking the slush from his skates, he explained that he had need of my services. "You are Rainer, the cutter?" he asked me in a low, conspiratorial voice. I told him that was what the people of the city called me. "I want you to use all your skills," he said. "I want to become an Alaloi."

I led him into my tearoom where he ejected the blades from his skates and flopped his dripping mittens on top of the marble table which I had imported from Urradeth at great cost. And though I didn't feel much like playing the host—my white tunic was spattered with blood and brains and I had matters to attend to—I offered him kvass or coffee and was surprised that he chose coffee.

"Kvass fogs the brain," he said, ignoring the frescoes on the stone walls around him and staring me in the eyes. "Drink makes men forget their purpose."

I sent for the domestic and I asked the young man, "And your purpose is to look like an Alaloi?"

He shook his head. "My purpose is to *become* an Alaloi. Completely."

I laughed and I said, "You know I can't do that; you know the law. I can change your flesh as you please but——"

"What about Goshevan?"

"Goshevan!" I shouted. "Why do the young men always come asking about Goshevan?" The domestic came and I embarrassed myself by shouting out an order for coffee and kvass. As it rolled away, I said, "There are more stories told about Goshevan than dead stars in the Vild. What do you know about Goshevan?"

"I know that he wanted what I want. He was a man with a dream who——"

"He was a dreamer! Do you want to know about Goshevan? I'll tell you the story that I tell all the young men who come to me seeking nightmares. Are you sitting comfortably? Then listen well . . ."

The domestic brought our drink bubbling in two of those huge, insulated pots that they blow on Fostora. It clumsily poured the dark liquids into our delicate marble cups as I told the young man the story of Goshevan:

"There lived on Summerworld a young noble who took a greater interest in antiques and old books—some say he had been to Ksandaria and bribed the librarians into selling him part of the Kyoto collection of Old Earth—than he did in managing his estates. He was an erudite man who claimed that the proper study of man was man—not how to produce five tons more coffee per cubage. One day he tired of his life and said, 'My s-sons are weak-faced maggots who exist on the diseased flesh of this rotten civilization. They p-plot with my wives against me and laugh as my wives sleep with other men.' And so Goshevan sold his estates, freed his slaves, and told his family they would have to make their living by the sweat of their hands and the inspiration of their brains. He paid for passage on a Darghinni long ship and made his way toward the Vild.

"Now everyone knows the Darghinni are tricksters and so is it any wonder they didn't warn him of the laughing pools on Darkmoon? Well, warn him they didn't, and Goshevan spent two seasons on that dim, lukewarm planet coughing at the lungmelt in his chest while the surgeons painstakingly cut the spirulli from his muscles and waited and watched and cut some more.

"When he was well, he found a Fravashi trader who was willing to take him to Yarkona; on Yarkona he shaved his head and wrapped his body in rags so that the harijan pilgrims he befriended there would allow him a corner on one of their sluggish prayer ships in which to float. And so, gray of hair and stinking of years of his own sweat and filth, he came to Neverness like any other seeker.

"Though it was late midwinter spring, and warm for that season, he was stunned by the cold and dazzled by the brightness of our city. And so he paid too much money for snow goggles and the finest of shagshay furs lined with silk belly. 'The streets are colored ice,' he said disbelievingly, for the only ice he had ever seen had been brought to him in exotic drinks by his slaves. And he marvelled at the purples and greens of the glissades and the laughing children who chased each other up and down the orange and yellow slidderies on ice skates. The silvery spires and towers were frozen with the ever present verglas of that season, scattering the white spring light so that the whole city gleamed and sparkled in a most disconcerting manner. 'There is beauty here,' he said. 'The false beauty of artifice and a civilization gone to rot.' And so, dressed in deep winter furs and wobbling on his newly bought skates, he struck out into the streets to preach to the people.

"In the great square outside the Hofgarten where the people of the Unreal City, high and low, meet and take their refreshment, the scryers, eschatologists, and cantors as well as the harijan, splicers and whores, he said, 'I s-speak to that inside you which is less than m-man but also m-more.' And he raged because no one would listen to a short, overdressed farsider who stuttered and could barely stand on his skates. 'You p-pilots,' he said, 'you are the p-pride of the galaxy! You travel from Simoom to Urradeth and on to Jacaranda in less time than the Darghinni need to prepare the first of eighteen jumps from Summerworld to Darkmoon. You penetrate the Vild, lost in your mathematics and dreamtime and tell yourself you have seen something of the ineffable and eternal. But you have forgotten how to take pleasure in a simple flower! You foreswear marriage and children and thus you are more and less than men!'

"When the pilots turned away from him to drink their kvass and eiswein, he told the historians and fabulists that they knew nothing of the true nature of man. And they, those haughty professionals of our city, snubbed him and went on talking about Gaiea and Old Earth as if he were invisible. So Goshevan spoke to the programmers and holists, the Fravashi aliens and Friends of God, the harijan, the wormrunners, the splicers, and at last, because he was filled with a great sadness and longing, he zipped up his furs and went deep into the Farsiders' Quarter where he might pay for the company of a friendly ear.

"Because he was lonely and had been without a woman for many years, he took his pleasure among the whores of the lesser glidderies, which at that time were stained crimson and were narrow and twisted like snakes. Because his soul was empty he smoked toalache and awoke one fine morning to find himself in bed with four courtesans from Jacaranda. They asked him if all dark little men were as potent as he and advised him that the joys of conjoining with the alien Friends of Man were such that no man who had known only women could comprehend them. Goshevan, horrified at what he had done and forgetting where he was, began swearing and shouting and ordered that the courtesans be sold as field slaves. He threw a bag of diamonds at them, clipped in the blades to his skates, and raced up and down the back glissades for two days before he came to his right mind."

I paused here in my story to refill our cups. The young man was staring at me intently, watching my every move with those piercing brown eyes and, I felt, stripping my words bare for lies. The room was very quiet and cold; I could hear his slow, even breathing as he nodded his head and asked, "And then?"

"And then Goshevan made a decision. You see, he had hoped to win people over to his dream, which was to go out into the wasteland and live as what he called 'natural man.' The Alaloi, of course, had been his model. When he found he could not emulate them, he decided to join them."

"A noble vision," the young man said.

"It was insane!" I half-shouted. "Who were these Alaloi he so admired? Dreamers and madmen they were—and still are. They came to this world on the first wave of the swarming, when Old Earth was young and, some say, as radioactive as plutonium. Cavemen! They wanted to be cavemen! So they back-mutated their chromosomes, destroyed their ship, and went to live in the frozen forests. And now their great-grandchildren's great-great-grandchildren hunt mammoths for meat and die long before they've seen their hundredth winter."

"But they die happy," the young man said.

"Who knows how they die?" I said to him. "Goshevan wanted to know. He sought me out because it was said that once as a journeyman I had pioneered the operation he wanted, cutting on my very own self to prove my worth as a flesh changer. 'Make me into an Alaloi,' he begged me, in this very room where we presently drink our coffee and kvass. And I told him, 'Go to any of the cetics in this quarter and they will cure you of your delusions.' And he said, 'I will p-pay you ten million talanns!' But his farsider money was worthless in the Unreal City and I told him so. 'Diamonds,' he said. 'I've two thousand carats of Yarkona bluestars.' 'For that price,' I said, 'I can add eight inches to your spine or make you into a beautiful woman. I can lighten your skin and make your hair as white as a Jacaranda courtesan's.' Then he looked at me cunningly and said, 'I'll trade information for your services: I know the fixed-points of Agathange.' I laughed at him and asked, 'How is it you know what the pilots of our city have been seeking for three thousand years?'

"Well, it happened that he *did* know. With the riches from the sale of his estates, he had bought the secret of the location of that fabled world from a renegade pilot he had met on Darkmoon. I consulted our city archives; the librarians were *very* excited. They sent a young pilot to verify my information, and I told Goshevan we might have to wait two or three hundred days before we would know.

"Ten thousand city disks his information was worth! The pilot who rediscovered Agathange was very good. Phased into his light ship, the *Infinite Sloop,* proving the theorems of probalistic topology—or whatever it is that our famous pilots do when they wish to fall through the space that isn't space—he rushed through the fallaways, fenestering from window to window with such precision and elegance that he returned from Agathange in forty days.

"'You can be a rich man,' Goshevan said to me on a clear, sparkling day of false winter. 'Do as I ask and all the disks are yours.'

"I hesitated not for a moment. I took him into the changing room and I began to cut. It was a challenge, I lied to myself, a test of knowledge and skill—to a dedicated cutter, it wasn't disks that mattered. I enlarged the basal bone of his jaw and stimulated the alveolar bone to maximal growth so that his face could support the larger teeth I implanted. The angle of the face itself I broadened so that there would be more room for a chewing apparatus strong enough to crack marrowbones. And of course, since the face jutted out farther from the skull, I had to build up the brow ridge with synthetic bone to protect the eyes. And though this shaping took the better part of winter, it was only the beginning.

"As he writhed beneath my lasers and scalpels, all the while keeping his face as quiet and blank as a snowfield, I went to work on his body. To support his huge new muscles—which were grown by the Fravashi deep-space method—I built him new bones. I expanded the plates and spicules of the honeycombed interior and strengthened the shafts and tendon attachments, adding as much as three millimeters to the cortices of the longer bones such as his femur. I stippled his skin. I went beneath the dermis, excising most of his sweat glands to keep him from soaking his furs and freezing to death at the first hint of false winter. Because his dark skin would synthesize too little vitamin D to keep his bones calcified during the long twilight of deep winter, I inhibited his melanocytes—it is little known that all men, light or dark, have nearly the same number of melanocytes—I lightened his skin until he was as fair as a man from Thorskalle. The last thing I did for him, or so I thought at the time, was to grow out his fine, almost invisible body hair so that it covered him like brown fur from toe to eyebrow.

"I was very pleased with my handiwork and a little frightened because Goshevan had grown so strong—stronger, I think, than any Alaloi—that he could have torn my clavicle from my chest, had he so desired. But *he* was not pleased and he said, 'The most important thing there is, this thing you didn't do.' And I told him, 'I've made you so that no one among the Alaloi could tell you from his brother.' But he looked at me with his dark fanatic's eyes and asked me, 'And my s-sons, should my s-seed by some chance be compatible with the Alaloi women, who will there be to call my weak-jawed half-breed sons brother?' I had no answer for him other than a dispirited repeating of the law: 'A man may do with his flesh as he pleases,' I said, 'but his DNA belongs to his species.' And then he grabbed my forearm so tightly that I thought my muscles would split away from the bone and said, 'Strong men make their own laws.'

"Then, because I felt a moment of pity for this strange man who only wanted what all men want—which is a son after his own image and a few moments of peace—I broke the law of the civilized worlds. It was a challenge, do you understand? I irradiated his testes and bathed them with sonics, killing off the sperm. I couldn't, of course, engage the services of a master splicer because all my colleagues shunned such criminal activity. But I *was* a master cutter—some will tell you the best in the city—and what is gene-splicing but surgery on a molecular scale? So I went into his tubules and painstakingly sectioned out and mutated segments of his stem cells' DNA so that the newly produced germ cells would make for him sons after his new image.

"When I finished this most delicate of delicate surgeries, which took the better part of two years, Goshevan regarded himself in the mirror of my changing room and announced, 'Behold *Homo neandertalis.* Now I am less than a man but also more.'

"'You look as savage as any savage,' I said. And then, thinking to scare him, I told him what was commonly believed about the Alaloi. 'They live in caves and have no language,' I said. 'They are bestially cruel to their children; they eat strangers, and perhaps each other.'

"Goshevan laughed as I said this and then he told me, 'On Old Earth during the holocaust century, a neanderthal burial site was discovered in a place called Shanidar near the Zagros mountains of Irak. The archeologists found the skeleton of a forty-year-old m-man who was missing his lower right arm. Shanidar I, they named him, and they determined he had lost his arm long before he died. In the burial site of another neanderthal, Shanidar IV, was the pollen of several kinds of flowers, mixed in with all the bone fragments, pebbles and dust. The question I have for you, Cutter, is: how savage could these people have been if they supported a cripple and honored their dead with bright colored wildflowers?' So I answered, 'The Alaloi are not the same.' And he said, 'We will see, we will see.'

"Here I freely admit I had underestimated him. I had supposed him to be a lunatic or at best, a self-deluder who hadn't a chance of getting ten miles away from our city. The covenant between the founder of Neverness and the Alaloi allows us this single island—large though it might be—and to our city fathers, this covenant is holy. Boats are useless because of the icebergs of the Sound, and the windjammers of would-be poachers and smugglers are shot from the air. Because I couldn't picture Goshevan walking out onto the Starnbergersee when it freezes over in deep winter, I asked him somewhat smugly how he intended to find his Alaloi.

"'Dogs,' he said. 'I will attach dogs to a sled and let them pull me across the frozen sea.' And I asked, 'What are dogs?' 'Dogs are carnivorous mammals from Old Earth,' he said. 'They are like human slaves, only friendly and eager to please.' And I said, 'Oh, you mean huzgies,' which is what the Alaloi call their sled dogs. I laughed at him then and watched the white skin beneath his hairy face turn red as if slapped by a sudden cold wind. 'And how will you smuggle such beasts into our city?' I asked him.

"So Goshevan parted the hair of his abdomen to show me a thin band of hard white skin I had taken for an appendectomy scar. 'Cut here,' he said, and after nerve-blocking him, cut I did until I came to a strange-looking organ adjoining the large intestine where his appendix should have been. 'It's a false ovary,' he said. 'Clever are the breeders of Darkmoon. Come. Cut again and see what I've brought with me.' I removed the false organ, which was red and slippery and made of one of those pungently sweet-smelling bioplastics they synthesize on Darkmoon. I made a quick incision and out spilled thousands of un-fertilized ova and a sac of sperm floating in krydda suspension to keep them fresh and vital. He pointed at the milky sperm sac and said, 'The seed of Darkmoon's finest Mutts. I had originally hoped to train hun-dreds of sled teams.'

"How Goshevan brought the dogs to term and trained them, I do not know because I didn't see him again for two winters. I thought perhaps that he'd been caught and banished or had his head split open and had his plasm sucked out by some filthy slel necker.

"But as you will see, Goshevan was a resourceful man and hard to kill. He came again to my shop on the deepest of deep winter nights when the air was so black and cold that even on the greatest of the glis-sades and slidderies, The Run and The Way, nothing moved. In the hallway of my shop he stood like a white bear, opening his shagshay furs and removing the balaclava from his face with powerful, sweeping motions. I could see beneath his furs one of those black and gold, heated kamelaikas that the racers wear on festival days when they wish to keep warm and still have their limbs free for stroking. 'This is my noble savage?' I said to him as I fingered his wonderfully warm under-suit. 'Even a f-fanatic such as I must make some concessions to sur-vival,' he said. And I asked him, 'What will you do when the batteries die?' He gave me a look that was at once fearful and bursting with ex-citement, and he said, 'When the batteries die, I will either be dead or I will have found my home.'

"He said goodbye to me and went out onto the gliddery where his dogs were up on their hind legs, straining at their harnesses as they whined and barked and pushed their black noses into his parka. From my window, I could see him fumbling with the stiff leather straps and thumping the side of the lead dog with his huge mittens. He adjusted the load three times before he had it to his liking, taking pains that the sacks of dog meal were balanced and tightly lashed to the wooden frame. Then he was off, whistling in a curious manner as he glided around the corner of the cetic's shop and disappeared into the cold."

The tearoom felt cold as I said these words. I noticed that the young man was pursing his narrow lips tightly as he fiddled with his coffee. All at once, he let out his breath in a puff of steam that seemed to hang in the air. "But that isn't the end of your story, is it, Cutter? You haven't told the moral: how poor Goshevan died on the ice broken-hearted and disavowing his dream."

"Why is it you young people always want an ending? Does our universe come to an *end* or does it fold in upon itself? Are the Agathanians at the end of human evolution or do they represent a new species? And so on, and so on. Is there any end to the questions impatient young men ask?"

I took a quick gulp of the bitter kvass, burning my lips and throat so that I sat there dumbly sucking in the cold air like an old bellows. "No, you are right," I gasped out. "That is not the end of my story."

"Goshevan drove his dogs straight out onto the frozen Starnbergersee. Due west he went, running fast across the wind-packed snow for six hundred miles. He came to the first of the Thousand Islands and found mountains shrouded in evergreen forests where the thallows nested atop the steep granite cliffs filling the air for miles with their harsh cawings. But he found no Alaloi, and he urged his dogs carefully across the crevasses of the Fairleigh ice-shelf, back out onto the sea.

"Fifteen islands he crossed without finding a trace of a human being. He had been gone sixty-two days when the crushing, deadly silent cold of deep winter began yielding to the terrible storms of midwinter spring. During a snow so heavy and wet that he had to stop every hundred yards to scrape the frozen slush from the steel runners of his sled, his lead dog, Yuri the Fierce, pulled them into a crevasse. Though he dug his boots into the sloppy snow and held on to the sled with all his strength, the pendulating weight of Yuri, Sasha and Ali as they swung back and forth over the lip of the ice was such that he felt himself being slowly dragged into the crevasse. It was only by the quick slashing of his hunting knife that he saved himself and the rest of his team. He cut the harness from which his strongest dogs dangled and watched helplessly as they tried to dig their black claws into the sides of the crevasse, all the while yelping pitifully as they fell to the ice below.

"Goshevan was stunned. Though the snow had stopped and he was within sight of the sixteenth and largest of the Thousand Islands, he realized he could go no farther without rest. He erected his tent and fed the dogs from the crumbly remnants of the last bag of food. There came a distant hissing that quickly grew into a roar as the storm returned, blasting across the Starnbergersee with such ferocity that he spent all that day and night tending the ice-screws of his tent so that he wouldn't be blown away. For nine days he lay there shivering inside his sleeping sack as the wind-whipped ice crystals did their work. By the tenth day, the batteries to his heated kamelaika were so low that he threw them in disgust against the shredded, useless walls of his tent. He dug a cave in the snow and pulled the last two of his starving dogs into the hole so that they might huddle close and keep each other warm. But Gasherbrum the Friendly, the smartest of his dogs, died on the eleventh day. And on the morning of the twelfth day, his beloved Kanika, whose paws were crusted with ice and blood, was as still as a deep winter night.

"When the storm broke on the fifteenth day, Goshevan was so crazy with thirst that he burned his frostbitten lips upon the metal cup in which he was melting snow. And though he was famished and weak as a snow worm, he could not bring himself to eat his dogs because he was both father and mother to them, and the thought of it made him so sick he would rather have died.

"From the leather and wood of his sled he fashioned a crude pair of snowshoes and set out across the drifts for a huge blue and white mountain he could see in the distance puncturing the sky. Kweitkel it was called, as he would later learn. Kweitkel, which meant 'white mountain' in the language of the Devaki, who were the tribe of Alaloi who found him dying in the thick forests of its eastern slope.

"His rescuers—five godlike men dressed in angelic white, or so it seemed to his fevered, delirious mind—brought him to a huge cave. Some days later he came awake to the wonderful smells of hot soup and roasting nuts. He heard soft voices speaking a strange, musical language that was a delight to his ear. Two children, a boy and a girl he thought, were sitting at the corners of the luxurious fur which covered him, peeking at him coyly through the spread-out fingers of their little hands and giggling

"A man with great shoulders and a beard as black as a furfly came over to him. Between his blunt, scarred fingers he held a soup bowl made from yellowed bone and scrimshawed with intricate figures of diving whales. As Goshevan gulped the soup, the man asked, 'Marek? Patwin? Olorun? Nodin? Mauli?' Goshevan, half-snowblind and weak in the head as he was, forgot that I had made him so that no one among the Alaloi could tell him from his brothers. He thought he was being accused of being an alien so he shook his head furiously back and forth at the sound of each name. At last, when Lokni, which was the big man's name, had given up trying to discover the tribe to which he belonged, Goshevan pointed to his chest and said, 'I am man. I'm just a man.' 'Iaman,' Lokni repeated. 'Ni luria la Devaki.' And so it was that Lokni of the Devaki welcomed Goshevan of the Iaman tribe to his new home.

"Goshevan gained strength quickly, gorging upon a salty cheese curdled from shagshay milk and the baldo nuts the Devaki stored against the storms of midwinter spring. And though Katerina, who was Lokni's wife, offered him thick mammoth steaks running red with the life's blood beneath a charcoaled crust, he would eat no meat. He, who all his life had eaten only soft, decerebrated cultured meats, was horrified that such gentle people took their nourishment from the flesh of living animals. 'I don't think I can teach these savages the few right-actioned ways of civilized man,' he said to himself. 'Why should they listen to me, a total stranger?' And so for the first time since Summerworld he came to question the wisdom of what he had done.

"By the time Goshevan had put on fifty pounds of new muscle, the storms of midwinter spring had given way to the fine weather of false winter. There came cool sunny days; the occasional powdery snows were too light to cover the alpine fireweed and snow dahlia which blanketed the lower slopes of Kweitkel. The thallows were molting and the furflys laying eggs. For Tuwa, the mammoth, came calving time, and for the Devaki, it was time to slaughter mammoth.

"Goshevan was sick. Though he had quickly learned the language of the Devaki, and learned also to tolerate his body lice and filthy hair, he did not know how he could kill an animal. But when Lokni unsmilingly slapped a spear into his hand, he knew he would have to hunt with the eighteen other men, many of whom had come to wonder about his strange ways and questioned his manhood.

"At first the hunt went well. In one of the lovely valleys of Kweitkel's southern foothills, they spotted a mammoth herd gorging on arctic timothy and overripe, half-fermented snow apple. The great hairy beasts were carousing and drunkenly trampling through the acres of alpine fireweed which were everywhere aflame with bright reds and oranges and so beautiful that Goshevan wanted to cry. They drove the trumpeting mammoths down the valley and into a bog where three calves fell quickly beneath flint-tipped spears. But then Lokni mired himself near the edge of the bog, and Wemilo was trampled by an enraged cow. It fell to Goshevan to help Lokni. Though he reached out with his spear into the bog until his shoulder joint popped, he failed to close the distance. He heard voices and shouting and thunder and felt the ground moving beneath him. As he looked up to see the red-eyed cow almost upon him, he realized that the men were praying for his ghost, for it was known that no single man could stand against Tuwa's charge.

"Goshevan was terrified. He cast his spear at the mammoth's eye with such a desperate force that the point drove into the brain, and the great beast fell like a mountain. The Devaki were stunned. Never had they seen such a thing, and Haidar and Alani, who had doubted his bravery, said that he was more than a man. But Goshevan knew his feat was the result of blind luck and my surgery, and thus he came to despise himself because he had killed a magnificent being and was therefore less than a man.

"In the cave that night, the Devaki made a feast to mourn the passing of Tuwa's anima and to wish Wemilo's ghost enlightenment on the other side of day. Lokni sliced his own ear off his head with a sharp obsidian flake and laid the bloody flap of skin on Wemilo's cold forehead so that he might always hear the prayers of the tribe. Katerina bound her husband's wound with feather moss while the other women scattered snow dahlias over Wemilo's crushed body.

"Then Lokni turned to Goshevan and said, 'A man, to be a man, must have a woman, and you are too old to take a virgin bride.' He went over to Lara, who was sobbing over Wemilo's grave. 'Look at this poor woman. Long ago her father, Arani, deserted her to live with the hairless people of the Unreal City. She has no brothers. And now Wemilo dances with the stars. Look at this poor beautiful woman whose hair is still black and shiny and whose teeth are straight and white. Who will be a man to this woman?'

"Goshevan looked at Lara and though her eyes were full of tears, they were also hot and dark, full of beauty and life. He felt very excited and said, 'A man would be a fool not to desire this woman.' And then he thought to comfort her by saying, 'We'll be married and have many fine children to love.'

"A hush fell over the cave. The Devaki looked at each other as if they couldn't believe their ears. And Ushi wondered aloud, 'How can he not know that Lara has three daughters and one son?' 'Of course I know,' Goshevan said. 'It only means she is very fertile and will have no trouble bearing me sons.' Then Ushi let out a cry and began tearing at her hair. Katerina hid her eyes beneath her hand and Lokni asked,

'How can it be, Goshevan, that you do not know the Law?' And Goshevan, who was angry and confused, replied, 'How can I know your
law when I'm from a faraway tribe?' Lokni looked at him and there
was death in his eyes. 'The Law is the Law,' he said, 'and it is the same
for every Alaloi. It can only be that the storm stole away your memory
and froze part of your soul.' And then, because Lokni didn't want to
kill the man who had saved his life and was about to marry his sister,
he explained the Law.

"'She may have but one more child. A woman may have five children: One child to give to the Serpent's Breath of deep winter, one
child for the tusks of Tuwa, the mammoth. One child for the fever that
comes in the night.' Lokni paused a moment as the Law passed from
lip to lip, and all the tribe except Goshevan were chanting: 'A boy to
become a man; a girl to become Devaki, Mother of the People.'

"Lokni cupped his hand around the back of Goshevan's neck and
squeezed as he said, 'If we become too many, we will kill all the mammoth and have to hunt silk belly and shagshay for food. And when they
are gone, we will have to cut holes in the ice of the sea so to spear the
seals when they come up to breathe. When the seals are gone, we will
be forced to murder Kikilia, the whale, who is wiser than we and as
strong as God. When all the animals are gone, we will dig tangleroot
and eat the larvae of furflys and break our teeth as we gnaw the lichen
from the rocks. At last we will be so many, we will murder the forests
to plant snow apple so that men will come to lust for land, and some
men will come to have more land than others. And when there is no
land left, the stronger men will get their sustenance from the labor of
weaker men, who will have to sell their women and children so that
they might have mash to eat. The strongest men will make war on each
other so that they might have still more land. Thus we will become
hunters of men and be doomed to hell in living and hell on the other
side. And then, as it did on Earth in the time before the swarming, fire
will rain from the sky, and the Devaki will be no more."

"And so Goshevan, who really wanted only one son, came to accept
the Law of the Alaloi, for who knew better than he the evils of owning
slaves and lying with whores?

"He married Lara at the end of false winter. In her long black hair,
she replaced the snow dahlias of her mourning time with the fire flowers of the new bride and set to sewing him the new shagshay parka he
would need when deep winter came. Each Devaki made them a wedding gift. Eirene and Jael, the two giggling children who had first

greeted him so many months before, gave him a pair of mittens and a carved tortrix horn for him to fill with the potent beer that was brewed each winter from mashed tangleroot. His finest gift, a work of breath-taking art and symmetry, was the spear that Lokni gave him. It was long and heavy and tipped with a blade of flint so sharp that it cut through cured mammoth hide as easily as cheese."

I finished my drink, pausing a moment to catch my breath. The sounds the young man's marble cup made against the cold hard table seemed gritty and overloud. I smelled cinnamon and honey; a minute later the domestic served raisin bread spread with honey-cheese and brought us fresh pots of coffee. Outside the tearoom, I could hear the soft clack-clack of steel skates against the ice of the gliddery. I wondered who would be so foolish, or desperate, to be out on such a night. The young man took my hand in his, staring at me so intently that I had to look away. "And Goshevan?" he asked. "He was happy with the beautiful Lara? He was happy, wasn't he?"

"He was happy," I said, trying to slip my old hand from the young man's grip. "He was so happy he came to regard his body lice as his 'little pets' and didn't care that he would have to pass the rest of his days without a bath. His stuttering, which had embarrassed him all his life and caused him great shame, came to a sudden end as he found the liquid vowels and smooth consonants of the Devaki language rolling easily off his tongue. He loved Lara's children as his own and loved Lara as only a desperate and romantic man can love a woman. Though she had none of the exotic skills of the courtesans with whom he had been so familiar, she loved him with such a strength and passion that he came to divide his life into two parts: the time before Lara, which was murky and dim and full of confused memories, and the time after, which was full of light and joy and laughter. So it happened that when, the following midwinter spring, she pointed to her belly and smiled, he knew with a sureness that he had not spent his life in vain and was as happy as a man could be.

"The deep powder snows of winter were falling as Lara swelled like the ripened baldo nuts which the women picked and stored in great barrels staved with mammoth ribs and covered with mammoth hides. 'It will be a boy,' she said to him one night in early deep winter when the slopes of Kweitkel were silvery with the light of the moons. 'When I was carrying my girls I was sick every morning of the three seasons of growing. But with this one I wake up as hungry as Tuwa in midwinter spring.'

"When her time came, Katerina shooed Lokni and Goshevan, uncle and father, to the front of the cave where they waited while the women did their secret things. It was a night of such coldness that old Amalia said comes but twice every hundredyear. To the north, they could see green curtains of light hanging down from the black starry sky. 'The firefalls,' Lokni said. 'Sometimes they are faint and green as you see and other times as red as blood. The spirit of Wemilo and all our ancestors light the deep winter night to give us hope against the darkness.' And then he pointed at a bright triangle of stars twinkling brightly above the eastern horizon. 'Wakanda, Eanna, and Farfara,' he said. 'Men live there, I think. Shadow men without bodies. It is said they have no souls and take their nourishment from light.' And so they sat there for a long time shivering in their shagshay furs, talking of the things men talk about when they are full of strange longing and wonder at the mystery of life.

"There came a squalling from the cave. Goshevan clapped Lokni on the back and started laughing. But the cries of his newborn son were followed by a low wailing and then a whole chorus of women crying. He felt a horrible fear and leapt to his feet even as Lokni tried to hold him back.

"He ran to the warmest, deepest part of the cave where the men were not supposed to go. There, in the sick yellow light of the oilstones, on a blood-soaked newl fur, he saw his son lying all wet and slippery and pink between Lara's bent legs. Katerina knelt over the struggling infant, holding a corner of the gray fur over his face. Goshevan knocked her away from his son so that she fell to the floor, winded and gasping for air. As Haidar and Palani grabbed his arms, Lokni came to him and with such a sadness that his voice broke and tears ran from his eyes, he said, 'It is the Law, my friend. Any born such as he must immediately make the journey to the other side.' Then Goshevan, who had been full of blind panic and rage, looked at his son. He saw that growing from the hips were two tiny red stumps, twitching pathetically where they should have been kicking. His son had no legs. And to Lokni, who had gathered up the baby in his arms, he said, 'The Devaki do not kill each other.' And Lokni said, 'A baby is not a Devaki until he is named.' Then Goshevan raged so that Einar and Pauli had to come hold him as well. 'I name him Shanidar,' he said. 'Shanidar, my son, whom I love more than life.' But Lokni shook his head because life is so hard the Devaki do not name their children until four

winters have passed. With his forefinger, he made a star above the
screaming baby's head and went out to bury him in the snow.

"Lokni, whose white parka was stained crimson with frozen blood,
returned alone with his hands shielding his eyes as if to protect them
from false winter's noonday sun. Goshevan broke free and picked up
the mammoth spear which had been his wedding gift. He threw it at
Lokni in desperation, too blind with pain and fear to see the point enter his stomach and emerge from his back. And he ran outside to find
his son.

"An hour later he returned. And in his arms, frozen as hard as a
mammoth leg, he held his quiet, motionless son. 'Lara,' he said. And
like a drunkard, he stumbled towards his wife. But Lara, who had seen
what had passed between her legs and what her husband had done,
opened the great artery of her throat with her hide scraper before he
could get too close. And when he cried out that he loved her and
would die if she died, she told him that the essence of the Law is that
life must be lived with honor and joy or not lived at all. So Lara died as
he watched and the best part of him died with her. Knowing that his
life had come to an end, he unknotted the ties of his parka, exposing
the black matted hair of his chest so that Einar and Alani and the others might more easily spear him. But Goshevan had learned nothing.
Lokni, lying on his back with the blood running from a great hole in his
abdomen, said, Go back to the City, foolish man. We will not kill you;
we are not hunters of men.'

"They gave Goshevan a team of snarling dogs and a barrel of baldo
nuts and sent him out onto the ice. And he, who should have died a
hundred times, did not die because he was full of the madness which
protects desperate men, and a new idea had come into his head. So he
made his way back across the ice of the Starnbergersee. This time, he
ate his dogs when they died and didn't care that his beard was crusted
with their black, frozen blood. He came once again to Neverness as a
seeker; he came to my cutting shop, wretched, starving, covered with
filth and dead, frostbitten skin rotting on his face. He came to me and
said, 'I seek life for my son.'

"He stood in this very room, above this table. From a leather bag
full of snow and rimed with frost, he removed a twisted, pinkish lump
of frozen meat and laid it on the table. 'This is my son,' he said. 'Use all
your skills, Cutter, and return my son to me.'

"Goshevan told me his story, all the while cradling in his arms the leather bag to which he had returned his poor son's corpse. He was mad, so mad that I had to shout and repeat myself over and over before he would cease his ranting. 'There isn't a single cryologist in the city,' I told him, 'who can bring your son back to life.'

"But he never understood me. He went out onto the slidderies and glissades, telling his story to every cutter, splicer and cetic who would listen to him. Thus it came to be known throughout the city that I had tampered with his DNA and tampered badly. I was brought before the akashics and their accursed optical computers which laid bare my brain and recorded my actions and memories for all to see. 'If you ever again break the laws of our city,' the master akashic told me, 'you will be banished.' To ensure that I would obey the law, he ordered me to submit to their computer on the first day of each new year 'so long as you live.' Curiously, although I had scandalized most of the city, my 'Neanderthal Procedure' became immediately popular among the many farsiders who come to Neverness seeking to be other than what they are. For many years thereafter, the glidderies of our quarter were filled with squat hairy supermen who looked as if they could have been Goshevan's brother.

"And Goshevan, poor Goshevan—though he pleaded with and threatened every cryologist in the quarter—death is death, and no one could do more for him than give him a hot meal and a little toalache and send him on his way. The last I heard of him, he was trying to bribe his way to Agathange, where, he said, the men were no longer men and miracles were free to anyone who would surrender up his humanity. But everyone knows Agathanian resurrection is just a myth dreamed up by some fabulist drunk with the fire of toalache, no more real than the telepaths of The Golcanda. And so Goshevan disappeared into the back alleys of our Unreal City, no doubt freezing to death one dark winter's night. And there, my young friend, my story ends."

Painfully, I stood up to indicate that our conversation was over. But the young man kept to his chair, staring at me silently. His eyes grew so intense, so dark and disturbed, I thought that, perhaps, all men who desire the unobtainable must be touched with some degree of madness. I felt the acids of the kvass and coffee burning in my stomach as I said, "You must go now. You understand now, you understand why."

Suddenly, he slapped the table. The tearoom echoed with the loud rattle of teacups and the young man's trembling voice. "There the story does *not* end," he said. "This is the end, the true end of Goshevan's story that they tell in the silver mines of Summerworld."

I smiled at him then because the story of Goshevan is now a legend, and the endings to his story are as many as the Thousand Islands. Although I was certain to be bored by one of the fabulist myths in which Goshevan returns triumphantly to the Patwin or Basham or some other tribe of the Alaloi, one can never be *truly* certain. As I am a collector of such myths, I said, "Tell me your ending."

"Goshevan found Agathange," the young man said with conviction. "You yourself said he was hard to kill, Cutter. He found Agathange where the men—I guess I really shouldn't call them men because they were many-sexed and looked more like seals than men—where the Agathanians brought Shanidar back to life. They fitted him with mechanical legs stronger than real legs. They made him fifty sets of replacement legs, in graduated lengths to accommodate his growth. They offered Goshevan the peace of Agathange's oceans, the wisdom and bliss of cortically implanted bio-chips. But Goshevan, he said he wasn't fit for an ice-world that was less than civilized and that he certainly wasn't worthy of a water world that was beyond civilization. He thanked his hosts and said, 'Shanidar will grow up to be a prince. I will bring him home to Summerworld where men such as we belong.'

"To Summerworld he came many years later as an old man with white hair and a stooped back. He called upon the favor of his old friends, asking for the loan of rich delta land so that he could reestablish his estates. But no one recognized him. They, those wily, arrogant lords swathed in their white summer silks, they saw only an old madman—who I guess must have looked more like a beast to them than a man—and a strange-looking boy with proscribed Agathanian legs. 'Goshevan,' said Leonid the Just, who had once helped Goshevan put down Summerworld's forty-eighth servile revolt 'was as hairless as an elephant. He stuttered, too, if my poor memory serves me right.' And then—are you listening, Cutter?—then Leonid ordered them sold into the silver mines. Sondevan, the obese slavemaster, removed Shanidar's legs and strapped a cart to his abdomen so that he could wheel himself along the steel tracks that led into the ground. And though Goshevan was old, he was as strong as a water buffalo. They shoved a pick at him and set him hacking at a vein of sylvanite. 'Goshevan,' said the slavemaster, 'was my father's name. He was small and weak and let the Delta Lords buy his land for a tenth a talann per cubage. This ugly animal is not he.'

"The mines were cooler than the rice paddies, but they were hellishly hot compared with the frozen forests of Kweitkel. Goshevan—do you remember how you removed his sweat glands, Cutter?—Goshevan lasted two hours before he keeled over from heatstroke and fell into delirium. But before he died, he told his son the story of his birth and explained the Law of the Devaki. His last words before the slavemaster's silver mallet caved in his head were, 'Go back!'

"So I've come back," the young man said. The cutting shop was silent around us. As I stood there on the cold tile floor, I could hear the ragged hissing of my breath and taste the bittersweet tang of coffee coating my tongue and teeth. Suddenly, the young man rose to his feet so quickly that he bumped the table with his hip, sending one of my priceless teacups shattering against the floor. He opened his furs and dropped his trousers. There, badly fitted to his hips as if by some ignorant apprentice cutter, I could see the prosthetic legs—the kind they make badly on Fostora or Kainan—where they disappeared beneath reddened flaps of skin.

"I've come back to you, Grandfather," he said. "And you must do for me what you failed to do for Goshevan, who was my father."

And there my story really and truly ends. I do not know if the young man who came to me was the real Shanidar. I do not know if the story he told of Goshevan's death is really true. I prefer to believe his story, though it isn't stories that matter. What matters is precision and skill, the growing of new limbs for the legless and the altering, despite the law of civilization, the tampering with a young man's DNA when the need to tamper and heal is great. What matters is men who aren't afraid to change the shape and substance of their flesh so that they might seek out new beginnings.

When, on the first day of midwinter spring, I am brought before the master akashic and banished from my mysterious and beloved city, I will not seek out Agathange, tempting though the warmth of their oceans might be. I am too old to take on the body of a seal; I do not wish for the wisdom of cortically implanted biochips. To paraphrase the law: A man may do with his DNA as he pleases but his soul belongs to his people. It is to my people, the Devaki, that I must return. I have bitterly missed all these years the quiet white beauty of Kweitkel and besides, I must put flowers on my daughter Lara's grave. I, Arani, who once came to Neverness from the sixteenth and largest of the Thousand Islands like any other seeker, will take my grandson back across the frozen Starnbergersee. And for Goshevan, child of my lasers and microscopes, for my poor, brave, restless son-in-law I will pray as we pray for all who make the great journey: Goshevan, mi alasharia la shantih Devaki, may your spirit rest in peace on the other side of day.

Introduction to "Speech Sounds"
by Octavia E. Butler

People sometimes ask me who, in my opinion, is the best science fiction writer working today. This is an impossible question, of course. Best at what kind of science fiction? For what audience? Do we include the average quality of all an author's works, or just his or her best? For sheer gung-ho swashbuckling sci-fi adventure, maybe Mike Resnick's Santiago *but maybe Dave Wolverton's* Golden Queen *series; but that category does grave injustice to both writers because it seems to suggest that that's all their novels are. How about best writer of "hard" sf? Well, how hard? Or the best writer of good prose? Define "good," please. The questions quickly evaporate as soon as they're given any serious thought. Who is the best science fiction writer today? Don't waste my time.*

Except . . . there's this nagging feeling that the question does have an answer, and the answer is, quite possibly, Octavia Butler.

It's not an accident that when I was writing a book on how to write science fiction and fantasy, and needed an example of how to unfold exposition at the opening of a story or novel, I turned to a book by Octavia Butler. Her science is rigorous, her extrapolation at once wide-ranging and profound. Her characterizations are plausible yet quirky, her philosophy compelling and intelligent. As adventures her stories are gripping; the reader can't wait to find out what happens next. Tragedy infuses her work, along with a deep morality against which all other moralities may properly be judged.

Indeed, it's hard to find a kind of science fiction of which Octavia Butler is not a first-rate practitioner. (I suspect that if this shy, soft-spoken woman had ever donned mirrorshades and colored her hair, she'd have been claimed by the cyberpunks.) Does that make her best? Oh, who cares? If she isn't, she's close enough to being best that I now routinely use her as the easy, short answer to the question. It saves me having to go through a whole lecture about why there can't possibly be a "best" science fiction writer. I just say "Octavia Butler" and go on.

And I've never had anybody come back and argue with me about it. Not even the MacArthur Foundation people, who give out the "genius grants." In fact, they agreed with me and gave her one.

If that doesn't raise your expectations for this story impossibly high, I don't know what will. But I'm not worried. You won't be disappointed.

SPEECH SOUNDS

Octavia E. Butler

There was trouble aboard the Washington Boulevard bus. Rye had expected trouble sooner or later in her journey. She had put off going until loneliness and hopelessness drove her out. She believed she might have one group of relatives left alive—a brother and his two children twenty miles away in Pasadena. That was a day's journey one-way, if she were lucky. The unexpected arrival of the bus as she left her Virginia Road home had seemed to be a piece of luck—until the trouble began.

Two young men were involved in a disagreement of some kind, or, more likely, a misunderstanding. They stood in the aisle, grunting and gesturing at each other, each in his own uncertain "T" stance as the bus lurched over the potholes. The driver seemed to be putting some effort into keeping them off balance. Still, their gestures stopped just short of contact—mock punches, handgames of intimidation to replace lost curses.

People watched the pair, then looked at each other and made small anxious sounds. Two children whimpered.

Rye sat a few feet behind the disputants and across from the back door. She watched the two carefully, knowing the fight would begin when someone's nerve broke or someone's hand slipped or someone came to the end of his limited ability to communicate. These things could happen any time.

One of them happened as the bus hit an especially large pothole and one man, tall, thin, and sneering, was thrown into his shorter opponent.

Instantly, the shorter man drove his left fist into the disintegrating sneer. He hammered his larger opponent as though he neither had nor needed any weapon other than his left fist. He hit quickly enough, hard enough to batter his opponent down before the taller man could regain his balance or hit back even once.

People screamed or squawked in fear. Those nearby scrambled to get out of the way. Three more young men roared in excitement and gestured wildly. Then, somehow, a second dispute broke out between two of these three—probably because one inadvertently touched or hit the other.

As the second fight scattered frightened passengers, a woman shook the driver's shoulder and grunted as she gestured toward the fighting.

The driver grunted back through bared teeth. Frightened, the woman drew away.

Rye, knowing the methods of bus drivers, braced herself and held on to the crossbar of the seat in front of her. When the driver hit the brakes, she was ready and the combatants were not. They fell over seats and onto screaming passengers, creating even more confusion. At least one more fight started.

The instant the bus came to a full stop, Rye was on her feet, pushing the back door. At the second push, it opened and she jumped out, holding her pack in one arm. Several other passengers followed, but some stayed on the bus. Buses were so rare and irregular now, people rode when they could, no matter what. There might not be another bus today—or tomorrow. People started walking, and if they saw a bus they flagged it down. People making intercity trips like Rye's from Los Angeles to Pasadena made plans to camp out, or risked seeking shelter with locals who might rob or murder them.

The bus did not move, but Rye moved away from it. She intended to wait until the trouble was over and get on again, but if there was shooting, she wanted the protection of a tree. Thus, she was near the curb when a battered, blue Ford on the other side of the street made a U-turn and pulled up in front of the bus. Cars were rare these days—as rare as a severe shortage of fuel and of relatively unimpaired mechanics could make them. Cars that still ran were as likely to be used as weapons as they were to serve as transportation. Thus, when the driver of the Ford beckoned to Rye, she moved away warily. The driver got out—a big man, young, neatly bearded with dark, thick hair. He wore a long overcoat and a look of wariness that matched Rye's. She stood several feet from him, waiting to see what he would do. He looked at the bus, now rocking with the combat inside, then at the small cluster of passengers who had gotten off. Finally he looked at Rye again.

She returned his gaze, very much aware of the old forty-five automatic her jacket concealed. She watched his hands.

He pointed with his left hand toward the bus. The dark-tinted windows prevented him from seeing what was happening inside.

His use of the left hand interested Rye more than his obvious question. Left-handed people tended to be less impaired, more reasonable and comprehending, less driven by frustration, confusion, and anger.

She imitated his gesture, pointing toward the bus with her own left hand, then punching the air with both fists.

The man took off his coat revealing a Los Angeles Police Department uniform complete with baton and service revolver.

Rye took another step back from him. There was no more LAPD, no more *any* large organization, governmental or private. There were neighborhood patrols and armed individuals. That was all.

The man took something from his coat pocket, then threw the coat into the car. Then he gestured Rye back, back toward the rear of the bus. He had something made of plastic in his hand. Rye did not understand what he wanted until he went to the rear door of the bus and beckoned her to stand there. She obeyed mainly out of curiosity. Cop or not, maybe he could do something to stop the stupid fighting.

He walked around the front of the bus, to the street side where the driver's window was open. There, she thought she saw him throw something into the bus. She was still trying to peer through the tinted glass when people began stumbling out the rear door, choking and weeping. Gas.

Rye caught an old woman who would have fallen, lifted two little children down when they were in danger of being knocked down and trampled. She could see the bearded man helping people at the front door. She caught a thin old man shoved out by one of the combatants. Staggered by the old man's weight, she was barely able to get out of the way as the last of the young men pushed his way out. This one, bleeding from nose and mouth, stumbled into another and they grappled blindly, still sobbing from the gas.

The bearded man helped the bus driver out through the front door, though the driver did not seem to appreciate his help. For a moment, Rye thought there would be another fight. The bearded man stepped back and watched the driver gesture threateningly, watched him shout in wordless anger.

The bearded man stood still, made no sound, refused to respond to clearly obscene gestures. The least impaired people tended to do this—stand back unless they were physically threatened and let those with less control scream and jump around. It was as though they felt it beneath them to be as touchy as the less comprehending. This was an attitude of superiority and that was the way people like the bus driver perceived it. Such "superiority" was frequently punished by beatings, even by death. Rye had had close calls of her own. As a result, she never went unarmed. And in this world where the only likely common language was body language, being armed was often enough. She had rarely had to draw her gun or even display it.

The bearded man's revolver was on constant display. Apparently that was enough for the bus driver. The driver spat in disgust, glared at the bearded man for a moment longer, then strode back to his gas-filled bus. He stared at it for a moment, clearly wanting to get in, but the gas was still too strong. Of the windows, only his tiny driver's window actually opened. The front door was open, but the rear door would not stay open unless someone held it. Of course, the air conditioning had failed long ago. The bus would take some time to clear. It was the driver's property, his livelihood. He had pasted old magazine pictures of items he would accept as fare on its sides. Then he would use what he collected to feed his family or to trade. If his bus did not run, he did not eat. On the other hand, if the inside of his bus were torn apart by senseless fighting, he would not eat very well either. He was apparently unable to preceive this. All he could see was that it would be some time before he could use his bus again. He shook his fist at the bearded man and shouted. There seemed to be words in his shout, but Rye could not understand them. She did not know whether this was his fault or hers. She had heard so little coherent human speech for the past three years, she was no longer certain how well she recognized it, no longer certain of the degree of her own impairment.

The bearded man sighed. He glanced toward his car, then beckoned to Rye. He was ready to leave, but he wanted something from her first. No. No, he wanted her to leave with him. Risk getting into his car when, in spite of his uniform, law and order were nothing—not even words any longer.

She shook her head in a universally understood negative, but the man continued to beckon.

She waved him away. He was doing what the less-impaired rarely did—drawing potentially negative attention to another of his kind. People from the bus had begun to look at her.

One of the men who had been fighting tapped another on the arm, then pointed from the bearded man to Rye, and finally held up the first two fingers of his right hand as though giving two-thirds of a Boy Scout salute. The gesture was very quick, its meaning obvious even at a distance. She had been grouped with the bearded man. Now what?

The man who had made the gesture started toward her.

She had no idea what she intended, but she stood her ground. The man was half-a-foot taller than she was and perhaps ten years younger. She did not imagine she could outrun him. Nor did she expect anyone to help her if she needed help. The people around her were all strangers.

She gestured once—a clear indication to the man to stop. She did not intend to repeat the gesture. Fortunately, the man obeyed. He gestured obscenely and several other men laughed. Loss of verbal language had spawned a whole new set of obscene gestures. The man, with stark simplicity, had accused her of sex with the bearded man and had suggested she accommodate the other men present—beginning with him.

Rye watched him wearily. People might very well stand by and watch if he tried to rape her. They would also stand and watch her shoot him. Would he push things that far?

He did not. After a series of obscene gestures that brought him no closer to her, he turned contemptuously and walked away.

And the bearded man still waited. He had removed his service revolver, holster and all. He beckoned again, both hands empty. No doubt his gun was in the car and within easy reach, but his taking it off impressed her. Maybe he was all right. Maybe he was just alone. She had been alone herself for three years. The illness had stripped her, killing her children one by one, killing her husband, her sister, her parents. . . .

The illness, if it was an illness, had cut even the living off from one another. As it swept over the country, people hardly had time to lay blame on the Soviets (though they were falling silent along with the rest of the world), on a new virus, a new pollutant, radiation, divine retribution. . . . The illness was stroke-swift in the way it cut people down and strokelike in some of its effects. But it was highly specific. Language was always lost or severely impaired. It was never regained. Often there was also paralysis, intellectual impairment, death.

Rye walked toward the bearded man, ignoring the whistling and applauding of two of the young men and their thumbs-up signs to the bearded man. If he had smiled at them or acknowledged them in any way, she would almost certainly have changed her mind. If she had let herself think of the possible deadly consequences of getting into a stranger's car, she would have changed her mind. Instead, she thought of the man who lived across the street from her. He rarely washed since his bout with the illness. And he had gotten into the habit of urinating wherever he happened to be. He had two women already—one tending each of his large gardens. They put up with him in exchange for his protection. He had made it clear that he wanted Rye to become his third woman.

She got into the car and the bearded man shut the door. She watched as he walked around to the driver's door—watched for his sake because his gun was on the seat beside her. And the bus driver and a pair of young men had come a few steps closer. They did nothing, though, until the bearded man was in the car. Then one of them threw a rock. Others followed his example, and as the car drove away, several rocks bounced off it harmlessly.

When the bus was some distance behind them, Rye wiped sweat from her forehead and longed to relax. The bus would have taken her more than halfway to Pasadena. She would have had only ten miles to walk. She wondered how far she would have to walk now—and wondered if walking a long distance would be her only problem.

At Figuroa and Washington where the bus normally made a left turn, the bearded man stopped, looked at her, and indicated that she should choose a direction. When she directed him left and he actually turned left, she began to relax. If he was willing to go where she directed, perhaps he was safe.

As they passed blocks of burned, abandoned buildings, empty lots, and wrecked or stripped cars, he slipped a gold chain over his head and handed it to her. The pendant attached to it was a smooth, glassy, black rock. Obsidian. His name might be Rock or Peter or Black, but she decided to think of him as Obsidian. Even her sometimes useless memory would retain a name like Obsidian.

She handed him her own name symbol—a pin in the shape of a large golden stalk of wheat. She had bought it long before the illness and the silence began. Now she wore it, thinking it was as close as she was likely to come to Rye. People like Obsidian who had not known her before probably thought of her as Wheat. Not that it mattered. She would never hear her name spoken again.

Obsidian handed her pin back to her. He caught her hand as she reached for it and rubbed his thumb over her calluses.

He stopped at First Street and asked which way again. Then, after turning right as she had indicated, he parked near the Music Center. There, he took a folded paper from the dashboard and unfolded it. Rye recognized it as a street map, though the writing on it meant nothing to her. He flattened the map, took her hand again, and put her index finger on one spot. He touched her, touched himself, pointed toward the floor. In effect, "We are here." She knew he wanted to know where she was going. She wanted to tell him, but she shook her head sadly. She had lost reading and writing. That was her most serious impairment and her most painful. She had taught history at UCLA. She had done freelance writing. Now she could not even read her own manuscripts. She had a house full of books that she could neither read nor bring herself to use as fuel. And she had a memory that would not bring back to her much of what she had read before.

She stared at the map, trying to calculate. She had been born in Pasadena, had lived for fifteen years in Los Angeles. Now she was near L.A. Civic Center. She knew the relative positions of the two cities, knew streets, directions, even knew to stay away from freeways which might be blocked by wrecked cars and destroyed overpasses. She ought to know how to point out Pasadena even though she could not recognize the word.

Hesitantly, she placed her hand over a pale orange patch in the upper right corner of the map. That should be right. Pasadena.

Obsidian lifted her hand and looked under it, then folded the map and put it back on the dashboard. He could read, she realized belatedly. He could probably write, too. Abruptly, she hated him—deep, bitter hatred. What did literacy mean to him—a grown man who played cops and robbers? But he was literate and she was not. She never would be. She felt sick to her stomach with hatred, frustration, and jealousy. And only a few inches from her hand was a loaded gun.

She held herself still, staring at him, almost seeing his blood. But her rage crested and ebbed and she did nothing.

Obsidian reached for her hand with hesitant familiarity. She looked at him. Her face had already revealed too much. No person still living in what was left of human society could fail to recognize that expression, that jealousy.

She closed her eyes wearily, drew a deep breath. She had experienced longing for the past, hatred of the present, growing hopelessness, purposelessness, but she had never experienced such a powerful urge to kill another person. She had left her home, finally, because she had come near to killing herself. She had found no reason to stay alive. Perhaps that was why she had gotten into Obsidian's car. She had never before done such a thing.

He touched her mouth and made chatter motions with thumb and fingers. Could she speak?

She nodded and watched his milder envy come and go. Now both had admitted what it was not safe to admit, and there had been no violence. He tapped his mouth and forehead and shook his head. He did not speak or comprehend spoken language. The illness had played with them, taking away, she suspected, what each valued most.

She plucked at his sleeve, wondering why he had decided on his own to keep the LAPD alive with what he had left. He was sane enough otherwise. Why wasn't he at home raising corn, rabbits, and children? But she did not know how to ask. Then he put his hand on her thigh and she had another question to deal with.

She shook her head. Disease, pregnancy, helpless, solitary agony . . . no.

He massaged her thigh gently and smiled in obvious disbelief.

No one had touched her for three years. She had not wanted anyone to touch her. What kind of world was this to chance bringing a child into even if the father were willing to stay and help raise it? It was too bad, though. Obsidian could not know how attractive he was to her—young, probably younger than she was, clean, asking for what he wanted rather than demanding it. But none of that mattered. What were a few moments of pleasure measured against a lifetime of consequences?

He pulled her closer to him and for a moment she let herself enjoy the closeness. He smelled good—male and good. She pulled away reluctantly.

He sighed, reached toward the glove compartment. She stiffened, not knowing what to expect, but all he took out was a small box. The writing on it meant nothing to her. She did not understand until he broke the seal, opened the box, and took out a condom. He looked at her and she first looked away in surprise. Then she giggled. She could not remember when she had last giggled.

He grinned, gestured toward the back seat, and she laughed aloud. Even in her teens, she had disliked back seats of cars. But she looked around at the empty streets and ruined buildings, then she got out and into the back seat. He let her put the condom on him, then seemed surprised at her eagerness.

Sometime later, they sat together, covered by his coat, unwilling to become clothed near-strangers again just yet. He made rock-the-baby gestures and looked questioningly at her.

She swallowed, shook her head. She did not know how to tell him her children were dead.

He took her hand and drew a cross in it with his index finger, then made his baby-rocking gesture again.

She nodded, held up three fingers, then turned away, trying to shut out a sudden flood of memories. She had told herself that the children growing up now were to be pitied. They would run through the downtown canyons with no real memory of what the buildings had been or even how they had come to be. Today's children gathered books as well as wood to be burned as fuel. They ran through the streets chasing each other and hooting like chimpanzees. They had no future. They were now all they would ever be.

He put his hand on her shoulder and she turned suddenly, fumbling for his small box, then urging him to make love to her again. He could give her forgetfulness and pleasure. Until now, nothing had been able to do that. Until now, every day had brought her closer to the time when she would do what she had left home to avoid doing: putting her gun in her mouth and pulling the trigger.

She asked Obsidian if he would come home with her, stay with her.

He looked surprised and pleased once he understood. But he did not answer at once. Finally he shook his head as she had feared he might. He was probably having too much fun playing cops and robbers and picking up women.

She dressed in silent disappointment, unable to feel any anger toward him. Perhaps he already had a wife and a home. That was likely. The illness had been harder on men than on women—had killed more men, had left male survivors more severely impaired. Men like Obsidian were rare. Women either settled for less or stayed alone. If they found an Obsidian, they did what they could to keep him. Rye suspected he had someone younger, prettier keeping him.

He touched her while she was strapping her gun on and asked with a complicated series of gestures whether it was loaded.

She nodded grimly.

He patted her arm.

She asked once more if he would come home with her, this time using a different series of gestures. He had seemed hesitant. Perhaps he could be courted.

He got out and into the front seat without responding.

She took her place in front again, watching him. Now he plucked at his uniform and looked at her. She thought she was being asked something, but did not know what it was.

He took off his badge, tapped it with one finger, then tapped his chest. Of course.

She took the badge from his hand and pinned her wheat stalk to it. If playing cops and robbers was his only insanity, let him play. She would take him, uniform and all. It occurred to her that she might eventually lose him to someone he would meet as he had met her. But she would have him for a while.

He took the street map down again, tapped it, pointed vaguely northeast toward Pasadena, then looked at her.

She shrugged, tapped his shoulder then her own, and held up her index and second fingers tight together, just to be sure.

He grasped the two fingers and nodded. He was with her.

She took the map from him and threw it onto the dashboard. She pointed back southwest—back toward home. Now she did not have to go to Pasadena. Now she could go on having a brother there and two nephews—three right-handed males. Now she did not have to find out for certain whether she was as alone as she feared. Now she was not alone.

Obsidian took Hill Street south, then Washington west, and she leaned back, wondering what it would be like to have someone again. With what she had scavenged, what she had preserved, and what she grew, there was easily enough food for him. There was certainly room enough in a four-bedroom house. He could move his possessions in. Best of all, the animal across the street would pull back and possibly not force her to kill him.

Obsidian had drawn her closer to him and she had put her head on his shoulder when suddenly he braked hard, almost throwing her off the seat. Out of the corner of her eye, she saw that someone had run across the street in front of the car. One car on the street and someone had to run in front of it.

Straightening up, Rye saw that the runner was a woman, fleeing from an old frame house to a boarded-up storefront. She ran silently, but the man who followed her a moment later shouted what sounded like garbled words as he ran. He had something in his hand. Not a gun. A knife, perhaps.

The woman tried a door, found it locked, looked around desperately, finally snatched up a fragment of glass broken from the storefront window. With this she turned to face her pursuer. Rye thought she would be more likely to cut her own hand than to hurt anyone else with the glass.

Obsidian jumped from the car, shouting. It was the first time Rye had heard his voice—deep and hoarse from disuse. He made the same sound over and over the way some speechless people did, "Da, da, da!"

Rye got out of the car as Obsidian ran toward the couple. He had drawn his gun. Fearful, she drew her own and released the safety. She looked around to see who else might be attracted to the scene. She saw the man glance at Obsidian, then suddenly lunge at the woman. The woman jabbed his face with her glass, but he caught her arm and managed to stab her twice before Obsidian shot him.

The man doubled, then toppled, clutching his abdomen. Obsidian shouted, then gestured Rye over to help the woman.

Rye moved to the woman's side, remembering that she had little more than bandages and antiseptic in her pack. But the woman was beyond help. She had been stabbed with a long, slender, boning knife.

She touched Obsidian to let him know the woman was dead. He had bent to check the wounded man who lay still and also seemed dead. But as Obsidian looked around to see what Rye wanted, the man opened his eyes. Face contorted, he seized Obsidian's just-holstered revolver and fired. The bullet caught Obsidian in the temple and he collapsed.

It happened just that simply, just that fast. An instant later, Rye shot the wounded man as he was turning the gun on her.

And Rye was alone—with three corpses.

She knelt beside Obsidian, dry-eyed, frowning, trying to understand why everything had suddenly changed. Obsidian was gone. He had died and left her—like everyone else.

Two very small children came out of the house from which the man and woman had run—a boy and girl perhaps three years old. Holding hands, they crossed the street toward Rye. They stared at her, then edged past her and went to the dead woman. The girl shook the woman's arm as though trying to wake her.

This was too much. Rye got up, feeling sick to her stomach with grief and anger. If the children began to cry, she thought she would vomit.

They were on their own, those two kids. They were old enough to scavenge. She did not need any more grief. She did not need a stranger's children who would grow up to be hairless chimps.

She went back to the car. She could drive home, at least. She remembered how to drive.

The thought that Obsidian should be buried occurred to her before she reached the car, and she did vomit.

She had found and lost the man so quickly. It was as though she had been snatched from comfort and security and given a sudden, inexplicable beating. Her head would not clear. She could not think.

Somehow, she made herself go back to him, look at him. She found herself on her knees beside him with no memory of having knelt. She stroked his face, his beard. One of the children made a noise and she looked at them, at the woman who was probably their mother. The children looked back at her, obviously frightened. Perhaps it was their fear that reached her finally.

She had been about to drive away and leave them. She had almost done it, almost left two toddlers to die. Surely there had been enough dying. She would have to take the children home with her. She would not be able to live with any other decision. She looked around for a place to bury three bodies. Or two. She wondered if the murderer were the children's father. Before the silence, the police had always said some of the most dangerous calls they went out on were domestic disturbance calls. Obsidian should have known that—not that the knowledge would have kept him in the car. It would not have held her back either. She could not have watched the woman murdered and done nothing.

She dragged Obsidian toward the car. She had nothing to dig with here, and no one to guard for her while she dug. Better to take the bodies with her and bury them next to her husband and her children. Obsidian would come home with her after all.

When she had gotten him onto the floor in the back, she returned for the woman. The little girl, thin, dirty, solemn, stood up and unknowingly gave Rye a gift. As Rye began to drag the woman by her arms, the little girl screamed, "No!"

Rye dropped the woman and stared at the girl.

"No!" the girl repeated. She came to stand beside the woman. "Go away!" she told Rye.

"Don't talk," the little boy said to her. There was no blurring or confusing of sounds. Both children had spoken and Rye had understood. The boy looked at the dead murderer and moved farther from him. He took the girl's hand. "Be quiet," he whispered.

Fluent speech! Had the woman died because she could talk and had taught her children to talk? Had she been killed by a husband's festering anger or by a stranger's jealous rage? And the children . . . they must have been born after the silence. Had the disease run its course, then? Or were these children simply immune? Certainly they had had time to fall sick and silent. Rye's mind leaped ahead. What if children of three or fewer years were safe and able to learn language? What if all they needed were teachers? Teachers and protectors.

Rye glanced at the dead murderer. To her shame, she thought she could understand some of the passions that must have driven him, whoever he was. Anger, frustration, hopelessness, insane jealousy . . . how many more of him were there—people willing to destroy what they could not have?

Obsidian had been the protector, had chosen that role for who knew what reason. Perhaps putting on an obsolete uniform and patrolling the empty streets had been what he did instead of putting a gun into his mouth. And now that there was something worth protecting, he was gone.

She had been a teacher. A good one. She had been a protector, too, though only of herself. She had kept herself alive when she had no reason to live. If the illness let these children alone, she could keep them alive.

Somehow she lifted the dead woman into her arms and placed her on the back seat of the car. The children began to cry, but she knelt on the broken pavement and whispered to them, fearful of frightening them with the harshness of her long unused voice.

"It's all right," she told them. "You're going with us, too. Come on." She lifted them both, one in each arm. They were so light. Had they been getting enough to eat?

The boy covered her mouth with his hand, but she moved her face away. "It's all right for me to talk," she told him. "As long as no one's around, it's all right." She put the boy down on the front seat of the car and he moved over without being told to, to make room for the girl.

When they were both in the car Rye leaned against the window, looking at them, seeing that they were less afraid now that they watched her with at least as much curiosity as fear.

"I'm Valerie Rye," she said, savoring the words. "It's all right for you to talk to me."

Introduction to "Snow"

by John Crowley

I first saw Crowley's name on the cover of a novel called The Deep. There was a cover quote from Harlan Ellison that said, if I remember correctly, that anyone who didn't buy and read this book immediately was too stupid to walk and hold their pants up. Or something like that. Anyway, I've always made it a practice in my life to do just what Harlan Ellison says, so I bought the book.

The thing had all the earmarks of an intellectual puzzle; there was a roster of players at the beginning, so you could tell—literally—the red team from the black. It was a game of checkers, eh? Kings getting crowned and hopping all over the board.

But in the reading of it, I discovered that it was far more than a mere intellectual exercise. Crowley was a writer of extraordinary power, and whatever his abstract plan, his characters emerged human and took hold of my heart. That it was sometimes hard to tell just what was going on was a minor flaw. Ellison was right—Crowley was a writer who sprayed brilliance the way dogs shake off rain.

Since then he has added ever-worthier books to his oeuvre—Engine Summer, a science fiction pastoral; Aegypt; the much-renowned Little, Big; others. It is, without question, his novels that have made him one of the most respected and influential writers in science fiction. But in the tight confines of a short story like "Snow," he can take the Heisenberg Uncertainty Principle and make a crystal out of it, small but complex and multifaceted, beautiful even as the breath of entropy melts it before your eyes.

SNOW

John Crowley

I don't think Georgie would ever have got one for herself: She was at
once unsentimental and a little in awe of death. No, it was her first
husband—an immensely rich and (from Georgie's description) a
strangely weepy guy, who had got it for her. Or for himself, actually, of
course. He was to be the beneficiary. Only he died himself shortly after it was installed. If *installed* is the right word. After he died, Georgie
got rid of most of what she'd inherited from him, liquidated it. It was
cash that she had liked best about that marriage anyway; but the Wasp
couldn't really be got rid of. Georgie ignored it.

In fact the thing really was about the size of a wasp of the largest
kind, and it had the same lazy and mindless fight. And of course it
really was a bug, not of the insect kind but of the surveillance kind.
And so its name fit all around: one of those bits of accidental poetry
the world generates without thinking. O Death, where is thy sting?

Georgie ignored it, but it was hard to avoid; you had to be a little
careful around it; it followed Georgie at a variable distance, depending
on her motions and the numbers of other people around her, the level
of light; and the tone of her voice. And there was always the danger
you might shut it in a door or knock it down with a tennis racket.

It cost a fortune (if you count the access and the perpetual care
contract, all prepaid), and though it wasn't really fragile, it made you
nervous.

It wasn't recording all the time. There had to be a certain amount
of light, though not much. Darkness shut it off. And then sometimes it
would get lost. Once when we hadn't seen it hovering around for a
time, I opened a closet door, and it flew out, unchanged. It went off
looking for her, humming softly. It must have been shut in there for
days.

Eventually it ran out, or down. A lot could go wrong, I suppose,
with circuits that small, controlling that many functions. It ended up

spending a lot of time bumping gently against the bedroom ceiling, over and over, like a winter fly. Then one day the maids swept it out from under the bureau, a husk. By that time it had transmitted at least eight thousand hours (eight thousand was the minimum guarantee) of Georgie: of her days and hours, her comings in and her goings out, her speech and motion, her living self—all on file, taking up next to no room, at The Park. And then, when the time came, you could go there, to The Park, say on a Sunday afternoon; and in quiet landscaped surroundings (as The Park described it) you would find her personal resting chamber, and there, in privacy, through the miracle of modern information storage and retrieval systems, you could access her, her alive, her as she was in every way, never changing or growing any older, fresher (as The Park's brochure said) than in memory ever green.

I married Georgie for her money, the same reason she married her first, the one who took out The Park's contract for her. She married me, I think, for my looks; she always had a taste for looks in men. I wanted to write. I made a calculation that more women than men make, and decided that to be supported and paid for by a rich wife would give me freedom to do so, to "develop." The calculation worked out no better for me than it does for most women who make it. I carried a typewriter and a case of miscellaneous paper from Ibiza to Gstaad to Bial to London, and typed on beaches, and learned to ski. Georgie liked me in ski clothes.

Now that those looks are all but gone, I can look back on myself as a young hunk and see that I was in a way a rarity, a type that you run into often among women, far less among men, the beauty unaware of his beauty, aware that he affects women profoundly and more or less instantly but doesn't know why; thinks he is being listened to and understood, that his soul is being seen, when all that's being seen is long-lashed eyes and a strong, square, tanned wrist turning in a lovely gesture, stubbing out a cigarette. Confusing. By the time I figured out why I had for so long been indulged and cared for and listened to, why I was interesting, I wasn't as interesting as I had been. At about the same time I realized I wasn't a writer at all. Georgie's investment stopped looking as good to her, and my calculation had ceased to add up; only by that time I had come, pretty unexpectedly, to love Georgie a lot, and she just as unexpectedly had come to love and need me too, as much as she needed anybody. We never really parted, even though when she died I hadn't seen her for years. Phone calls, at dawn or four

A.M. because she never, for all her travel, really grasped that the world turns and cocktail hour travels around with it. She was a crazy, wasteful, happy woman, without a trace of malice or permanence or ambition in her—easily pleased and easily bored and strangely serene despite the hectic pace she kept up. She cherished things and lost them and forgot them: things, days, people. She had fun, though, and I had fun with her; that was her talent and her destiny, not always an easy one. Once, hung over in a New York hotel, watching a sudden snowfall out the immense window, she said to me, "Charlie, I'm going to die of fun."

And she did. Snow-foiling in Austria, she was among the first to get one of those snow leopards, silent beasts as fast as speedboats. Alfredo called me in California to tell me, but with the distance and his accent and his eagerness to tell me *he* wasn't to blame, I never grasped the details. I was still her husband, her closest relative, heir to the little she still had, and beneficiary, too, of The Park's access concept. Fortunately, The Park's services included collecting her from the morgue in Gstaad and installing her in her chamber at The Park's California unit. Beyond signing papers and taking delivery when Georgie arrived by freight airship at Van Nuys, there was nothing for me to do. The Park's representative was solicitous and made sure I understood how to go about accessing Georgie, but I wasn't listening. I am only a child of my time, I suppose. Everything about death, the fact of it, the fate of the remains, and the situation of the living faced with it, seems grotesque to me, embarrassing, useless. And everything done about it only makes it more grotesque, more useless: Someone I loved is dead; let me therefore dress in clown's clothes, talk backwards, and buy expensive machinery to make up for it. I went back to L.A.

A year or more later, the contents of some safe-deposit boxes of Georgie's arrived from the lawyer's: some bonds and such stuff and a small steel case, velvet lined, that contained a key, a key deeply notched on both sides and headed with smooth plastic, like the key to an expensive car.

Why did I go to The Park that first time? Mostly because I had forgotten about it: Getting that key in the mail was like coming across a pile of old snapshots you hadn't cared to look at when they were new but which after they have aged come to contain the past, as they did not contain the present. I was curious.

I understood very well that The Park and its access concept were very probably only another cruel joke on the rich, preserving the illusion that they can buy what can't be bought, like the cryonics fad of thirty years ago. Once in Ibiza, Georgie and I met a German couple who also had a contract with The Park; their Wasp hovered over them like a Paraclete and made them self-conscious in the extreme—they seemed to be constantly rehearsing the eternal show being stored up for their descendants. Their deaths had taken over their lives, as though they were pharaohs. Did they, Georgie wondered, exclude the Wasp from their bedroom? Or did its presence there stir them to greater efforts, proofs of undying love and admirable vigor for the unborn to see?

No, death wasn't to be cheated that way, any more than by pyramids, by masses said in perpetuity. It wasn't Georgie saved from death that I would find. But there were eight thousand hours of her life with me, genuine hours, stored there more carefully than they could be in my porous memory; Georgie hadn't excluded the Wasp from her bedroom, our bedroom, and she who had never performed for anybody could not have conceived of performing for it. And there would be me, too, undoubtedly, caught unintentionally by the Wasp's attention: Out of those thousands of hours there would be hundreds of myself, and myself had just then begun to be problematic to me, something that had to be figured out, something about which evidence had to be gathered and weighed. I was thirty-eight years old.

That summer, then, I borrowed a Highway Access Permit (the old HAPpy cards of those days) from a county lawyer I knew and drove the coast highway up to where The Park was, at the end of a pretty beach road, all alone above the sea. It looked from the outside like the best, most peaceful kind of Italian country cemetery, a low stucco wall topped with urns, amid cypresses, an arched gate in the center. A small brass plaque on the gate: PLEASE USE YOUR KEY. The gate opened, not to a square of shaded tombstones but onto a ramped corridor going down: The cemetery wall was an illusion, the works were underground. Silence, or nameless Muzak-like silence: solitude—whether the necessary technicians were discreetly hidden or none were needed. Certainly the access concept turned out to be simplicity itself, in operation anyway. Even I, who am an idiot about information technology, could tell that. The Wasp was genuine state-of-the-art stuff, but what we mourners got was as ordinary as home movies, as old letters tied up in ribbon.

A display screen near the entrance told me down which corridor to find Georgie, and my key let me into a small screening room where there was a moderate-size TV monitor, two comfortable chairs, and dark walls of chocolate-brown carpeting. The sweet-sad Muzak. Georgie herself was evidently somewhere in the vicinity, in the wall or under the floor, they weren't specific about the charnel-house aspect of the place. In the control panel before the TV were a keyhole for my key and two bars: ACCESS and RESET.

I sat, feeling foolish and a little afraid, too, made more uncomfortable by being so deliberately soothed by neutral furnishings and sober tools. I imagined, around me, down other corridors, in other chambers, others communed with their dead as I was about to do, that the dead were murmuring to them beneath the stream of Muzak; that they wept to see and hear, as I might, but I could hear nothing. I turned my key in its slot, and the screen lit up. The dim lights dimmed further, and the Muzak ceased. I pushed ACCESS, obviously the next step. No doubt all these procedures had been explained to me long ago at the dock when Georgie in her aluminum box was being off-loaded, and I hadn't listened. And on the screen she turned to look at me—only not at me, though I started and drew breath—at the Wasp that watched her. She was in mid-sentence, mid-gesture. Where? When? *Or put it on the same card with the others,* she said, turning away. Someone said something, Georgie answered, and stood up, the Wasp panning and moving erratically with her, like an amateur with a home-video camera. A white room, sunlight, wicker. Ibiza. Georgie wore a cotton blouse, open; from a table she picked up lotion, poured some on her hand, and rubbed it across her freckled breastbone. The meaningless conversation about putting something on a card went on, ceased. I watched the room, wondering what year, what season I had stumbled into. Georgie pulled off her shirt—her small round breasts tipped with large, childlike nipples, child's breasts she still had at forty, shook delicately. And she went out onto the balcony, the Wasp following, blinded by sun, adjusting. *If you want to do it that way,* someone said. The someone crossed the screen, a brown blur, naked. It was me. Georgie said: *Oh, look, hummingbirds.*

She watched them, rapt, and the Wasp crept close to her cropped blond head, rapt too, and I watched her watch. She turned away, rested her elbows on the balustrade. I couldn't remember this day. How should I? One of hundreds, of thousands. . . . She looked out to the bright sea, wearing her sleepwalking face, mouth partly open, and absently stroked her breast with her oiled hand. An iridescent glitter among the flowers was the hummingbird.

Without really knowing what I did—I felt hungry, suddenly, hungry for pastness, for more—I touched the RESET bar. The balcony in Ibiza vanished, the screen glowed emptily. I touched ACCESS.

At first there was darkness, a murmur; then a dark back moved away from before the Wasp's eye, and a dim scene of people resolved itself. Jump. Other people, or the same people, a party? Jump. Apparently the Wasp was turning itself on and off according to the changes in light levels here, wherever *here* was. Georgie in a dark dress having her cigarette lit: brief flare of the lighter. She said, *Thanks.* Jump. A foyer or hotel lounge. Paris? The Wasp jerkily sought for her among people coming and going; it couldn't make a movie, establishing shots, cutaways—it could only doggedly follow Georgie, like a jealous husband, seeing nothing else. This was frustrating. I pushed RESET. ACCESS. Georgie brushed her teeth, somewhere, somewhen.

I understood, after one or two more of these terrible leaps. Access was random. There was no way to dial up a year, a day, a scene. The Park had supplied no program, none; the eight thousand hours weren't filed at all, they were a jumble, like a lunatic's memory, like a deck of shuffled cards. I had supposed, without thinking about it, that they would begin at the beginning and go on till they reached the end. Why didn't they?

I also understood something else. If access was truly random, if I truly had no control, then I had lost as good as forever those scenes I had seen. Odds were on the order of eight thousand to one (more? far more? probabilities are opaque to me) that I would never light on them again by pressing this bar. I felt a pang of loss for that afternoon in Ibiza. It was doubly gone now. I sat before the empty screen, afraid to touch ACCESS again, afraid of what I would lose.

I shut down the machine (the light level in the room rose, the Muzak poured softly back in) and went out into the halls, back to the display screen in the entranceway. The list of names slowly, greenly, rolled over like the list of departing flights at an airport: Code numbers were missing from beside many, indicating perhaps that they weren't yet in residence, only awaited. In the *D*s, three names, and DIRECTOR—hidden among them as though he were only another of the dead. A chamber number. I went to find it and went in. The director looked more like a janitor or a night watchman, the semiretired type you often see caretaking little-visited places. He wore a brown smock like a monk's robe and was making coffee in a corner of his small office, out of which little business seemed to be done. He looked up startled, caught out, when I entered.

"Sorry," I said, "but I don't think I understand this system right."

"A problem?" he said. "Shouldn't be a problem." He looked at me a little wide-eyed and shy, hoping not to be called on for anything difficult. "Equipment's all working?"

"I don't know," I said. "It doesn't seem that it could be." I described what I thought I had learned about The Park's access concept. "That can't be right, can it?" I said. "That access is totally random . . ."

He was nodding, still wide-eyed, paying close attention.

"Is it?" I asked.

"Is it what?"

"Random."

"Oh, yes. Yes, sure. If everything's in working order."

I could think of nothing to say for a moment, watching him nod reassuringly. Then, "Why?" I asked. "I mean why is there no way at all to, to organize, to have some kind of organized access to the material?" I had begun to feel that sense of grotesque foolishness in the presence of death, as though I were haggling over Georgie's effects. "That seems stupid, if you'll pardon me."

"Oh no, oh no," he said. "You've read your literature? You've read all your literature?"

"Well, to tell the truth . . ."

"It's all just as described," the director said. "I can promise you that. If there's any problem at all. . . ."

"Do you mind," I said, "if I sit down?" I smiled. He seemed so afraid of me and my complaint, of me as mourner, possibly grief crazed and unable to grasp the simple limits of his responsibilities to me, that he needed soothing himself. "I'm sure everything's fine," I said. "I just don't think I understand. I'm kind of dumb about these things."

"Sure. Sure. Sure." He regretfully put away his coffee makings and sat behind his desk, lacing his fingers together like a consultant. "People get a lot of satisfaction out of the access here," he said, "a lot of comfort, if they take in the right spirit." He tried a smile. I wondered what qualifications he had had to show to get this job. "The random part. Now, it's all in the literature. There's the legal aspect—you're not a lawyer are you, no, no, sure, no offense. You see, the material here isn't for anything, except, well, except for communing. But suppose the stuff were programmed, searchable. Suppose there was a problem about taxes or inheritance or so on. There could be subpoenas, lawyers all over the place, destroying the memorial concept completely."

I really hadn't thought of that. Built-in randomness saved past lives from being searched in any systematic way. And no doubt saved The Park from being in the records business and at the wrong end of a lot of suits. "You'd have to watch the whole eight thousand hours," I said, "and even if you found what you were looking for there'd be no way to replay it. It would have gone by." It would slide into the random past even as you watched it, like that afternoon in Ibiza, that party in Paris. Lost. He smiled and nodded. I smiled and nodded.

"I'll tell you something," he said. "They didn't predict that. The randomness. It was a side effect, an affect of the storage process. Just luck." His grin turned down, his brows knitted seriously. "See, we're storing here at the molecular level. We have to go that small, for space problems. I mean your eight-thousand-hour guarantee. If we had gone tape or conventional, how much room would it take up? If the access concept caught on. A lot of room. So we went vapor trap and endless tracking. Size of my thumbnail. It's all in the literature." He looked at me strangely. I had a sudden intense sensation that I was being fooled, tricked, that the man before me in his smock was no expert, no technician; he was a charlatan, or maybe a madman impersonating a director and not belonging here at all. It raised the hair on my neck and passed. "So the randomness," he was saying. "It was an effect of going molecular. Brownian movement. All you do is lift the endless tracking for a microsecond and you get a rearrangement at the molecular level. We don't randomize. The molecules do it for us."

I remembered Brownian movement, just barely, from physics class. The random movement of molecules, the teacher said; it has a mathematical description. It's like the movement of dust motes you see swimming in a shaft of sunlight, like the swirl of snowflakes in a glass paperweight that shows a cottage being snowed on. "I see," I said. "I guess I see."

"Is there," he said, "any other problem?" He said it as though there might be some other problem and that he knew what it might be and that he hoped I didn't have it. "You understand the system, key lock, two bars, ACCESS, RESET. . . . ."

"I understand," I said. "I understand now."

"Communing," he said, standing, relieved, sure I would be gone soon. "I understand. It takes a while to relax into the communing concept."

"Yes," I said. "It does."

I wouldn't learn what I had come to learn, whatever that was. The Wasp had not been good at storage after all, no, no better than my young soul had been. Days and weeks had been missed by its tiny eye. It hadn't seen well, and in what it had seen it had been no more able to distinguish the just-as-well-forgotten from the unforgettable than my own eye had been. No better and no worse—the same.

And yet, and yet—she stood up in Ibiza and dressed her breasts with lotion, and spoke to me: *Oh, look, hummingbirds.* I had forgotten, and the Wasp had not; and I owned once again what I hadn't known I had lost, hadn't known was precious to me.

The sun was setting when I left The Park, the satin sea foaming softly, randomly around the rocks.

I had spent my life waiting for something, not knowing what, not even knowing I waited. Killing time. I was still waiting. But what I had been waiting for had already occurred and was past.

It was two years, nearly, since Georgie had died; two years until, for the first and last time, I wept for her—for her and for myself.

Of course I went back. After a lot of work and correctly placed dollars, I netted a HAPpy card of my own. I had time to spare, like a lot of people then, and often on empty afternoons (never on Sunday) I would get out onto the unpatched and weed-grown freeway and glide up the coast. The Park was always open. I relaxed into the communing concept.

Now, after some hundreds of hours spent there underground, now, when I have long ceased to go through those doors (I have lost my key, I think; anyway I don't know where to look for it), I know that the solitude I felt myself to be in was real. The watchers around me, the listeners I sensed in other chambers, were mostly my imagination. There was rarely anyone there.

These tombs were as neglected as any tombs anywhere usually are. Either the living did not care to attend much on the dead—when have they ever?—or the hopeful buyers of the contracts had come to discover the flaw in the access concept—as I discovered it, in the end.

ACCESS, and she takes dresses one by one from her closet, and holds them against her body, and studies the effect in a tall mirror, and puts them back again. She had a funny face, which she never made except when looking at herself in the mirror, a face made for no one but herself, that was actually quite unlike her. The mirror Georgie.

RESET.

ACCESS. By a bizarre coincidence here she is looking in another mirror. I think the Wasp could be confused by mirrors. She turns away, the Wasp adjusts; there is someone asleep, tangled in bedclothes on a big hotel bed, morning, a room-service cart. Oh, the Algonquin: myself. Winter. Snow is falling outside the tall window. She searches her handbag, takes out a small vial, swallows a pill with coffee, holding the cup by its body and not its handle. I stir, show a tousled head of hair. Conversation—unintelligible. Gray room, whitish snow light, color degraded. Would I now (I thought, watching us) reach out for her? Would I in the next hour take her, or she me, push aside the bedclothes, open her pale pajamas? She goes into the john, shuts the door. The Wasp watches stupidly, excluded, transmitting the door.

RESET, finally.

But what (I would wonder) if I had been patient, what if I had watched and waited?

Time, it turns out, takes an unconscionable time. The waste, the footless waste—it's no spectator sport. Whatever fun there is in sitting idly looking at nothing and tasting your own being for a whole afternoon, there is no fun in replaying it. The waiting is excruciating. How often, in five years, in eight thousand hours of daylight or lamplight, might we have coupled, how much time expended in lovemaking? A hundred hours, two hundred? Odds were not high of my coming on such a scene; darkness swallowed most of them, and the others were lost in the interstices of endless hours spent shopping, reading, on planes and in cars, asleep, apart. Hopeless.

ACCESS. She has turned on a bedside lamp. Alone. She hunts amid the Kleenex and magazines on the bedside table, finds a watch, looks at it dully, turns it right side up, looks again, and puts it down. Cold. She burrows in the blankets, yawning, staring, then puts out a hand for the phone but only rests her hand on it, thinking. Thinking at four A.M. She withdraws her hand, shivers a child's deep, sleepy shiver, and shuts off the light. A bad dream. In an instant it's morning, dawn; the Wasp slept, too. She sleeps soundly, unmoving, only the top of her blond head showing out of the quilt—and will no doubt sleep so for hours, watched over more attentively, more fixedly, than any peeping Tom could ever have watched over her.

RESET.

ACCESS.

"I can't hear as well as I did at first," I told the director. "And the definition is getting softer."

"Oh sure," the director said. "That's really in the literature. We have to explain that carefully. That this might be a problem."

"It isn't just my monitor?" I asked. "I thought it was probably only the monitor."

"No, no, not really, no," he said. He gave me coffee. We'd gotten to be friendly over the months. I think, as well as being afraid of me he was glad I came around now and then; at least one of the living came here, one at least was using the services. "There's a *slight* degeneration that does occur."

"Everything seems to be getting gray."

His face had shifted into intense concern, no belittling this problem. "Mm-hm, mm-hm, see, at the molecular level where we're at, there is degeneration. It's just in the physics. It randomizes a little over time. So you lose—you don't lose a minute of what you've got, but you lose a little definition. A little color. But it levels off."

"It does?"

"We think it does. Sure it does, we promise it does. We *predict* that it will."

"But you don't know."

"Well, well you see we've only been in this business a short while. This concept is new. There were things we couldn't know." He still looked at me, but seemed at the same time to have forgotten me. Tired. He seemed to have grown colorless himself lately, old, losing definition. "You might start getting some snow," he said softly.

ACCESS RESET ACCESS.

A gray plaza of herringbone-laid stones, gray, clicking palms. She turns up the collar of her sweater, narrowing her eyes in a stern wind. Buys magazines at a kiosk: *Vogue, Harper's, La Mode. Cold,* she says to the kiosk girl. *Frio.* The young man I was takes her arm: they walk back along the beach, which is deserted and strung with cast seaweed, washed by a dirty sea. Winter in Ibiza. We talk, but the Wasp can't hear, the sea's sound confuses it; it seems bored by its duties and lags behind us.

RESET.

ACCESS. The Algonquin, terribly familiar morning, winter. She turns away from the snow window. I am in bed, and for a moment watching this I felt suspended between two mirrors, reflected endlessly. I had seen this before; I had lived it once and remembered it once, and remembered the memory, and here it was again, or could it be nothing but another morning, a similar morning. There were far more than one like this, in this place. But no; she turns from the window, she gets out her vial of pills, picks up the coffee cup by its body: I had seen this moment before, not months before, weeks before, here in this chamber. I had come upon the same scene twice.

What are the odds of it, I wondered, what are the odds of coming upon the same minutes again, these minutes.

I stir within the bedclothes.

I leaned forward to hear, this time, what I would say; it was something like *but fun anyway,* or something.

Fun, she says, laughing, harrowed, the degraded sound a ghost's twittering. *Charlie, someday I'm going to die of fun.*

She takes her pill. The Wasp follows her to the john and is shut out.

Why am I here? I thought, and my heart was beating hard and slow. *What am I here for? What?*

RESET.

ACCESS.

Silvered icy streets, New York, Fifth Avenue. She is climbing, shouting from a cab's dark interior. *Just don't shout at me,* she shouts at someone; her mother I never met, a dragon. She is out and hurrying away down the sleety street with her bundles, the Wasp at her shoulder. I could reach out and touch her shoulder and make her turn and follow me out. Walking away, lost in the colorless press of traffic and people, impossible to discern within the softened snowy image.

Something was very wrong.

Georgie hated winter, she escaped it most of the time we were together, about the first of the year beginning to long for the sun that had gone elsewhere; Austria was all right for a few weeks, the toy villages and sugar snow and bright, sleek skiers were not really the winter she feared, though even in fire-warmed chalets it was hard to get her naked without gooseflesh and shudders from some draft only she could feel. We were chaste in winter. So Georgie escaped it: Antigua and Bali and two months in Ibiza when the almonds blossomed. It was continual false, flavorless spring all winter long.

How often could snow have fallen when the Wasp was watching her?

Not often; countable times, times I could count up myself if I could remember as the Wasp could. Not often. Not always.

"There's a problem," I said to the director.

"It's peaked out, has it?" he said. "That definition problem?"

"Actually," I said, "it's gotten worse."

He was sitting behind his desk, arms spread wide across his chair's back, and a false, pinkish flush to his cheeks like undertaker's makeup. Drinking.

"Hasn't peaked out, huh?" he said.

"That's not the problem," I said. "The problem is the access. It's not random like you said."

"Molecular level," he said. "It's in the physics."

"You don't understand. It's not getting more random. It's getting less random. It's getting selective. It's freezing up."

"No, no, no," he said dreamily. "Access is random. Life isn't all summer and fun, you know. Into each life some rain must fall."

I sputtered, trying to explain. "But but . . ."

"You know," he said. "I've been thinking of getting out of access." He pulled open a drawer in the desk before him; it made an empty sound. He stared within it dully for a moment and shut it. "The Park's been good for me, but I'm just not used to this. Used to be you thought you could render a service, you know? Well, hell, you know, you've had fun, what do you care?"

He was mad. For an instant I heard the dead around me; I tasted on my tongue the stale air of underground.

"I remember," he said, tilting back in his chair and looking elsewhere, "many years ago, I got into access. Only we didn't call it that then. What I did was, I worked for a stock-footage house. It was going out of business, like they all did, like this place here is going to do, shouldn't say that, but you didn't hear it. Anyway, it was a big warehouse with steel shelves for miles, filled with film cans, film cans filled with old plastic film, you know? Film of every kind. And movie people, if they wanted old scenes of past time in their movies, would call up and ask for what they wanted, find me this, find me that. And we had everything, every kind of scene, but you know what the hardest thing to find was? Just ordinary scenes of daily life. I mean people just doing things and living their lives. You know what we *did* have? Speeches. People giving speeches. Like presidents. You could have hours of speeches, but not just people, whatchacallit, oh, washing clothes, sitting in a park . . ."

"It might just be the reception," I said. "Somehow."

He looked at me for a long moment as though I had just arrived. "Anyway," he said at last, turning away again, "I was there awhile learning the ropes. And producers called and said, 'Get me this, get me that.' And one producer was making a film, some film of the past, and he wanted old scenes, *old,* of people long ago, in the summer; having fun; eating ice cream; swimming in bathing suits; riding in convertibles. Fifty years ago. Eighty years ago."

He opened his empty drawer again, found a toothpick, and began to use it.

"So I accessed the earliest stuff. Speeches. More speeches. But I found a scene here and there—people in the street, fur coats, window-shopping, traffic. Old people, I mean they were young then, but people of the past; they have these pinched kind of faces, you get to know them. Sad, a little. On city streets, hurrying, holding their hats. Cities were sort of black then, in film; black cars in the streets, black derby hats. Stone. Well, it wasn't what they wanted. I found summer for them, color summer, but new. They wanted old. I kept looking back. I kept looking. I did. The further back I went, the more I saw these pinched faces, black cars, black streets of stone. Snow. There isn't any summer there."

With slow gravity he rose and found a brown bottle and two coffee cups. He poured sloppily. "So it's not your reception," he said. "Film takes longer, I guess, but it's the physics. All in the physics. A word to the wise is sufficient."

The liquor was harsh, a cold distillate of past sunlight. I wanted to go, get out, not look back. I would not stay watching until there was only snow.

So I'm getting out of access," the director said. "Let the dead bury the dead, right? Let the dead bury the dead."

I didn't go back. I never went back, though the highways opened again and The Park isn't far from the town I've settled in. Settled; the right word. It restores your balance, in the end, even in a funny way your cheerfulness, when you come to know, without regrets, that the best thing that's going to happen in your life has already happened. And I still have some summer left to me.

I think there are two different kinds of memory, and only one kind gets worse as I get older: the kind where, by an effort of will, you can reconstruct your first car or your serial number or the name and figure of your high school physics teacher—a Mr. Holm, in a gray suit, a bearded guy, skinny, about thirty. The other kind doesn't worsen; if anything it grows more intense. The sleepwalking kind, the kind you stumble into as into rooms with secret doors and suddenly find yourself sitting not on your front porch but in a classroom. You can't at first think where or when, and a bearded, smiling man is turning in his hand a glass paperweight, inside which a little cottage stands in a swirl of snow.

There is no access to Georgie, except that now and then, unpredictably, when I'm sitting on the porch or pushing a grocery cart or standing at the sink, a memory of that kind will visit me, vivid and startling, like a hypnotist's snap of fingers.

Or like that funny experience you sometimes have, on the point of sleep, of hearing your name called softly and distinctly by someone who is not there.

Introduction to "Klein's Machine"
by Andrew Weiner

I've heard theories about how British science fiction differs in some systematic way from American science fiction, and there is some plausibility to the idea. After all, they grew out of separate evolutionary tracks, interbreeding frequently, but forced to grow in quite different soils. American science fiction was magazine-driven, pulpy, masked in lurid covers that protected it from the smothering embrace of academia but also drove off many of the serious-minded people who might have written, read, and commented within the field. British science fiction, however, was regarded as a continuation of the tradition of H. G. Wells, and included such writers as Aldous Huxley, George Orwell, and C. S. Lewis, all of whom exploited science fiction's power as a medium of satire and allegory. So British science fiction can include within its penumbra such older works as Frankenstein, Gulliver's Travels, Utopia, and Erewhon, while American science fiction, in search of roots, can only seize with any plausibility upon the works of Jules Verne, and before him the Thrilling Wonder stories from travelers and promoters like John Smith and Marco Polo and, of course, the extravagantly fictional claims of inventors filing for patents on perpetual motion machines.

So . . . what is Canadian science fiction? Some kind of averaging of the two traditions? Perelandra with Eve in a strategically torn dress? Brave New World, only the new machines are really really cool?

On the contrary, without fanfare or any detectable "movement," there seems to be a Canadian sensibility that is neither British nor American. As practiced by Andrew Weiner, Terence Green, Robert Charles Wilson, Charles de Lint, and even William Gibson (when we use our polarized mirrorshades to filter out the distracting cyberpunkery surrounding him), Canadian *speculative fiction has a way of making large issues intensely personal and individual, while imbuing individual lives with a sense of tragedy. Dare I say that it's a Shakespearian kind of storytelling?*

Or maybe I'm just imagining all this, and these writers have nothing in common except a propensity for pronouncing out *and* about *more in the front of their mouths than Americans do.*

Even if Weiner were from some remote godforsaken spot like Pasadena or Pensacola, "Klein's Machine" would be an effective tale of a quiet tragedy, of a possible reason why Cassandra isn't believed.

KLEIN'S MACHINE

Andrew Weiner

1.

They took him off the bus in Mt. Vernon, Ohio. His eyes were blank, and he had been sobbing quietly to himself for the past fifty miles. He was holding the crushed remains of a bright green flower in his left hand.

The driver turned him over to the ticket clerk, who called the local police. He was unresponsive to their questions. He had no identification, and no possessions except a one-way ticket to San Francisco and a crumpled $20 bill.

They threw the flower in the garbage and took him to the emergency ward of the local hospital.

"He's spaced out," one of the police officers told the intern. "Flying high."

Subsequent blood and urine analysis, however, showed no trace of drugs.

2.

"Could be a travel psychosis," said the senior psychiatrist. "Haven't seen one in years."

"Travel psychosis?" asked the intern.

"During the war," the psychiatrist said, "they would send soldiers cross-country by bus, transferring from base to base. Some of them would just disintegrate. The monotony got to them, you see. They had nowhere to look except inside. And they realized that they didn't know who they were. Of course, these were people who never had a very good grip in the first place."

He turned to the blank-eyed patient.

"Been travelling far, kid?"

The patient spoke for the first time.

"Oh yes," he said. "Very far."

3.

The patient was identified on the basis of his fingerprints. He had a minor criminal record in New York State, having been picked up several times at political demonstrations for disturbing the peace. He also had an active file at the FBI, documenting his involvement with several fringe leftist groups, although there were no recent entries.

The patient's name was Philip Herbert Klein. He was a resident of New York City. He had been reported missing three weeks before by his mother, Mrs. Alice Klein.

4.

Klein was transferred to a state mental hospital, and given antipsychotic medication.

Within a few days he was able to converse normally, although he appeared fatigued and withdrawn. He claimed to have no memory of leaving New York City, nor of how he had come to be on a cross-country bus.

The duty psychiatrist modified the diagnosis from psychosis to hysterical reaction, dissociative type, and arranged for his immediate discharge.

"Amnesia," he told the patient's mother, when she came to take him home.

"Like on *Another World*?" she asked.

"Something like that," he said. "Although in this case he doesn't seem to have hit his head."

"But where has he been?" she asked. "Where has he been all this time?"

"Maybe it will come back to him," the duty psychiatrist said.

5.

On his return to New York City, Mrs. Klein, on the recommendation of the duty psychiatrist, arranged for a home visit by a psychiatric social worker.

While Klein sat on the couch watching a *Star Trek* rerun, Mrs. Klein explained the situation.

"He never did anything like this before," she told the social worker. "He was always a good boy. A little nervous, maybe. High strung. Perhaps a bit over-imaginative. But always such a good boy."

After taking a family history, the social worker asked to speak with Klein in private.

6.

Report of the psychiatric social worker
   Philip Herbert Klein

I interviewed the client on the morning of July 24th, three days after his return from Ohio. I also interviewed the client's mother, Mrs. Alice Klein.

The client is 23 years old. He has never lived outside his family's home, and continues to reside with his widowed mother in a rent-controlled apartment on the Upper West Side. He has never held regular employment. He failed to complete his studies in accountancy at the City University, dropping out at the end of the first year. He told me that he had wished to study physics, but had been urged by his mother towards a more "practical" field.

Neither the client not his mother were forthcoming as to the circumstances surrounding him leaving university, although Mrs. Klein noted on several occasions that her son was troubled at times by "nerves" and was "highly strung."

The family has never sought psychiatric assistance for the client, although he was treated briefly for enuresis by a pediatrician at the age of nine, soon after his father's death.

The client and his mother subsist on a modest income from the estate of the late Mr. Harry Klein, a clothing manufacturer. The client is the only child. Mr. Klein was a refugee from eastern Europe, considerably older and rather less educated than his wife. Mrs. Klein recalls that her parents felt she had married "beneath" her, a verdict which she only superficially disclaims. Mrs. Klein came from a family with some pretensions to social standing, although little wealth after setbacks in the market.

At the time of their marriage, Mr. Klein was quite successful in his business, but later he suffered considerable reverses. This change in their fortunes, in some way a repetition of Mrs. Klein's own childhood experiences, coincided with the birth of their son. It seems that the client grew up in an atmosphere of some tension and economic insecurity, and that these conflicts between the parents were transmitted to him.

Philip himself claims to recall little about his father, who worked long hours and was rarely home. He does recall that Mr. Klein spoke with a marked accent, and had no knowledge of or interest in popular sports such as baseball, which caused him some embarrassment with his peer group. He "does not remember" how he felt when his father died, although his mother says that he "took it badly." As already noted, his enuresis first became severe at that time.

The mother, in any case, has apparently always been the dominant figure within this family constellation. Currently, she appears less concerned about her son's condition *per se* as with the fact that he was outside her surveillance and control for so lengthy a period.

Mrs. Klein suggested, in fact, that Philip might have been "kidnapped" and "brainwashed" by some radical group, although she was quite unable to suggest any motive for such an action. She has, apparently, warned her son repeatedly of the dangers of mixing with "bad company."

The boy (it is very difficult to think of him as a man) has little social life, and rarely leaves the apartment. For some period of time he was involved with peripheral socialist groups, but left following a disagreement he appears to have gone out of his way to engineer. He has no close friends of either sex, although he is a prolific letter-writer. He spends much of his time tinkering with fantastic and apparently useless machinery, styling himself an "inventor." (His mother recalls that in his teens he attempted to obtain a patent for a "space drive," an incident she found enormously comical.)

His other great interest is reading popular fiction, specifically science fiction. His room is littered with paperbacks of this description. His interest in this literature goes back to early adolescence, and at one time he himself produced an amateur journal of criticism and discussion for circulation to similarly anomic and obsessive individuals.

"There is nothing like (these books)," he told me. "Nothing in the world."

The client has been diagnosed as suffering a classical dissociative reaction, of amnesia coupled with fugue state. On the occasion of the home visit, the client still claimed to be unable to recall any details of his experiences during his absence from home. He did, however, offer a hypothetical explanation of his disappearance, one so bizarre as to raise the question of a more severe pathology. The client told me that he believed that he had been "travelling in time." He attempted to substantiate this claim through reference to his personal journal.

I have referred the client for further psychiatric treatment on an outpatient basis.

7.

Excerpts from the journal of Philip Herbert Klein
February 7, 198-

Freezing cold today, arse-freezing cold, highest wind chill factor for the day in eleven years, got to be a screw-up in the sunspot cycle. Almost died of exposure getting over to Claude's place for the Progressive League meeting. Big argument with Ma before I left, why am I wasting my life hanging around with commie creeps, why am I doing this to her, and etc. You just can't win. Last year it was, get out of the house, find an interest, make new friends.

Lousy attendance at the meeting, not even the whole Central Committee. Claude is a lousy speaker, and "Capital Movements in West Africa" is not exactly a crowd-puller. I could have done without it myself. All his usual stuff about the Rockefellers and the Chase-Manhattan and the Trilateral Commission. No facts, just speculation. Claude has always been flipped-out on the Rockefellers. Always has to *personalize* everything.

"Come on," I said, when I couldn't take it anymore. "We have to be scientific, here. We're supposed to be *scientific* socialists, aren't we?"

"What do you know about science?" Claude asked.

"More than you," I said.

He didn't like that at all.

I've got to admit I'm getting sick of all these personality conflicts. How are we ever going to establish socialism in this country when we can't even agree on when to take a coffee break? They say every personality conflict is really a political conflict, but I'm starting to wonder.

I haven't told anyone in the League about my project. I've got to have some concrete proof first. Otherwise, they're going to laugh in my face.

February 24th, 198-

Long letter from Sam Gold, replying to a letter of comment I wrote about an article on Heinlein which appeared in *Space Potatoes*. It's so long since I wrote the letter I can't even remember what I said, but I guess I was attacking Sam for attacking Heinlein's *Time Enough For Love*, which I still think is a great book. I guess Sam is on a literary kick these days.

Sam also asked if I was ever going to put out another issue of *Kleinlight*. The truth of it is, ever since Ma smashed my Gestetner, I've sort of lost the urge. Also, I really don't have the time anymore. Maybe that's what growing up is all about.

March 2nd, 198-

Leafletted with Penny outside the local supermarket, in support of the union local. It rained the whole time, I'm probably going to get pneumonia. I was almost glad when the union goons chased us away, although you'd think they would know who their friends are. I've had it up to here with leafletting, anyway. There's got to be a faster way to make a revolution.

Coffee with Penny afterwards; she was wearing a green blouse, looked very pretty. She told me I should go back to college, maybe study pol-sci. That's what she's doing at Columbia. I guess she thinks I just fritter away most of my time. I almost told her about my machine, but then I got worried about what she would think.

I thought about asking her to a movie, but I decided to go home and work on my project instead. There'll be more time later. All the time in the world.

March 7th 198-

The hamster didn't come back. I sat and watched the cage for two hours straight, and it didn't come back. Then I crashed out, and when I woke up it was past noon, and still no hamster. Now I have to figure out where it went.

March 10th 198-

Another big blow-up with Ma. We're back on my reading habits of all things. The stuff I read is ruining my mind, driving me crazy, making me blind, and like that. She should know how crazy. I almost felt like walking out of the house and never coming back. But I'm too close to success now to have to worry about finding a place to live, and a job and all that stuff.

Why do I have to put up with this shit? I'm *twenty-three years old.*

March 18th, 198-

League meeting. Dick presented his paper on "Technology in a Socialist Society." Against capital-intensive energy resources, in favor of small localized power units and an overall reduction in energy consumption. The usual hippy-dippy stuff.

What kind of future, I asked, are we going to have with less energy?

Nearly got kicked out on my ear.

Walking to the subway, Penny told me that my position in the League is insecure, and urged me to keep quiet for awhile. Apparently Claude is looking to start a schism. Wants to expel me and a few others who have crossed him. I'm not even sure that I care, although I'm glad that she seems to.

March 26th, 198-

The hamster is back. Also my wristwatch, which I strapped on its back. The watch appears to have stopped at the moment the field was induced. The hamster seems fine, though a bit sleepy. Have begun follow-up observations.

April 2nd, 198-

Well, I got expelled from the League. Deviationism. Big surprise. I guess I'm more relieved than anything else. In fact I should have quit first. I'm only sorry because I think I was starting to get close to Penny and now she can't be seen consorting with a deviationist.

Of course, this changes everything concerning the project. I was almost ready to make my pitch, lay it all out for the League.

"We *can* change the future," I was going to tell them. "And fast."

Maybe I should have tried it anyway. Probably they would have dumped all over it, but I could have tried.

Maybe I'm not such a principled type after all. Maybe I wanted to keep all this to myself all along. But now I really do have to think things through, decide where I go from here.

April 3rd, 198-

Went out to pick up some magazines, and when I came back I found that Ma had poisoned the hamster. Said she couldn't stand the smell.

Thomas Alva Edison never had to put up with this shit!

Post-test follow-up incomplete. Should repeat the whole performance, make sure the hamster wouldn't have eventually dropped dead. But I'm not sure I can wait that long.

8.

"So you built a time machine," said the psychiatrist, whose name was Dr. Lawrence Segal.

"That's right," Klein said.

"Where is this machine?"

"In my apartment," Klein said. "But it doesn't work anymore."

"Why not?"

"I don't know," Klein said. "Maybe Ma tampered with it. Maybe something burned out. I can't make it work anymore."

"But it did work at least once?"

"Twice. Once for the hamster, and once for me."

"Tell me, Philip, what made you want to travel in time?"

"I don't know," Klein said. "It's something I thought about for years. I used to daydream about it, even back in high school. It came from reading all those stories about people travelling in time, into the future, into the past. People changing history. I used to wish I could do that too. Not change history, exactly. Just a few details here and there."

"What sort of details?"

"I don't know. It's like people always say, *if I could do it all again.* Go back before things went wrong and make them right. Things I said and wished I hadn't. Places I went to when I wanted to stay home, or go someplace else. Dumb, embarrassing scenes with girls. Like that. Go back and short-circuit all the pain.

"And then I started to thinking about bigger things. Like maybe going back to Dallas and saving Kennedy. I used to think that the world would have been a much better place if only Kennedy had lived.

"That was naive, of course. Saving Kennedy wouldn't really have changed anything. That was something I realized when I got into being a socialist. It would all have been the same. The same misery, the same wars, same everything. Only the names of the presidents would have been different.

"And then I thought about something my mother said. She used to point to this picture of Franklin Roosevelt, we always had a picture of him on the wall, and she would say, 'Without that man, there would have been a revolution in this country.' She thought that was great, of course, that old FDR stuck his finger in the dike. But I could see how Roosevelt had really been an obstacle to genuine social progress in this country.

"So that was my plan. To build a time machine, and get the League to knock off Roosevelt. And if that didn't help, we would try knocking off somebody else.

"I don't know if I was serious about all this. I don't know if I could actually bring myself to kill anyone, let alone FDR, who was always revered in my family as something approaching a goddam saint. And I never even tried to win over the League. So I don't know if I was ever really serious about all this political stuff. I think probably it was always personal, really.

"So in the end, I decided to go forward rather than back. To try and find a place for myself somewhere in the future. Because I wasn't happy here, that was for sure, and I don't think that even a revolution would have changed that much.

"I suppose my mother thought I was just beating off in there, all those months. But that was what I was doing. Building a time machine. And I did it. I really did it. I travelled in time."

"Except," Dr. Segal said, "that you don't remember a thing about it."

9.

With Philip Klein's consent, Dr. Segal scheduled a session using sodium pentathol in attempt to bring back his lost memory and lead him through and beyond whatever traumatic event or events might have precipitated his fugue.

"Philip," Dr. Segal said, once the drug had taken hold. "I want you to think back to the night of July 5th. Do you remember that night?"

"Of course," Philip said. "Tonight's the night. The night I test my machine."

"How do you feel?"

"Good," Philip said. "Excited. I can hardly wait. Should have done this months ago. I was nervous, I guess. And then I wanted to wait for July 4th. For the fireworks. I always did like the fireworks."

"Where are you, Philip?"

"I'm at home. In my room. I'm inducing the field."

"And then what?"

"I'm . . . travelling. Into the future."

"Tell me about it. Tell me about the future."

Klein appeared agitated. He shifted in his seat.

"What's happening, Philip.?"

"I don't know. I don't remember . . ."

"Go with it, Philip. Don't fight it. You remember the future. You're there now. In the future now . . ."

"The walls are high . . ."

"Yes?"

"Very high. And white, sheer white. Dazzling in the sun. The swollen sun. I see no one, no one at all. The air . . . the air is hard to breathe. Thin. Harsh." Klein's breathing became labored. "There's something wrong with the air."

"Easy, Philip. Take it easy."

Klein's expression changed. He became alert, jerked his head back.

"I see something in the sky. Some kind of flying machine. It makes no noise, no noise at all. The shape is strange, I can't describe the shape. The machine is getting closer. The machine is firing at me. Firing some sort of ray . . ."

"And?"

"Now I'm inside the machine. The walls are smooth. Dark. There is no one else inside the flying machine. I can see out the window. We are flying above the city. The city of the future. Glass, concrete. Stripped, massed, streamlined. Overhead roads link the towers. The golden towers. But the city is empty."

"Empty?"

"There is no one, no sign of life."

"Then who guides the flying machine?"

"Machines guide the flying machine. Nothing but machines. I am taken to the Hall of the Central Computer. The Computer speaks to me. It tells me that the people have gone now, all gone away to other worlds circling other stars. But the people will return. They have promised that they will return."

"And then?"

"I move on. Onwards into the future. I travel on."

"And what do you see?"

"I see the sun explode. The wind burns my skin. My hair is matted with a fine ash. I move back. I watch the children swim in the decaying flower gardens. I stoop down to smell the sweet green flowers. I pick a flower, I hold it in my hand . . . I move on, to visit the golden city. The buildings are crystal, so very high. And the people fly! Faces are yellow this year, this wonderful year." Tears welled up in his eyes. "The ice! I see and will remember the ice! And the fire. I will not forget the fire."

10.

"It was amazing the way it all came back," Klein told Dr. Segal at the next session. "All came flooding back. In no coherent order. No pattern. But the future. The actual future."

Dr. Segal's expression was noncommittal.

"You think it's a delusion, don't you?" Klein asked. "A hallucination. From your perspective, that's all it could be. You think this is some private fantasy. Like the guy in *The Fifty-Minute Hour.* The one who thought he travelled in time and space."

Dr. Segal raised his eyebrows.

"You've read Lindner?"

"Oh sure. And Freud, and Rogers, and Skinner. I liked Lindner's book. But you know, I couldn't help thinking. What if the guy was right?"

11.

Excerpt from the notebook of Dr. Lawrence Segal

I had asked Philip Klein to bring in a selection of his favorite science fiction books, and have now spent the better part of a weekend in reading them. Most of the authors were unknown to me, although I had heard of, if not actually read, Kurt Vonnegut Jr. Somehow I am always suspicious of a man who calls himself "Jr.," but it is hardly surprising that he should be so much better known than his contemporaries. He can, at least, manipulate the language.

Leaving aside the question of literary quality, I was both fascinated and repelled by these materials. This is, in many ways, a literature steeped in pathology, and there would surely be an article here if I could find the time.

Behind the veneer of reasoned "scientific" speculation, sometimes tiresomely detailed, more often as thin and perfunctory as the plot of some pornographic movie, one finds, almost inevitably, an enormous and overweening narcissism, luxuriating in the most joyously infantile fantasies of limitlessness and omnipotence.

Machines are everywhere in this literature. Phallic and magical machines, powered only by our most secret wishes and fears, penetrating the thin webs of space and time.

The most central and repetitious vision is one of escape, of mobility without limit, of a freedom never defined except by the absence of all civilized constraints. Characters rip themselves free of their proper place in the social and familial framework to achieve a personal transcendence.

It should go without saying that this is a profoundly oedipal literature although typically these yearnings are at least somewhat masked. The parent or parent-figure is merely vilified, escaped, left behind.

But, almost an embarrassment of riches, there are actually stories in which we see a complete return of the repressed. The incest drive itself breaks surface, like some great white whale billowing water. Here a spaceman who travels to far stars and returns to make love to his own great-granddaughter. And there, yes, a time traveller who goes back to kill the hated father figure, to seduce his unsuspecting mother, even to become his own father.

Confronted even with such explicit material, Klein demonstrates absolutely no insight into his attachment to this literature.

"It's not a question of being for or against incest," he told me, in reference to one such story. "It's only a *speculation*. To provoke thought about the socio-cultural taboos surrounding the incest taboo."

"To provoke thought?" I said. "I see."

Klein places great importance on having his thoughts provoked. Contrary to the report of the psychiatric social worker, he is actually exceptionally well-read. He has been a voracious consumer of organized knowledge, has set himself upon a course of relentless self-education, seeking to understand intellectually a world in which he has always felt out of place. He has read physics, chemistry, biology, history, even psychology. On several occasions he has attempted to draw me into a discussion of Pepper's critique of psychoanalysis. Yet his reading has been without discrimination, mixing relativity theory and kaballah, Mendel and the mail-order wisdom of the Rosicrucians.

His idol is the English polymath and socialist H. G. Wells, perhaps best known as an early writer of these scientific romances. Klein, too, claims to be a "socialist," despite a profound aversion for his fellow man. But essentially his philosophy is one of self-improvement. Not only must man evolve as a species, but each one of us must evolve as a person. "There must be progress," he told me. "There must be."

Socially awkward, distanced from his peers, dominated always by his mother, Klein has set out deliberately to expand his mind the way that others might expand their muscle tissue, through exercise, training, and rigor. He has kept journals of his every waking thought, scraps of time and broken insights hoarded to chew over again and again, playing constantly with his own ideas, not so much stimulating his imagination as masturbating it.

He is, in fact, exactly the sort of alienated individual to whom this literature of science fiction would most powerfully appeal. Passive and detached, he seeks refuge from the storm of life in these Faustian fantasies of superiority, of an understanding which transcends normal understanding. In reality, of course, Klein is only dizzied and intoxicated by these restless, pointless dreams.

"What did you think the future would be like?" I asked him.

"I don't know," he said. "Different. I thought things would be different. Like California, maybe. Only better."

He rambled on, then, about a world in which abundance has replaced scarcity, automation has removed the need to work, love has replaced greed, where individuals live their lives only to create. No doubt all this came from his reading of these utopian tales of magic kingdoms at the end of the warp, where one floats in sweetness and light, where generations merge and smear themselves immortally across all space and time and even death itself is defeated.

And yet one must be careful not to accept these surface notions, these relatively simple and obvious yearnings of a desperately alienated individual, at face value. Far more real and urgent wishes, however unacknowledged, lay behind the construction of his supposed machine. His desire to travel forward in time, then, screens out his shameful and inexpressible wish to travel backwards in time and reunite with his own narcissistic vision of the pre-Oedipal mother. He toys with various rationalizations that might justify this voyage back, but in the end is unable to sustain them, for they bring him too close to recognizing his real desires. His fantasy of saving Kennedy, for example, shields his repressed wish to kill Kennedy, kill the primal father. Later disguised as a "scientific socialist" he actually permits himself partial expression of these aggressive impulses, in his extraordinary scheme for the assassination of Franklin Roosevelt. But this plan, too, is quickly repressed, discarded, thrown away.

It is a truism, of course, that time does not exist in the unconscious. We may travel back there, at will, back to infancy, back to our primal paradise of infantile omnipotence, of unlimited control and unqualified love. Klein's longing to return is not in itself unusual. Yet typically such wishes are displaced upon the social environment. The effort to recover lost infancy is channeled into the drive for economic or social transcendence, or else dissipated in nostalgic and romantic illusion. Klein, however, has become fixated on this matter of changing the very flow of time.

12.

"You picked a flower, Philip. Do you remember the flower?"

"It was green," Klein said. "Amazingly green. I held it in my hand."

"What happened to it?"

"I don't know," Klein said. "I don't know."

13.

"The machine, Philip. How is your machine?"

"It doesn't work, anymore."

"Where is it? Is it still in your apartment?"

"It's here."

"Where?"

"Here. I am the machine. The time machine. I am it."

14.

On the advice of his psychiatrist, Philip Klein moved out of his mother's apartment.

He got a furnished room, and supported himself through a job in a bookstore.

He began taking night school classes in Business Administration.

He read very little science fiction.

He began dating.

His therapy continued, but they no longer spoke of Klein's machine. They explored his childhood, and his current relationships with the world.

He was, according to Dr. Segal, developing good insight into himself and his world.

15.

The garbage from the Mt. Vernon bus station found its way, eventually, to the city dump.

Strange green flowers bloomed there briefly, then withered away, before being covered under new loads of garbage.

16.

"The Earth is all gone now, all gone away," Klein said. He was deep under the drug now, breathing very slowly. "And the Sun, the Sun is a long time gone. And yet the light is still bright, brighter than you could imagine. But soft, so it doesn't hurt my eyes. And I'm floating, floating inside the light. Floating on some fixed path. Moving through the space and the time. And now the light is pulsing. It's breaking down. There's darkness in between the light. And the lights are shrinking, moving away from me. Slowly. Very slowly. All going away now. All."

Introduction to "Pots"
by C. J. Cherryh

The skeleton of this story, if you saw it bleached and wired together in a museum, could easily be taken as one of those unforgettable idea stories we sometimes call Campbellian and which were epitomized in classic stories like "The Star" and "The Nine Billion Names of God" and "Nightfall." When we first read those stories, they blew us away by the sheer power of the idea; only later, upon reexamining the story, do we realize that the idea is really all there is in this kind of tale. All the characters, all the dialogue, all the actual events exist solely in order to explain or expose the idea to the reader. They do not matter in themselves.

So much for what we can learn from skeletons. For "Pots" is by C. J. Cherryh, and the rules have changed. The creature does not have to be skin and bone, it can be fully fleshed, full of life. "Pots" can be reread even after you know the cool idea, because Cherryh is incapable of writing a story without a fully imagined society peopled with interesting characters who are worth reading about in their own right. Furthermore, there are resonances with the real world that qualify this story as biting satire along with all the other jobs it does.

In fact, with "Pots" I think it's safe to say that gosh-wow sci-fi is fully dead. Unlike the lenslike science of Campbellian days, which enabled us to focus on Truth, Cherryh shows us science as it is really practiced, caught up in the turmoil of personalities, with Truth always out of reach and truths too often limping along, wounded in the turf wars and drive-bys of gangs of Ph.D.-totin' grant-heads. Or maybe I'm reading too much social criticism into a story that is, after all, just sci-fi.

POTS

C. J. Cherryh

It was a most bitter trip, the shuttle-descent to the windy surface. Suited, encumbered by lifesupport, Desan stepped off the platform and waddled onward into the world, waving off the attentions of small spidery service robots: "Citizen, this way, this way, citizen, have a care—do watch your step; a suit tear is hazardous."

Low-level servitors. Desan detested them. The chief of operations had plainly sent these creatures accompanied only by an AI eight-wheel transport, which inconveniently chose to park itself a good five hundred paces beyond the shuttle blast zone, an uncomfortably long walk across the dusty pan in the crinkling, pack-encumbered oxy-suit. Desan turned, casting a forlorn glance at the shuttle waiting there on its landing gear, silver, dip-nosed wedge under a gunmetal sky, at rest on an ochre and rust landscape. He shivered in the sky-view, surrendered himself and his meager luggage to the irritating ministries of the service robots, and waddled on his slow way down to the waiting AI transport.

"Good day," the vehicle said inanely, opening a door. "My passenger compartment is not safe atmosphere; do you understand, Lord Desan?"

"Yes, yes." Desan climbed in and settled himself in the front seat, a slight give of the transport's suspensors. The robots fussed about in insectile hesitance, delicately setting his luggage case just so, adjusting, adjusting until it conformed with their robotic, template-compared notion of their job. Maddening. Typical robotic efficiency. Desan slapped the pressure-sensitive seating. "Come, let's get this moving, shall we?"

The AI talked to its duller cousins, a single squeal that sent them scuttling, "Attention to the door, citizen." It lowered and locked. The AI started its noisy drive motor. "Will you want the windows dimmed, citizen?"

"No. I want to see this place."

"A pleasure, Lord Desan."

Doubtless for the AI, it was.

The station was situated a long drive across the pan, across increasingly softer dust that rolled up to obscure the rearview—softer, looser dust, occasionally a wind-scooped hollow that made the transport flex—("Do forgive me, citizen. Are you comfortable?")

"Quite, quite, you're very good."

"Thank you, citizen."

And finally—*finally!*—something other than flat appeared, the merest humps of hills, and one anomalous mountain, a massive, long bar that began as a haze and became solid; became a smooth regularity before the gentle brown folding of hills hardly worthy of the name.

Mountain. The eye indeed took it for a volcanic or sedimentary formation at distance, some anomalous and stubborn outcrop in this barren reach, where all else had declined to entropy; absolute, featureless, flat. But when the AI passed along its side this mountain had joints and seams, had the marks of *making* on it; and even knowing in advance what it was, driving along within view of the jointing, this work of Ancient hands—chilled Desan's well-traveled soul. The station itself came into view against the weathered hills, a collection of shocking green domes on a brown lifeless world. But such domes Desan had seen. With only the AI for witness, Desan turned in his seat, pressed the flexible bubble of the helmet to the double-seal window, and stared and stared at the stonework until it passed to the rear and the dust obscured it.

"Here, Lord," said the AI, eternally cheerful. "We are almost at the station—a little climb. I do it very smoothly."

Flex and lean; sway and turn. The domes lurched closer in the forward window and the motor whined. "I've very much enjoyed serving you."

"Thank you," Desan murmured, seeing another walk before him, ascent of a plastic grid to an airlock and no sight of a welcoming committee.

More service robots, scuttling toward them as the transport stopped and adjusted itself with a pneumatic wheeze.

"Thank you, Lord Desan, do watch your helmet, watch your life-support connections, watch your footing please. The dust is slick. . . ."

"Thank you." With an AI one had no recourse.

"Thank *you*, my lord." The door came up; Desan extricated himself from the seat and stepped to the dusty ground, carefully shielding the oxy-pack from the doorframe and panting with the unaccustomed weight of it in such gravity. The service robots moved to take his luggage while Desan waddled doggedly on, up the plastic gridwork path to the glaringly lime-green domes. Plastics. Plastics that could not even originate in this desolation, but which came from their ships' spare biomass. Here all was dead, frighteningly void: Even the signal that guided him to the lakebed was robotic, like the advertisement that a transport would meet him.

The airlock door shot open ahead; and living, suited personnel appeared, three of them, at last, at long last, flesh-and-blood personnel came walking toward him to offer proper courtesy. But before that mountain of stone, before these glaring green structures and the robotic paraphernalia of research that made all the reports real—Desan still felt the deathliness of the place. He trudged ahead, touched the offered, gloved hands, acknowledged the expected salutations, and proceeded up the jointed-plastic walk to the open airlock. His marrow refused to be warmed. The place refused to come into clear focus, like some bad dream with familiar elements hideously distorted.

A hundred years of voyage since he had last seen this world and then only from orbit, receiving reports thirdhand. A hundred years of work on this planet preceded this small trip from port to research center, under that threatening sky, in this place by a mountain that had once been a dam on a lake that no longer existed.

There had been the findings of the moon, of course. A few artifacts. A cloth of symbols. Primitive, unthinkably primitive. First omen of the findings of this sere, rust-brown world.

He accompanied the welcoming committee into the airlock of the main dome, waited through the cycle, and breathed a sigh of relief as the indicator lights went from white to orange and the inner door admitted them to the interior. He walked forward, removed the helmet and drew a deep breath of air unexpectedly and unpleasantly tainted. The foyer of this centermost dome was businesslike—plastic walls, visible ducting. A few plants struggled for life in a planter in the center of the floor. Before it, a black pillar and a common enough emblem: a plaque with two naked alien figures, the diagrams of a starsystem—reproduced even to its scars and pitting. In some places it might be mundane, unnoticed.

It belonged here, *belonged* here, and it could never be mundane, this message of the Ancients.

"Lord Desan," a female voice said, and he turned, awkward in the suit.

It was Dr. Gothon herself, unmistakable aged woman in science blues. The rare honor dazed him, and wiped away all failure of hospitality thus far. She held out her hand. Startled, he reacted in kind, remembered the glove, and hastily drew back his hand to strip the glove. Her gesture was gracious and he felt the very fool and very much off his stride, his hand touching—no, firmly grasped by the callused, aged hand of the legendary intellect. Age-soft and hard-surfaced at once. Age and vigor. His tongue quite failed him, and he felt, recalling his purpose, utterly daunted.

"Come in, let them rid you of that suit, Lord Desan. Will you rest after your trip, a nap, a cup of tea, perhaps. The robots are taking your luggage to your room. Accommodations here aren't luxurious, but I think you'll find them comfortable."

Deeper and deeper into courtesies. One could lose all sense of direction in such surroundings, letting oneself be disarmed by gentleness, by pleasantness—by embarrassed reluctance to resist.

"I want to see what I came to see, doctor." Desan unfastened more seams and shed the suit into waiting hands, smoothed his coveralls. Was that too brusque, too unforgiveably hasty? "I don't think I *could* rest, Dr. Gothon. I attended my comfort aboard the shuttle. I'd like to get my bearings here at least, if one of your staff would be so kind to take me in hand—"

"Of course, of course. I rather expected as much—do come, please, let me show you about. I'll explain as much as I can. Perhaps I can convince you as I go."

He was overwhelmed from the start; he had expected *some* high official, the director of operations most likely, not Gothon. He walked slightly after the doctor, the stoop-shouldered presence that passed like a benison among the students and lesser staff—*I saw the Doctor,* the young ones had been wont to say in hushed tones, aboard the ship, when Gothon strayed absently down a corridor in her rare intervals of waking. *I saw the Doctor.*

In that voice one might claim a theophany.

They had rarely waked her, lesser researchers being sufficient for most worlds; while he was the fifth lord-navigator, the fourth born on the journey, a time-dilated trifle, fifty-two waking years of age and a mere two thousand years of voyage against—aeons of Gothon's slumberous life.

And Desan's marrow ached now at such gentle grace in this bowed, mottle-skinned old scholar, this sleuth patiently deciphering the greatest mystery of the universe. Pity occurred to him. He suffered personally in this place; but not as Gothon would have suffered here, in that inward quiet where Gothon carried on thoughts the ship crews were sternly admonished never to disturb.

Students rushed now to open doors for them, pressed themselves to the walls and allowed their passage into deeper and deeper halls within the maze of the domes. Passing hands brushed Desan's sleeves, welcome offered the current lord-navigator; he reciprocated with as much attention as he could devote to courtesy in his distress. His heart labored in the unaccustomed gravity, his nostrils accepted not only the effluvium of dome plastics and the recyclers and so many bodies dwelling together; but a flinty, bitter air, like electricity or dry dust. He imagined some hazardous leakage of the atmosphere into the dome: unsettling thought. The hazards of the place came home to him, and he wished already to be away.

Gothon had endured here, during his further voyages—seven years more of her diminishing life; waked four times, and this was the fourth, continually active now for five years, her longest stint yet in any waking. She had found data finally worth the consumption of her life, and she burned it without stint. *She* believed. She believed enough to die pursuing it.

He shuddered up and down and followed Gothon through a seal-door toward yet another dome, and his gut tightened in dismay; for there were shelves on either hand, and those shelves were lined with yellow skulls, endless rows of staring dark sockets and grinning jaws. Some were long-nosed; some were short. Some small, virtually noseless skulls had fangs which gave them a wise and intelligent look—*Like miniature people, like babies with grown up features,* must be the initial reaction to anyone seeing them in the holos or viewing the specimens brought up to the orbiting labs. But cranial capacity in these was much too small. The real sapient occupied further shelves, row upon row of eyeless, generously domed skulls, grinning in their flat-toothed way, in permanent horror—provoking profoundest horror in those who discovered them here, in this desolation.

Here Gothon paused, selected one of the small sapient skulls, much reconstructed: Desan had at least the skill to recognize the true bone from the plassbone bonded to it. This skull was far more delicate than the others, the jaw smaller. The front two teeth were restructs. So was one of the side.

"It was a child," Gothon said. "We call her Missy. The first we found at this site, up in the hills, in a streambank. Most of Missy's feet were gone, but she's otherwise intact. Missy was all alone except for a little animal all tucked up in her arms. We keep them together—never mind the cataloging." She lifted an anomalous and much-reconstructed skull from the shelf among the sapients; fanged and delicate. "Even archaeologists have sentiment."

"I—see—" Helpless, caught in courtesy, Desan extended an unwilling finger and touched the skull.

"Back to sleep." Gothon set both skulls tenderly back on the shelf, and dusted her hands and walked further, Desan following, beyond a simple door and into a busy room of workbenches piled high with a clutter of artifacts.

Staff began to rise from their dusty work in a sudden startlement. "No, no, go on," Gothon said quietly. "We're only passing through; ignore us. —Here, do you see, Lord Desan?" Gothon reached carefully past a researcher's shoulder and lifted from the counter an elongate ribbed bottle with the opalescent patina of long burial. "We find a great many of these. Mass production. Industry. Not only on this continent. This same bottle exists in sites all over the world, in the uppermost strata. Same design. Near the time of the calamity. We trace global alliances and trade by such small things." She set it down and gathered up a virtually complete vase, much patched. "It always comes to pots, Lord Desan. By pots and bottles we track them through the ages. Many layers. They had a long and complex past."

Desan reached out and touched the corroded brown surface of the vase, discovering a single bright remnant of the blue glaze along with the gray encrustations of long burial. "How long—how long does it take to reduce a thing to this?"

"It depends on the soil—on moisture, on acidity. This came from hereabouts." Gothon tenderly set it back on a shelf, walked on, frail, hunch-shouldered figure among the aisles of the past. "But very long, very long to obliterate so much—almost all the artifacts are gone. Metals oxidize; plastics rot; cloth goes very quickly; paper and wood last quite long in a desert climate, but they go, finally. Moisture dissolves the details of sculpture. Only the noble metals survive intact. Soil creep warps even stone; crushes metal. We find even the best pots in a matrix of pieces, a puzzle-toss. Fragile as they are, they outlast monuments, they last as long as the earth that holds them, drylands, wetlands, even beneath the sea—where no marine life exists to trouble them. That bottle and that pot are as venerable as that great dam. The makers wouldn't have thought that, would they?"

"But—" Desan's mind reeled at the remembrance of the great plain, the silt and the deep buried secrets.

"But?"

"You surely might miss important detail. A world to search. You might walk right over something and misinterpret everything."

"Oh, yes, it can happen. But *finding* things where we expect them is an important clue, Lord Desan, a confirmation—One only has to suspect where to look. We locate our best hope first—a sunken, a raised place in those photographs we trouble the orbiters to take; but one gets a *feeling* about the lay of the land—more than the mechanical probes, Lord Desan." Gothon's dark eyes crinkled in the passage of thoughts unguessed, and Desan stood lost in Gothon's unthinkable mentality. What did a mind *do* in such age? Wander? Could the great doctor lapse into mysticism? To report such a thing—would solve one difficulty. But to have that regrettable duty—

"It's a feeling for living creatures, Lord Desan. It's reaching out to the land and saying—if this were long ago, if I thought to build, if I thought to trade—where would I go? Where would my neighbors live?"

Desan coughed delicately, wishing to draw things back to hard fact. "And the robot probes, of course, do assist."

"Probes, Lord Desan, are heartless things. A robot can be very skilled, but a researcher directs it only at distance, blind to opportunities and the true sense of the land. But you were born to space. Perhaps it makes no sense."

"I take your word for it," Desan said earnestly. He felt the weight of the sky on his back. The leaden, awful sky, leprous and unhealthy cover between them and the star and the single moon. Gothon remembered homeworld. *Remembered homeworld.* Had been renowned in her field even there. The old scientist claimed to come to such a landscape and locate things by seeing things that robot eyes could not, by thinking thoughts those dusty skulls had held in fleshy matter—

—how long ago?

"We look for mounds," Gothon said, continuing in her brittle gait down the aisle, past the bowed heads and shy looks of staff and students at their meticulous tasks. The work of tiny electronic needles proceeded about them, the patient ticking away at encrustations to bring ancient surfaces to light. "They built massive structures. Great skyscrapers. Some of them must have lasted, oh, thousands of years intact; but when they went unstable, they fell, and their fall made rubble; and the wind came and the rivers shifted their courses around the ruin, and of course the weight of sediment piled up, wind- and water driven. From that point, its own weight moved it and warped it and complicated our work." Gothon paused again beside a further table, where holo plates stood inactive. She waved her hand and a landscape showed itself, a serpented row of masonry across a depression. "See the wall there. They didn't build it that way, all wavering back and forth and up and down. Gravity and soil movement deformed it. It was buried until we unearthed it. Otherwise, wind and rain alone would have destroyed it ages ago. As it will do, now, if time doesn't rebury it."

"And this great pile of stone—" Desan waved an arm, indicating the imagined direction of the great dam and realizing himself disoriented. "How old is it?"

"Old as the lake it made."

"But contemporaneous with the fall?"

"Yes. Do you know, that mass may be standing when the star dies. The few great dams; the pyramids we find here and there around the world—One only guesses at their age. They'll outlast any other surface feature except the mountains themselves."

"Without life."

"Oh, but there is."

"Declining."

"No, no. Not declining." The doctor waved her hand and a puddle appeared over the second holo plate, all green with weed waving feathery tendrils back and forth in the surge. "The moon still keeps this world from entropy. There's water, not as much as this dam saw— It's the weed, this little weed that gives one hope for this world. The little life, the things that fly and crawl—the lichens and the life on the flatlands."

"But nothing *they* knew."

"No. Life's evolved new answers here. Life's starting over."

"It certainly hasn't much to start with, has it?"

"Not very much. It's a question that interests Dr. Bothogi—whether the life making a start here has the time left, and whether the consumption curve doesn't add up to defeat—But life doesn't know that. We're very concerned about contamination. But we fear it's inevitable. And who knows, perhaps it will have added something beneficial." Dr. Gothon lit yet another holo with the wave of her hand. A streamlined six-legged creature scuttled energetically across a surface of dead moss, frantically waving antennae and making no apparent progress.

"The inheritors of the world." Despair chilled Desan's marrow.

"But each generation of these little creatures is an unqualified success. The last to perish perishes in profound tragedy, of course, but without consciousness of it. The awareness will have, oh, half a billion years to wait—then, maybe it will appear; if the star doesn't fail; it's already far advanced down the sequence." Another holo, the image of desert, of blowing sand, beside the holo of the surge of weed in a pool. "Life makes life. That weed you see is busy making life. It's taking in and converting and building a chain of support that will enable things to feed on it, while more of its kind grows. That's what life does. It's busy, all unintended, of course, but fortuitously building itself a way off the planet."

Desan cast her an uncomfortable look askance.

"Oh, indeed. Biomass. Petrochemicals. The storehouse of aeons of energy all waiting the use of consciousness. And that consciousness, if it arrives, dominates the world because awareness is a way of making life more efficiently. But consciousness is a perilous thing, Lord Desan. Consciousness is a computer loose with its own perceptions and performing calculations on its own course, in the service of that little weed; billions of such computers all running and calculating faster and faster, adjusting themselves and their ecological environment, and what if there were the smallest, the most insignificant software error at the outset?"

"You don't believe such a thing. You don't reduce us to that." Desan's faith was shaken; this good woman had not gone unstable, this great intellect had had her faith shaken, that was what—the great and gentle doctor had, in her unthinkable age, acquired cynicism, and he fought back with his fifty-two meager years. "Surely, but surely this isn't the proof, doctor, this could have been a natural calamity."

"Oh, yes, the meteor strike." The doctor waved past a series of holos on a fourth plate, and a vast crater showed in aerial view, a crater so vast the picture showed planetary curvature. It was one of the planet's main features, shockingly visible from space. "But this solar system shows scar after scar of such events. A many-planeted system like this, a star well-attended by debris in its course through the galaxy—Look at the airless bodies, the moons, consider the number of meteor strikes that crater them. Tell me, spacefarer: am I not right in that?"

Desan drew in a breath, relieved to be questioned in his own element. "Of course, the system is prone to that kind of accident. But that crater is ample cause—"

"If it came when there was still sapience here. But that hammerblow fell on a dead world."

He gazed on the eroded crater, the sandswept crustal melting, eloquent of age. "You have proof."

"Strata. Pots. Ironic, they must have feared such an event very greatly. One thinks they must have had a sense of doom about them, perhaps on the evidence of their moon; or understanding the mechanics of their solar system; or perhaps primitive times witnessed such falls and they remembered. One catches a glimpse of the mind that reached out from here . . . what impelled it, what it sought."

"How can we know that? We overlay our mind on their expectations—" Desan silenced himself, abashed, terrified. It was next to heresy. In a moment more he would have committed irremediable indiscretion; and the lords-magistrate on the orbiting station would hear it by suppertime, to his eternal detriment.

"We stand in their landscape, handle their bones, we hold their skulls in our fleshly hands and try to think in their world. Here we stand beneath a threatening heaven. What will we do?"

"Try to escape. Try to get off this world. They *did* get off. The celestial artifacts—"

"Archaelogy is ever so much easier in space. A million years, two, and a thing still shines. Records still can be read. A color can blaze out undimmed after aeons, when first a light falls on it. One surface chewed away by microdust, and the opposing face pristine as the day it had its maker's hand on it. You keep asking me about the age of these ruins. But we know that, don't we truly suspect it, in the marrow of our bones—at what age they fell silent?"

"It *can't* have happened then!"

"Come with me, Lord Desan." Gothon waved a hand, extinguishing all the holos, and, walking on, opened the door into yet another hallway. "So much to catalog. That's much of the work in that room. They're students, mostly. Restoring what they can; numbering, listing. A librarian's job, just to know where things are filed. In five hundred years more of intensive cataloguing and restoring, we may know them well enough to know something of their minds, though we may never find more of their written language than that of those artifacts on the moon. A place of wonders. A place of ongoing wonders, in Dr. Bothogi's work. A little algae beginning the work all over again. Perhaps not for the first time—interesting thought."

"You mean—" Desan overtook the aged doctor in the narrow, sterile hall, a series of ringing steps. "You mean—before the sapients evolved—there were other calamities, other re-beginnings."

"Oh, well before. It sends chills up one's back, doesn't it, to think how incredibly stubborn life might be here, how persistent in the calamity of the skies— The algae and then the creeping things and the slow, slow climb to dominance—"

"Previous sapients?"

"Interesting question in itself. But a thing need not be sapient to dominate a world, Lord Desan. Only tough. Only efficient. Haven't the worlds proven that? High sapience is a rare jewel. So many successes are dead ends. Flippers and not hands; lack of vocal apparatus—unless you believe in telepathy, which I assuredly don't. No. Vocalizing is necessary. Some sort of long-distance communication. Light-flashes; sound; something. Else your individuals stray apart in solitary discovery and rediscovery and duplication of effort. Oh, even with awareness—even granted that rare attribute—how many species lack something essential, or have some handicap that will stop them before civilization; before technology—"

"—before they leave the planet. But they *did* that, they were the one in a thousand— Without them—"

"Without them. Yes." Gothon turned her wonderful soft eyes on him at close range and for a moment he felt a great and terrible stillness like the stillness of a grave. "Childhood ends here. One way or the other, it ends."

He was struck speechless. He stood there, paralyzed a moment, his mind tumbling freefall; then blinked and followed the doctor like a child, helpless to do otherwise.

Let me rest, he thought then, *let us forget this beginning and this day, let me go somewhere and sit down and have a warm drink to get the chill from my marrow and let us begin again. Perhaps we can begin with facts and not fancies—*

But he would not rest. He feared that there was no rest to be had in this place, that once the body stopped moving, the weight of the sky would come down, the deadly sky that had boded destruction for all the history of this lost species, and the age of the land would seep into their bones and haunt his dreams as the far greater scale of stars did not.

All the years I've voyaged, Dr. Gothon, all the years of my life searching from star to star. Relativity has made orphans of us. The world will have sainted you. Me it never knew. In a quarter of a million years—they'll have forgotten; o doctor, you know more than I how a world ages. A quarter of a million years you've seen—and we're both orphans. Me endlessly cloned. You in your long sleep, your several clones held aeons waiting in theirs—o doctor, we'll recreate you. And not truly you, ever again. No more than I'm a Desanprime. I'm only the fifth lord-navigator.

In a quarter of a million years, has not our species evolved beyond us, might they not, may they not, find some faster transport and find us, their aeons-lost precursors; and we will not know each other, Dr. Gothon—how could we know each other—if they had, but they have not; we have become the wavefront of a quest that never overtakes, never surpasses us.

In a quarter of a million years, might some calamity have befallen us and our world be like this world, ocher and deadly rust?

While we are clones and children of clones, genetic fossils, anomalies of our kind?

What are they to us and we to them? We seek the Ancients, the makers of the probe.

Desan's mind reeled; adept as he was at time-relativity calculations, accustomed as he was to stellar immensities, his mind tottered and he fought to regain the corridor in which they walked, he and the doctor. He widened his stride yet again, overtaking Gothon at the next door.

"Doctor." He put out his hand, preventing her, and then feared his own question, his own skirting of heresy and tempting of hers. "Are you beyond doubt? You can't be beyond doubt. They could have simply abandoned this world in its calamity."

Again the impact of those gentle eyes, devastating. "Tell me, tell me, Lord Desan. In all your travels, in all the several near stars you've visited in a century of effort, have you found traces?"

"No. But they could have gone—"

"—leaving no traces, except on their moon?"

"There may be others. The team in search on the fourth planet—"

"Finds nothing."

"You yourself say that you have to stand in that landscape, you have to think with their mind—Maybe Dr. Ashodt hasn't come to the right hill, the right plain—"

"If there are artifacts there they only are a few. I'll tell you why I know so. Come, come with me." Gothon waved a hand and the door gaped on yet another laboratory.

Desan walked. He would rather have walked out to the deadly surface than through this simple door, to the answer Gothon promised him . . . but habit impelled him; habit, duty—necessity. He had no other purpose for his life but this. He had been left none, lord-navigator, fifth incarnation of Desan Das. They had launched his original with none, his second incarnation had had less, and time and successive incarnations had stripped everything else away. So he went, into a place at once too mundane and too strange to be quite sane—mundane because it was sterile as any lab, a well-lit place of littered tables and a few researchers; and strange because hundreds and hundreds of skulls and bones were piled on shelves in heaps on one wall, silent witnesses. An articulated skeleton hung in its frame; the skeleton of a small animal scampered in macabre rigidity on a tabletop.

He stopped. He stared about him, lost for the moment in the stare of all those eyeless sockets of weathered bone.

"Let me present my colleagues," Gothon was saying; Desan focused on the words late, and blinked helplessly as Gothon rattled off names. Bothogi the zoologist was one, younger than most, seventeenth incarnation, burning himself out in profligate use of his years: so with all the incarnations of Bothogi Nan. The rest of the names slid past his ears ungathered—true strangers, the truly-born, sons and daughters of the voyage. He was lost in their stares like the stares of the skulls, eyes behind which shadows and dust were truth, gazes full of secrets and heresies.

They knew him and he did not know them, not even Lord Bothogi. He felt his solitude, the helplessness of his convictions all lost in the dust and the silences.

"Kagodte," said Gothon, to a white-eared, hunched individual, "Kagodte—the Lord Desan has come to see your model."

"Ah." The aged eyes flicked, nervously.

"Show him, pray, Dr. Kagodte."

The hunched man walked over to the table, spread his hands. A holo flared and Desan blinked, having expected some dreadful image, some confrontation with a reconstruction. Instead, columns of words rippled in the air, green and blue. Numbers ticked and multiplied. In his startlement he lost the beginning and failed to follow them. "I don't see—"

"We speak statistics here," Gothon said. "We speak data; we couch our heresies in mathematical formulae."

Desan turned and stared at Gothon in fright. "Heresies I have nothing to do with, doctor. I deal with facts. I come here to find facts."

"Sit down," the gentle doctor said. "Sit down, Lord Desan. There, move the bones over, do; the owners won't mind, there, that's right."

Desan collapsed onto a stool facing a white worktable. Looked up reflexively, eye drawn by a wall-mounted stone that bore the blurred image of a face, eroded, time-dulled—

The juxtaposition of image and bones overwhelmed him. The two whole bodies portrayed on the plaque. The sculpture. The rows of fleshless skulls.

Dead. World hammered by meteors, life struggling in its most rudimentary forms. Dead.

"Ah," Gothon said. Desan looked around and saw Gothon looking up at the wall in his turn. "Yes. That. We find very few sculptures. A few—a precious few. Occasionally the fall of stone will protect a surface. Confirmation. Indeed. But the skulls tell us as much. With our measurements and our holos we can flesh them. We can make them—even more vivid. Do you want to see?"

Desan's mouth worked. "No." A small word. A coward word. "Later. So this was *one* place— You still don't convince me of your thesis, doctor, I'm sorry."

"The place. The world of origin. A many-layered world. The last layers are rich with artifacts of one period, one global culture. Then silence. Species extinguished. Stratum upon stratum of desolation. Millions of years of geological record—"

Gothon came round the end of the table and sat down in the opposing chair, elbows on the table, a scatter of bone between them. Gothon's green eyes shone watery in the brilliant light, her mouth was wrinkled about the jowls and trembled in minute cracks, like aged clay. "The statistics, Lord Desan, the dry statistics tell us. They tell us centers of production of artifacts, such as we have; they tell us compositions, processes the Ancients knew—and there was no progress into advanced materials. None of the materials we take for granted, metals that would have lasted—"

"And perhaps they went to some new process, materials that degraded completely. Perhaps their information storage was on increasingly perishable materials. Perhaps they developed these materials in space."

"Technology has steps. The dry numbers, the dusty dry numbers, the incidences and concentration of items, the numbers and the pots—always the pots, Lord Desan; and the imperishable stones; and the very fact of the meteors—the undeniable fact of the meteor strikes. Could we not avert such a calamity for our own world? Could we not have done it—oh, a half a century before we left?"

"I'm sure you remember, Dr. Gothon. I'm sure you have the advantage of me. But—"

"You see the evidence. You want to cling to your hopes. But there is only one question—no, two. Is this the species that launched the probe?—Yes. Or evolution and coincidence have cooperated mightily. Is this the only world they inhabited? Beyond all doubt. If there are artifacts on the fourth planet they are scoured by its storms, busied, lost."

"But they may *be* there."

"There is no abundance of them. There is no *progression*, Lord Desan. That is the key thing. There is nothing beyond these substances, these materials. This was not a star-faring civilization. They launched their slow, unmanned probes, with their cameras, their robot eyes—not for us. We always knew that. We were the recipients of flotsam. Mere wreckage on the beach."

"It was purposeful!" Desan hissed, trembling, surrounded by them all, a lone credent among the quiet heresy in this room. "Dr. Gothon, your unique position—is a position of trust, of profound trust; I beg you to consider the effect you have—"

"Do you threaten me, Lord Desan? Are you here for that, to silence me?"

Desan looked desperately about him, at the sudden hush in the room. The minute tickings of probes and picks had stopped. Eyes stared. "Please." He looked back. "I came here to gather data; I expected a simple meeting, a few staff meetings—to consider things at leisure—"

"I have distressed you. You wonder how it would be if the lords-magistrate fell at odds with me. I am aware of myself as an institution, Lord Desan. I remember Desan Das. I remember launch, the original five ships. I have waked to all but one of your incarnations. Not to mention the numerous incarnations of the lords-magistrate."

"You cannot discount them! Even you—Let me plead with you, Dr. Gothon, be patient with us."

"You do not need to teach me patience, Desan-Five."

He shivered convulsively. Even when Gothon smiled that gentle, disarming smile. "You have to give me facts, doctor, not mystical communings with the landscape. The lords-magistrate accept that this is the world of origin. I assure you they never would have devoted so much time to creating a base here if that were not the case."

"Come, lord, those power systems on the probe, so long dead— What was it truly for, but to probe something very close at hand? Even orthodoxy admits that. And what is close at hand but their own solar system? Come, I've *seen* the original artifact and the original tablet. Touched it with my hands. This was a *primitive* venture, designed to cross their own solar system—*which they had not the capability to do.*"

Desan blinked. "But the purpose—"

"Ah. The purpose."

"You say that you stand in a landscape and you think in their mind. Well, doctor, use this skill you claim. What did the Ancients intend? Why did they send it out with a message?"

The old eyes flickered, deep and calm and pained. "An oracular message, Lord Desan. A message into the dark of their own future, unaimed, unfocused. Without answer. Without hope of answer. We know its voyage time. Eight million years. They spoke to the universe at large. This probe went out, and they fell silent shortly afterward— the depth of this dry lake of dust, Lord Desan, is eight and a quarter million years."

"I will not believe that."

"Eight and a quarter million years ago, Lord Desan. Calamity fell on them, calamity global and complete within a century, perhaps within a decade of the launch of that probe. Perhaps calamity fell from the skies; but demonstrably it was atomics and their own doing. They were at that precarious stage. And the destruction in the great centers is catastrophic and of one level. Destruction centered in places of heavy population. Trace elements. That is what those statistics say. Atomics, Lord Desan."

"I cannot accept this!"

"Tell me, space-farer—do you understand the workings of weather? What those meteor strikes could do, the dust raised by atomics could do with equal efficiency. Never mind the radiation that alone would have killed millions—never mind the destruction of centers of government: We speak of global calamity, the dimming of the sun in dust, the living oceans and lakes choking in dying photosynthetes in a sunless winter, killing the food chain from the bottom up—"

"You have no proof!"

"The universality, the ruin of the population-centers. Arguably, they had the capacity to prevent meteor-impact. That may be a matter of debate. But beyond a doubt in my own mind, simultaneous destruction of the population centers indicates atomics. The statistics, the pots and the dry numbers, Lord Desan, doom us to that answer. The question is answered. There were no descendants, there was no escape from the world. They destroyed themselves before that meteor hit them."

Desan rested his mouth against his joined hands. Stared helplessly at the doctor. "A lie. Is that what you're saying? We pursued a lie?"

"Is it their fault that we needed them so much?"

Desan pushed himself to his feet and stood there by mortal effort. Gothon sat staring up at him with those terrible dark eyes.

"What will you do, lord-navigator? Silence me? The old woman's grown difficult at last: wake my clone after, tell it—what the lords-magistrate select for it to be told?" Gothon waved a hand about the room, indicating the staff, the dozen sets of living eyes among the dead. "Bothogi too, those of us who have clones— But what of the rest of the staff? How much will it take to silence all of us?"

Desan stared about him, trembling. "Dr. Gothon—" He leaned his hands on the table to look at Gothon. "You mistake me. You utterly mistake me— The lords-magistrate may have the station, but I have the ships, *I*, I and my staff. I propose no such thing. I've come home—" The unaccustomed word caught in his throat; he considered it, weighed it accepted it, at least in the emotional sense. "—*home*, Dr.

Gothon, after a hundred years of search, to discover this argument and this dissension."

"Charges of heresy—"

"They dare not make them against *you*." A bitter laugh welled up. "Against *you* they have no argument and you well know it, Dr. Gothon."

"Against their violence, lord-navigator, I have no defense."

"But she has," said Dr. Bothogi.

Desan turned, flicked a glance from the hardness in Bothogi's green eyes to the even harder substance of the stone in Bothogi's hand. He flung himself about again, hands on the table, abandoning the defense of his back. "Dr. Gothon! I appeal to you! I am your friend!"

"For myself," said Dr. Gothon, "I would make no defense at all. But, as you say—they have no argument against me. So it must be a general catastrophe—the lords-magistrate have to silence everyone, don't they? *Nothing* can be left on this base. Perhaps they've quietly dislodged an asteroid or two and put them on course. In the guise of mining, perhaps they will silence this poor old world forever—myself and the rest of the relics. Lost relics and the distant dead are always safer to venerate, aren't they?"

"That's absurd!"

"Or perhaps they've become more hasty now that your ships are here and their judgement is in question. *They* have atomics within their capability, lord-navigator. They can disable your shuttle with beam-fire. They can simply welcome you to the list of casualties—a charge of heresy. A thing taken out of context, who knows? After all— all lords are immediately duplicatable, the captains accustomed to obey the lords-magistrate—what few of them are awake—am I not right? If an institution like myself can be threatened—where is the fifth lord-navigator in their plans? And of a sudden those plans will be moving in haste."

Desan blinked. "Dr. Gothon—I assure you—"

"If you are my friend, lord-navigator, I hope for your survival. The robots are theirs, do you understand? Their powerpacks are sufficient for transmission of information to the base AIs; and from the communications center it goes to satellites; and from satellites to the station and the lords-magistrate. This room is safe from their monitoring. We have seen to that. They cannot hear you."

"I cannot believe these charges, I cannot accept it—"

"Is murder so new?"

"Then come with me! Come with me to the shuttle, we'll confront them—"

"The transportation to the port is theirs. It would not permit. The transport AI would resist. The planes have AI components. And we might never reach the airfield."

"My luggage. Dr. Gothon, my luggage—my com unit!" And Desan's heart sank, remembering the service-robots. "*They* have it."

Gothon smiled, a small, amused smile. "O space-farer. So many scientists clustered here, and could we not improvise so simple a thing? *We* have a receiver-transmitter. Here. In this room. We broke one. We broke another. They're on the registry as broken. What's another bit of rubbish—on this poor planet? We meant to contact the ships, to call *you*, lord-navigator, when you came back. But you saved us the trouble. You came down to us like a thunderbolt. Like the birds you never saw, my spaceborn lord, swooping down on prey. The conferences, the haste you must have inspired up there on the station—if the lords-magistrate planned what I most suspect! I congratulate you. But knowing we have a transmitter—with your shuttle sitting on this world vulnerable as this building—what will you do, lord-navigator, since *they* control the satellite relay?"

Desan sank down on his chair. Stared at Gothon. "You never meant to kill me. All this—you schemed to enlist me."

"I entertained that hope, yes. I knew your predecessors. I also know your personal reputation—a man who burns his years one after the other as if there were no end of them. Unlike his predecessors. What are you, lord-navigator? Zealot? A man with an obsession? Where do you stand in this?"

"To what—" His voice came hoarse and strange. "To what are you trying to convert me, Dr. Gothon?"

"To our rescue from the lords-magistrate. To the rescue of truth."

"Truth!" Desan waved a desperate gesture. "I don't believe you, I cannot believe you, and you tell me about plots as fantastical as your research and try to involve me in your politics. I'm trying to find the trail the Ancients took—one clue, one artifact to direct us—"

"A new tablet?"

"You make light of me. Anything. Any indication where they went. And they *did* go, doctor. You will not convince me with your statistics. The unforeseen and the unpredicted aren't in your statistics."

"So you'll go on looking—for what you'll never find. You'll serve the lords-magistrate. They'll surely cooperate with you. They'll approve your search and leave this world . . . after the great catastrophe. After the catastrophe that obliterates us and all the records. An asteroid. Who but the robots chart their course? Who knows how close it is at this moment?"

"People would know a murder! They could never hide it!"

"I tell you, Lord Desan, you stand in a place and you look around you and you say—what would be natural to this place? In this cratered, devastated world, in this chaotic, debris-ridden solar system—could not an input error by an asteroid miner be more credible an accident than atomics? I tell you when your shuttle descended, we thought you might be acting for the lords-magistrate. That you might have a weapon in your baggage that their robots would deliberately fail to detect. But I believe you, lord-navigator. You're as trapped as we. With only the transmitter and a satellite relay system they control. What will you do? Persuade the lords-magistrate that you support them? Persuade them to support you on this further voyage—in return for your backing them? Perhaps they'll listen to you and let you leave."

"But they will," Desan said. He drew in a deep breath and looked from Gothon to the others and back again. "My shuttle is my own. *My* robotics, Dr. Gothon. From my ship and linked to it. And what I need is that transmitter. Appeal to *me* for protection if you think it so urgent. Trust me. Or trust nothing and we will all wait here and see what truth is."

Gothon reached into a pocket, held up an odd metal object. Smiled. Her eyes crinkled round the edges. "An old-fashioned thing, lord-navigator. We say *key* nowadays and mean something quite different, but I'm a relic myself, remember. Baffles hell out of the robots. Bothogi. Link up that antenna and unlock the closet and let's see what the lord-navigator and his shuttle can do."

"Did it hear you?" Bothogi asked, a boy's honest worry on his unlined face. He still had the rock, as if he had forgotten it. Or feared robots. Or intended to use it if he detected treachery. "Is it moving?"

"I assure you it's moving," Desan said, and shut the transmitter down. He drew a great breath, shut his eyes and saw the shuttle lift, a silver wedge spreading wings for home. Deadly if attacked. *They will not attack it, they must not attack it, they will query us when they know the shuttle is launched and we will discover yet that this is all a ridiculous error of understanding.* And looking at nowhere: "Relays have gone; *nothing* stops it and its defenses are considerable. The lords-navigator have not been fools, citizens: we probe worlds with our shuttles, and we plan to get them back." He turned and faced Gothon and the other staff. "The message is *out.* And because I am a prudent man—are there suits enough for your staff? I advise we get to them. In the case of an accident."

"The alarm," said Gothon at once. "Neoth, sound the alarm." And as a senior staffer moved: "The dome pressure alert," Gothon said. "*That* will confound the robots. All personnel to pressure suits; all robots to seek damage. I agree about the suits. Get them."

The alarm went, a staccato shriek from overhead. Desan glanced instinctively at an uncommunicative white ceiling—

—darkness, darkness above, where the shuttle reached the thin blue edge of space. The station now knew that things had gone greatly amiss. It should inquire, there should be inquiry immediate to the planet—

Staffers had unlocked a second closet. They pulled out suits, not the expected one or two for emergency exit from this pressure-sealable room; but a tightly jammed lot of them. The lab seemed a mine of defenses, a stealthily equipped stronghold that smelled of conspiracy all over the base, throughout the staff—*everyone* in on it—

He blinked at the offering of a suit, ears assailed by the siren. He looked into the eyes of Bothogi who had handed it to him. There would be no call, no inquiry from the lords-magistrate. He began to know that, in the earnest, clear-eyed way these people behaved—not lunatics, not schemers. Truth. They had told their truth as they believed it, as the whole base believed it. And the lords-magistrate named it heresy.

His heart beat steadily again. Things made sense again. His hands found familiar motions, putting on the suit, making the closures.

"There's that AI in the controller's office," said a senior staffer. "I have a key."

"What will they do?" a younger staffer asked, panic-edged. "Will the station's weapons reach here?"

"It's quite distant for sudden actions," said Desan. "Too far for beams and missiles are slow." His heartbeat steadied further. The suit was about him; familiar feeling; hostile worlds and weapons: more familiar ground. He smiled, not a pleasant kind of smile, a parting of lips on strong, long teeth. "And one more thing, young citizen, the ships they have are transports. Miners. Mine are hunters. I regret to say we've carried weapons for the last two hundred thousand years, and my crews know their business. If the lords-magistrate attack that shuttle it will be their mistake. Help Dr. Gothon."

"I've got it, quite, young lord." Gothon made the collar closure. "I've been handling these things longer than—"

Explosion thumped somewhere away. Gothon looked up. All motion stopped. And the air-rush died in the ducts.

"The oxygen system—" Bothogi exclaimed. "O *damn* them—!"

"We have," said Desan coldly. He made no haste. Each final fitting of the suit he made with care. Suit-drill; example to the young: the lord-navigator, youngsters, demonstrates his skill. Pay attention. "And we've just had our answer from the lords-magistrate. We need to get to that AI and shut it down. Let's have no panic here. Assume that my shuttle has cleared atmosphere—"

—well above the gray clouds, the horror of the surface. Silver needle aimed at the heart of the lords-magistrate.

Alert, alert, it would shriek, *alert, alert, alert*—With its transmission relying on no satellites, with its message shoved out in one high-powered bow-wave. *Crew on the world is in danger.* And, code that no lord-navigator had ever hoped to transmit, a series of numbers in syntaxical link: *Treachery; the lords-magistrate are traitors; aid and rescue—Alert, alert, alert—*

—anguished scream from a world of dust; a place of skulls; the grave of the search.

Treachery, alert, alert, alert!

Desan was not a violent man; he had never thought of himself as violent. He was a searcher, a man with a quest.

He knew nothing of certainty. He believed a woman a quarter of a million years old, because—because Gothon was Gothon. He cried traitor and let loose havoc all the while knowing that here might be the traitor, this gentle-eyed woman, this collector of skulls.

O Gothon, he would ask if he dared, *which of you is false? To force the lords-magistrate to strike with violence enough to damn them—Is that what you wish? Against a quarter million years of unabated life— what are my five incarnations: mere genetic congruency, without memory. I am helpless to know your perspectives.*

Have you planned this a thousand years, ten thousand?

Do you stand in this place and think in the mind of creatures dead longer even than you have lived? Do you hold their skulls and think their thoughts?

Was it purpose eight million years ago?

Was it, is it—horror upon horror—a mistake on both sides?

"Lord Desan," said Bothogi, laying a hand on his shoulder. "Lord Desan, we have a master key. We have weapons. We're waiting, Lord Desan."

Above them the holocaust.

It was only a service robot. It had never known its termination. Not like the base AI, in the director's office, which had fought them with locked doors and release of atmosphere, to the misfortune of the director—

"Tragedy, tragedy," said Bothogi, standing by the small dented corpse, there on the ocher sand before the buildings. Smoke rolled up from a sabotaged lifesupport plant to the right of the domes; the world's air had rolled outward and inward and mingled with the breaching of the central dome—the AI transport's initial act of sabotage, ramming the plastic walls. "Microorganisms let loose on this world—the fools, the arrogant *fools!*"

It was not the microorganisms Desan feared. It was the AI eight-wheeled transport, maneuvering itself for another attack on the cold-sleep facilities. Prudent to have set themselves inside a locked room with the rest of the scientists and hope for rescue from offworld; but the AI would batter itself against the plastic walls, and living targets kept it distracted from the sleeping, helpless clones—Gothon's junior-most; Bothogi's; those of a dozen senior staffers.

And keeping it distracted became more and more difficult.

Hour upon hour they had evaded its rushes, clumsy attacks and retreats in their encumbering suits. They had done it damage where they could while staff struggled to come up with something that might slow it . . . it limped along now with a great lot of metal wire wrapped around its rearmost right wheel.

"Damn!" cried a young biologist as it maneuvered for her position. It was the agile young who played this game; and one aging lord-navigator who was the only fighter in the lot.

Dodge, dodge and dodge. "It's going to catch you against the oxy-plant, youngster! *This* way!" Desan's heart thudded as the young woman thumped along in the cumbersome suit in a losing race with the transport. "Oh, *damn,* it's got it figured! Bothogi!"

Desan grasped his probe-spear and jogged on—"Divert it!" he yelled. Diverting it was all they could hope for.

It turned their way, a whine of the motor, a serpentine flex of its metal body and a flurry of sand from its eight-wheeled drive. "Run, lord!" Bothogi gasped beside him; and it was still turning—it aimed for them now, and at another tangent a white-suited figure hurled a rock, to distract it yet again.

It kept coming at them. AI. An eight-wheeled, flex-bodied intelligence that had suddenly decided its behavior was not working and altered the program, refusing distraction. A pressure-windowed juggernaut tracking every turn they made.

Closer and closer. "Sensors!" Desan cried, turning on the slick dust—his footing failed him and he caught himself, gripped the probe and aimed it straight at the sensor array clustered beneath the front window.

Thum-p! The dusty sky went blue and he was on his back, skidding in the sand with the great balloon tires churning sand on either side of him.

The suit, he thought with a spaceman's horror of the abrading, while it dawned on him at the same time he was being dragged beneath the AI, and that every joint and nerve center was throbbing with the high voltage shock of the probe.

Things became very peaceful then, a cessation of commotion. He lay dazed, staring up at a rusty blue sky, and seeing it laced with a silver thread.

They're coming, he thought, and thought of his eldest clone, sleeping at a well-educated twenty years of age. Handsome lad. He talked to the boy from time to time. *Poor lad, the lordship is yours. Your predecessor was a fool—*

A shadow passed above his face. It was another suited face peering down into his. A weight rested on his chest.

"Get off," he said.

"He's alive!" Bothogi's voice cried. "Dr. Gothon, he's still alive!"

The world showed no more scars than it had at the beginning—red and ocher where clouds failed. The algae continued its struggle in sea and tidal pools and lakes and rivers—with whatever microscopic addenda the breached dome had let loose in the world. The insects and the worms continued their blind ascent to space, dominant life on this poor, cratered globe. The research station was in function again, repairs complete.

Desan gazed on the world from his ship: it hung as a sphere in the holotank by his command station. A wave of his hand might show him the darkness of space; the floodlit shapes of ten hunting ships, lately returned from the deep and about to seek it again in continuation of the Mission, sleek fish rising and sinking again in a figurative black sea. A good many suns had shone on their hulls, but this one sun had seen them more often than any since their launching.

Home.

The space station was returning to function. Corpses were consigned to the sun the Mission had sought for so long. And power over the Mission rested solely at present in the hands of the lord-navigator, in the unprecedented circumstance of the demise of all five lords-magistrate simultaneously. Their clones were not yet activated to begin their years of majority—"Later will be time to wake the new lords-magistrate," Desan decreed, "at some further world of the search. Let them hear this event as history."

When I can manage them personally, he thought. He looked aside at twenty-year-old Desan Six and the youth looked gravely back with the face Desan had seen in the mirror thirty-two waking years ago.

"Lord-navigator?"

"You'll wake your brother after we're away, Six. Directly after. I'll be staying awake much of this trip."

"*Awake,* sir?"

"Quite. There are things I want you to think about. I'll be talking to you and Seven both."

"About the lords-magistrate, sir?"

Desan lifted brows at this presumption. "You and I are already quite well attuned, Six. You'll succeed young. Are you sorry you missed this time?"

"No, lord-navigator! I assure you not!"

"Good brain. I ought to know. Go to your post, Six. Be grateful you don't have to cope with a new lordship *and* five new lords-magistrate and a recent schism."

Desan leaned back in his chair as the youth crossed the bridge and settled at a crew-post, beside the captain. The lord-navigator was more than a figurehead to rule the seventy ships of the Mission, with their captains and their crews. Let the boy try his skill on this plotting. Desan intended to check it. He leaned aside with a wince—the electric shock that had blown him flat between the AI's tires had saved him from worse than a broken arm and leg; and the medical staff had seen to that: the arm and the leg were all but healed, with only a light wrap to protect them. The ribs were tightly wrapped too; and they cost him more pain than all the rest.

A scan had indeed located three errant asteroids, three courses the station's computers had not accurately recorded as inbound for the planet—until personnel from the ships began to run their own observation. Those were redirected.

Casualties. Destruction. Fighting within the Mission. The guilt of the lords-magistrate was profound and beyond dispute.

"Lord-navigator," the communications officer said. "Dr. Gothon returning your call."

Goodbye, he had told Gothon. *I don't accept your judgment, but I shall devote my energy to pursuit of mine, and let any who want to join you—reside on the station. There are some volunteers; I don't profess to understand them. But you may trust them. You may trust the lords-magistrate to have learned a lesson. I will teach it. No member of this mission will be restrained in any opinion while my influence lasts. And I shall see to that. Sleep again and we may see each other once more in our lives.*

"I'll receive it," Desan said, pleased and anxious at once that Gothon deigned reply; he activated the com-control. Ship-electronics touched his ear, implanted for comfort. He heard the usual blip and chatter of com's mechanical protocols, then Gothon's quiet voice. "Lord-navigator."

"I'm hearing you, doctor."

"Thank you for your sentiment. I wish you well, too. I wish you very well."

The tablet was mounted before him, above the console. Millions of years ago a tiny probe had set out from this world, bearing the original. Two aliens standing naked, one with hand uplifted. A series of diagrams which, partially obliterated, had still served to guide the Mission across the centuries. A probe bearing a greeting. Ages-dead cameras and simple instruments.

Greetings, stranger. We come from this place, this star system.

See, the hand, the appendage of a builder—This we will have in common.

The diagrams: we speak knowledge; we have no fear of you, strangers who read this, whoever you be.

Wise fools.

There had been a time, long ago, when fools had set out to seek them . . . In a vast desert of stars. Fools who had desperately needed proof, once upon a quarter million years ago, that they were not alone. One dust-covered alien artifact they found, so long ago, on a lonely drifting course.

Hello, it said.

The makers, the peaceful Ancients, became a legend. They became purpose, inspiration.

The overriding, obsessive *Why* that saved a species, pulled it back from war, gave it the stars.

"I'm very serious—I do hope you rest, doctor—save a few years for the unborn."

"My eldest's awake. I've lost my illusions of immortality, lord-navigator. She hopes to meet you."

"You might still abandon this world and come with us, doctor."

"To search for a myth?"

"Not a myth. We're bound to disagree. Doctor, doctor, what *good* can your presence there do? What if you're right? It's a dead end. What if I'm wrong? I'll never stop looking. *I'll* never know."

"But we know their descendants, lord-navigator. We. We are. We've spread their legend from star to star—they've become a fable. The Ancients. The Pathfinders. A hundred civilizations have taken up that myth. A hundred civilizations have lived out their years in that belief and begotten others to tell their story. What if you should find them? Would you know them—or where evolution had taken them? Perhaps we've already met them, somewhere along the worlds we've visited, and we failed to know them."

It was irony. Gentle humor. "Perhaps, then," Desan said in turn, "we'll find the track leads home again. Perhaps we *are* their children—eight and a quarter million years removed."

"O ye makers of myths. Do your work, space-farer. Tangle the skein with legends. Teach fables to the races you meet. Brighten the universe with them. I put my faith in you. Don't you know—this world is all I came to find, but you—child of the voyage, you have to have more. For you the voyage is the Mission. Goodbye to you. Fare well. Nothing is complete calamity. The equation here is different, by a multitude of microorganisms let free—Bothogi has stopped grieving and begun to have quite different thoughts on the matter. His algae-pools may turn out a different breed this time—the shift of a protein here and there in the genetic chain—who knows what it will breed? Different software this time, perhaps. Good voyage to you, lord-navigator. Look for your Ancients under other suns. We're waiting for their offspring here, under this one."

Introduction to "Press Enter ■"

by John Varley

Okay, I'll tell you right now, my favorite John Varley story wasn't even published under his name, it came out as a story by "Herb Boehm." But that story didn't belong in this anthology for several reasons. First, it's already too familiar—it has been turned into a novel and then into an HBO movie. Second, it was published in the 1970s, just like another of Varley's best stories, "The Persistence of Vision," and so is ineligible for this book.

But that's all right. No loss. Because any decade in which John Varley publishes at all, there will be a John Varley story worthy of inclusion in any anthology that pretends to be definitive. This is Varley's monument to the 1980s, when personal computers first became a pervasive part of the American experience.

When this story came out, most home computers were crumby little VICs and Commodore 64s doomed to gather dust on the closet shelves, or graphically and computationally crippled IBM PCs that software designers were desperately trying to turn into useful tools of business and industry. The people who understood computers weren't writing stories, and the people writing stories didn't understand computers. Thus you got end-of-the-world nonsense like War Games, *in which a computer somehow got a mind of its own and decided to blow up the world, or romanticized computer networks as in* Neuromancer, *where "virtual" people lived as electronic cowboys on the open range, now and then roping a cow or holding up a train. These works might well have been entertaining, and even, in some cases, good art; but what they definitely were* not *was an exploration of what computers can actually do. (To their credit, however,* War Games *and* Neuromancer *were infinitely smarter than* Tron, *which, despite its humiliating dumbness, continues to be remade again and again, in films and stories in which people somehow get trapped inside computers, or computers somehow leap out and run amok in our world.)*

Even if "Press Enter ■" did nothing else, it would be remarkable for having found a believable way that a computer might actually wreak havoc in the real world. And, because it's Varley's story, "Press Enter ■" does do something else. It draws you through the twists and turns of real lives, so that even though it is structured as a mystery story, it can be reread many times as a story of character.

PRESS ENTER ■

John Varley

"This is a recording. Please do not hang up until—"

I slammed the phone down so hard it fell onto the floor. Then I stood there, dripping wet and shaking with anger. Eventually, the phone started to make that buzzing noise they make when a receiver is off the hook. It's twenty times as loud as any sound a phone can normally make, and I always wondered why. As though it was such a terrible disaster: "Emergency! Your telephone is off the hook!!!"

Phone answering machines are one of the small annoyances of life. Confess, do you really *like* to talk to a machine? But what had just happened to me was more than a petty irritation. I had just been called by an automatic dialing machine.

They're fairly new. I'd been getting about two or three such calls a month. Most of them come from insurance companies. They give you a two-minute spiel and then a number to call if you are interested. (I called back, once, to give them a piece of my mind, and was put on hold, complete with Muzak.) They use lists. I don't know where they get them.

I went back to the bathroom, wiped water droplets from the plastic cover of the library book, and carefully lowered myself back into the water. It was too cool. I ran more hot water and was just getting my blood pressure back to normal when the phone rang again.

So I sat through fifteen rings, trying to ignore it.

Did you ever try to read with the phone ringing?

On the sixteenth ring I got up. I dried off, put on a robe, walked slowly and deliberately into the living room. I stared at the phone for a while.

On the fiftieth ring I picked it up.

"This is a recording. Please do not hang up until the message has been completed. This call originates from the house of your next-door neighbor, Charles Kluge. It will repeat every ten minutes. Mister

Kluge knows he has not been the best of neighbors, and apologizes in advance for the inconvenience. He requests that you go immediately to his house. The key is under the mat. Go inside and do what needs to be done. There will be a reward for your services. Thank you."

Click. Dial tone.

I'm not a hasty man. Ten minutes later, when the phone rang again, I was still sitting there thinking it over. I picked up the receiver and listened carefully.

It was the same message. As before, it was not Kluge's voice. It was something synthesized, with all the human warmth of a Speak'n'Spell.

I heard it out again, and cradled the receiver when it was done.

I thought about calling the police. Charles Kluge had lived next door to me for ten years. In that time I may have had a dozen conversations with him, none lasting longer than a minute. I owed him nothing.

I thought about ignoring it. I was still thinking about that when the phone rang again. I glanced at my watch. Ten minutes. I lifted the receiver and put it right back down.

I could disconnect the phone. It wouldn't change my life radically.

But in the end I got dressed and went out the front door, turned left, and walked toward Kluge's property.

My neighbor across the street, Hal Lanier, was out mowing the lawn. He waved to me, and I waved back. It was about seven in the evening of a wonderful August day. The shadows were long. There was the smell of cut grass in the air. I've always liked that smell. About time to cut my own lawn, I thought.

It was a thought Kluge had never entertained. His lawn was brown and knee-high and choked with weeds.

I rang the bell. When nobody came I knocked. Then I sighed, looked under the mat, and used the key I found there to open the door.

"Kluge?" I called out as I stuck my head in.

I went along the short hallway, tentatively, as people do when unsure of their welcome. The drapes were drawn, as always, so it was dark in there, but in what had once been the living room ten television screens gave more than enough light for me to see Kluge. He sat in a chair in front of a table, with his face pressed into a computer keyboard and the side of his head blown away.

✦   ✦   ✦

Hal Lanier operates a computer for the L.A.P.D., so I told him what I had found and he called the police. We waited together for the first car to arrive. Hal kept asking if I'd touched anything, and I kept telling him no, except for the front door knob.

An ambulance arrived without the siren. Soon there were police all over, and neighbors standing out in their yards or talking in front of Kluge's house. Crews from some of the television stations arrived in time to get pictures of the body, wrapped in a plastic sheet, being carried out. Men and women came and went. I assumed they were doing all the standard police things, taking fingerprints, collecting evidence. I would have gone home, but had been told to stick around.

Finally I was brought in to see Detective Osborne, who was in charge of the case. I was led into Kluge's living room. All the television screens were still turned on. I shook hands with Osborne. He looked me over before he said anything. He was a short guy, balding. He seemed very tired until he looked at me. Then, though nothing really changed in his face, he didn't look tired at all.

"You're Victor Apfel?" he asked. I told him I was. He gestured at the room. "Mister Apfel, can you tell if anything has been taken from this room?"

I took another look around, approaching it as a puzzle.

There was a fireplace and there were curtains over the windows. There was a rug on the floor. Other than those items, there was nothing else you would expect to find in a living room.

All the walls were lined with tables, leaving a narrow aisle down the middle. On the tables were monitor screens, keyboards, disc drives —all the glossy bric-a-brac of the new age. They were interconnected by thick cables and cords. Beneath the tables were still more computers, and boxes full of electronic items. Above the tables were shelves that reached the ceiling and were stuffed with boxes of tapes, discs, cartridges . . . there was a word for it which I couldn't recall just then. It was software.

"There's no furniture, is there? Other than that . . ."

He was looking confused.

"You mean there was furniture here before?"

"How would I know?" Then I realized what the misunderstanding was. "Oh. You thought I'd been here before. The first time I ever set foot in this room was about an hour ago."

He frowned, and I didn't like that much.

"The medical examiner says the guy had been dead about three hours. How come you came over when you did, Victor?"

I didn't like him using my first name, but didn't see what I could do about it. And I knew I had to tell him about the phone call.

He looked dubious. But there was one easy way to check it out, and we did that. Hal and Osborne and I and several others trooped over to my house. My phone was ringing as we entered.

Osborne picked it up and listened. He got a very sour expression on his face. As the night wore on, it just got worse and worse.

We waited ten minutes for the phone to ring again. Osborne spent the time examining everything in my living room. I was glad when the phone rang again. They made a recording of the message, and we went back to Kluge's house.

Osborne went into the back yard to see Kluge's forest of antennas. He looked impressed.

"Mrs. Madison down the street thinks he was trying to contact Martians," Hal said, with a laugh. "Me, I just thought he was stealing HBO." There were three parabolic dishes. There were six tall masts, and some of those things you see on telephone company buildings for transmitting microwaves.

Osborne took me to the living room again. He asked me to describe what I had seen. I didn't know what good that would do, but I tried.

"He was sitting in that chair, which was here in front of this table. I saw the gun on the floor. His hand was hanging down toward it."

"You think it was suicide?"

"Yes, I guess I did think that." I waited for him to comment, but he didn't. "Is that what you think?"

He sighed. "There wasn't any note."

"They don't always leave notes," Hal pointed out.

"No, but they do often enough that my nose starts to twitch when they don't." He shrugged. "It's probably nothing."

"That phone call," I said. "That might be a kind of suicide note."

Osborne nodded. "Was there anything else you noticed?"

I went to the table and looked at the keyboard. It was made by Texas Instruments, model TI-99/4A. There was a large bloodstain on the right side of it, where his head had been resting.

"Just that he was sitting in front of this machine." I touched a key, and the monitor screen behind the keyboard immediately filled with words. I quickly drew my hand back, then stared at the message there.

PROGRAM NAME: GOODBYE REAL WORLD

DATE: 8/20

CONTENTS: LAST WILL AND TESTAMENT;
              MISC. FEATURES

PROGRAMER: "CHARLES KLUGE"

TO RUN

PRESS ENTER ■

The black square at the end flashed on and off. Later I learned it was called a cursor.

Everyone gathered around. Hal, the computer expert, explained how many computers went blank after ten minutes of no activity, so the words wouldn't be burned into the television screen. This one had been green until I touched it, then displayed black letters on a blue background.

"Has this console been checked for prints?" Osborne asked. Nobody seemed to know, so Osborne took a pencil and used the eraser to press the *ENTER* key.

The screen cleared, stayed blue for a moment, then filled with little ovoid shapes that started at the top of the screen and descended like rain. There were hundreds of them in many colors.

"Those are pills," one of the cops said, in amazement. "Look, that's gotta be a Quaalude. There's a Nembutal." Other cops pointed out other pills. I recognized the distinctive red stripe around the center of a white capsule that had to be a Dilantin. I had been taking them every day for years

Finally the pills stopped falling, and the damn thing started to play music at us. "Nearer My God To Thee," in three-part harmony.

A couple people laughed. I don't think any of us thought it was funny—it was creepy as hell listening to that eerie dirge—but it sounded like it had been scored for pennywhistle, calliope, and kazoo. What could you do but laugh?

As the music played a little figure composed entirely of squares entered from the left of the screen and jerked spastically toward the center. It was like one of those human figures from a video game, but not as detailed. You had to use your imagination to believe it was a man.

A shape appeared in the middle of the screen. The "man" stopped in front of it. He bent in the middle, and something that might have been a chair appeared under him

"What's that supposed to be?"

"A computer. Isn't it?"

It must have been, because the little man extended his arms, which jerked up and down like Liberace at the piano. He was typing. The words appeared above him.

SOMEWHERE ALONG THE LINE I MISSED SOMETHING. I SIT HERE, NIGHT AND DAY. A SPIDER IN THE CENTER OF A COAXIAL WEB, MASTER OF ALL I SURVEY . . . AND IT IS NOT ENOUGH. THERE MUST BE MORE.

ENTER YOUR NAME HERE ■

"Jesus Christ," Hal said. "I don't believe it. An interactive suicide note."

"Come on, we've got to see the rest of this."

I was nearest the keyboard, so I leaned over and typed my name. But when I looked up, what I had typed was VICT9R.

"How do you back this up?" I asked.

"Just enter it," Osborne said. He reached around me and pressed ENTER.

DO YOU EVER GET THAT FEELING, VICT9R? YOU HAVE WORKED ALL YOUR LIFE TO BE THE BEST THERE IS AT WHAT YOU DO, AND ONE DAY YOU WAKE UP TO WONDER WHY YOU ARE DOING IT? THAT IS WHAT HAPPENED TO ME.

DO YOU WANT TO HEAR MORE, VICT9R? Y/N ■

The message rambled from that point. Kluge seemed to be aware of it, apologetic about it, because at the end of each forty- or fifty-word paragraph the reader was given the Y/N option.

I kept glancing from the screen to the keyboard, remembering

Kluge slumped across it. I thought about him sitting here alone, writing this.

He said he was despondent. He didn't feel like he could go on. He was taking too many pills (more of them rained down the screen at this point), and he had no further goal. He had done everything he set out to do. We didn't understand what he meant by that. He said he no longer existed. We thought that was a figure of speech

ARE YOU A COP, VICT9R? IF YOU ARE NOT, A COP WILL BE HERE SOON. SO TO YOU OR THE COP: I WAS NOT SELLING NARCOTICS. THE DRUGS IN MY BEDROOM WERE FOR MY OWN PERSONAL USE. I USED A LOT OF THEM AND NOW I WILL NOT NEED THEM ANYMORE.

PRESS ENTER ■

Osborne did, and a printer across the room began to chatter, scaring the hell out of all of us. I could see the carriage zipping back and forth, printing in both directions, when Hal pointed at the screen and shouted.

"Look! Look at that!"

The compugraphic man was standing again. He faced us. He had something that had to be a gun in his hand, which he now pointed at his head.

"Don't do it!" Hal yelled.

The little man didn't listen. There was a denatured gunshot sound, and the little man fell on his back. A line of red dripped down the screen. Then the green background turned to blue, the printer shut off, and there was nothing left but the little black corpse lying on its back and the word °°DONE°° at the bottom of the screen.

I took a deep breath, and glanced at Osborne. It would be an understatement to say he did not look happy.

"What's this about drugs in the bedroom?" he said.

We watched Osborne pulling out drawers in dressers and beside the tables. He didn't find anything. He looked under the bed, and in the closet. Like all the other rooms in the house, this one was full of computers. Holes had been knocked in walls for the thick sheaves of cables.

I had been standing near a big cardboard drum, one of several in the room. It was about thirty gallon capacity, the kind you ship things in. The lid was loose, so I lifted it. I sort of wished I hadn't.

"Osborne," I said. "You'd better look at this."

The drum was lined with a heavy-duty garbage bag. And it was two-thirds full of Quaaludes.

They pried the lids off the rest of the drums. We found drums of amphetamines, of Nembutals, of Valium. All sorts of things.

With the discovery of the drugs a lot more police returned to the scene. With them came the television camera crews.

In all the activity no one seemed concerned about me, so I slipped back to my own house and locked the door. From time to time I peeked out the curtains. I saw reporters interviewing the neighbors. Hal was there, and seemed to be having a good time. Twice crews knocked on my door, but I didn't answer. Eventually they went away.

I ran a hot bath and soaked in it for about an hour. Then I turned the heat up as high as it would go and got in bed, under the blankets.

I shivered all night.

Osborne came over about nine the next morning. I let him in. Hal followed, looking very unhappy. I realized they had been up all night. I poured coffee for them.

"You'd better read this first," Osborne said, and handed me the sheet of computer printout. I unfolded it, got out my glasses, and started to read.

It was in that awful dot-matrix printing. My policy is to throw any such trash into the fireplace, un-read, but I made an exception this time.

It was Kluge's will. Some probate court was going to have a lot of fun with it.

He stated again that he didn't exist, so he could have no relatives. He had decided to give all his worldly property to somebody who deserved it.

But who was deserving? Kluge wondered. Well, not Mr. and Mrs. Perkins, four houses down the street. They were child abusers. He cited court records in Buffalo and Miami, and a pending case locally.

Mrs. Radnor and Mrs. Polonski, who lived across the street from each other five houses down, were gossips.

The Andersons' oldest son was a car thief.

Marian Flores cheated on her high school algebra tests.

There was a guy nearby who was diddling the city on a freeway construction project. There was one wife in the neighborhood who made out with door-to-door salesmen, and two having affairs with men other than their husbands. There was a teenage boy who got his girl-friend pregnant, dropped her, and bragged about it to his friends.

There were no fewer than nineteen couples in the immediate area who had not reported income to the IRS, or who padded their deductions.

Kluge's neighbors in back had a dog that barked all night.

Well, I could vouch for the dog. He'd kept me awake often enough. But the rest of it was *crazy!* For one thing, where did a guy with two hundred gallons of illegal narcotics get the right to judge his neighbors so harshly? I mean, the child abusers were one thing, but was it right to tar a whole family because their son stole cars? And for another . . . how did he *know* some of this stuff?

But there was more. Specifically, four philandering husbands. One was Harold "Hal" Lanier, who for three years had been seeing a woman named Toni Jones, a co-worker at the L.A.P.D. Data Process-ing facility. She was pressuring him for a divorce; he was "waiting for the right time to tell his wife."

I glanced up at Hal. His red face was all the confirmation I needed.

Then it hit me. What had Kluge found out about *me?*

I hurried down the page, searching for my name. I found it in the last paragraph.

". . . for thirty years Mr. Apfel has been paying for a mistake he did not even make. I won't go so far as to nominate him for sainthood, but by default—if for no other reason—I hereby leave all deed and title to my real property and the structure thereon to Victor Apfel."

I looked at Osborne, and those tired eyes were weighing me.

"But I don't *want* it!"

"Do you think this is the reward Kluge mentioned in the phone call?"

"It must be," I said. "What else could it be?"

Osborne sighed, and sat back in his chair. "At least he didn't try to leave you the drugs. Are you still saying you didn't know the guy?"

"Are you accusing me of something?"

He spread his hands. "Mister Apfel, I'm simply asking a question. You're never one hundred per cent sure in a suicide. Maybe it was a murder. If it was, you can see that, so far, you're the only one we know of that's gained by it."

"He was almost a stranger to me."

He nodded, tapping his copy of the computer printout. I looked back at my own, wishing it would go away.

"What's this . . . mistake you didn't make?"

I was afraid that would be the next question.

"I was a prisoner of war in North Korea," I said.

Osborne chewed that over a while.

"They brainwash you?"

"Yes." I hit the arm of my chair, and suddenly had to be up and moving. The room was getting cold. "No. I don't . . . there's been a lot of confusion about the word. Did they 'brainwash' me? Yes. Did they succeed? Did I offer a confession of my war crimes and denounce the U.S. Government? No."

Once more, I felt myself being inspected by those deceptively tired eyes.

"You still seem to have . . . strong feelings about it."

"It's not something you forget."

"Is there anything you want to say about it?"

"It's just that it was all so . . . no. No, I have nothing further to say. Not to you, not to anybody."

"I'm going to have to ask you more questions about Kluge's death."

"I think I'll have my lawyer present for those." Christ. Now I was going to have to get a lawyer. I didn't know where to begin.

Osborne just nodded again. He got up and went to the door.

"I was ready to write this one down as a suicide," he said. "The only thing that bothered me was there was no note. Now we've got a note." He gestured in the direction of Kluge's house, and started to look angry.

"This guy not only writes a note, he programs the fucking thing into his computer, complete with special effects straight out of Pac-Man.

"Now, I know people do crazy things. I've seen enough of them. But when I heard the computer playing a hymn, that's when I knew this was murder. Tell you the truth, Mr. Apfel, I don't think you did it. There must be two dozen motives for murder in that printout. Maybe he was blackmailing people around here. Maybe that's how he bought all those machines. And people with that amount of drugs usually die violently. I've got a lot of work to do on this one, and I'll find who did it." He mumbled something about not leaving town, and that he'd see me later, and left.

"Vic . . ." Hal said. I looked at him.

"About that printout," he finally said. "I'd appreciate it . . . well, they said they'd keep it confidential. If you know what I mean." He had eyes like a basset hound. I'd never noticed that before.

"Hal, if you'll just go home, you have nothing to worry about from me."

He nodded, and scuttled for the door.

"I don't think any of that will get out," he said.

It all did, of course.

It probably would have even without the letters that began arriving a few days after Kluge's death, all postmarked Trenton, New Jersey, all computer-generated from a machine no one was ever able to trace. The letters detailed the matters Kluge had mentioned in his will.

I didn't know about any of that at the time. I spent the rest of the day after Hal's departure lying in my bed, under the electric blanket. I couldn't get my feet warm. I got up only to soak in the tub or to make a sandwich.

Reporters knocked on the door but I didn't answer. On the second day I called a criminal lawyer—Martin Abrams, the first in the book— and retained him. He told me they'd probably call me down to the police station for questioning. I told him I wouldn't go, popped two Dilantin, and sprinted for the bed.

A couple of times I heard sirens in the neighborhood. Once I heard a shouted argument down the street. I resisted the temptation to look. I'll admit I was a little curious, but you know what happened to the cat.

I kept waiting for Osborne to return, but he didn't. The days turned into a week. Only two things of interest happened in that time.

The first was a knock on my door. This was two days after Kluge's death. I looked through the curtains and saw a silver Ferrari parked at the curb. I couldn't see who was on the porch, so I asked who it was.

"My name's Lisa Foo," she said. "You asked me to drop by."

"I certainly don't remember it."

"Isn't this Charles Kluge's house?"

"That's next door."

"Oh. Sorry."

I decided I ought to warn her Kluge was dead, so I opened the door. She turned around and smiled at me. It was blinding.

Where does one start in describing Lisa Foo? Remember when newspapers used to run editorial cartoons of Hirohito and Tojo, when the *Times* used the word "Jap" without embarrassment? Little guys with faces wide as footballs, ears like jug handles, thick glasses, two big rabbity buck teeth, and pencil-thin moustaches . . .

Leaving out only the moustache, she was a dead ringer for a cartoon Tojo. She had the glasses, and the ears, and the teeth. But her teeth had braces, like piano keys wrapped in barbed wire. And she was five-eight or five-nine and couldn't have weighed more than a hundred and ten. I'd have said a hundred, but added five pounds for each of her breasts, so improbably large on her scrawny frame that all I could read of the message on her T-shirt was "POCK LIVE."

It was only when she turned sideways that I saw the esses before and after.

She thrust out a slender hand.

"Looks like I'm going to be your neighbor for a while," she said. "At least until we get that dragon's lair next door straightened out." If she had an accent, it was San Fernando Valley.

"That's nice."

"Did you know him? Kluge, I mean. Or at least that's what he called himself."

"You don't think that was his name?"

"I doubt it. 'Kluge' means clever in German. And it's hacker slang for being tricky. And he sure was a tricky bugger. Definitely some glitches in the wetware." She tapped the side of her head meaningfully. "Viruses and phantoms and demons jumping out every time they try to key in, software rot, bit buckets overflowing onto the floor . . ."

She babbled on in that vein for a time. It might as well have been Swahili.

"Did you say there were demons in his computers?"

"That's right."

"Sounds like they need an exorcist."

She jerked her thumb at her chest and showed me another half-acre of teeth.

"That's me. Listen, I gotta go. Drop in and see me anytime."

The second interesting event of the week happened the next day. My bank statement arrived. There were three deposits listed. The first was the regular check from the V.A., for $487.00. The second was for

$392.54, interest on the money my parents had left me fifteen years ago.

The third deposit had come in on the twentieth, the day Charles Kluge died. It was for $700,083.04.

A few days later Hal Lanier dropped by.

"Boy, what a week," he said. Then he flopped down on the couch and told me all about it.

There had been a second death on the block. The letters had stirred up a lot of trouble, especially with the police going house to house questioning everyone. Some people had confessed to things when they were sure the cops were closing in on them. The woman who used to entertain salesmen while her husband was at work had admitted her infidelity, and the guy had shot her. He was in the County Jail. That was the worst incident, but there had been others, from fist-fights to rocks thrown through windows. According to Hal, the IRS was thinking of setting up a branch office in the neighborhood, so many people were being audited.

I thought about the seven hundred thousand and eighty-three dollars.

And four cents.

I didn't say anything, but my feet were getting cold.

"I suppose you want to know about me and Betty," he said, at last. I didn't. I didn't want to hear *any* of this, but I tried for a sympathetic expression.

"That's all over," he said, with a satisfied sigh. "Between me and Toni, I mean. I told Betty all about it. It was real bad for a few days, but I think our marriage is stronger for it now." He was quiet for a moment, basking in the warmth of it all. I had kept a straight face under worse provocation, so I trust I did well enough then.

He wanted to tell me all they'd learned about Kluge, and he wanted to invite me over for dinner, but I begged off on both, telling him my war wounds were giving me hell. I just about had him to the door when Osborne knocked on it. There was nothing to do but let him in. Hal stuck around, too.

I offered Osborne coffee, which he gratefully accepted. He looked different. I wasn't sure what it was at first. Same old tired expression . . . no, it wasn't. Most of that weary look had been either an act or a cop's built-in cynicism. Today it was genuine. The tiredness had moved from his face to his shoulders, to his hands, to the way he walked and the way he slumped in the chair. There was a sour aura of defeat around him.

"Am I still a suspect?" I asked.

"You mean should you call your lawyer? I'd say don't bother. I checked you out pretty good. That will ain't gonna hold up, so your motive is pretty half-assed. Way I figure it, every coke dealer in the Marina had a better reason to snuff Kluge than you." He sighed. "I got a couple questions. You can answer them or not."

"Give it a try."

"You remember any unusual visitors he had? People coming and going at night?"

"The only visitors I ever recall were deliveries. Post Office, Federal Express, freight companies . . . that sort of thing. I suppose the drugs could have come in any of those shipments."

"That's what we figure, too. There's no way he was dealing nickel and dime bags. He must have been a middle man. Ship it in, ship it out." He brooded about that for a while, and sipped his coffee.

"So are you making any progress?" I asked.

"You want to know the truth? The case is going in the toilet. We've got too many motives, and not a one of them that works. As far as we can tell, nobody on the block had the slightest idea Kluge had all that information. We've checked bank accounts and we can't find evidence of blackmail. So the neighbors are pretty much out of the picture. Though if he were alive, most people around here would like to kill him now."

"Damn straight," Hal said.

Osborne slapped his thigh. "If the bastard was alive, *I'd* kill him," he said. "But I'm beginning to think he never was alive."

"I don't understand."

"If I hadn't seen the goddamn body . . ." He sat up a little straighter. "He said he didn't exist. Well, he practically didn't. PG&E never heard of him. He's hooked up to their lines and a meter reader came by every month, but they never billed him for a single kilowatt. Same with the phone company. He had a whole exchange in that house that was *made* by the phone company, and delivered by them, and installed by them, but they have no record of him. We talked to the guy who hooked it all up. He turned in his records, and the computer swallowed them. Kluge didn't have a bank account anywhere in California, and apparently he didn't need one. We've tracked down a hundred companies that sold things to him, shipped them out, and then either marked his account paid or forgot they ever sold him anything. Some of them have check numbers and account numbers in their books, for accounts or even *banks* that don't exist."

He leaned back in his chair, simmering at the perfidy of it all.

"The only guy we've found who ever heard of him was the guy who delivered his groceries once a month. Little store down on Sepulveda. They don't have a computer, just paper receipts. He paid by check. Wells Fargo accepted them and the checks never bounced. But Wells Fargo never heard of him."

I thought it over. He seemed to expect something of me at this point, so I made a stab at it.

"He was doing all this by computers?"

"That's right. Now, the grocery store scam I can understand, almost. But more often than not, Kluge got right into the basic programming of the computers and wiped himself out. The power company was never paid, by check or any other way, because as far as they were concerned, they weren't selling him anything.

"No government agency has ever heard of him. We've checked him with everybody from the Post Office to the CIA."

"Kluge was probably an alias, right?" I offered.

"Yeah. But the FBI doesn't have his fingerprints. We'll find out who he was, eventually. But it doesn't get us any closer to whether or not he was murdered."

He admitted there was pressure to simply close the felony part of the case, label it suicide, and forget it. But Osborne would not believe it. Naturally, the civil side would go on for some time, as they attempted to track down all Kluge's deceptions.

"It's all up to the dragon lady," Osborne said. Hal snorted.

"Fat chance," Hal said, and muttered something about boat people.

"That girl? She's still over there? Who is she?"

"She's some sort of giant brain from Cal Tech. We called out there and told them we were having problems, and she's what they sent." It was clear from Osborne's face what he thought of any help she might provide.

I finally managed to get rid of them. As they went down the walk I looked over at Kluge's house. Sure enough, Lisa Foo's silver Ferrari was sitting in his driveway.

I had no business going over there. I knew that better than anyone.

So I set about preparing my evening meal. I made a tuna casserole—which is not as bland as it sounds, the way I make it—put it in the oven and went out to the garden to pick the makings for a salad. I was slicing cherry tomatoes and thinking about chilling a bottle of white wine when it occurred to me that I had enough for two.

Since I never do anything hastily, I sat down and thought it over for a while. What finally decided me was my feet. For the first time in a week, they were warm. So I went to Kluge's house.

The front door was standing open. There was no screen. Funny how disturbing that can look, the dwelling wide open and unguarded. I stood on the porch and leaned in, but all I could see was the hallway.

"Miss Foo?" I called. There was no answer.

The last time I'd been here I had found a dead man. I hurried in.

Lisa Foo was sitting on a piano bench before a computer console. She was in profile, her back very straight, her brown legs in lotus position, her fingers poised at the keys as words sprayed rapidly onto the screen in front of her. She looked up and flashed her teeth at me.

"Somebody told me your name was Victor Apfel," she said.

"Yes. Uh, the door was open . . ."

"It's hot," she said, reasonably, pinching the fabric of her shirt near her neck and lifting it up and down like you do when you're sweaty. "What can I do for you?"

"Nothing, really." I came into the dimness, and stumbled on something. It was a cardboard box, the large flat kind used for delivering a jumbo pizza.

"I was just fixing dinner, and it looks like there's plenty for two, so I was wondering if you . . ." I trailed off, as I had just noticed something else. I had thought she was wearing shorts. In fact, all she had on was the shirt and a pair of pink bikini underpants. This did not seem to make her uneasy.

". . . would you like to join me for dinner?"

Her smile grew even broader.

"I'd love to," she said. She effortlessly unwound her legs and bounced to her feet, then brushed past me, trailing the smells of perspiration and sweet soap. "Be with you in a minute."

I looked around the room again but my mind kept coming back to her. She liked Pepsi with her pizza; there were dozens of empty cans. There was a deep scar on her knee and upper thigh. The ashtrays were empty . . . and the long muscles of her calves bunched strongly as she walked. Kluge must have smoked, but Lisa didn't, and she had fine, downy hairs in the small of her back just visible in the green computer light. I heard water running in the bathroom sink, looked at a yellow notepad covered with the kind of penmanship I hadn't seen in decades, and smelled soap and remembered tawny brown skin and an easy stride.

She appeared in the hall, wearing cut-off jeans, sandals and a new T-shirt. The old one had advertised BURROUGHS OFFICE SYS-TEMS. This one featured Mickey Mouse and Snow White's Castle and smelled of fresh bleached cotton. Mickey's ears were laid back on the upper slopes of her incongruous breasts.

I followed her out the door. Tinkerbell twinkled in pixie dust from the back of her shirt.

"I like this kitchen," she said.

You don't really look at a place until someone says something like that.

The kitchen was a time capsule. It could have been lifted bodily from an issue of *Life* in the early fifties. There was the hump-shouldered Frigidaire, of a vintage when that word had been a generic term, like Xerox or Coke. The counter tops were yellow tile, the sort that's only found in bathrooms these days. There wasn't an ounce of Formica in the place. Instead of a dishwasher I had a wire rack and a double sink. There was no electric can opener, Cuisinart, trash compacter, or micro-wave oven. The newest thing in the whole room was a fifteen-year-old blender.

I'm good with my hands. I like to repair things.

"This bread is terrific," she said.

I had baked it myself. I watched her mop her plate with a crust, and she asked if she might have seconds.

I understand cleaning one's plate with bread is bad manners. Not that I cared; I do it myself. And other than that, her manners were im-peccable. She polished off three helpings of my casserole and when she was done the plate hardly needed washing. I had a sense of a rav-enous appetite barely held in check.

She settled back in her chair and I refilled her glass with white wine.

"Are you sure you wouldn't like some more peas?"

"I'd bust." She patted her stomach contentedly. "Thank you so much, Mister Apfel. I haven't had a home-cooked meal in ages."

"You can call me Victor."

"I just love American food."

"I didn't know there was such a thing. I mean, not like Chinese or . . . you *are* American, aren't you?" She just smiled. "What I meant—"

"I know what you meant, Victor. I'm a citizen, but not native-born. Would you excuse me for a moment? I know it's impolite to jump right up, but with these braces I find I have to brush *instantly* after eating."

I could hear her as I cleared the table. I ran water in the sink and started doing the dishes. Before long she joined me, grabbed a dish towel, and began drying the things in the rack, over my protests.

"You live alone here?" she asked.

"Yes. Have ever since my parents died."

"Ever married? If it's none of my business, just say so."

"That's all right. No. I never married."

"You do pretty good for not having a woman around."

"I've had a lot of practice. Can I ask you a question?"

"Shoot."

"Where are you from? Taiwan?"

"I have a knack for languages. Back home, I spoke pidgen American, but when I got here I cleaned up my act. I also speak rotten French, illiterate Chinese in four or five varieties, gutter Vietnamese, and enough Thai to holler 'Me wanna see American Consul, pretty-damn-quick, you!'"

I laughed. When she said it, her accent was thick.

"I been here eight years now. You figured out where home is?"

"Vietnam?" I ventured.

"The sidewalks of Saigon, fer shure. Or Ho Chi Minh's Shitty, as the pajama-heads renamed it, may their dinks rot off and their buns be filled with jagged punjee-sticks. Pardon my French."

She ducked her head in embarrassment. What had started out light had turned hot very quickly. I sensed a hurt at least as deep as my own, and we both backed off from it.

"I took you for a Japanese," I said.

"Yeah, ain't it a pisser? I'll tell you about it some day. Victor, is that a laundry room through that door there? With an electric washer?"

"That's right."

"Would it be too much trouble if I did a load?"

                              ❄   ❄   ❄

It was no trouble at all. She had seven pairs of faded jeans, some with the legs cut away, and about two dozen T-shirts. It could have been a load of boys' clothing except for the frilly underwear.

We went into the back yard to sit in the last rays of the setting sun, then she had to see my garden. I'm quite proud of it. When I'm well, I spend four or five hours a day working out there, year-round, usually in the morning hours. You can do that in southern California. I have a greenhouse I built myself.

She loved it, though it was not in its best shape. I had spent most of the week in bed or in the tub. As a result, weeds were sprouting here and there.

"We had a garden when I was little," she said. "And I spent two years in a rice paddy."

"That must be a lot different than this."

"Damn straight. Put me off rice for *years*."

She discovered an infestation of aphids, so we squatted down to pick them off. She had that double-jointed Asian peasant's way of sitting that I remembered so well and could never imitate. Her fingers were long and narrow, and soon the tips of them were green from squashed bugs.

We talked about this and that. I don't remember quite how it came up, but I told her I had fought in Korea. I learned she was twenty-five. It turned out we had the same birthday, so some months back I had been exactly twice her age.

The only time Kluge's name came up was when she mentioned how she liked to cook. She hadn't been able to at Kluge's house.

"He has a freezer in the garage full of frozen dinners," she said. "He had one plate, one fork, one spoon, and one glass. He's got the best microwave oven on the market. And that's *it,* man. Ain't nothing else in his kitchen at *all*." She shook her head, and executed an aphid. "He was one weird dude."

When her laundry was done it was late evening, almost dark. She loaded it into my wicker basket and we took it out to the clothesline. It got to be a game. I would shake out a T-shirt and study the picture or message there. Sometimes I got it, and sometimes I didn't. There were pictures of rock groups, a map of Los Angeles, Star Trek tie-ins . . . a little of everything.

"What's the L5 Society?" I asked her.

"Guys that want to build these great big farms in space. I asked 'em if they were gonna grow rice, and they said they didn't think it was the best crop for zero gee, so I bought the shirt."

"How many of these things do you have?"

"Wow, it's gotta be four or five hundred. I usually wear 'em two or three times and then put them away."

I picked up another shirt, and a bra fell out. It wasn't the kind of bra girls wore when I was growing up. It was very sheer, though somehow functional at the same time.

"You like, Yank?" Her accent was very thick. "You oughtta see my sister!"

I glanced at her, and her face fell.

"I'm sorry, Victor," she said. "You don't have to blush." She took the bra from me and clipped it to the line.

She must have misread my face. True, I had been embarrassed, but I was also pleased in some strange way. It had been a long time since anybody had called me anything but Victor or Mr. Apfel.

The next day's mail brought a letter from a law firm in Chicago. It was about the seven hundred thousand dollars. The money had come from a Delaware holding company which had been set up in 1933 to provide for me in my old age. My mother and father were listed as the founders. Certain long-term investments had matured, resulting in my recent windfall. The amount in my bank was *after* taxes.

It was ridiculous on the face of it. My parents had never had that kind of money. I didn't want it. I would have given it back if I could find out who Kluge had stolen it from.

I decided that, if I wasn't in jail this time next year, I'd give it all to some charity. Save The Whales, maybe, or the L5 Society.

I spent the morning in the garden. Later I walked to the market and bought some fresh ground beef and pork. I was feeling good as I pulled my purchases home in my fold-up wire basket. When I passed the silver Ferrari I smiled.

She hadn't come to get her laundry. I took it off the line and folded it, then knocked on Kluge's door.

"It's me. Victor."

"Come on in, Yank."

She was where she had been before, but decently dressed this time. She smiled at me, then hit her forehead when she saw the laundry basket. She hurried to take it from me.

"I'm sorry, Victor. I meant to get this—"

"Don't worry about it," I said. "It was no trouble. And it gave me the chance to ask if you'd like to dine with me again."

Something happened to her face which she covered quickly. Perhaps she didn't like "American" food as much as she professed to. Or maybe it was the cook.

"Sure, Victor, I'd love to. Let me take care of this. And why don't you open those drapes? It's like a tomb in here."

She hurried away. I glanced at the screen she had been using. It was blank, but for one word: intercourse-p. I assumed it was a typo.

I pulled the drapes open in time to see Osborne's car park at the curb. Then Lisa was back, wearing a new T-shirt. This one said A CHANGE OF HOBBIT, and had a picture of a squat, hairy-footed creature. She glanced out the window and saw Osborne coming up the walk.

"I say, Watson," she said. "It's Lestrade of the Yard. Do show him in."

That wasn't nice of her. He gave me a suspicious glance as he entered. I burst out laughing. Lisa sat on the piano bench, pokerfaced. She slumped indolently, one arm resting near the keyboard.

"Well, Apfel," Osborne started. "We've finally found out who Kluge really was."

"Patrick William Gavin," Lisa said.

Quite a time went by before Osborne was able to close his mouth. Then he opened it right up again.

"How the hell did you find that out?"

She lazily caressed the keyboard beside her.

"Well, of course I got it when it came into your office this morning. There's a little stoolie program tucked away in your computer that whispers in my ear every time the name Kluge is mentioned. But I didn't need that. I figured it out five days ago."

"Then why the . . . why didn't you tell me?"

"You didn't ask me."

They glared at each other for a while. I had no idea what events had led up to this moment, but it was quite clear they didn't like each other even a little bit. Lisa was on top just now, and seemed to be enjoying it. Then she glanced at her screen, looked surprised, and quickly tapped a key. The word that had been there vanished. She gave me an inscrutable glance, then faced Osborne again.

"If you recall, you brought me in because all your own guys were getting was a lot of crashes. This system was brain-damaged when I got here, practically catatonic. Most of it was down and your guys couldn't get it up." She had to grin at that.

"You decided I couldn't do any worse than your guys were doing. So you asked me to try and break Kluge's codes without frying the system. Well, I did it. All you had to do was come by and interface and I would have downloaded N tons of wallpaper right in your lap."

Osborne listened quietly. Maybe he even knew he had made a mistake.

"What did you get? Can I see it now?"

She nodded, and pressed a few keys. Words started to fill her screen, and one close to Osborne. I got up and read Lisa's terminal.

It was a brief bio of Kluge/Gavin. He was about my age, but while I was getting shot at in a foreign land, he was cutting a swath through the infant computer industry. He had been there from the ground up, working at many of the top research facilities. It surprised me that it had taken over a week to identify him.

"I compiled this anecdotally," Lisa said, as we read. "The first thing you have to realize about Gavin is that he exists nowhere in any computerized information system. So I called people all over the country—interesting phone system he's got, by the way; it generates a new number for each call, and you can't call back or trace it—and started asking who the top people were in the fifties and sixties. I got a lot of names. After that, it was a matter of finding out who no longer existed in the files. He faked his death in 1967. I located one account of it in a newspaper file. Everybody I talked to who had known him knew of his death. There is a paper birth certificate in Florida. That's the only other evidence I found of him. He was the only guy so many people in the field knew who left no mark on the world. That seemed conclusive to me."

Osborne finished reading, then looked up.

"All right, Ms. Foo. What else have you found out?"

"I've broken some of his codes. I had a piece of luck, getting into a basic rape-and-plunder program he'd written to attack *other* people's programs, and I've managed to use it against a few of his own. I've unlocked a file of passwords with notes on where they came from. And I've learned a few of his tricks. But it's the tip of the iceberg."

She waved a hand at the silent metal brains in the room.

"What I haven't gotten across to anyone is just what this *is*. This is the most devious electronic weapon ever devised. It's armored like a battleship. It has to be; there's a lot of very slick programs out there that grab an invader and hang on like a terrier. If they ever got this far Kluge could deflect them. But usually they never even knew they'd been burgled. Kluge'd come in like a cruise missile, low and fast and twisty. And he'd route his attack through a dozen cut-offs.

"He had a lot of advantages. Big systems these days are heavily protected. People use passwords and very sophisticated codes. But Kluge helped *invent* most of them. You need a damn good lock to keep out a locksmith. He helped install a lot of the major systems. He left informants behind, hidden in the software. If the codes were changed, the computer *itself* would send the information to a safe system that Kluge could tap later. It's like you buy the biggest, meanest, best-trained watchdog you can. And that night, the guy who *trained* the dog comes in, pats him on the head, and robs you blind."

There was a lot more in that vein. I'm afraid that when Lisa began talking about computers, ninety percent of my head shut off.

"I'd like to know something, Osborne," Lisa said.

"What would that be?"

"What is my status here? Am I supposed to be solving your crime for you, or just trying to get this system back to where a competent user can deal with it?"

Osborne thought it over.

"What worries me," she added, "is that I'm poking around in a lot of restricted data banks. I'm worried about somebody knocking on the door and handcuffing me. *You* ought to be worried, too. Some of these agencies wouldn't like a homicide cop looking into their affairs."

Osborne bridled at that. Maybe that's what she intended.

"What do I have to do?" he snarled. "Beg you to stay?"

"No. I just want your authorization. You don't have to put it in writing. Just say you're behind me."

"Look. As far as L.A. County and the State of California are concerned, this house doesn't exist. There is no lot here. It doesn't appear in the tax assessor's records. This place is in a legal limbo. If anybody can authorize you to use this stuff, it's me, because I believe a murder was committed in it. So you just keep doing what you've been doing."

"That's not much of a commitment," she mused.

"It's all you're going to get. Now, what else have you got?"

She turned to her keyboard and typed for a while. Pretty soon a printer started, and Lisa leaned back. I glanced at her screen. It said: osculate posterior-p. I remembered that osculate meant kiss. Well, these people have their own language. Lisa looked up at me and grinned.

"Not you," she said, quietly. *"Him."*

I hadn't the faintest notion of what she was talking about.

Osborne got his printout and was ready to leave. Again, he couldn't resist turning at the door for final orders.

"If you find anything to indicate he didn't commit suicide, let me know."

"Okay. He didn't commit suicide."

Osborne didn't understand for a moment.

"I want proof."

"Well, I have it, but you probably can't use it. He didn't write that ridiculous suicide note."

"How do you know that?"

"I knew my first day here. I had the computer list the program. Then I compared it to Kluge's style. No *way* he could have written it. It's tighter'n a bug's ass. Not a spare line in it. Kluge didn't pick his alias for nothing. You know what it means?"

"Clever," I said.

"Literally. But it means . . . a Rube Goldberg device. Something overly complex. Something that works, but for the wrong reason. You 'kluge around' bugs in a program. It's the hacker's Vaseline."

"So?" Osborne wanted to know.

"So Kluge's programs were really crocked. They were full of bells and whistles he never bothered to clean out. He was a genius, and his programs worked, but you wonder why they did. Routines so bletcherous they'd make your skin crawl. Real crufty bagbiters. But good programming's so rare, even his diddles were better than most people's super-moby hacks."

I suspect Osborne understood about as much of that as I did.

"So you base your opinion on his programming style."

"Yeah. Unfortunately, it's gonna be ten years or so before that's admissable in court, like graphology or fingerprints."

We eventually got rid of him, and I went home to fix the dinner. Lisa joined me when it was ready. Once more she had a huge appetite.

I fixed lemonade and we sat on my small patio and watched evening gather around us.

＊　＊　＊

I woke up in the middle of the night, sweating. I sat up thinking it out, and I didn't like my conclusions. So I put on my robe and slippers and went over to Kluge's.

The front door was open again. I knocked anyway. Lisa stuck her head around the corner.

"Victor? is something wrong?"

"I'm not sure," I said. "May I come in?"

She gestured, and I followed her into the living room. An open can of Pepsi sat beside her console. Her eyes were red as she sat on her bench.

"What's up?" she said, and yawned.

"You should be asleep, for one thing," I said.

She shrugged, and nodded.

"Yeah. I can't seem to get in the right phase. Just now I'm in day mode. But Victor, I'm used to working odd hours, and long hours, and you didn't come over here to lecture me about that, did you?"

"No. You say Kluge was murdered."

"He didn't write his suicide note. That seems to leave murder."

"I was wondering why someone would kill him. He never left the house, so it was for something he did here with his computers. And now you're . . . well, I don't know *what* you're doing, frankly, but you seem to be poking into the same things. Isn't there a danger the same people will come after you?"

"People?" She raised an eyebrow.

I felt helpless. My fears were not well-formed enough to make sense.

"I don't know . . . you mentioned agencies . . ."

"You notice how impressed Osborne was with that? You think there's some kind of conspiracy Kluge tumbled to, or you think the CIA killed him because he found out too much about something, or . . ."

"I don't know, Lisa. But I'm worried the same thing could happen to you."

Surprisingly, she smiled at me.

"Thank you so much, Victor. I wasn't going to admit it to Osborne, but I've been worried about that, too."

"Well, what are you going to do?"

"I want to stay here and keep working. So I gave some thought to what I could do to protect myself. I decided there wasn't anything."

"Surely there's something."

"Well, I got a gun, if that's what you mean. But think about it. Kluge was offed in the middle of the day. Nobody saw anybody enter or leave the house. So I asked myself, who can walk into a house in broad daylight, shoot Kluge, program that suicide note, and walk away, leaving no traces he'd ever been there?"

"Somebody very good."

"Goddamn good. So good there's not much chance one little gook's gonna be able to stop him if he decides to waste her."

She shocked me, both by her words and by her apparent lack of concern for her own fate. But she had said she was worried.

"Then you have to stop this. Get out of here."

"I won't be pushed around that way," she said. There was a tone of finality to it. I thought of things I might say, and rejected them all.

"You could at least . . . lock your front door," I concluded, lamely.

She laughed, and kissed my cheek.

"I'll do that, Yank. And I appreciate your concern. I really do."

I watched her close the door behind me, listened to her lock it, then trudged through the moonlight toward my house. Halfway there I stopped. I could suggest she stay in my spare bedroom. I could offer to stay with her at Kluge's.

No, I decided. She would probably take that the wrong way.

I was back in bed before I realized, with a touch of chagrin and more than a little disgust at myself, that she had every reason to take it the wrong way.

And me exactly twice her age.

I spent the morning in the garden, planning the evening's menu. I have always liked to cook, but dinner with Lisa had rapidly become the high point of my day. Not only that, I was already taking it for granted. So it hit me hard, around noon, when I looked out the front and saw her car gone.

I hurried to Kluge's front door. It was standing open. I made a quick search of the house. I found nothing until the master bedroom, where her clothes were stacked neatly on the floor.

Shivering, I pounded on the Laniers' front door. Betty answered, and immediately saw my agitation.

"The girl at Kluge's house," I said. "I'm afraid something's wrong. Maybe we'd better call the police."

"What happened?" Betty asked, looking over my shoulder. "Did she call you? I see she's not back yet."

"Back?"

"I saw her drive away about an hour ago. That's quite a car she has."

Feeling like a fool, I tried to make nothing of it, but I caught a look in Betty's eye. I think she'd have liked to pat me on the head. It made me furious.

But she'd left her clothes, so surely she was coming back.

I kept telling myself that, then went to run a bath, as hot as I could stand it.

When I answered the door she was standing there with a grocery bag in each arm and her usual blinding smile on her face.

"I wanted to do this yesterday but I forgot until you came over, and I know I should have asked first, but then I wanted to surprise you, so I just went to get one or two items you didn't have in your garden and a couple of things that weren't in your spice rack . . ."

She kept talking as we unloaded the bags in the kitchen. I said nothing. She was wearing a new T-shirt. There was a big V, and under it a picture of a screw, followed by a hyphen and a small-case "p." I thought it over as she babbled on. V, screw-p. I was determined not to ask what it meant.

"Do you like Vietnamese cooking?"

I looked at her, and finally realized she was very nervous.

"I don't know," I said. "I've never had it. But I like Chinese, and Japanese, and Indian. I like to try new things." The last part was a lie, but not as bad as it might have been. I do try new recipes, and my tastes in food are catholic. I didn't expect to have much trouble with southeast Asian cuisine.

"Well, when I get through you *still* won't know," she laughed. "My momma was half-Chinese. So what you're gonna get here is a mongrel meal." She glanced up, saw my face, and laughed.

"I forgot. You've been to Asia. No, Yank. I ain't gonna serve any dog meat."

There was only one intolerable thing, and that was the chopsticks. I used them for as long as I could, then put them aside and got a fork.

"I'm sorry," I said. "Chopsticks happen to be a problem for me."

"You use them very well."

"I had plenty of time to learn how."

It was very good, and I told her so. Each dish was a revelation, not quite like anything I had ever had. Toward the end, I broke down halfway.

"Does the V stand for victory?" I asked.

"Maybe."

"Beethoven? Churchill? World War Two?"

She just smiled.

"Think of it as a challenge, Yank."

"Do I frighten you, Victor?"

"You did at first."

"It's my face, isn't it?"

"It's a generalized phobia of Orientals. I suppose I'm a racist. Not because I want to be."

She nodded slowly, there in the dark. We were on the patio again, but the sun had gone down a long time ago. I can't recall what we had talked about for all those hours. It had kept us busy, anyway.

"I have the same problem," she said.

"Fear of Orientals?" I had meant it as a joke.

"Of Cambodians." She let me take that in for a while, then went on. "I fled to Cambodia when Saigon fell. I walked across it. I'm lucky to be alive really. They had me in labor camps."

"I thought they called it Kampuchea now."

She spat. I'm not even sure she was aware she had done it.

"It's the People's Republic of Syphilitic Dogs. The North Koreans treated you very badly, didn't they, Victor?"

"That's right."

"Koreans are pus suckers." I must have looked surprised, because she chuckled.

"You Americans feel so guilty about racism. As if you had invented it and nobody else—except maybe the South Africans and the Nazis—had ever practiced it as heinously as you. And you can't tell one yellow face from another, so you think of the yellow races as one homogeneous block. When in fact Orientals are among the most racist peoples on the earth. The Vietnamese have hated the Cambodians for a thousand years. The Chinese hate the Japanese. The Koreans hate everybody. And *everybody* hates the 'ethnic Chinese.' The Chinese are the Jews of the east."

"I've heard that."

She nodded, lost in her own thoughts.

"And I hate all Cambodians," she said, at last. "Like you, I don't wish to. Most of the people who suffered in the camps were Cambodians. It was the genocidal leaders, the Pol Pot scum, who I should hate." She looked at me. "But sometimes we don't get a lot of choice about things like that, do we, Yank?"

The next day I visited her at noon. It had cooled down, but was still warm in her dark den. She had not changed her shirt.

She told me a few things about computers. When she let me try some things on the keyboard I quickly got lost. We decided I needn't plan on a career as a computer programmer.

One of the things she showed me was called a telephone modem, whereby she could reach other computers all over the world. She "interfaced" with someone at Stanford whom she had never met, and who she knew only as "Bubble Sorter." They typed things back and forth at each other.

At the end, Bubble Sorter wrote "bye-p." Lisa typed T.

"What's T?" I asked.

"True. Means yes, but yes would be too straightforward for a hacker."

"You told me what a byte is. What's a byep?"

She looked up at me seriously.

"It's a question. Add p to a word, and you make it a question. So bye-p means Bubble Sorter was asking if I wanted to log out. Sign off."

I thought that over.

"So how would you translate 'osculate posterior-p'?"

"'You wanna kiss my ass?' But remember, that was for Osborne."

I looked at her T-shirt again, then up to her eyes, which were quite serious and serene. She waited, hands folded in her lap.

Intercourse-p.

"Yes," I said. "I would."

She put her glasses on the table and pulled her shirt over her head.

We made love in Kluge's big waterbed.

I had a certain amount of performance anxiety—it had been a long, *long* time. After that, I was so caught up in the touch and smell and taste of her that I went a little crazy. She didn't seem to mind.

At last we were done, and bathed in sweat. She rolled over, stood, and went to the window. She opened it, and a breath of air blew over me. Then she put one knee on the bed, leaned over me, and got a pack of cigarettes from the bedside table. She lit one.

"I hope you're not allergic to smoke," she said.

"No. My father smoked. But I didn't know you did."

"Only afterwards," she said, with a quick smile. She took a deep drag. "Everybody in Saigon smoked, I think." She stretched out on her back beside me and we lay like that, soaking wet, holding hands. She opened her legs so one of her bare feet touched mine. It seemed enough contact. I watched the smoke rise from her right hand.

"I haven't felt warm in thirty years," I said. "I've been hot, but I've never been warm. I feel warm now."

"Tell me about it," she said.

So I did, as much as I could, wondering if it would work this time. At thirty years' remove, my story does not sound so horrible. We've seen so much in that time. There were people in jails at that very moment, enduring conditions as bad as any I encountered. The paraphernalia of oppression is still pretty much the same. Nothing physical happened to me that would account for thirty years lived as a recluse.

"I *was* badly injured," I told her. "My skull was fractured. I still have . . . problems from that. Korea can get very cold, and I was never warm enough. But it was the other stuff. What they call brainwashing now.

"We didn't know what it was. We couldn't understand that even after a man had told them all he knew they'd keep on at us. Keeping us awake. Disorienting us. Some guys signed confessions, made up all sorts of stuff, but even that wasn't enough. They'd just keep on at you.

"I never did figure it out. I guess I couldn't understand an evil that big. But when they were sending us back and some of the prisoners wouldn't go . . . they really didn't *want* to go, they really believed . . ."

I had to pause there. Lisa sat up, moved quietly to the end of the bed, and began massaging my feet.

"We got a taste of what the Vietnam guys got, later. Only for us it was reversed. The G.I.'s were heroes, and the prisoners were . . ."

"You didn't break," she said. It wasn't a question.

"No, I didn't."

"That would be worse."

I looked at her. She had my foot pressed against her flat belly, holding me by the heel while her other hand massaged my toes.

"The country was shocked," I said. "They didn't understand what brainwashing was. I tried telling people how it was. I thought they were looking at me funny. After a while, I stopped talking about it. And I didn't have anything else to talk about.

"A few years back the Army changed its policy. Now they don't expect you to withstand psychological conditioning. It's understood you can say anything or sign anything."

She just looked at me, kept massaging my foot, and nodded slowly. Finally she spoke.

"Cambodia was hot," she said. "I kept telling myself when I finally got to the U.S. I'd live in Maine or someplace, where it snowed. And I did go to Cambridge, but I found out I didn't like snow."

She told me about it. The last I heard, a million people had died over there. It was a whole country frothing at the mouth and snapping at anything that moved. Or like one of those sharks you read about that, when its guts are ripped out, bends in a circle and starts devouring itself.

She told me about being forced to build a pyramid of severed heads. Twenty of them working all day in the hot sun finally got it ten feet high before it collapsed. If any of them stopped working, their own heads were added to the pile.

"It didn't mean anything to me. It was just another job. I was pretty crazy by then. I didn't start to come out of it until I got across the Thai border."

That she had survived it at all seemed a miracle. She had gone through more horror than I could imagine. And she had come through it in much better shape. It made me feel small. When I was her age, I was well on my way to building the prison I have lived in ever since. I told her that.

"Part of it is preparation," she said, wryly. "What you expect out of life, what your life has been so far. You said it yourself. Korea was new to you. I'm not saying I was ready for Cambodia, but my life up to that point hadn't been what you'd call sheltered. I hope you haven't been thinking I made a living in the streets by selling apples."

She kept rubbing my feet, staring off into scenes I could not see.

"How old were you when your mother died?"

"She was killed during Tet, 1968. I was ten."

"By the Viet Cong?"

"Who knows? Lot of bullets flying, lot of grenades being thrown."

She sighed, dropped my foot, and sat there, a scrawny Buddha without a robe.

"You ready to do it again, Yank?"

"I don't think I can, Lisa. I'm an old man."

She moved over me and lowered herself with her chin just below my sternum, settling her breasts in the most delicious place possible.

"We'll see," she said, and giggled. "There's an alternative sex act I'm pretty good at, and I'm pretty sure it would make you a young man again. But I haven't been able to do it for about a year on account of these." She tapped her braces. "It'd be sort of like sticking it in a buzz saw. So now I do this instead. I call it 'touring the silicone valley.'" She started moving her body up and down, just a few inches at a time. She blinked innocently a couple times, then laughed.

"At last, I can see you," she said. "I'm awfully myopic."

I let her do that for a while, then lifted my head.

"Did you say silicone?"

"Uh-huh. You didn't think they were real, did you?"

I confessed that I had.

"I don't think I've ever been so happy with anything I ever bought. Not even the car."

"Why did you?"

"Does it bother you?"

It didn't, and I told her so. But I couldn't conceal my curiosity.

"Because it was safe to. In Saigon I was always angry that I never developed. I could have made a good living as a prostitute, but I was always too tall, too skinny, and too ugly. Then in Cambodia I was lucky. I managed to pass for a boy some of the time. If not for that I'd have been raped a lot more than I was. And in Thailand I knew I'd get to the West one way or another, and when I got there, I'd get the best car there was, eat anything I wanted any time I wanted to, and purchase the best tits money could buy. You can't imagine what the West looks like from the camps. A place where you can buy tits!"

She looked down between them, then back at my face.

"Looks like it was a good investment," she said.

"They do seem to work okay," I had to admit.

We agreed that she would spend the nights at my house. There were certain things she had to do at Kluge's, involving equipment that had to be physically loaded, but many things she could do with a remote terminal and an armload of software. So we selected one of Kluge's best computers and about a dozen peripherals and installed her at a cafeteria table in my bedroom.

I guess we both knew it wasn't much protection if the people who got Kluge decided to get her. But I know I felt better about it, and I think she did, too.

The second day she was there a delivery van pulled up outside, and two guys started unloading a king-size waterbed. She laughed and laughed when she saw my face.

"Listen, you're not using Kluge's computers to—"

"Relax, Yank. How'd you think I could afford a Ferrari?"

"I've been curious."

"If you're really good at writing software you can make a lot of money. I own my own company. But every hacker picks up tricks here and there. I used to run a few Kluge scams, myself."

"But not anymore?"

She shrugged. "Once a thief, always a thief, Victor. I told you I couldn't make ends meet selling my bod."

Lisa didn't need much sleep.

We got up at seven, and I made breakfast every morning. Then we would spend an hour or two working in the garden. She would go to Kluge's and I'd bring her a sandwich at noon, then drop in on her several times during the day. That was for my own peace of mind; I never stayed more than a minute. Sometime during the afternoon I would shop or do household chores, then at seven one of us would cook dinner. We alternated. I taught her "American" cooking, and she taught me a little of everything. She complained about the lack of vital ingredients in American markets. No dogs, of course, but she claimed to know great ways of preparing monkey, snake, and rat. I never knew how hard she was pulling my leg, and didn't ask.

After dinner she stayed at my house. We would talk, make love, bathe.

She loved my tub. It is about the only alteration I have made in the house, and my only real luxury. I put it in—having to expand the bathroom to do so—in 1975, and never regretted it. We would soak for twenty minutes or an hour, turning the jets and bubblers on and off, washing each other, giggling like kids. Once we used bubble bath and made a mountain of suds four feet high, then destroyed it, splashing water all over the place. Most nights she let me wash her long black hair.

She didn't have any bad habits—or at least none that clashed with mine. She was neat and clean, changing her clothes twice a day and never so much as leaving a dirty glass on the sink. She never left a mess in the bathroom. Two glasses of wine was her limit.

I felt like Lazarus.

Osborne came by three times in the next two weeks. Lisa met him at Kluge's and gave him what she had learned. It was getting to be quite a list.

"Kluge once had an account in a New York bank with nine *trillion* dollars in it," she told me after one of Osborne's visits. "I think he did it just to see if he could. He left it in for one day, took the interest and fed it to a bank in the Bahamas, then destroyed the principal. Which never existed anyway."

In return, Osborne told her what was new on the murder investigation—which was nothing—and on the status of Kluge's property, which was chaotic. Various agencies had sent people out to look the place over. Some FBI men came, wanting to take over the investigation. Lisa, when talking about computers, had the power to cloud men's minds. She did it first by explaining exactly what she was doing, in terms so abstruse that no one could understand her. Sometimes that was enough. If it wasn't, if they started to get tough, she just moved out of the driver's seat and let them try to handle Kluge's contraption. She let them watch in horror as dragons leaped out of nowhere and ate up all the data on a disc, then printed "You Stupid Putz!" on the screen.

"I'm cheating them," she confessed to me. "I'm giving them stuff I *know* they're gonna step in, because I already stepped in it myself. I've lost about forty percent of the data Kluge had stored away. But the others lose a hundred percent. You ought to see their faces when Kluge drops a logic bomb into their work. That second guy threw a three thousand dollar printer clear across the room. Then tried to bribe me to be quiet about it."

When some Federal agency sent out an expert from Stanford, and he seemed perfectly content to destroy everything in sight in the firm belief that he was *bound* to get it right sooner or later, Lisa let him get tangled up in the Internal Revenue Service's computer. He couldn't get out, because some sort of watchdog program noticed him. During his struggles, it seemed he had erased all the tax records from the letter S down into the W's. Lisa let him think that for half an hour.

"I thought he was having a heart attack," she told me. "All the blood drained out of his face and he couldn't talk. So I showed him where I had—with my usual foresight—arranged for that data to be recorded, told him how to put it back where he found it, and how to pacify the watchdog. He couldn't get out of that house fast enough. Pretty soon he's gonna realize you *can't* destroy that much information with anything short of dynamite because of the backups and the limits of how much can be running at any one time. But I don't think he'll be back."

"It sounds like a very fancy video game," I said.

"It is, in a way. But it's more like Dungeons and Dragons. It's an endless series of closed rooms with dangers on the other side. You don't dare take it a step at a time. You take it a *hundredth* of a step at a time. Your questions are like, 'Now this isn't a question, but if it entered my mind to *ask* this question—which I'm not about to do—concerning what might happen if I looked at this door here—and I'm not touching it, I'm not even in the next room—what do you suppose you might do?' And the program crunches on that, decides if you fulfilled the conditions for getting a great big cream pie in the face, then either throws it or allows as how it *might* just move from step A to step A Prime. Then you say, 'Well, maybe I am looking at that door.' And sometimes the program says 'You looked, you looked, you dirty crook!' And the fireworks start."

Silly as all that sounds, it was very close to the best explanation she was ever able to give me about what she was doing.

"Are you telling him everything, Lisa?" I asked her.

"Well, not *every*thing. I didn't mention the four cents."

Four cents? Oh my god.

"Lisa, I didn't want that, I didn't ask for it, I wish he'd never—"

"Calm down, Yank. It's going to be all right."

"He kept records of all that, didn't he?"

"That's what I spend most of my time doing. Decoding his records."

"How long have you known?"

"About the seven hundred thousand dollars? It was in the first disc I cracked."

"I just want to give it back."

She thought that over, and shook her head.

"Victor, it'd be more dangerous to get rid of it now than it would be to keep it. It was imaginary money at first. But now it's got a history. The IRS thinks it knows where it came from. The taxes are paid on it. The State of Delaware is convinced that a legally chartered corporation disbursed it. An Illinois law firm has been paid for handling it. Your bank had been paying you interest on it. I'm not saying it would be impossible to go back and wipe all that out, but I wouldn't like to try. I'm good, but I don't have Kluge's touch."

"How could he *do* all that? You say it was imaginary money. That's not the way I thought money worked. He could just pull it out of thin air?"

Lisa patted the top of her computer console, and smiled at me.

"This is money, Yank," she said, and her eyes glittered.

At night she worked by candlelight so she wouldn't disturb me. That turned out to be my downfall. She typed by touch and needed the candle only to locate software.

So that's how I'd go to sleep every night, looking at her slender body bathed in the glow of the candle. I was always reminded of melting butter dripping down a roasted ear of corn. Golden light on golden skin.

Ugly, she called herself. Skinny. It was true she was thin. I could see her ribs when she sat with her back impossibly straight, her tummy sucked in, her chin up. She worked in the nude these days, sitting in lotus position. For long periods she would not move, her hand lying on her thighs, then she would poise, as if to pound the keys. But her touch was light, almost silent. It looked more like yoga than programming. She said she went into a meditative state for her best work.

I had expected a bony angularity, all sharp elbows and knees. She wasn't like that. I had guessed her weight ten pounds too low, and still didn't know where she put it. But she was soft and rounded, and strong beneath.

No one was ever going to call her face glamorous. Few would even go so far as to call her pretty. The braces did that, I think. They caught the eye and held it, drawing attention to that unsightly jumble.

But her skin was wonderful. She had scars. Not as many as I had expected. She seemed to heal quickly, and well.

I thought she was beautiful.

I had just completed my nightly survey when my eye was caught by the candle. I looked at it, then tried to look away.

Candles do that sometimes. I don't know why. In still air, with the flame perfectly vertical, they begin to flicker. The flame leaps up then squats down, up and down, up and down, brighter and brighter in regular rhythm, two or three beats to the second—

—and I tried to call out to her, wishing the candle would stop its flickering, but already I couldn't speak—

—I could only gasp, and I tried once more, as hard as I could, to yell, to scream, to tell her not to worry, and felt the nausea building . . .

I tasted blood. I took an experimental breath, did not find the smells of vomit, urine, feces. The overhead lights were on.

Lisa was on her hands and knees leaning over me, her face very close. A tear dropped on my forehead. I was on the carpet, on my back.

"Victor, can you hear me?"

I nodded. There was a spoon in my mouth. I spit it out.

"What happened? Are you going to be all right?"

I nodded again, and struggled to speak.

"You just lie there. The ambulance is on its way."

"No. Don't need it."

"Well, it's on its way. You just take it easy and—"

"Help me up."

"Not yet. You're not ready."

She was right. I tried to sit up, and fell back quickly. I took deep breaths for a while. Then the doorbell rang.

She stood up and started to the door. I just managed to get my hand around her ankle. Then she was leaning over me again, her eyes as wide as they would go.

"What is it? What's wrong now?"

"Get some clothes on," I told her. She looked down at herself, surprised.

"Oh. Right."

She got rid of the ambulance crew. Lisa was a lot calmer after she made coffee and we were sitting at the kitchen table. It was one o'clock, and I was still pretty rocky. But it hadn't been a bad one.

I went to the bathroom and got the bottle of Dilantin I'd hidden when she moved in. I let her see me take one.

"I forgot to do this today," I told her.

"It's because you hid them. That was stupid."

"I know." There must have been something else I could have said. It didn't please me to see her look hurt. But she was hurt because I wasn't defending myself against her attack, and that was a bit too complicated for me to dope out just after a grand mal.

"You can move out if you want to," I said. I was in rare form.

So was she. She reached across the table and shook me by the shoulders. She glared at me.

"I won't take a lot more of that kind of shit," she said, and I nodded, and began to cry.

She let me do it. I think that was probably best. She could have babied me, but I do a pretty good job of that myself.

"How long has this been going on?" she finally said. "Is that why you've stayed in your house for thirty years?"

I shrugged. "I guess it's part of it. When I got back they operated, but it just made it worse."

"Okay. I'm mad at you because you didn't tell me about it, so I didn't know what to do. I want to stay, but you'll have to tell me how. Then I won't be mad anymore."

I could have blown the whole thing right there. I'm amazed I didn't. Through the years I've developed very good methods for doing things like that. But I pulled through when I saw her face. She really did want to stay. I didn't know why, but it was enough.

"The spoon was a mistake," I said. "If there's time, and you can do it without risking your fingers, you could jam a piece of cloth in there. Part of a sheet, or something. But nothing hard." I explored my mouth with a finger. "I think I broke a tooth."

"Serves you right," she said. I looked at her, and smiled, then we were both laughing. She came around the table and kissed me, then sat on my knee.

"The biggest danger is drowning. During the first part of the seizure, all my muscles go rigid. That doesn't last long. Then they all start contracting and relaxing at random. It's *very* strong."

"I know. I watched, and I tried to hold you."

"Don't do that. Get me on my side. Stay behind me, and watch out for flailing arms. Get a pillow under my head if you can. Keep me away from things I could injure myself on." I looked her square in the eye. "I want to emphasize this. Just *try* to do all those things. If I'm getting too violent, it's better you stand off to the side. Better for both of us. If I knock you out, you won't be able to help me if I start strangling on vomit."

I kept looking at her eyes. She must have read my mind, because she smiled slightly.

"Sorry, Yank. I am not freaked out. I mean, like, it's totally gross, you know, and it barfs me out to the max, you could—"

"—gag me with a spoon, I know. Okay, right, I know I was dumb. And that's about it. I might bite my tongue or the inside of my cheek. Don't worry about it. There is one more thing."

She waited, and I wondered how much to tell her. There wasn't a lot she could do, but if I died on her I didn't want her to feel it was her fault.

"Sometimes I have to go to the hospital. Sometimes one seizure will follow another. If that keeps up for too long, I won't breathe, and my brain will die of oxygen starvation."

"That only takes about five minutes," she said, alarmed.

"I know. It's only a problem if I start having them frequently, so we could plan for it if I do. But if I don't come out of one, start having another right on the heels of the first, or if you can't detect any breathing for three or four minutes, you'd better call an ambulance."

"Three or four minutes? You'd be dead before they got here."

"It's that or live in a hospital. I don't like hospitals."

"Neither do I."

The next day she took me for a ride in her Ferrari. I was nervous about it, wondering if she was going to do crazy things. If anything, she was too slow. People behind her kept honking. I could tell she hadn't been driving long from the exaggerated attention she put into every movement.

"A Ferrari is wasted on me, I'm afraid," she confessed at one point. "I never drive it faster than fifty-five."

We went to an interior decorator in Beverly Hills and she bought a low-watt gooseneck lamp at an outrageous price.

I had a hard time getting to sleep that night. I suppose I was afraid of having another seizure, though Lisa's new lamp wasn't going to set it off.

Funny about seizures. When I first started having them, everyone called them fits. Then, gradually, it was seizures, until fits began to sound dirty.

I guess it's a sign of growing old, when the language changes on you.

There were rafts of new words. A lot of them were for things that didn't even exist when I was growing up. Like software. I always visualized a limp wrench.

"What got you interested in computers, Lisa?" I asked her.

She didn't move. Her concentration when sitting at the machine was pretty damn good. I rolled onto my back and tried to sleep.

"It's where the power is, Yank." I looked up. She had turned to face me.

"Did you pick it all up since you got to America?"

"I had a head start. I didn't tell you about my Captain, did I?"

"I don't think you did."

"He was strange. I knew that. I was about fourteen. He was an American, and he took an interest in me. He got me a nice apartment in Saigon. And he put me in school."

She was studying me, looking for a reaction. I didn't give her one.

"He was surely a pedophile, and probably had homosexual tendencies, since I looked so much like a skinny little boy."

Again the wait. This time she smiled.

"He was good to me. I learned to read well. From there on, anything is possible."

"I didn't actually ask you about your Captain. I asked why you got interested in computers."

"That's right. You did."

"Is it just a living?"

"It started that way. It's the future, Victor."

"God knows I've read that enough times."

"It's true. It's already here. It's power, if you know how to use it. You've seen what Kluge was able to do. You can make money with one of these things. I don't mean earn it, I mean *make* it, like if you had a printing press. Remember Osborne mentioned that Kluge's house didn't exist? Did you think what that means?"

"That he wiped it out of the memory banks."

"That was the first step. But the lot exists in the county plat books, wouldn't you think? I mean, this country hasn't *entirely* given up paper."

"So the county really does have a record of the house."

"No. That page was torn out of the records."

"I don't get it. Kluge never left the house."

"Oldest way in the world, friend. Kluge looked through the L.A.P.D. files until he found a guy known as Sammy. He sent him a cashier's check for a thousand dollars, along with a letter saying he could earn twice that if he'd go to the hall of records and do something. Sammy didn't bite, and neither did McGee, or Molly Unger. But Little Billy Phipps did, and he got a check just like the letter said, and he and Kluge had a wonderful business relationship for many years. Little Billy drives a new Cadillac now, and hasn't the faintest notion who Kluge was or where he lived. It didn't matter to Kluge how much he spent. He just pulled it out of thin air."

I thought that over for a while. I guess it's true that with enough money you can do just about anything, and Kluge had all the money in the world.

"Did you tell Osborne about Little Billy?"

"I erased that disc, just like I erased your seven hundred thousand. You never know when you might need somebody like Little Billy."

"You're not afraid of getting into trouble over it?"

"Life is risk, Victor. I'm keeping the best stuff for myself. Not because I intend to use it, but because if I ever needed it badly and didn't have it, I'd feel like such a fool."

She cocked her head and narrowed her eyes, which made them practically disappear.

"Tell me something, Yank. Kluge picked you out of all your neighbors because you'd been a boy scout for thirty years. How do you react to what I'm doing?"

"You're cheerfully amoral, and you're a survivor, and you're basically decent. And I pity anybody who gets in your way."

She grinned, stretched, and stood up.

"'Cheerfully amoral.' I like that." She sat beside me, making a great sloshing in the bed. "You want to be amoral again?"

"In a little bit." She started rubbing my chest. "So you got into computers because they were the wave of the future. Don't you ever worry about them . . . I don't know, I guess it sounds corny . . . do you think they'll take over?"

"Everybody thinks that until they start to use them," she said. "You've got to realize just how stupid they are. Without programming they are good for nothing, literally. Now, what I do believe is that the people who *run* the computers will take over. They already have. That's why I study them."

"I guess that's not what I meant. Maybe I can't say it right."

She frowned. "Kluge was looking into something. He'd been eavesdropping in artificial intelligence labs, and reading a lot of neurological research. I think he was trying to find a common thread."

"Between human brains and computers?"

"Not quite. He was thinking of computers and neurons. Brain cells." She pointed to her computer. "That thing, or any other com-

puter, is light-years away from being a human brain. It can't general-
ize, or infer, or categorize, or invent. With good programming it can
appear to do some of those things, but it's an illusion.

"There's an old speculation about what would happen if we finally
built a computer with as many transistors as the brain has neurons.
Would there be self-awareness? I think that's baloney. A transistor isn't
a neuron, and a quintillion of them aren't any better than a dozen.

"So Kluge—who seems to have felt the same way—started looking
into the possible similarities between a neuron and a 16-bit computer.
That's why he had all that consumer junk sitting around his house,
those Trash-80's and Atari's and TI's and Sinclair's, for chrissake. He
was used to *much* more powerful instruments. He ate up the home
units like candy."

"What did he find out?"

"Nothing, it looks like. A 16-bit unit is more complex than a neuron, and no computer is in the same galaxy as an organic brain. But
see, the words get tricky. I said an Atari is more complex than a neuron, but it's hard to really compare them. It's like comparing a direction with a distance, or a color with a mass. The units are different.
Except for one similarity."

"What's that?"

"The connections. Again, it's different, but the concept of net-
working is the same. A neuron is connected to a lot of others. There
are trillions of them, and the way messages pulse through them determine what we are and what we think and what we remember. And
with that computer I can reach a million others. It's bigger than the
human brain, really, because the information in that network is more
than all humanity could cope with in a million years. It reaches from
Pioneer Ten, out beyond the orbit of Pluto, right into every living
room that has a telephone in it. With that computer you can tap tons
of data that has been collected but nobody's even had the time to
look at.

"That's what Kluge was interested in. The old 'critical mass computer' idea, the computer that becomes aware, but with a new angle.
Maybe it wouldn't be the size of the computer, but the *number* of
computers. There used to be thousands of them. Now there's millions.
They're putting them in cars. In wristwatches. Every home has several, from the simple timer on a microwave oven up to a video game or
home terminal. Kluge was trying to find out if critical mass could be
reached that way."

"What did he think?"

"I don't know. He was just getting started." She glanced down at me. "But you know what, Yank? I think you've reached critical mass while I wasn't looking."

"I think you're right." I reached for her.

Lisa liked to cuddle. I didn't, at first, after fifty years of sleeping alone. But I got to like it pretty quickly.

That's what we were doing when we resumed the conversation we had been having. We just lay in each other's arms and talked about things. Nobody had mentioned love yet, but I knew I loved her. I didn't know what to do about it, but I would think of something.

"Critical mass," I said. She nuzzled my neck, and yawned.

"What about it?"

"What would it be like? It seems like it would be such a vast intelligence. So quick, so omniscient. God-like."

"Could be."

"Wouldn't it . . . run our lives? I guess I'm asking the same questions I started off with. Would it take over?"

She thought about it for a long time.

"I wonder if there would be anything to take over. I mean, why should it care? How could we figure what its concerns would be? Would it want to be worshipped, for instance? I doubt it. Would it want to 'rationalize all human behavior, to eliminate all emotion,' as I'm sure some sci-fi film computer must have told some damsel in distress in the fifties.

"You can use a word like awareness, but what does it mean? An amoeba must be aware. Plants probably are. There may be a level of awareness in a neuron. Even in an integrated circuit chip. We don't even know what our own awareness really is. We've never been able to shine a light on it, dissect it, figure out where it comes from or where it goes when we're dead. To apply human values to a thing like this hypothetical computer-net consciousness would be pretty stupid. But I don't see how it could interact with human awareness at all. It might not even notice us, any more than we notice cells in our bodies, or neutrinos passing through us, or the vibrations of the atoms in the air around us."

So she had to explain what a neutrino was. One thing I always provided her with was an ignorant audience. And after that, I pretty much forgot about our mythical hyper-computer.

✿　✿　✿

"What about your Captain?" I asked much later.

"Do you really want to know, Yank?" she mumbled sleepily.

"I'm not afraid to know."

She sat up and reached for her cigarettes. I had come to know she sometimes smoked them in times of stress. She had told me she smoked after making love but that first time had been the only time. The lighter flared in the dark. I heard her exhale.

"My Major, actually. He got a promotion. Do you want to know his name?"

"Lisa, I don't want to know any of it if you don't want to tell it. But if you do, what I want to know is did he stand by you?"

"He didn't marry me, if that's what you mean. When he knew he had to go, he said he would, but I talked him out of it. Maybe it was the most noble thing I ever did. Maybe it was the most stupid.

"It's no accident I look Japanese. My grandmother was raped in '42 by a Jap soldier of the occupation. She was Chinese, living in Hanoi. My mother was born there. They went south after Dien Bien Phu. My grandmother died. My mother had it hard. Being Chinese was tough enough, but being half Chinese and half Japanese was worse. My father was half French and half Annamese. Another bad combination. I never knew him. But I'm sort of a capsule history of Vietnam."

The end of her cigarette glowed brighter once more.

"I've got one grandfather's face and the other grandfather's height. With tits by Goodyear. About all I missed was some American genes, but I was working on that for my children.

"When Saigon was falling I tried to get to the American Embassy. Didn't make it. You know the rest, until I got to Thailand, and when I finally got Americans to notice me, it turned out my Major was still looking for me. He sponsored me over here, and I made it in time to watch him die of cancer. Two months I had with him, all of it in the hospital."

"My god." I had a horrible thought. "That wasn't the war, too, was it? I mean, the story of your life—"

"—is the rape of Asia. No, Victor. Not that war, anyway. But he was one of those guys who got to see atom bombs up close, out in Nevada. He was too Regular Army to complain about it, but I think he knew that's what killed him."

"Did you love him?"

"What do you want me to say? He got me out of hell."

Again the cigarette flared, and I saw her stub it out.

"No," she said. "I didn't love him. He knew that. I've never loved anybody. He was very dear, very special to me. I would have done almost anything for him. He was fatherly to me." I felt her looking at me in the dark. "Aren't you going to ask how old he was?"

"Fiftyish," I said.

"On the nose. Can I ask you something?"

"I guess it's your turn."

"How many girls have you had since you got back from Korea?"

I held up my hand and pretended to count on my fingers.

"One," I said, at last.

"How many before you went?"

"One. We broke up before I left for the war."

"How many in Korea?"

"Nine. All at Madame Park's jolly little whorehouse in Pusan."

"So you've made love to one white and ten Asians. I bet none of the others were as tall as me."

"Korean girls have fatter cheeks too. But they all had your eyes."

She nuzzled against my chest, took a deep breath, and sighed.

"We're a hell of a pair, aren't we?"

I hugged her, and her breath came again, hot on my chest.

I wondered how I'd lived so long without such a simple miracle as that.

"Yes, I think we really are."

Osborne came by again about a week later. He seemed subdued. He listened to the things Lisa had decided to give him without much interest. He took the printout she handed him, and promised to turn it over to the departments that handled those things. But he didn't get up to leave.

"I thought I ought to tell you, Apfel," he said, at last. "The Gavin case has been closed."

I had to think a moment to remember Kluge's real name had been Gavin.

"The coroner ruled suicide a long time ago. I was able to keep the case open quite a while on the strength of my suspicions." He nodded toward Lisa. "And on what she said about the suicide note. But there was just no evidence at all."

"It probably happened quickly," Lisa said. "Somebody caught him, tracked him back—it can be done; Kluge was lucky for a long time—and did him the same day."

"You don't think it was suicide?" I asked Osborne.

"No. But whoever did it is home free unless something new turns up."

"I'll tell you if it does," Lisa said.

"That's something else," Osborne said. "I can't authorize you to work over there anymore. The county's taken possession of house and contents."

"Don't worry about it," Lisa said, softly.

There was a short silence as she leaned over to shake a cigarette from the pack on the coffee table. She lit it, exhaled, and leaned back beside me, giving Osborne her most inscrutable look. He sighed.

"I'd hate to play poker with you, lady," he said. "What do you mean, 'Don't worry about it'?"

"I bought the house four days ago. And its contents. If anything turns up that would help you reopen the murder investigation, I will let you know."

Osborne was too defeated to get angry. He studied her quietly for a while.

"I'd like to know how you swung that."

"I did nothing illegal. You're free to check it out. I paid good cash money for it. The house came onto the market. I got a good price at the Sheriff's sale."

"How'd you like it if I put my best men on the transaction? See if they can dig up some funny money? Maybe fraud. How about I get the F.B.I. in to look it all over?"

She gave him a cool look.

"You're welcome to. Frankly, Detective Osborne, I could have stolen that house, Griffith Park, and the Harbor Freeway and I don't think you could have caught me."

"So where does that leave me?"

"Just where you were. With a closed case, and a promise from me."

"I don't like you having all that stuff, if it can do the things you say it can do."

"I didn't expect you would. But that's not your department, is it? The county owned it for a while, through simple confiscation. They didn't know what they had, and they let it go."

"Maybe I can get the Fraud detail out here to confiscate your software. There's criminal evidence on it."

"You could try that," she agreed.

They stared at each other for a while. Lisa won. Osborne rubbed his eyes and nodded. Then he heaved himself to his feet and slumped to the door.

Lisa stubbed out her cigarette. We listened to him going down the walk.

"I'm surprised he gave up so easy," I said. "Or did he? Do you think he'll try a raid?"

"It's not likely. He knows the score."

"Maybe you could tell it to me."

"For one thing, it's not his department, and he knows it."

"Why did you buy the house?"

"You ought to ask *how*."

I looked at her closely. There was a gleam of amusement behind the poker face.

"Lisa. What did you do?"

"That's what Osborne asked himself. He got the right answer, because he understands Kluge's machines. And he knows how things get done. It was no accident that house going on the market, and no accident I was the only bidder. I used one of Kluge's pet councilmen."

"You bribed him?"

She laughed, and kissed me.

"I think I finally managed to shock you, Yank. That's gotta be the biggest difference between me and a native-born American. Average citizens don't spend much on bribes over here. In Saigon, everybody bribes."

"Did you bribe him?"

"Nothing so indelicate. One has to go in the back door over here. Several entirely legal campaign contributions appeared in the accounts of a State Senator, who mentioned a certain situation to someone, who happened to be in the position to do legally what I happened to want done." She looked at me askance. "Of *course* I bribed him, Victor. You'd be amazed to know how cheaply. Does that bother you?"

"Yes," I admitted. "I don't like bribery."

"I'm indifferent to it. It happens, like gravity. It may not be admirable, but it gets things done."

"I assume you covered yourself."

"Reasonably well. You're never entirely covered with a bribe, because of the human element. The councilman might geek if they got him in front of a grand jury. But they won't, because Osborne won't pursue it. That's the second reason he walked out of here without a fight. *He* knows how the world wobbles, he knows what kind of force I now possess, and he knows he can't fight it."

There was a long silence after that. I had a lot to think about, and I didn't feel good about most of it. At one point Lisa reached for the pack of cigarettes, then changed her mind. She waited for me to work it out.

"It is a terrific force, isn't it," I finally said.

"It's frightening," she agreed. "Don't think it doesn't scare me. Don't think I haven't had fantasies of being superwoman. Power is an awful temptation, and it's not easy to reject. There's so much I could do."

"Will you?"

"I'm not talking about stealing things, or getting rich."

"I didn't think you were."

"This is political power. But I don't know how to wield it . . . it sounds corny, but to use it for good. I've seen so much evil come from good intentions. I don't think I'm wise enough to do any good. And the chances of getting torn up like Kluge did are large. But I'm not wise enough to walk away from it. I'm still a street urchin from Saigon, Yank. I'm smart enough not to use it unless I have to. But I can't give it away, and I can't destroy it. Is that stupid?"

I didn't have a good answer for that one. But I had a bad feeling.

My doubts had another week to work on me. I didn't come to any great moral conclusions. Lisa knew of some crimes, and she wasn't reporting them to the authorities. That didn't bother me much. She had at her fingertips the means to commit more crimes, and that bothered me a lot. Yet I really didn't think she planned to do anything. She was smart enough to use the things she had only in a defensive way—but with Lisa that could cover a lot of ground.

When she didn't show up for dinner one evening, I went over to Kluge's and found her busy in the living room. A nine-foot section of shelving had been cleared. The discs and tapes were stacked on a table. She had a big plastic garbage can and a magnet the size of a softball. I watched her wave a tape near the magnet, then toss it in the garbage can, which was almost full. She glanced up, did the same operation with a handful of discs, then took off her glasses and wiped her eyes.

"Feel any better now, Victor?" she asked.

"What do you mean? I feel fine."

"No you don't. And I haven't felt right, either. It hurts me to do it, but I have to. You want to go get the other trash can?"

I did, and helped her pull more software from the shelves.

"You're not going to wipe it all, are you?"

"No. I'm wiping records, and . . . something else."

"Are you going to tell me what?"

"There are things it's better not to know," she said, darkly.

I finally managed to convince her to talk over dinner. She had said little, just eating and shaking her head. But she gave in.

"Rather dreary, actually," she said. "I've been probing around some delicate places the last couple days. These are places Kluge visited at will, but they scare the hell out of me. Dirty places. Places where they know things I thought I'd like to find out."

She shivered, and seemed reluctant to go on.

"Are you talking about military computers? The C.I.A.?"

"The C.I.A. is where it starts. It's the easiest. I've looked around at NORAD—that's the guys who get to fight the next war. It makes me shiver to see how easy Kluge got in there. He cobbled up a way to start World War Three, just as an exercise. That's one of the things we just erased. The last two days I was nibbling around the edges of the big boys. The Defense Intelligence Agency and the National Security . . . something. DIA and NSA. Each of them is bigger than the CIA. Something knew I was there. Some watchdog program. As soon as I realized that I got out quick, and I've spent the last five hours being sure it didn't follow me. And now I'm sure, and I've destroyed all that, too."

"You think they're the one who killed Kluge?"

"They're surely the best candidates. He had tons of their stuff. I know he helped design the biggest installations at NSA, and he'd been poking around in there for years. One false step is all it would take."

"Did you get it all? I mean are you sure?"

"I'm sure they didn't track me. I'm not sure I've destroyed all the records. I'm going back now to take a last look."

"I'll go with you."

※　　※　　※

We worked until well after midnight. Lisa would review a tape or a disc, and if she was in any doubt, toss it to me for the magnetic treatment. At one point, simply because she was unsure, she took the magnet and passed it in front of an entire shelf of software.

It was amazing to think about it. With that one wipe she had randomized billions of bits of information. Some of it might not exist anywhere else in the world. I found myself confronted by even harder questions. Did she have the right to do it? Didn't knowledge exist for everyone? But I confess I had little trouble quelling my protests. Mostly I was happy to see it go. The old reactionary in me found it easier to believe There Are Things We Are Not Meant To Know.

We were almost through when her monitor screen began to malfunction. It actually gave off a few hisses and pops, so Lisa stood back from it for a moment, then the screen started to flicker. I stared at it for a while. It seemed to me there was an image trying to form in the screen. Something three-dimensional. Just as I was starting to get a picture of it I happened to glance at Lisa, and she was looking at me. Her face was flickering. She came to me and put her hands over my eyes.

"Victor, you shouldn't look at that."

"It's okay," I told her. And when I said it, it was, but as soon as I had the words out I knew it wasn't. And that is the last thing I remembered for a long time.

I'm told it was a very bad two weeks. I remember very little of it. I was kept under high dosages of drugs, and my few lucid periods were always followed by a fresh seizure.

The first thing I recall clearly was looking up at Dr. Stuart's face. I was in a hospital bed. I later learned it was in Cedars-Sinai, not the Veteran's Hospital. Lisa had paid for a private room.

Stuart put me through the usual questions. I was able to answer them, though I was very tired. When he was satisfied as to my condition he finally began to answer some of my questions. I learned how long I had been there, and how it had happened.

"You went into consecutive seizures," he confirmed. "I don't know why, frankly. You haven't been prone to them for a decade. I was thinking you were well under control. But nothing is ever really stable, I guess."

"So Lisa got me here in time."

"She did more than that. She didn't want to level with me at first. It seems that after the first seizure she witnessed she read everything she could find. From that day, she had a syringe and a solution of Valium handy. When she saw you couldn't breathe she injected you, and there's no doubt it saved your life."

Stuart and I had known each other a long time. He knew I had no prescription for Valium, though we had talked about it the last time I was hospitalized. Since I lived alone, there would be no one to inject me if I got in trouble.

He was more interested in results than anything else, and what Lisa did had the desired result. I was still alive.

He wouldn't let me have any visitors that day. I protested, but soon was asleep. The next day she came. She wore a new T-shirt. This one had a picture of a robot wearing a gown and mortarboard, and said "Class of 11111000000." It turns out that was 1984 in binary notation.

She had a big smile and said "Hi, Yank!" and as she sat on the bed I started to shake. She looked alarmed and asked if she should call the doctor.

"It's not that," I managed to say. "I'd like it if you just held me."

She took off her shoes and got under the covers with me. She held me tightly. At some point a nurse came in and tried to shoo her out. Lisa gave her profanities in Vietnamese, Chinese, and few startling ones in English, and the nurse left. I saw Dr. Stuart glance in later.

I felt much better when I finally stopped crying. Lisa's eyes were wet, too.

"I've been here every day," she said. "You look awful, Victor."

"I feel a lot better."

"Well, you look better than you did. But your doctor says you'd better stick around another couple of days, just to make sure."

"I think he's right."

"I'm planning a big dinner for when you get back. You think we should invite the neighbors?"

I didn't say anything for a while. There were so many things we hadn't faced. Just how long could it go on between us? How long before I got sour about being so useless? How long before she got tired of being with an old man? I don't know just when I had started to think of Lisa as a permanent part of my life. And I wondered how I could have thought that.

"Do you want to spend more years waiting in hospitals for a man to die?"

"What do you want, Victor? I'll marry you if you want me to. Or I'll live with you in sin. I prefer sin, myself, but if it'll make you happy—"

"I don't know why you want to saddle yourself with an epileptic old fart."

"Because I love you."

It was the first time she had said it. I could have gone on questioning—bringing up her Major again, for instance—but I had no urge to. I'm very glad I didn't. So I changed the subject.

"Did you get the job finished?"

She knew which job I was talking about. She lowered her voice and put her mouth close to my ear.

"Let's don't be specific about it here, Victor. I don't trust any place I haven't swept for bugs. But, to put your mind at ease, I did finish, and it's been a quiet couple of weeks. No one is any wiser, and I'll never meddle in things like that again."

I felt a lot better. I was also exhausted. I tried to conceal my yawns, but she sensed it was time to go. She gave me one more kiss, promising many more to come, and left me.

It was the last time I ever saw her.

At about ten o'clock that evening Lisa went into Kluge's kitchen with a screwdriver and some other tools and got to work on the microwave oven.

The manufacturers of those appliances are very careful to insure they can't be turned on with the door open, as they emit lethal radiation. But with simple tools and a good brain it is possible to circumvent the safety interlocks. Lisa had no trouble with them. About ten minutes after she entered the kitchen she put her head in the oven and turned it on.

It is impossible to say how long she held her head in there. It was long enough to turn her eyeballs to the consistency of boiled eggs. At some point she lost voluntary muscle control and fell to the floor, pulling the microwave down with her. It shorted out, and a fire started.

The fire set off the sophisticated burglar alarm she had installed a month before. Betty Lanier saw the flames and called the fire department as Hal ran across the street and into the burning kitchen. He dragged what was left of Lisa out onto the grass. When he saw what the fire had done to her upper body, and in particular her breasts, he threw up.

She was rushed to the hospital. The doctors there amputated one arm and cut away the frightful masses of vulcanized silicone, pulled all her teeth, and didn't know what to do about the eyes. They put her on a respirator.

It was an orderly who first noticed the blackened and bloody T-shirt they had cut from her. Some of the message was unreadable, but it began, "I can't go on this way anymore . . ."

There is no other way I could have told all that. I discovered it piece-meal, starting with the disturbed look on Dr. Stuart's face when Lisa didn't show up the next day. He wouldn't tell me anything, and I had another seizure shortly after.

The next week is a blur. Betty was very good to me. They gave me a tranquilizer called Tranxene, and it was even better. I ate them like candy. I wandered in a drugged haze, eating only when Betty insisted, sleeping sitting up in my chair, coming awake not knowing where or who I was. I returned to the prison camp many times. Once I recall helping Lisa stack severed heads.

When I saw myself in the mirror, there was a vague smile on my face. It was Tranxene, caressing my frontal lobes. I knew that if I was to live much longer, me and Tranxene would have to become very good friends.

I eventually became capable of something that passed for rational thought. I was helped along somewhat by a visit from Osborne. I was trying, at that time, to find reasons to live, and wondered if he had any.

"I'm very sorry," he started off. I said nothing. "This is on my own time," he went on. "The department doesn't know I'm here."

"Was it suicide?" I asked him.

"I brought along a copy of the . . . the note. She ordered it from a shirt company in Westwood, three days before the . . . accident."

He handed it to me, and I read it. I was mentioned, though not by name. I was "the man I love." She said she couldn't cope with my problems. It was a short note. You can't get too much on a T-shirt. I read it through five times, then handed it back to him.

"She told you Kluge didn't write his note. I tell you she didn't write this."

He nodded reluctantly. I felt a vast calm, with a howling nightmare just below it. Praise Tranxene.

"Can you back that up?"

"She saw me in the hospital shortly before the . . . accident. She was full of life and hope. You say she ordered the shirt three days before. I would have felt that. And that note is pathetic. Lisa was never pathetic."

He nodded again.

"Some things I want to tell you. There were no signs of a struggle. Mrs. Lanier is sure no one came in the front. The crime lab went over the whole place and we're sure no one was in there with her. I'd stake my life on the fact that no one entered or left that house. Now, *I* don't believe it was suicide either, but do you have any suggestions?"

"The NSA," I said.

I explained about the last things she had done while I was still there. I told him of her fear of the government spy agencies. That was all I had.

"Well, I guess they're the ones who could do a thing like that, if anyone could. But I'll tell you, I have a hard time swallowing it. I don't know why, for one thing. Maybe you believe those people kill like you and I'd swat a fly." His look made it into a question.

"I don't know what I believe."

"I'm not saying they wouldn't kill for national security. Or some such shit. But they'd have taken the computers, too. They wouldn't have left her alone, they wouldn't even have let her *near* that stuff after they killed Kluge."

"What you're saying makes sense."

He muttered on about it for quite some time. Eventually I offered him some wine. He accepted thankfully. I considered joining him—it would be a quick way to die—but did not. He drank the whole bottle, and was comfortably drunk when he suggested we go next door and look it over one more time. I was planning on visiting Lisa the next day, and knew I had to start somewhere building myself up for that, so I agreed to go with him.

We inspected the kitchen. The fire had blackened the counters and melted some linoleum, but not much else. Water had made a mess of the place. There was a brown stain on the floor which I was able to look at with no emotion.

So we went back to the living room, and one of the computers was turned on. There was a short message on the screen.

IF YOU WISH TO KNOW MORE

PRESS ENTER ■

"Don't do it," I told him. But he did. He stood, blinking solemnly, as the words wiped themselves out and a new message appeared.

YOU LOOKED

The screen started to flicker and I was in my car, in darkness, with a pill in my mouth and another in my hand. I spit out the pill, and sat for a moment, listening to the old engine ticking over. In my hand was the plastic pill bottle. I felt very tired, but opened the car door and shut off the engine. I felt my way to the garage door and opened it. The air outside was fresh and sweet. I looked down at the pill bottle and hurried into the bathroom

When I got through what had to be done there were a dozen pills floating in the toilet that hadn't even dissolved. There were the wasted shells of many more, and a lot of other stuff I won't bother to describe. I counted the pills in the bottle, remembered how many there had been, and wondered if I would make it.

I went over to Kluge's house and could not find Osborne. I was getting tired, but I made it back to my house and stretched out on the couch to see if I would live or die.

The next day I found the story in the paper. Osborne had gone home and blown out the back of his head with his revolver. It was not a big story. It happens to cops all the time. He didn't leave a note.

I got on the bus and rode out to the hospital and spent three hours trying to get in to see Lisa. I wasn't able to do it. I was not a relative and the doctors were quite firm about her having no visitors. When I got angry they were as gentle as possible. It was then I learned the extent of her injuries. Hal had kept the worst from me. None of it would have mattered, but the doctors swore there was nothing left in her head. So I went home.

She died two days later.

She had left a will, to my surprise. I got the house and contents. I picked up the phone as soon as I learned of it, and called a garbage company. While they were on the way over I went for the last time into Kluge's house.

The same computer was still on, and it gave the same message.

PRESS ENTER ▇

I cautiously located the power switch, and turned it off. I had the garbage people strip the place to the bare walls.

I went over my own house very carefully, looking for anything that was even the first cousin to a computer. I threw out the radio. I sold the car, and the refrigerator, and the stove, and the blender, and the electric clock. I drained the waterbed and threw out the heater.

Then I bought the best propane stove on the market, and hunted a long time before I found an old icebox. I had the garage stacked to the ceiling with firewood. I had the chimney cleaned. It would be getting cold soon.

One day I took the bus to Pasadena and established the Lisa Foo Memorial Scholarship fund for Vietnamese refugees and their children. I endowed it with seven hundred thousand eighty-three dollars and four cents. I told them it could be used for any field of study except computer science. I could tell they thought me eccentric.

And I really thought I was safe, until the phone rang.

I thought it over for a long time before answering it. In the end, I knew it would just keep on going until I did. So I picked it up.

For a few seconds there was a dial tone, but I was not fooled. I kept holding it to my ear, and finally the tone turned off. There was just silence. I listened intently. I heard some of those far-off musical tones that live in phone wires. Echoes of conversations taking place a thousand miles away. And something infinitely more distant and cool.

I do not know what they have incubated out there at the NSA. I don't know if they did it on purpose, or if it just happened or if it even has anything to do with them, in the end. But I know it's out there, because I heard its soul breathing on the wires. I spoke very carefully.

"I do not wish to know any more," I said. "I won't tell anyone anything. Kluge, Lisa, and Osborne all committed suicide. I am just a lonely man, and I won't cause you any trouble."

There was a click, and a dial tone.

Getting the phone taken out was easy. Getting them to remove all the wires was a little harder, since once a place is wired they expect it to be wired forever. They grumbled, but when I started pulling them out myself, they relented, though they warned me it was going to cost.

PG&E was harder. They actually seemed to believe there was a regulation requiring each house to be hooked up to the grid. They were willing to shut off my power—though hardly pleased about it—but they just weren't going to take the wires away from my house. I went up on the roof with an axe and demolished four feet of eaves as they gaped at me. Then they coiled up their wires and went home.

I threw out all my lamps, all things electrical. With hammer, chisel, and handsaw I went to work on the drywall just above the baseboards.

As I stripped the house of wiring I wondered many times why I was doing it. Why was it worth it? I couldn't have very many more years before a final seizure finished me off. Those years were not going to be a lot of fun.

Lisa had been a survivor. She would have known why I was doing this. She had once said I was a survivor, too. I survived the camp. I survived the death of my mother and father and managed to fashion a solitary life. Lisa survived the death of just about everything. No survivor expects to live through it all. But while she was alive, she would have worked to stay alive.

And that's what I did. I got all the wires out of the walls, went over the house with a magnet to see if I had missed any metal, then spent a week cleaning up, fixing the holes I had knocked in the walls, ceiling, and attic. I was amused trying to picture the real-estate agent selling this place after I was gone.

It's a great little house, folks. No electricity . . .

Now I live quietly, as before.

I work in my garden during most of the daylight hours. I've expanded it considerably, and even have things growing in the front yard now.

I live by candlelight, and kerosene lamp. I grow most of what I eat.

It took a long time to taper off the Tranxene and the Dilantin, but I did it, and now take the seizures as they come. I've usually got bruises to show for it.

In the middle of a vast city I have cut myself off. I am not part of the network growing faster than I can conceive. I don't even know if it's dangerous to ordinary people. It noticed me, and Kluge, and Osborne. And Lisa. It brushed against our minds like I would brush away a mosquito, never noticing I had crushed it. Only I survived.

But I wonder.

It would be very hard . . . Lisa told me how it can get in through the wiring. There's something called a carrier wave that can move over wires carrying household current. That's why the electricity had to go.

I need water for my garden. There's just not enough rain here in southern California, and I don't know how else I could get the water.

Do you think it could come through the pipes?

Introduction to "Dinosaurs"

by Walter Jon Williams

Imagine if Cortez could have sat down and negotiated with Moctezuma, or Pizarro with Atahualpa, or John Smith with Powhatan.

Wait. Come to think of it, they did. Hmmm.

If there's one kind of story that science fiction is notorious for doing very, very badly, it's the "ruling class" story. Ambassadors, generals, presidents, corporate CEOs, congressmen, judges, politicians as a group and as individuals: As soon as they take the stage in a science fiction story, we find our eyes glazing over as the author inadvertently reveals his or her ignorance of how power is actually wielded, or of the delicacy with which the powerful must treat each other.

So here's this story, which is entirely devoted to a negotiation between two species in an interstellar war. Yes, folks, it's a couple of ambassadors talking to each other, the one a calm representative of a mature species, the other a barbarian barely able to hold the hotheads of his species in check. A recipe for disaster! What is this story doing in this book?

Well, see, sometimes even science fiction writers can do it right. This story could have been told no other way. No "deep characterization" was needed—in fact, it would have distracted. And yet this is no one-idea story with placeholder characters serving merely to provide exposition. On the contrary, the irony is layered so thick that it takes surgical tools to separate them.

Oh, yeah. Walter Jon Williams is known as a cyberpunk. I've even heard him claim the dubious title himself. But not here, not in these pages. Here he's just a storyteller with a finely tuned sense of appropriate despair.

DINOSAURS

Walter Jon Williams

The Shars seethed in the dim light of their ruddy sun. Pointed faces raised to the sky, they sniffed the faint wind for sign of the stranger and scented only hydrocarbons, far-off vegetation, damp fur, the sweat of excitement and fear. Weak eyes peered upward, glistened with hope, anxiety, apprehension, and saw only the faint pattern of stars. Short, excited barking sounds broke out here and there, but mostly the Shars crooned, a low ululation that told of sudden onslaught, destruction, war in distant reaches, and now the hope of peace.

The crowds surged left, then right. Individuals bounced high on their third legs, seeking a view, seeing only the wide sea of heads, the ears and muzzles pointed to the stars.

Suddenly, a screaming. High-pitched howls, a bright chorus of barks. The crowds surged again.

Something was crossing the field of stars.

The human ship was huge, vaster than anything they'd seen, a moonlet descending. Shars closed their eyes and shuddered in terror. The screaming turned to moans. Individuals leaped high, baring their teeth, barking in defiance of their fear. The air smelled of terror, incipient panic, anger.

War! cried some. *Peace!* cried others.

The crooning went on. *We mourn, we mourn,* it said, *we mourn our dead billions.*

We fear, said others.

Soundlessly, the human ship neared them, casting its vast shadow. Shars spilled outward from the spot beneath, bounding high on their third legs.

The human ship came to a silent rest. Dully, it reflected the dim red sun.

The Shars crooned their fear, their sorrow. And waited for the humans to emerge.

⚘ ⚘ ⚘

These? Yes. These. Drill, the human ambassador, gazed through his video walls at the sea of Shars, the moaning, leaping thousands that surrounded him. Through the mass a group was moving with purpose, heading for the airlock as per his instructions. His new Memory crawled restlessly in the armored hollow atop his skull. *Stand by,* he broadcast.

His knees made painful crackling noises as he walked toward the airlock, the silver ball of his translator rolling along the ceiling ahead of him. The walls mutated as he passed, showing him violet sky, far-off polygonal buildings, cold distant green . . . and here, nearby, a vast, dim plain covered with a golden tissue of Shars.

He reached the airlock and it began to open. Drill snuffed wetly at the alien smells—heat, dust, the musky scent of the Shars themselves.

Drill's heart thumped in his chest. His dreams were coming true. He had waited all his life for this.

Mash, whimpered Lowbrain. Drill told it to be silent. Lowbrain protested vaguely, then obeyed.

Drill told Lowbrain to move. Cool, alien air brushed his skin. The Shars cried out sharply, moaned, fell back. They seemed a wild, sibilant ocean of pointed ears and dark, questing eyes. The group heading for the airlock vanished in the general retrograde movement, a stone washed by a pale tide. Beneath Drill's feet was soft vegetation. His translator floated in the air before him. His mind flamed with wonder, but Lowbrain kept him moving.

The Shars fell back, moaning.

Drill stood eighteen feet tall on his two pillarlike legs, each with a splayed foot that displayed a horny underside and vestigial nails. His skin was ebony and was draped in folds over his vast naked body. His pendulous maleness swung loosely as he walked. As he stepped across the open space he was conscious of the fact that he was the ultimate product of nine million years of human evolution, all leading to the expansion, diversification, and perfection that was now humanity's manifest existence.

He looked down at the little Shars, their white skin and golden fur, their strange, stiff tripod legs, the muzzles raised to him as if in awe. *If your species survives,* he thought benignly, *you can look like me in another few million years.*

The group of Shars that had been forging through the crowd were suddenly exposed when the crowd fell back from around them. On the perimeter were several Shars holding staffs—weapons, perhaps—in their clever little hands. In the center of these were a group of Shars wearing decorative ribbon to which metal plates had been attached. *Badges of rank,* Memory said. *Ignore.* The shadow of the translator bobbed toward them as Drill approached. Metallic geometries rose from the group and hovered over them.

Recorders, Memory said. *Artificial similarities to myself. Or possibly security devices. Disregard.*

Drill was getting closer to the party, speeding up his instructions to Lowbrain, eventually entering Zen Synch. It would make Lowbrain hungrier but lessen the chance of any accidents.

The Shars carrying the staffs fell back. A wailing went up from the crowd as one of the Shars stepped toward Drill. The ribbons draped over her sloping shoulders failed to disguise four mammalian breasts. Clear plastic bubbles covered her weak eyes. In Zen Synch with Memory and Lowbrain, Drill ambled up to her and raised his hands in friendly greeting. The Shar flinched at the expanse of the gesture.

"I am Ambassador Drill," he said. "I am a human."

The Shar gazed up at him. Her nose wrinkled as she listened to the booming voice of the translator. Her answer was a succession of sharp sounds, made high in the throat, somewhat unpleasant. Drill listened to the voice of his translator.

"I am President Gram of the InterSharian Sociability of Nations and Planets." That's how it came through in translation, anyway. Memory began feeding Drill referents for the word "nation."

"I welcome you to our planet, Ambassador Drill."

"Thank you, President Gram," Drill said. "Shall we negotiate peace now?"

President Gram's ears pricked forward, then back. There was a pause, and then from the vast circle of Shars came a mad torrent of hooting noises. The awesome sound lapped over Drill like the waves of a lunatic sea.

They approve your sentiment, said Memory.

I thought that's what it meant, Drill said. *Do you think we'll get along?*

Memory didn't answer, but instead shifted to a more comfortable position in the saddle of Drill's skull. Its job was to provide facts, not draw conclusions.

"If you could come into my Ship," Drill said, "we could get started."

"Will we then meet the other members of your delegation?"

Drill gazed down at the Shar. The fur on her shoulders was rising in odd tufts. She seemed to be making a concerted effort to calm it.

"There are no other members," Drill said. "Just myself."

His knees were paining him. He watched as the other members of the Shar party cast quick glances at each other.

"No secretaries? No assistants?" the President was saying.

"No," Drill said. "Not at all. I'm the only conscious mind on Ship. Shall we get started?"

Eat! Eat! said Lowbrain. Drill ordered it to be silent. His stomach grumbled.

"Perhaps," said President Gram, gazing at the vastness of the human ship, "it would be best should we begin in a few hours. I should probably speak to the crowd. Would you care to listen?"

No need. Memory said. *I will monitor.*

"Thank you, no," Drill said. "I shall return to Ship for food and sex. Please signal me when you are ready. Please bring any furniture you may need for your comfort. I do not believe my furniture would fit you, although we might be able to clone some later."

The Shars' ears all pricked forward. Drill entered Zen Synch, turned his huge body, and began accelerating toward the airlock. The sound of the crowd behind him was like the murmuring of wind through a stand of trees.

Peace, he thought later, as he stood by the mash bins and fed his complaining stomach. *It's a simple thing. How long can it take to arrange?*

Long, said Memory. *Very long.*

The thought disturbed him. He thought the first meeting had gone well.

After his meal, when he had sex, it wasn't very good.

Memory had been monitoring the events outside Ship, and after Drill had completed sex, Memory showed him the outside events. *They have been broadcast to the entire population,* Memory said.

President Gram had moved to a local elevation and had spoken for some time. Drill found her speech interesting—it was rhythmic and incantorial, rising and falling in tone and volume, depending heavily on repetition and melody. The crowd participated, issuing forth with excited barks or low moans in response to her statements or questions, sometimes babbling in confusion when she posed them a conundrum.

Memory only gave the highlights of the speech. "Unknown . . . attackers . . . billions dead . . . preparations advanced . . . ready to defend ourselves . . . offer of peace . . . hope in the darkness . . . unknown . . . willing to take the chance . . . peace . . . peace . . . hopeful smell . . . peace." At the end the other Shars were all singing "Peace! Peace!" in chorus while President Gram bounced up and down on her sturdy rear leg.

It sounds pretty, Drill thought. *But why does she go on like that?*
Memory's reply was swift.
Remember that the Shars are a generalized and social species, it said. *President Gram's power, and her ability to negotiate, derives from the degree of her popular support. In measures of this significance she must explain herself and her actions to the population in order to maintain their enthusiasm for her policies.*
Primitive, Drill thought.
That is correct.
Why don't they let her get on with her work? Drill asked.
There was no reply.

After an exchange of signals the Shar party assembled at the airlock. Several Shars had been mobilized to carry tables and stools. Drill sent a Frog to escort the Shars from the airlock to where he waited. The Frog met them inside the airlock, turned, and hopped on ahead through Ship's airy, winding corridors. It had been trained to repeat "Follow me, follow me" in the Shars' own language.

Drill waited in a semi-reclined position on a Slab. The Slab was an organic sub-species used as furniture, with an idiot brain capable of responding to human commands. The Shars entered cautiously, their weak eyes twitching in the bright light. "Welcome, Honorable President," Drill said. "Up, Slab." Slab began to adjust itself to place Drill on his feet. The Shars were moving tables and stools into the vast room.

Frog was hopping in circles, making a wet noise at each landing. "Follow me, follow me," it said.

The members of the Shar delegation who bore badges of rank stood in a body while the furniture-carriers bustled around them. Drill noticed, as Slab put him on his feet, that they were wrinkling their noses. He wondered what it meant.

His knees crackled as he came fully upright. "Please make yourselves comfortable," he said. "Frog will show your laborers to the air-lock."

"Does your Excellency object to a mechanical recording of the proceedings?" President Gram asked. She was shading her eyes with her hand.

"Not at all." As a number of devices rose into the air above the party, Drill wondered if it were possible to give the Shars detachable Memories. Perhaps human bioengineers could adapt the Memories to the Shar physiology. He asked Memory to make a note of the question so that he could bring it up later.

"Follow me, follow me," Frog said. The workers who had carried the furniture began to follow the hopping Frog out of the room.

"Your Excellency," President Gram said, "may I have the honor of presenting to you the other members of my delegation?"

There were six in all, with titles like Secretary for Syncopated Speech and Special Executive for External Coherence. There was also a Minister for the Dissemination of Convincing Lies, whose title Drill suspected was somehow mistranslated, and an Opposite Secretary-General for the Genocidal Eradication of Alien Aggressors, at whom Drill looked with more than a little interest. The Opposite Secretary-General was named Vang, and was small even for a Shar. He seemed to wrinkle his nose more than the others. The Special Executive for External Coherence, whose name was Cup, seemed a bit piebald, patches of white skin showing through the golden fur covering his shoulders, arms, and head.

He is elderly, said Memory.

That's what I thought.

"Down, Slab," Drill said. He leaned back against the creature and began to move to a more relaxed position.

He looked at the Shars and smiled. Fur ruffled on shoulders and necks. "Shall we make peace now?" he asked.

"We would like to clarify something you said earlier," President Gram said. "You said that you were the only, ah, conscious entity on the ship. That you were the only member of the human delegation. Was that translated correctly?"

"Why, yes," Drill said. "Why would more than one diplomat be necessary?"

The Shars looked at each other. The Special Executive for External Coherence spoke cautiously.

"You will not be needing to consult with your superiors? You have full authority from your government?"

Drill beamed at them. "We humans do not have a government, of course," he said. "But I am a diplomat with the appropriate Memory and training. There is no problem that I can foresee."

"Please let me understand, your Excellency," Cup said. He was leaning forward, his small eyes watering. "I am elderly and may be slow in comprehending the situation. But if you have no government, who accredited you with this mission?"

"I am a diplomat. It is my specialty. No accreditation is necessary. The human race will accept my judgment on any matter of negotiation, as they would accept the judgment of any specialist in his area of expertise."

"But why *you*. As an individual?"

Drill shrugged massively. "I was part of the nearest diplomatic enclave, and the individual without any other tasks at the moment." He looked at each of the delegation in turn. "I am incredibly happy to have this chance, honorable delegates," he said. "The vast majority of human diplomats never have the chance to speak to another species. Usually we mediate only in conflicts of interest between the various groups of human specialties."

"But the human species will abide by your decisions?"

"Of course." Drill was surprised at the Shar's persistence. "Why wouldn't they?"

Cup settled back in his chair. His ears were down. There was a short silence.

"We have an opening statement prepared," President Gram said. "I would like to enter it into our record, if I may. Or would your Excellency prefer to go first?"

"I have no opening statement," Drill said. "Please go ahead."

Cup and the President exchanged glances. President Gram took a deep breath and began.

Long. Memory said. *Very long.*

The opening statement seemed very much like the address President Gram had been delivering to the crowd, the same hypnotic rhythms, more or less the same content. The rest of the delegation made muted responses. Drill drowsed through it, enjoying it as music.

"Thank you, Honorable President," he said afterwards. "That was very nice."

"We would like to propose an agenda for the conference," Gram said. "First, to resolve the matter of the cease-fire and its provisions for an ending to hostilities. Second, the establishment of a secure border between our two species, guaranteeing both species room for expansion. Third, the establishment of trade and visitation agreements. Fourth, the matter of reparations, payments, and return of lost territory."

Drill nodded. "I believe," he said, "that resolution of the second through fourth points will come about as a result of an understanding reached on the first. That is, once the cease-fire is settled, that resolution will imply a settlement of the rest of the situation."

"You accept the agenda?"

"If you like. It doesn't matter."

Ears pricked forward, then back. "So you accept that our initial discussions will consist of formalizing the disengagement of our forces?"

"Certainly. Of course I have no way of knowing what forces you have committed We humans have committed none."

The Shars were still for a long time. "Your species attacked our planets, Ambassador. Without warning, without making yourselves known to us." Gram's tone was unusually flat. Perhaps, Drill thought, she was attempting to conceal great emotion.

"Yes," Drill said. "But those were not our military formations. Your species were contacted only by our terraforming Ships. They did not attack your people, as such—they were only peripherally aware of your existence. Their function was merely to seed the planets with life-forms favorable to human existence. Unfortunately for your people, part of the function of these lifeforms is to destroy the native life of the planet."

The Shars conferred with one another. The Opposite Secretary-General seemed particularly vehement. Then President Gram turned to Drill.

"We cannot accept your statement, your Excellency," she said. "Our people were attacked. They defended themselves, but were overcome."

"Our terraforming Ships are very good at what they do," Drill said. "They are specialists. Our Shrikes, our Shrews, our Sharks—each is a master of its element. But they lack intelligence. They are not conscious entities, such as ourselves. They weren't aware of your civilization at all. They only saw you as food."

"You're claiming that you *didn't notice us?*" demanded Secretary-General Vang. *"They didn't notice us as they were killing us?"* He was shouting. President Gram's ears went back.

"Not as such, no," Drill said.

President Gram stood up. "I am afraid, your Excellency, your explanations are insufficient," she said. "This conference must be postponed until we can reach a united conclusion concerning your remarkable attitude."

Drill was bewildered. "What did I say?" he asked.

The other Shars stood. President Gram turned and walked briskly on her three legs toward the exit. The others followed.

"Wait," Drill said. "Don't go. Let me send for Frog. Up, Slab, up!"

The Shars were gone by the time Slab had got Drill to his feet. The Ship told him they had found their own way to the airlock. Drill could think of nothing to do but order the airlock to let them out.

"Why would I lie?" he asked. "Why would I lie to them?" Things were so very simple, really.

He shifted his vast weight from one foot to the other and back again. Drill could not decide whether he had done anything wrong. He asked Memory what to do next, but Memory held no information to comfort him, only dry recitations of past negotiations. Annoyed at the lifeless monologue, Drill told Memory to be silent and began to walk restlessly through the corridors of his Ship. He could not decide where things had gone bad.

Sensing his agitation, Lowbrain began to echo his distress. *Mash,* Lowbrain thought weakly. *Food. Sex.*

Be silent, Drill commanded.

Sex, sex, Lowbrain thought.

Drill realized that Lowbrain was beginning to give him an erection. Acceding to the inevitable, he began moving toward Surrogate's quarters.

Surrogate lived in a dim, quiet room filled with the murmuring sound of its own heartbeat. It was a human subspecies, about the intelligence of Lowbrain, designed to comfort voyagers on long journeys through space, when carnal access to their own subspecies might necessarily be limited. Surrogate had a variety of sexual equipment designed for the accommodation of the various human subspecies and their sexes. It also had large mammaries that gave nutritious milk, and a rudimentary head capable of voicing simple thoughts.

Tiny Mice, that kept Surrogate and the ship clean, scattered as Drill entered the room. Surrogate's little head turned to him.

"It's good to see you again," Surrogate said.

"I am Drill."

"It's good to see you again, Drill," said Surrogate. "It's good to see you again."

Drill began to nuzzle its breasts. One of Surrogate's male parts began to erect. "I'm confused, Surrogate," he said. "I don't know what to do."

"Why are you confused, Drill?" asked Surrogate. It raised one of its arms and began to stroke Drill's head. It wasn't really having a conversation: Surrogate had only been programmed to make simple statements, or to analyze its partners' speech and ask questions.

"Things are going wrong," Drill said. He began to suckle. The warm milk flowed down his throat. Surrogate's male part had an orgasm. Mice jumped from hiding to clean up the mess.

"Why are things going wrong?" asked Surrogate. "I'm sure everything will be all right."

Lowbrain had an orgasm, perceived by Drill as scattered, faraway bits of pleasure. Drill continued to suckle, feeling a heavy comfort beginning to radiate from Surrogate, from the gentle sound of its heartbeat, its huge, wholesome, brainless body.

Everything will be all right, Drill decided.

"Nice to see you again, Drill," Surrogate said. "Drill, it's *nice* to see you again."

The vast crowds of Shars did not leave when night fell. Instead they stood beneath floating globes dispersing a cold reddish light that reflected eerily from pointed ears and muzzles. Some of them donned capes or skirts to help them keep warm. Drill, watching them on the video walls of the command center, was reminded of crowds standing in awe before some vast cataclysm.

The Shars were not quiet. They stood in murmuring groups, but sometimes they began the crooning chants they had raised earlier, or suddenly broke out in a series of shrill yipping cries.

President Gram spoke to them after she had left Ship. "The human has admitted his species' attacks," she said, "but has disclaimed responsibility. We shall urge him to adopt a more realistic position."

"Adopt a position," Drill repeated, not understanding. "It is not a position. It is the truth. Why don't they understand?"

Opposite Minister-General Vang was more vehement. "We now have a far more complete idea of the humans' attitude," he said. "It is opposed to ours in every way. We shall not allow the murderous atrocities which the humans have committed upon five of our planets to be forgotten, or understood to be the result of some inexplicable lack of attention on the part of our species' enemies."

"That one is obviously deranged," thought Drill.

He went to his sleeping quarters and ordered the Slab there to play him some relaxing music. Even with Slab's murmurs and comforting hums, it took Drill some time before his agitation subsided.

Diplomacy, he thought as slumber overtook him, was certainly a strange business.

In the morning the Shars were still there, chanting and crying, moving in their strange crowded patterns. Drill watched them on his video walls as he ate breakfast at the mash bins. "There is a communication from President Gram," Memory announced. "She wishes to speak with you by radio."

"Certainly."

"Ambassador Drill." She was using the flat tones again. A pity she was subject to such stress.

"Good morning, President Gram," Drill said. "I hope you spent a pleasant night."

"I must give you the results of our decision. We regret that we can see no way to continue the negotiations unless you, as a representative of your species, agree to admit responsibility for your peoples' attacks on our planets."

"Admit responsibility?" Drill said. "Of course. Why wouldn't I?"

Drill heard some odd, indistinct barking sounds that his translator declined to interpret for him. It sounded as if someone other than President Gram were on the other end of the radio link.

"You admit responsibility?" President Gram's amazement was clear even in translation.

"Certainly. Does it make a difference?"

President Gram declined to answer that question. Instead she proposed another meeting for that afternoon.

"I will be ready at any time."

Memory recorded President Gram's speech to her people, and Drill studied it before meeting the Shar party at the airlock. She made a great deal out of the fact that Drill had admitted humanity's responsibility for the war. Her people leaped, yipped, chanted their responses as if possessed. Drill wondered why they were so excited.

Drill met the party at the airlock this time, linked with Memory and Lowbrain in Zen Synch so as not to accidentally step on the President or one of her party. He smiled and greeted each by name and led them toward the conference room.

"I believe," said Cup, "we may avoid future misunderstandings, if your Excellency would consent to inform us about your species. We have suffered some confusion in regard to your distinction between 'conscious' and 'unconscious' entities. Could you please explain the difference, as you understand it?"

"A pleasure, your Excellency," Drill said. "Our species, unlike yours, is highly specialized. Once, eight million years ago, we were like you—a small, nonspecialized species type is very useful at a certain stage of evolution. But once a species reaches a certain complexity in its social and technological evolution, the need for specialists becomes too acute. Through both deliberate genetic manipulation and natural evolution, humanity turned away from a generalist species, toward highly specialized forms adapted to particular functions and environments. We understand this to be a natural function of species evolution.

"In the course of our explorations into manipulating our species, we discovered that the most efficient way of coding large amounts of information was in our own cell structure—our DNA. For tasks requiring both large and small amounts of data, we arranged that, as much as possible, these would be performed by organic entities, human subspecies. Since many of these tasks were boring and repetitive, we reasoned that advanced consciousness, such as that which we both share, was not necessary. You have met several unconscious entities. Frog, for example, and the Slab on which I lie. Many parts of my Ship are also alive, though not conscious."

"That would explain the smell," one of the delegation murmured.

"The terraforming Ships," Drill went on, "which attacked your planets—these were also designed so as not to require a conscious operator."

The Shars squinted up at Drill with their little eyes. "But why?" Cup asked.

"Terraforming is a dull process. It takes many years. No conscious mind could possibly enjoy it."

"But your species would find itself at war without knowing it. If your explanation for the cause of this war is correct, you already have."

Drill shrugged massively. "This happens from time to time. Sometimes other species which have reached our stage of development have attacked us in the same way. When it does, we arrange a peace."

"You consider these attacks normal?" Opposite Minister-General Vang was the one who spoke.

"These occasional encounters seem to be a natural result of species evolution," Drill said.

Vang turned to one of the Shars near him and spoke in several sharp barks. Drill heard a few words: "Billions lost . . . five planets . . . atrocities . . . *natural result!*"

"I believe," said President Gram, "that we are straying from the agenda."

Vang looked at her. "Yes, honorable President. Please forgive me."

"The matter of withdrawal," said President Gram, "to recognized truce lines."

Species at this stage of their development tend to be territorial, Memory reminded Drill. *Their political mentality is based around the concept of borders. The idea of a borderless community of species may be perceived as a threat.*

I'll try and go easy on them, Drill said.

"The Memories on our terraforming Ships will be adjusted to account for your species," Drill said. "After the adjustment, your people will no longer be in danger."

"In our case, it will take the disengage order several months to reach all our forces," President Gram said. "How long will the order take to reach your own Ships?"

"A century or so." The Shars stared. "Memories at our exploration basis in this area will be adjusted first, of course, and these will adjust the Memories of terraforming Ships as they come in for maintenance and supplies."

"We'll be subject to attack for *another hundred years?*" Vang's tone mixed incredulity and scorn.

"Our terraforming Ships move more or less at random, and only come into base when they run out of supplies. We don't know where they've been till they report back. Though they're bound to encounter a few more of your planets, your species will still survive, enough to continue your species evolution. And during that time you'll be searching for and occupying new planets on your own. You'll probably come out of this with a net gain."

"Have you no respect for life?" Vang demanded. Drill considered his answer.

"All individuals die, Opposite Minister-General," he said. "That is a fact of nature which no species has been able to alter. Only species can survive. Individuals are easily replaceable. Though you will lose some planets and a large number of individuals, your species as a whole will survive and may even prosper. What more could a species or its delegated representatives desire?"

Opposite Minister-General Vang was glaring at Drill, his ears pricked forward, lips drawn back from his teeth. He said nothing.

"We desire a cease-fire that is a true cease-fire," President Gram said. Her hands were clasping and unclasping rhythmically on the edge of her chair. "Not a slow, authorized extermination of our species. Your position has an unwholesome smell. I am afraid we must end these discussions until you alter it."

"Position? This is not a position, honorable President. It is truth."

"We have nothing further to say."

Unhappily, Drill followed the Shar delegation to the airlock. "I do not lie, honorable President," he said, but Gram only turned away and silently left the human Ship. The Shars in their pale thousands received her.

The Shar broadcasts were not heartening. Opposite Minister-General Vang was particularly vehement. Drill collected the highlights of the speeches as he speeded through Memory's detailed remembrance "Callous disregard . . . no common ground for communication . . . casual attitude toward atrocity . . . displays of obvious savagery . . . no respect for the individual . . . defend ourselves . . . this stinks in the nose."

The Shars leaped and barked in response. There were strange bubbling high-pitched laughing sounds that Drill found unsettling.

"We hope to find a formula for peace," President Gram said. "We will confer with all the ministers in session." That was all.

That night, the Shars surrounding Ship moaned, moving slowly in a giant circle, their arms linked. The laughing sounds that followed Vang's speech did not cease entirely. He did not understand why they did not all go home and sleep.

Long, long, Memory said. No comfort there.

❊   ❊   ❊

Early in the morning, before dawn, there was a communication from President Gram. "I would like to meet with you privately. Away from the recorders, the coalition partners."

"I would like nothing better," Drill said. He felt a small current of optimism begin to trickle into him.

"Can I use an airlock other than the one we've been using up till now?"

Drill gave President Gram instructions and met her in the other airlock. She was wearing a night cape with a hood. The Shars, circling and moaning, had paid her no attention.

"Thank you for seeing me under these conditions," she said, peering up at him from beneath the hood. Drill smiled. She shuddered.

"I am pleased to be able to cooperate," he said.

Mash! Lowbrain demanded. It had been silent until Drill entered Zen Synch. Drill told it to be silent with a snarling vehemence that silenced it for the present.

"This way, honorable President," Drill said. He took her to his sleeping chamber—a small room, only fifty feet square. "Shall I send a Frog for one of your chairs?" he asked.

"I will stand. Three legs seem to be more comfortable than two for standing."

"Yes."

"Is it possible, Ambassador Drill, that you could lower the intensity of the light here? I find it oppressive."

Drill felt foolish, knowing he should have thought of this himself. "I'm sorry," he said. "I will give the orders at once. I wish you had told me earlier." He smiled nervously as he dimmed the lights and arranged himself on his Slab.

"Honorable ambassador." President Gram's words seemed hesitant. "I wonder if it is possible . . . can you tell me the meaning of that facial gesture of yours, showing me your teeth?"

"It is called a smile. It is intended as a gesture of benevolent reassurance."

"Showing of the teeth is considered a threat here, honorable Ambassador. Some of us have considered this a sign that you wish to eat us."

Drill was astonished. "My goodness!" he said. "I don't even eat meat! Just a kind of vegetable mash."

"I pointed out that your teeth seemed unsuitable for eating meat, but still it makes us uneasy. I was wondering . . ."

"I will try to suppress the smile, yes. Eating meat! What an idea. Some of our military specialists, yes, and of course the Sharks and Shrikes and so on . . ." He told his Memory to enforce a strict ban against smiling in the presence of a Shar.

Gram leaned back on her sturdy rear leg. Her cape parted, revealing her ribbons and badges of office, her four furry dugs. "I wanted to inform you of certain difficulties here, Ambassador Drill," she said. "I am having difficulty holding together my coalition. Minister-General Vang's faction is gaining strength. He is attempting to create a perception in the minds of Shars that you are untrustworthy and violent. Whether he believes this, or whether he is using this notion as a means of destabilizing the coalition, is hardly relevant—considering your species' unprovoked attacks, it is not a difficult perception to reinforce. He is also trying to tell our people that the military is capable of dealing with your species."

Drill's brain swam with Memory's information on concepts such as "faction" and "coalition." The meaning of the last sentence, however, was clear.

"That is a foolish perception, honorable President," he said.

"His assurances on that score lack conviction." Gram's eyes were shiny. Her tone grew earnest. "You must give me something, ambassador. Something I can use to soothe the public mind. A way out of this dilemma. I tell you that it is impossible to expect us to sit idly by and accept the loss of an undefined number of planets over the next hundred years. I plead with you, ambassador. Give me something. Some way we can avoid attack. Otherwise . . ." She left the sentence incomplete.

Mash, Lowbrain wailed. Drill ignored it. He moved into Zen Synch with Memory, racing through possible solutions. Sweat gathered on his forehead, pouring down his vast shoulders.

"Yes," he said. "Yes, there is a possibility. If you could provide us with the location of all your occupied planets, we could dispatch a Ship to each with the appropriate Memories as cargo. If any of our terraforming Ships arrived, the Memories could be transferred at once, and your planets would be safe."

President Gram considered this. "Memories," she said. "You've been using the term, but I'm not sure I understand."

"Stored information is vast, and even though human bodies are large we cannot always have all the information we need to function efficiently even in our specialized tasks," Drill said. "Our human brains have been separated as to function. I have a Lowbrain, which is on my spinal cord above my pelvis. Lowbrain handles motor control of my lower body, routine monitoring of my body's condition, eating, excretion, and sex. My perceptual centers, short-term memory, personality, and reasoning functions are handled by the brain in my skull—the classical brain, if you like. Long-term and specialized memory is the function of the large knob you see moving on my head, my Memory. My Memory records all that happens in great detail, and can recapitulate it at any point. It has also been supplied with information concerning the human species' contacts with other nonhuman groups. It attaches itself easily to my nervous system and draws nourishment from my body. Specific memories can be communicated from one living Memory to another, or if it proves necessary I can simply give my Memory to another human, a complete transfer. I have another Memory aboard that I'm not using at the moment, a pilot Memory that can navigate and handle Ship, and I wore this Memory while in transit. I also have spare Memories in case my primary Memories fall ill. So you see, our specialization does not rule out adaptability—any piece of information needed by any of us can easily be transferred, and in far greater detail than by any mechanical medium."

"So you could return to your base and send out pilot Memories to our planets," Gram said. "Memories that could halt your terraforming ships."

"That is correct." Just in time, Memory managed to stop the twitch in Drill's cheeks from becoming a smile. Happiness bubbled up in him. He was going to arrange this peace after all!

"I am afraid that would not be acceptable, your Excellency," President Gram said. Drill's hopes fell.

"Whyever not?"

"I'm afraid the Minister-General would consider it a naïve attempt of yours to find out the location of our populated planets. So that your species could attack them, ambassador."

"I'm trying very hard, President Gram," Drill said.

"I'm sure you are."

Drill frowned and went into Zen Synch again, ignoring Lowbrain's plaintive cries for mash and sex, sex and mash. Concepts crackled through his mind. He began to develop an erection, but Memory was drawing off most of the available blood and the erection failed. The smell of Drill's sweat filled the room. President Gram wrinkled her nose and leaned back far onto her rear leg.

"Ah," Drill said. "A solution. Yes. I can have my Pilot memory provide the locations to an equivalent number of our own planets. We will have one another's planets as hostage."

"Bravo, ambassador," President Gram said quietly. "I think we may have a solution. But—forgive me—it may be said that we cannot trust your information. We will have to send ships to verify the location of your planets."

"If your ships go to my planet first," Drill said, "I can provide your people with one of my spare Memories that will inform my species what your people are doing, and instruct the humans to cooperate. We will have to construct some kind of link between your radio and my Memory . . . maybe I can have my Ship grow one."

President Gram came forward off her third leg and began to pace forward, moving in her strange, fast, hobbling way. "I can present it to the council this way, yes," she said. "There is hope here." She stopped her movement, peering up at Drill with her ears pricked forward. "Is it possible that you could allow me to present this to the council as my own idea?" she asked. "It may meet with less suspicion that way."

"Whatever way is best," said Drill. President Gram gazed into the darkened recesses of the room.

"This smells good," she said. Drill succeeded in suppressing his smile.

"It's nice to see you again."

"I am Drill."

"It's nice to see you again, Drill."

"I think we can make the peace work."

"Everything will be all right, Drill. Drill, I'm sure everything will be all right."

"I'm so glad I had this chance. This is the chance of a lifetime."

"Drill, it's *nice* to see you again."

The next day President Gram called and asked to present a new plan. Drill said he would be pleased to hear it. He met the party at the airlock, having already dimmed the lights. He was very rigid in his attempts not to smile.

They sat in the dimmed room while President Gram presented the plan. Drill pretended to think it over, then acceded. Details were worked out. First the location of one human planet would be given and verified—this planet, the Shar capital, would count as the first revealed Shar planet. After verification, each side would reveal the location of two planets, verify those, then reveal four, and so on. Even counting the months it would take to verify the location of planets, the treaty should be completed within less than five years.

That night the Shars went mad. At President Gram's urging, they built fires, danced, screamed, sang. Drill watched on his Ship's video walls. Their rhythms beat at his head.

He smiled. For hours.

The Ship obligingly grew a communicator and coupled it to one of Drill's spare Memories. The two were put aboard a Shar ship and sent in the direction of Drill's home. Drill remained in his ship, watching entertainment videos Ship received from the Shars' channels. He didn't understand the dramas very well, but the comedies were delightful. The Shars could do the most intricate, clever things with their flexible bodies and odd tripod legs—it was delightful to watch them.

Maybe I could take some home with me, he thought. *They can be very entertaining.*

The thousands of Shars waiting outside Ship began to drift away. Within a month only a few hundred were left. Their singing was quiet, triumphant, assured. Sometimes Drill had it piped into his sleeping chamber. It helped him relax.

President Gram visited informally every ten days or so. Drill showed her around Ship, showing her the pilot Memory, the Frog quarters, the giant stardrive engines with their human subspecies' implanted connections, Surrogate in its shadowed, pleasant room. The sight of Surrogate seemed to agitate the President.

"You do not use sex for procreation?" she asked. "As an expression of affection?"

"Indeed we do. I have scads of offspring. There are never enough diplomats, so we have a great many couplings among our subspecies. As for affection . . . I think I can say that I have enjoyed the company of each of my partners."

She looked up at him with solemn eyes. "You travel to the stars, Drill," she said. "Your species expands randomly in all directions, encountering other species, sometimes annihilating them. Do you have a reason for any of this?"

"A reason?" Drill mused. "It is natural to us. Natural to all intelligent species, so far as we know."

"I meant a conscious reason. Is it anything other than what you do in an automatic way?"

"I can't think of why we would need any such reasons."

"So you have no philosophy of constant expansion? No ideology?"

"I do not know what those words mean," Drill said.

Gram closed her eyes and lowered her head. "I am sorry," she said.

"No need. We have no conflicts in our ideas about ourselves, about our lives. We are happy with what we are."

"Yes. You couldn't be unhappy if you tried, could you?"

"No," Drill said cheerfully. "I see that you understand."

"Yes," Gram said. "I scent that I do."

"In a few million years," Drill said, "these things will become clear to you."

The first Shar ship returned from Drill's home, reporting a transfer of the Memory. The field around Ship filled again with thousands of Shars, crying their happiness to the skies. Other Memories were now taking instructions to all terraforming bases. The locations of two new planets were released. Ships carrying spare Memories leaped into the skies.

It's working, Drill told Memory.

Long, Memory said. *Very long.*

But Memory could not lower Drill's joy. This was what he had lived his life for, and he knew he was good at it. Memories of the future would take this solution as a model for negotiations with other species. Things were working out.

One night the Shars outside Ship altered their behavior. Their singing became once again a moaning, mixed with cries. Drill was disturbed.

A communication came from the President. "Cup is dead," she said.

"I understand," Drill said. "Who is his replacement?"

Drill could not read Gram's expression. "That is not yet known. Cup was a strong person, and did not like other strong people around him. Already the successors are fighting for the leadership, but they may not be able to hold his faction together." Her ears flickered. "I may be weakened by this."

"I regret things tend that way."

"Yes," she said. "So do I."

❀   ❀   ❀

The second set of ships returned. More Memories embarked on their journeys. The treaty was holding.

There was a meeting aboard Ship to formalize the agreement. Cup's successor was Brook, a tall, elderly Shar whose golden fur was darkened by age. A compromise candidate, President Gram said, his election determined after weeks of fighting for the successorship. He was not respected. Already pieces of Cup's old faction were breaking away.

"I wonder, your Excellency," Brook said, after the formal business was over, "if you could arrange for our people to learn your language. You must have powerful translation modules aboard your ship in order to learn our language so quickly. You were broadcasting your message of peace within a few hours of entering real space."

"I have no such equipment aboard Ship," Drill said. "Our knowledge of your language was acquired from Shar prisoners."

"Prisoners?" Shar ears pricked forward. "We were not aware of this," Brook said.

"After our base Memories recognized discrepancies," Drill said, "we sent some Ships out searching for you. We seized one of your ships and took it to my home world. The prisoners were asked about their language and the location of your capital planet. Otherwise it would have taken me months to find your world here, and learn to communicate with you."

"May we ask to arrange for the return of the prisoners?"

"Oh." Drill said. "That won't be possible. After we learned what we needed to know, we terminated their lives. They were being kept in an area reserved for a garden. The landscapers wanted to get to work." Drill bobbed his head reassuringly. "I am pleased to inform you that they proved excellent fertilizer for the gardens. The result was quite lovely."

"I think," said President Gram carefully, "that it would be best that this information not go beyond those of us in this room. I think it would disturb the process."

Minister-General Vang's ears went back. So did others'. But they acceded.

"I think we should take our leave," said President Gram.

"Have a pleasant afternoon," said Drill.

"It's important." It was not yet dawn. Ship had awakened Drill for a call from the President. "One of your ships has attacked another of our planets."

Alarm drove the sleep from Drill's brain. "Please come to the airlock," he said.

"The information will reach the population within the hour."

"Come quickly," said Drill.

The President arrived with a pair of assistants, who stayed inside the airlock. They carried staves. "My people will be upset," Gram said. "Things may not be entirely safe."

"Which planet was it?" Drill asked.

Gram rubbed her ears. "It was one of those whose location went out on the last peace shuttle."

"The new Memory must not have arrived in time."

"That is what we will tell the people. That it couldn't have been prevented. I will try to speed up the process by which the planets receive new Memories. Double the quota."

"That is a good idea."

"I will have to dismiss Brook. Opposite Minister-General Vang will have to take his job. If I can give Vang more power, he may remain in the coalition and not cause a split."

"As you think best."

President Gram looked up at Drill, her head rising reluctantly, as if held back by a great weight. "My son," she said. "He was on the planet when it happened."

"You have other offspring," Drill said.

Gram looked at him, the pain burning deep in her eyes. "Yes," she said. "I do."

The fields around Ship filled once again. Cries and howls rent the air, and dirges pulsed against Ship's uncaring walls. The Shar broadcasts in the next weeks seemed confused to Drill. Coalitions split and fragmented. Vang spoke frequently of readiness. President Gram succeeded in doubling the quota of planets. The decision was a near one.

Then, days later, another message. "One of our commanders," said President Gram, "was based on the vicinity of the attacked planet. He is one of Vang's creatures. On his own initiative he ordered our military forces to engage. Your terraforming Ship was attacked."

"Was it destroyed?" Drill asked. His tone was urgent. There is still hope, he reminded himself.

"Don't be anxious for your fellow humans," Gram said. "The Ship was damaged, but escaped."

"The loss of a few hundred billion unconscious organisms is no cause for anxiety," Drill said. "An escaped terraforming Ship is. The Ship will alert our military forces. It will be a real war."

President Gram licked her lips. "What does that mean?"

"You know of our Shrikes and so on. Our military people are worse. They are fully conscious and highly specialized in different modes of warfare. They are destructive, carnivorous, capable of taking enormous damage without impairing function. Their minds concentrate only on tactics, on destruction. Normally they are kept on planetoids away from the rest of humanity. Even other humans find their proximity too . . . disturbing." Drill put all the urgency in his speech that he could. "Honorable President, you must give me the locations of the remaining planets. If I can get Memories to each of them with news of the peace, we may yet save them."

"I will try. But the coalition . . ." She turned away from the transmitter. "Vang will claim a victory."

"It is the worst possible catastrophe," Drill said.

Gram's tone was grave. "I believe you," she said.

Drill listened to the broadcasts with growing anxiety. The Shars who spoke on the broadcasts were making angry comments about the execution of prisoners, about flower gardens and values Drill didn't understand. Someone had let the secret loose. President Gram went from group to group outside Ship, talking of the necessity of her plan. The Shars' responses were muted. Drill sensed they were waiting. It was announced that Vang had left the coalition. A chorus of triumphant yips rose from scattered members of the crowd. Others only moaned.

Vang, now simply General Vang, arrived at the field. His followers danced intoxicated circles around him as he spoke, howling their responses to his words. "Triumph! United will!" they cried. "The humans can be beaten! Treachery avenged! Dictate the peace from a position of strength! We smell the location of their planets!"

The Shars' weird cackling laughter followed him from point to point. The laughing and crying went on well into the night. In the morning the announcement came that the coalition had fallen. Vang was now President-General.

In his sleeping chamber, surrounded by his video walls, Drill began to weep.

✦   ✦   ✦

"I have been asked to bear Vang's message to you," Gram said. She seemed smaller than before, standing unsteadily even on her tripod legs. "It is his . . . humor."

"What is the message?" Drill said. His whole body seemed in pain. Even Lowbrain was silent, wrapped in misery.

"I had hoped," Gram said, "that he was using this simply as an issue on which to gain power. That once he had the Presidency, he would continue the diplomatic effort. It appears he really means what he's been saying. Perhaps he's no longer in control of his own people."

"It is war," Drill said.

"Yes."

You have failed, said Memory. Drill winced in pain.

"You will lose," he said.

"Vang says we are cleverer than you are."

"That may be the case. But cleverness cannot compete with experience. Humans have fought hundreds of these little wars, and never failed to wipe out the enemy. Our Memories of these conflicts are intact. Your people can't fight millions of years of specialized evolution."

"Vang's message doesn't end there. You have till nightfall to remove your Ship from the planet. Six days to get out of real space."

"I am to be allowed to live?" Drill was surprised.

"Yes. It is our . . . our custom."

Drill scratched himself. "I regret our efforts did not succeed."

"No more than I." She was silent for a while. "Is there any way we can stop this?"

"If Vang attacks any human planets after the Memories of the peace arrangement have arrived," Drill said, "the military will be unleashed to wipe you out. There is no stopping them after that point."

"How long," she asked, "do you think we have?"

"A few years. Ten at the most."

"Our species will be dead."

"Yes. Our military are very good at their jobs."

"You will have killed us," Gram said, "destroyed the culture that we have built for thousands of years, and you won't even give it any thought. Your species doesn't think about what it does any more. It just acts, like a single-celled animal, engulfing everything it can reach. You say that you are a conscious species, but that isn't true. Your every action is . . . instinct. Or reflex."

"I don't understand," said Drill.

Gram's body trembled. "That is the tragedy of it," she said.

An hour later Ship rose from the field. Shars laughed their defiance from below, dancing in crazed abandon.

I have failed, Drill told Memory.

You knew the odds were long, Memory said. *You knew that in negotiations with species this backward there have only been a handful of successes, and hundreds of failures.*

Yes, Drill acknowledged. *It's a shame, though. To have spent all these months away from home.*

Eat! Eat! said Lowbrain.

Far away, in their forty-mile-long Ships, the human soldiers were already on their way.

Introduction to "Face Value"

by Karen Joy Fowler

Fish-out-of-water stories are a staple of Hollywood. Sometimes they can lead to charming fables like Splash, *and sometimes to formulaic extravaganzas like* Beverly Hills Cop III. *But, while Hollywood finds humor in thrusting characters from one milieu into another, it's worth remembering that when fish are too long out of the water, they die. (They also begin to stink, which is an aspect that Hollywood has* not *neglected.)*

This is a waterless story, dusty as its desert setting, as its mothy aliens; but reading it is not a dry experience. It is liquid with life, hot with the suffering of a character who wavers between being un- and too-adaptable.

Karen Joy Fowler came to maturity as a writer via the academic route of literature and writing classes. Often this is where would-be sf writers are lost to our field, because the pressure against writing science fiction can be intense. But Fowler doesn't respond to pressure by complying; instead she combusts, and the result has been a series of unforgettable short stories that owe more to Faulkner than to Heinlein and yet are definitely science fiction—arguably could not exist except as science fiction.

Fowler is also a perceptive teacher of writing. It is not true that writing cannot be taught; the aphorism is widely believed because most writing teachers are incompetent. Just because someone knows how to write well, or even edit well, does not mean that she knows how to teach writing. It is a separate knack, and Fowler has it. So if you are ambitious to join the ranks of practitioners of this arcane magic, and you hear of her leading a writing workshop or teaching one of the weeks at Clarion, I assure you that she will actually help you toward your goal.

FACE VALUE

Karen Joy Fowler

It was almost like being alone. Taki, who had been alone one way or another most of his life, recognized this and thought he could deal with it. What choice did he have? It was only that he had allowed himself to hope for something different. A second star, small and dim, joined the sun in the sky, making its appearance over the rope bridge which spanned the empty river. Taki crossed the bridge in a hurry to get inside before the hottest part of the day began.

Something flashed briefly in the dust at his feet and he stooped to pick it up. It was one of Hesper's poems, half finished, left out all night. Taki had stopped reading Hesper's poetry. It reflected nothing, not a whisper of her life here with him, but was filled with longing for things and people behind her. Taki pocketed the poem on his way to the house, stood outside the door, and removed what dust he could with the stiff brush which hung at the entrance. He keyed his admittance; the door made a slight sucking sound as it resealed behind him.

Hesper had set out an iced glass of ade for him. Taki drank it at a gulp, superimposing his own dusty fingerprints over hers sketched lightly in the condensation on the glass. The drink was heavily sugared and only made him thirstier.

A cloth curtain separated one room from another, a blue sheet, Hesper's innovation since the dwelling was designed as a single, multifunctional space. Through the curtain Taki heard a voice and knew Hesper was listening again to her mother's letter—earth weather, the romances of her younger cousins. The letter had arrived weeks ago, but Taki was careful not to remind Hesper how old its news really was. If she chose to imagine the lives of her family moving along the same timeline as her own, then this must be a fantasy she needed. She knew the truth. In the time it had taken her to travel here with Taki, her mother had grown old and died. Her cousins had settled into marriages happy or unhappy or had faced life alone. The letters which continued to arrive with some regularity were an illusion. A lifetime later Hesper would answer them.

Taki ducked through the curtain to join her. "Hot," he told her as if this were news. She lay on their mat stomach down, legs bent at the knees, feet crossed in the air. Her hair, the color of dried grasses, hung over her face. Taki stared for a moment at the back of her head. "Here," he said. He pulled her poem from his pocket and laid it by her hand. "I found this out front."

Hesper switched off the letter and rolled onto her back away from the poem. She was careful not to look at Taki. Her cheeks were stained with irregular red patches so that Taki knew she had been crying again. The observation caused him a familiar mixture of sympathy and impatience. His feelings for Hesper always came in these uncomfortable combinations; it tired him.

"'Out front,'" Hesper repeated, and her voice held a practiced tone of uninterested nastiness. "And how did you determine that one part of this featureless landscape was the 'front'?"

"Because of the door. We have only the one door so it's the front door."

"No," said Hesper. "If we had two doors then one might arguably be the front door and the other the back door, but with only one it's just the door." Her gaze went straight upward. "You use words so carelessly. Words from another world. They mean nothing here." Her eyelids fluttered briefly, the lashes darkened with tears. "It's not just an annoyance to me, you know," she said. "It can't help but damage your work."

"My work is the study of the mene," Taki answered. "Not the creation of a new language," and Hesper's eyes closed.

"I really don't see the difference," she told him. She lay a moment longer without moving, then opened her eyes and looked at Taki directly. "I don't want to have this conversation. I don't know why I started it. Let's rewind, run it again. I'll be the wife this time. You come in and say, 'Honey, I'm home!' and I'll ask you how your morning was."

Taki began to suggest that this was a scene from another world and would mean nothing here. He had not yet framed the sentence when he heard the door seal release and saw Hesper's face go hard and white. She reached for her poem and slid it under the scarf at her waist. Before she could get to her feet the first of the mene had joined them in the bedroom. Taki ducked through the curtain to fasten the door before the temperature inside the house rose. The outer room was filled with dust and the hands which reached out to him as he went past left dusty streaks on his clothes and his skin. He counted eight of the mene, fluttering about him like large moths, moths the size of human children, but with furry vestigial wings, hourglass abdomens, sticklike limbs. They danced about him in the open spaces, looked through the cupboards, pulled the tapes from his desk. When they had their backs to him he could see the symmetrical arrangement of dark spots which marked their wings in a pattern resembling a human face. A very sad face, very distinct. Masculine, Taki had always thought, but Hesper disagreed.

The party which had made initial contact under the leadership of Hans Mene so many years ago had wisely found the faces too whimsical for mention in their report. Instead they had included pictures and allowed them to speak for themselves. Perhaps the original explorers had been asking the same question Hesper posed the first time Taki showed her the pictures. Was the face really there? Or was this only evidence of the ability of humans to see their own faces in everything? Hesper had a poem entitled "The Kitchen God," which recounted the true story of a woman about a century ago who had found the image of Christ in the burn-marks on a tortilla. "Do *they* see it, too?" she had asked Taki, but there was as yet no way to ask this of the mene, no way to know if they had reacted with shock and recognition to the faces of the first humans they had seen, though studies of the mene eye suggested a finer depth perception which might significantly distort the flat image.

Taki thought that Hesper's own face had changed since the day, only six months ago calculated as Traveltime, when she had said she would come here with him and he thought it was because she loved him. They had sorted through all the information which had been collected to date on the mene and her face had been all sympathy then. "What would it be like," she asked him, "to be able to fly and then to lose this ability? To outgrow it? What would a loss like that do to the racial consciousness of a species?"

"It happened so long ago, I doubt it's even noticed as a loss," Taki had answered. "Legends, myths not really believed perhaps. Probably not even that. In the racial memory not even a whisper."

Hesper had ignored him. "What a shame they don't write poetry," she had said. She was finding them less romantic now as she joined Taki in the outer room, her face stoic. The mene surrounded her, ran their string-fingered hands all over her body, inside her clothing. One mene attempted to insert a finger into her mouth, but Hesper tightened her lips together resolutely, dust on her chin. Her eyes were fastened on Taki. Accusingly? Beseechingly? Taki was no good at reading people's eyes. He looked away.

Eventually the mene grew bored. They left in groups, a few lingering behind to poke among the boxes in the bedroom, then following the others until Hesper and Taki were left alone. Hesper went to wash herself as thoroughly as their limited water supply allowed; Taki swept up the loose dust. Before he finished, Hesper returned, showing him her empty jewelry box without a word. The jewelry had all belonged to her mother.

"I'll get them when it cools," Taki told her.

"Thank you."

It was always Hesper's things that the mene took. The more they disgusted her, pawing over her, rummaging through her things, no way to key the door against clever mene fingers even if Taki had agreed to lock them out, which he had not, the more fascinating they seemed to find her. They touched her twice as often as they touched Taki and much more insistently. They took her jewelry, her poems, her letters, all the things she treasured most, and Taki believed, although it was far too early in his studies really to speculate with any assurance, that the mene read something off the objects. The initial explorers had concluded that mene communication was entirely telepathic, and if this was accurate, then Taki's speculation was not such a leap. Certainly the mene didn't value the objects for themselves. Taki always found them discarded in the dust on this side of the rope bridge.

The fact that everything would be easily recovered did nothing to soften Hesper's sense of invasion. She mixed herself a drink, stirring it with the metal straw which poked through the dust-proof lid. "You shouldn't allow it," she said at last, and Taki knew from the time that had elapsed that she had tried not to begin this familiar conversation. He appreciated her effort as much as he was annoyed by her failure.

"It's part of my job," he reminded her. "We have to be accessible to them. I study them. They study us. There's no way to differentiate the two activities and certainly no way to establish communication except simultaneously."

"You're letting them study us, but you're giving them a false picture. You're allowing them to believe that humans intrude on each other in this way. Does it occur to you that they may be involved in similar charades? If so, what can either of us learn?"

Taki took a deep breath. "The need for privacy may not be as intrinsically human as you imagine. I could point to many societies which afforded very little of this. As for any deliberate misrepresentations on their part—well, isn't that the whole rationale for not sending a study team? Wouldn't I be farther along if I were working with environmentalists, physiologists, linguists? But the risk of contamination increases exponentially with each additional human. We would be too much of a presence. Of course, I will be very careful. I am far from the stage in my study where I can begin to draw conclusions. When I visit them . . ."

"Reinforcing the notion that such visits are ordinary human behavior . . ." Hesper was looking at Taki with great coolness.

"When I visit them I am much more circumspect," Taki finished. "I conduct my study as unobtrusively as possible."

"And what do you imagine you are studying?" Hesper asked. She closed her lips tightly over the straw and drank. Taki regarded her steadily and with exasperation.

"Is this a trick question?" he asked. "I imagine I am studying the mene. What do you imagine I am studying?"

"What humans always study," said Hesper. "Humans."

You never saw one of the mene alone. Not ever. One never wandered off to watch the sun set or took its food to a solitary hole to eat without sharing. They did everything in groups and although Taki had been observing them for weeks now and was able to identify individuals and had compiled charts of the groupings he had seen, trying to isolate families or friendships or work-castes, still the results were inconclusive.

His attempts at communication were similarly discouraging. He had tried verbalizations, but had not expected a response to them; he had no idea how they processed audio information although they could hear. He had tried clapping and gestures, simple hand signals for the names of common objects. He had no sense that these efforts were noticed. They were so unfocused when he dealt with them, fluttering here, fluttering there. Taki's ESP quotient had never been measurable, yet he tried that route, too. He tried to send a simple command. He would trap a mene hand and hold it against his own cheek, trying to form in his mind the picture which corresponded to the action. When he released the hand, sticky mene fingers might linger for a moment or they might slip away immediately, tangle in his hair instead, or tap his teeth. Mene teeth were tiny and pointed like wires. Taki saw them only when the mene ate. At other times they were hidden inside the folds of skin which almost hid their eyes as well. Taki speculated that the skin flaps protected their mouths and eyes from the dust. Taki found mene faces less expressive than their backs. Head-on they appeared petaled and blind as flowers. When he wanted to differentiate one mene from another, Taki looked at their wings.

Hesper had warned him there would be no art and he had asked her how she could be so sure. "Because their communication system is perfect," she said. "Out of one brain and into the next with no loss of meaning, no need for abstraction. Art arises from the inability to communicate. Art is the imperfect symbol. Isn't it?" But Taki, watching the mene carry water up from their underground deposits, asked himself where the line between tools and art objects should be drawn. For no functional reason that he could see, the water containers curved in the centers like the shapes of the mene's own abdomens.

Taki followed the mene below ground, down some shallow, rough-cut stairs into the darkness. The mene themselves were slightly luminescent when there was no other light; at times and seasons some were spectacularly so and Taki's best guess was that this was sexual. Even with the dimmer members, Taki could see well enough. He moved through a long tunnel with a low ceiling which made him stoop. He could hear water at the other end of it, not the water itself, but a special quality to the silence which told him water was near. The lake was clearly artificial, collected during the rainy season which no human had seen yet. The tunnel narrowed sharply. Taki could have gone forward, but felt suddenly claustrophobic and backed out instead. What did the mene think, he wondered, of the fact that he came here without Hesper. Did they notice this at all? Did it teach them anything about humans that they were capable of understanding?

"Their lives together are perfect," Hesper said. "Except for those useless wings. If they are ever able to talk with us at all it will be because of those wings."

Of course Hesper was a poet. The world was all language as far as she was concerned.

When Taki first met Hesper, at a party given by a colleague of his, he had asked her what she did. "I name things," she had said. "I try to find the right names for things." In retrospect Taki thought it was bullshit. He couldn't remember why he had been so impressed with it at the time, a deliberate miscommunication, when a simple answer, "I write poetry," would have been so clear and easy to understand. He felt the same way about her poetry itself, needlessly obscure, slightly evocative, but it left the reader feeling that he had fallen short somehow, that it had been a test and he had flunked it. It was unkind poetry and Taki had worked so hard to read it then.

"Am I right?" he would ask her anxiously when he finished. "Is that what you're saying?" but she would answer that the poem spoke for itself.

"Once it's on the page, I've lost control over it. Then the reader determines what it says or how it works." Hesper's eyes were gray, the irises so large and intense within their dark rings, that they made Taki dizzy. "So you're always right. By definition. Even if it's not remotely close to what I intended."

What Taki really wanted was to find himself in Hesper's poems. He would read them anxiously for some symbol which could be construed as him, some clue as to his impact on her life. But he was never there.

It was against policy to send anyone into the field alone. There were pros and cons, of course, but ultimately the isolation of a single professional was seen as too cruel. For shorter projects there were advantages in sending a threesome, but during a longer study the group dynamics in a trio often became difficult. Two were considered ideal and Taki knew that Rawji and Heyen had applied for this post, a husband and wife team in which both members were trained for this type of study. He had never stopped being surprised that the post had been offered to him instead. He could not have even been considered if Hesper had not convinced the members of the committee of her willingness to accompany him, but she must have done much more. She must have impressed someone very much for them to decide that one trained xenologist and one poet might be more valuable than two trained xenologists. The committee had made some noises about "contamination" occurring between the two trained professionals, but Taki found this argument specious. "What did you say to them?" he asked her after her interview and she shrugged.

"You know," she said. "Words."

Taki had hidden things from the committee during his own interview. Things about Hesper. Her moods, her deep attachment to her mother, her unreliable attachment to him. He must have known it would never work out, but he walked about in those days with the stunned expression of a man who has been given everything. Could he be blamed for accepting it? Could he be blamed for believing in Hesper's unexpected willingness to accompany him? It made a sort of equation for Taki. *If* Hesper was willing to give up everything and come with Taki, *then* Hesper loved Taki. An ordinary marriage commitment was reviewable every five years; this was something much greater. No other explanation made any sense.

The equation still held a sort of inevitability for Taki. *Then* Hesper loved Taki, *if* Hesper were willing to come with him. So somehow, sometime, Taki had done something which lost him Hesper's love. If he could figure out what, perhaps he could make her love him again. "Do you love me?" he had asked Hesper, only once; he had too much pride for these thinly disguised pleadings. "Love is such a difficult word," she had answered, but her voice had been filled with a rare softness and had not hurt Taki as much as it might.

The daystar was appearing again when Taki returned home. Hesper had made a meal which suggested she was coping well today. It included a sort of pudding made of a local fruit they found themselves able to tolerate. Hesper called the pudding "boxty." It was apparently a private joke. Taki was grateful for the food and the joke, even if he didn't understand it. He tried to keep the conversation lighthearted, talking to Hesper about the mene water jars. Taki's position was that when the form of a practical object was less utilitarian than it might be, then it was art. Hesper laughed. She ran through a list of human artifacts and made him classify them.

"A paper clip," she said.

"The shape hasn't changed in centuries," he told her. "Not art."

"A safety pin."

Taki hesitated. How essential was the coil at the bottom of the pin? Very. "Not art," he decided.

"A hair brush."

"Boar bristle?"

"Wood handle."

"Art. Definitely."

She smiled at him. "You're confusing ornamentation with art. But why not? It's as good a definition as any," she told him. "Eat your boxty."

They spend the whole afternoon alone, uninterrupted. Taki transcribed the morning's notes into his files, reviewed his tapes. Hesper recorded a letter whose recipient would never hear it and sang softly to herself.

That night he reached for her, his hand along the curve at her waist. She stiffened slightly, but responded by putting her hand on his face. He kissed her and her mouth did not move. His movements became less gentle. It might have been passion; it might have been anger She told him to stop, but he didn't. Couldn't. Wouldn't. "Stop," she said again and he heard she was crying. "They're here. Please stop. They're watching us."

"Studying us," Taki said. "Let them," but he rolled away and released her. They were alone in the room. He would have seen the mene easily in the dark. "Hesper," he said. "There's no one here."

She lay rigid on her side of their bed. He saw the stitching of her backbone disappearing into her neck and had a sudden feeling that he could see everything about her, how she was made, how she was held together. It made him no less angry.

"I'm sorry," Hesper told him, but he didn't believe her. Even so, he was asleep before she was. He made his own breakfast the next morning without leaving anything out for her. He was gone before she had gotten out of bed.

The mene were gathering food, dried husks thick enough to protect the liquid fruit during the two-star dry season. They punctured the husks with their needle-thin teeth. Several crowded about him, greeting him with their fingers, checking his pockets, removing his recorder and passing it about until one of them dropped it in the dust. When they returned to work, Taki retrieved it, wiped it as clean as he could. He sat down to watch them, logged everything he observed. He noted in particular how often they touched each other and wondered what each touch meant. Affection? Communication? Some sort of chain of command?

Later he went underground again, choosing another tunnel, looking for one which wouldn't narrow so as to exclude him, but finding himself beside the same lake with the same narrow access ahead. He went deeper this time until it gradually became too close for his shoulders. Before him he could see a luminescence; he smelled the dusty odor of the mene and could just make out a sound, too, a sort of movement, a grass-rubbing-together sound. He stooped and strained his eyes to see something in the faint light. It was like looking into the wrong end of a pair of binoculars. The tunnel narrowed and narrowed. Beyond it must be the mene homes and he could never get into them.

He contrasted this with the easy access they had to his home. At the end of his vision he thought he could just see something move, but he wasn't sure. A light touch on the back of his neck and another behind his knee startled him. He twisted around to see a group of the mene crowded into the tunnel behind him. It gave him a feeling of being trapped and he had to force himself to be very gentle as he pushed his way back and let the mene go through. The dark pattern of their wings stood in high relief against the luminescent bodies. The human faces grew smaller and smaller until they disappeared.

"Leave me alone," Hesper told him. It took Taki completely by surprise. He had done nothing but enter the bedroom; he had not even spoken yet. "Just leave me alone."

Taki saw no signs that Hesper had ever gotten up. She lay against the pillow and her cheek was still creased from the wrinkles in the sheets. She had not been crying. There was something worse in her face, something which alarmed Taki.

"Hesper?" he asked. "Hesper? Did you eat anything? Let me get you something to eat."

It took Hesper a moment to answer. When she did, she looked ordinary again. "Thank you," she said. "I am hungry." She joined him in the outer room, wrapped in their blanket, her hair tangled around her face. She got a drink for herself, dropping the empty glass once, stooping to retrieve it. Taki had the strange impression that the glass fell slowly. When they had first arrived, the gravitational pull had been light, just perceptibly lighter than Earth's. Without quite noticing, this had registered on him in a sort of lightheartedness. But Hesper had complained of feelings of dislocation, disconnection. Taki put together a cold breakfast, which Hesper ate slowly, watching her own hands as if they fascinated her. Taki looked away. "Fork," she said. He looked back. She was smiling at him.

"What?"

"Fork."

He understood. "Not art."

"Four tines?"

He didn't answer.

"Roses carved on the handle."

"Well then, art. Because of the handle. Not because of the tines." He was greatly reassured.

The mene came while he was telling her about the tunnel. They put their dusty fingers in her food, pulled it apart. Hesper set her fork down and pushed the plate away. When they reached for her she pushed them away, too. They came back. Hesper shoved harder.

"Hesper," said Taki

"I just want to be left alone. They never leave me alone." Hesper stood up, towering above the mene. The blanket fell to the floor. "We flew here," Hesper said to the mene. "Did you see the ship? Didn't you see the pod? Doesn't that interest you? Flying?" She laughed and flapped her arms until they froze, horizontal at her sides. The mene reached for her again and she brought her arms in to protect her breasts, pushing the mene away repeatedly, harder and harder, until they tired of approaching her and went into the bedroom, reappearing with her poems in their hands. The door sealed behind them.

"I'll get them back for you," Taki promised, but Hesper told him not to bother.

"I haven't written in weeks," she said. "In case you hadn't noticed. I haven't finished a poem since I came here. I've lost that. Along with everything else." She brushed at her hair rather frantically with one hand. "It doesn't matter," she added. "My poems? Not art."

"Are you the best person to judge that?" Taki asked.

"Don't patronize me." Hesper returned to the table, looked again at the plate which held her unfinished breakfast, dusty from handling. "My critical faculties are still intact. It's just the poetry that's gone." She took the dish to clean it, scraped the food away. "I was never any good," she said. "Why do you think I came here? I had no poetry of my own so I thought I'd write the mene's. I came to a world without words. I hoped it would be clarifying. I knew there was a risk." Her hands moved very fast. "I want you to know I don't blame you."

"Come and sit down a moment, Hesper," Taki said, but she shook her head. She looked down at her body and moved her hands over it.

"They feel sorry for us. Did you know that? They feel sorry about our bodies."

"How do *you* know that?" Taki asked.

"Logic. We have these completely functional bodies. No useless wings. Not art." Hesper picked up the blanket and headed for the bedroom. At the cloth curtain she paused a moment. "They love our loneliness, though. They've taken all mine. They never leave me alone now." She thrust her right arm suddenly out into the air. It made the curtain ripple. "Go away," she said, ducking behind the sheet.

Taki followed her. He was very frightened. "No one is here but us,

Hesper," he told her. He tried to put his arms around her but she pushed him back and began to dress.

"Don't touch me all the time," she said. He sank onto the bed and watched her. She sat on the floor to fasten her boots.

"Are you going out, Hesper?" he asked and she laughed.

"Hesper is out," she said. "Hesper is out of place, out of time, out of luck, and out of her mind. Hesper has vanished completely. Hesper was broken into and taken."

Taki fastened his hands tightly together. "Please don't do this to me, Hesper," he pleaded. "It's really so unfair. When did I ask so much of you? I took what you offered me; I never took anything else. Please don't do this."

Hesper had found the brush and was pulling it roughly through her hair. He rose and went to her, grabbing her by the arms, trying to turn her to face him. "Please, Hesper!"

She shook loose from him without really appearing to notice his hands, continued to work through the worst of her tangles. When she did turn around, her face was familiar, but somehow not Hesper's face. It was a face which startled him.

"Hesper is gone," it said. "We have her. You've lost her. We are ready to talk to you. Even though you will never, never, never understand." She reached out to touch him, laying her open palm against his cheek and leaving it there.

Introduction to "Cabracan"

by Lewis Shiner

Lewis Shiner and Bruce Sterling are friends and, through playing ideas off each other, have come to have some opinions in common. Shiner also seemed to enjoy the early notoriety of the movement that later became "cyberpunk," but wore his mirrorshades as a joke, really. For at the same time that cyberpunk was first pene-trating the consciousness of a certain segment of the American cul-ture, Shiner was talking with real excitement about mainstream authors that he admired, and how he wanted to write something other than science fiction. Or perhaps I should say "in addition to" science fiction, for with Shiner there was no ringing declaration that he was not a sci-fi writer.

Which just goes to show you Shiner's class. He didn't have to reject one community in order to embrace another.

There are various reasons why some writers make vehement denials that what they write is science fiction, even though it is ob-vious that they have and they do. Sometimes it is snobbery—one thinks at once of Margaret Atwood, who, had she not been too ar-rogant to read science fiction in order to learn from it, might not have done such a clumsy job of handling exposition in The Hand-maid's Tale. *But so grimly determined is she not to confess to hav-ing perpetrated that loathsome thing, sci-fi, that she can't even manage ordinary civility when sharing a public platform with a known science fiction writer.*

Other writers, though, become quite frustrated at the science fiction label, because it limits what they can write and publish. Those limits are real. For instance, I have a story called "Feed the Baby of Love" that cries out to be a short novel. But it hasn't found a publisher because no one wants to take a chance on a completely mainstream smalltown love story by a "science fiction writer." Thus my relative success in science fiction has put serious road-

blocks in my way as a writer of other kinds of fiction. This is especially frustrating because at no point in my career has even half my writing been genuine science fiction and fantasy. But the public perception—or rather, the bookstore buyers' and publishers' and marketers' perception—means that I cannot write out of category, at least not under my own name.

That kind of narrow categorizing functions even within the genre of speculative fiction. A science fiction writer I very much admire has recently had to make the painful decision to publish his latest book, the start of a fantasy trilogy, under another name, for apparently fantasy readers won't embrace a writer perceived as a sci-fi guy. Or at least not in sufficient numbers.

Thus I understand perfectly why Harlan Ellison and Kurt Vonnegut both made ringing declarations of the non-science-fictional nature of their fiction—this despite the obvious fact that both of them had written within the genre and showed intense awareness of how it is properly done. Ellison has won about as many Hugos as you can win and not get lynched by the other writers. Vonnegut has always written science fiction as an insider, and his work has strayed less from the genre's boundaries than the work of, say, Ray Bradbury, who has never denied his science fiction roots.

But that's not a fair comparison, because Ray Bradbury, like Ursula K. Le Guin, was embraced by the academic-literary community without having to deny his previous work. This luxurious gift is bestowed only by whim, however, and is not to be had for the asking. Even those writers who most slavishly imitate the manners and methods of li-fi in their sci-fi are contemptuously ignored by the literati, for begging to be admitted to the "cool" group is the surest way to be despised by them—a lesson we all learned in middle school, I thought.

Harlan Ellison and Kurt Vonnegut were not begging for academic-literary respectability, however; to one degree or another, both of them already had it. What they wanted was to be published out of category. They wanted not to be shelved with the science fiction in some back corner of the bookstore. They felt that their audience was much wider than the dedicated aficionados of the genre, and correctly so. They wanted not to be limited in the way their books were presented to the public, in the kind of reader who would be permitted to find their work.

Lew Shiner, at that point in his career, was not yet well enough known as a science fiction writer to be confined within boundaries. He still had the freedom to choose what kind of writing he would do. So no public declaration was required, no furious negotiations with publishers to insist that certain labels not be placed on his books.

What Shiner was bound to run into was another wall: Science fiction is easier to break into than mainstream fiction.

Why is that? Because it's so easy to write?

Not at all. In fact, if it were easy to write science fiction, it would be one of the hardest fields to break into, because so many people want to write it that there would be far more competition for each slot in the magazines or in publishers' schedules. The reason science fiction is relatively easier to break into is partly because it's so hard to write that there is less competition for each slot—fewer competently written manuscripts vying for the editors' attention.

Another reason that science fiction is easier to break into is that we still have a short-story market—the magazines and anthologies—that functions as a kind of "farm club" for the big leagues of books. (This reflects the reality of publishing, not the relative artistic merit of novels and short stories—by aesthetic standards, the various lengths are similar in their capacity to embrace great art.) The sf magazines don't pay much, but they pay something, and they are read and taken seriously by readers, critics, and editors within the field. And the short-story market is constantly reopening because the writers who break in that way quickly find that writing novels pays so much better and reaches so much wider an audience that it makes more sense to develop ideas that can become novels than those that could only be short stories.

But even this does not explain entirely why sci-fi is an easier genre to enter. Another contributing factor is the contempt of American English departments for science fiction and fantasy.

Young people who love to read and want to write fiction are invariably steered by high school English teachers toward "creative writing," which puts the young writers under the thumbs of teachers who, with few exceptions, sneer at science fiction as being less than literature. Some, of course, being stubborn souls, know that science fiction is a viable and potentially powerful literary medium and so pay no attention to the disdain of their teachers. But that's a tough position to maintain, especially if every story you write that is not sci-fi gets lavishly praised, while your ventures into science fiction are ignored or criticized.

Thus a significant number of the talented young writers who, by taste and inclination, ought to be contributing to the science fiction community are drawn away into writing fiction that, ironically enough, usually reaches a much smaller audience than science fiction (i.e., academic-literary writing) and leads to book publication for a relatively smaller proportion of those who attempt it. This is why, when I visit college campuses, an astonishing number of English professors and graduate students confess to me that they'd really like to write science fiction, that they love reading in the genre (though they confess it to few of their colleagues), and that they want very much to publish a manuscript. Sadly, however, those few who actually write science fiction have become so imbued with the tenets of academic-literary writing while never having practiced or fully analyzed how science fiction is written, that they generally produce manuscripts that simply cannot be published within the sf community. Often their stories are marvelous, and if clearly told and reasonably paced they would do well. But, still true believers in the dogmas of the academic-literary establishment—or perhaps determined to show their colleagues that they haven't sold out completely by writing sci-fi—they make it a point to include a lot of purely literary elements in their novel or story.

It is rather as if a talented composer of operas, unable to get one of the few opera houses in the world to debut his atonal "experimental" (don't get me started) operas, finally realizes he should never have allowed his teachers in college to steer him away from his first love—Broadway-style musical comedy. That's what he grew up with; the names that make his heart pound are Richard Rodgers and either Hart or Hammerstein (take your pick), Cole Porter, Stephen Sondheim, Irving Berlin, George and Ira Gershwin, Lerner and Loewe, Jones and Schmidt. He knows that music. He can write it! So he works and works to produce his first Broadway score and script—but he has written it atonally! There is no chance that anyone will invest fourteen cents in producing a twelve-tone musical on Broadway—songs have to be memorable and singable! But this composer, frustrated as he is, *can't let go of the very tenets of "serious" music that have made the general public turn away in disgust. He loves Broadway and knows that the "serious musician's" rejection of that kind of music is stupid; but he has been made just a little stupid, too, through long association, and carries the stupidity with him.*

It breaks my heart to see how close some of these writers come—but then they refuse to let go of their handhold in academia, and so they never give themselves a fair trial. And, sadly enough, they take consolation by telling themselves (and their colleagues), "I guess I was just too literary for a commercial genre like that." Well, yes, I guess you were. But while you're congratulating/consoling yourself, remember that people read that "commercial" stuff out of love, while precious few of the "literary" works that are written are ever read at all—and even fewer are beloved.

And that's why science fiction is easier to break into—somebody has been poisoning half of the most talented competitors, taking them out of the competition.

So what happens to someone like Lewis Shiner, who can write science fiction—good science fiction—but wants to speak to other audiences as well? Well, he starts over, that's what. He plunges as a nonswimmer into a different pool, and finds that there are a lot more people here . . . and a lot more sharks. If he's tough enough and smart enough, he learns what he has to learn and sticks it out. And maybe—if we're lucky—now and then he'll continue to write science fiction for us.

And what about old farts like me, who are so tied to science fiction we can't get even our best work published in other genres? We duck. We fake. We write sideways into other genres. In my case, I write contemporary mainstream stories but with a fantasy element, so it is perceived by publishers as being "sort of" speculative fiction even as I begin to build some kind of audience for those books. And, slowly, it's working. I hear from more and more readers now who tell me that their first exposure to my work was my mainstreamish novel Lost Boys.

And the other strategy? We go to Hollywood.

Well, I'm doing that, too, but it's no cure for genre woes. For one thing, nobody wants to hear a pitch from me that isn't sci-fi. (Though if my TV series The Gate *actually makes it onto the schedule at the WB, I will suddenly be perceived as a writer of teenager television, another box that I'll have to break out of.) And in Hollywood it doesn't matter much how successful you've been as a novelist. Everything is considered on a project-by-project basis. And it's a different art. What works as a novel rarely works, unchanged, as a film.*

In short, these genre boundaries are hard to break.

And yet . . . that's not entirely bad. Because the existence of those boundaries is also the reason why science fiction has been able to develop into such a vibrant literary community, with highly developed structures of criticism and many subgenres, so that speculative fiction is larger inside than the rest of contemporary literature is outside. Without our own space on the shelves in the bookstores, without our ability to develop tropes and themes of our own that grow from book to book, story to story, author to author, decade to decade, it is doubtful that we would have achieved any of our finest work. Lacking such a category in Britain, Aldous Huxley, George Orwell, and C. S. Lewis did not advance "scientific romance" writing, per se, one iota beyond what H. G. Wells had done before them. There was no envelope to push, just a device to use.

Our lurid magazine covers in America may have brought us contempt, but they also brought us freedom, some room to learn and grow. We may live within literary ghetto walls, but, if we're determined enough, we can break out, to some degree, and hawk our wares on other streets.

Whatever Lewis Shiner is doing these days—and I'm not tracking science fiction well enough to know—he had more influence over me than he knows. He reminded me, a dozen years ago, that I don't have to write one kind of thing just because that's what people are determined to pay me for. And so I kept looking for and seizing upon chances to write non-genre material. Some of my books exist in part because of that conversation with Lew; maybe my musical comedy that ran this summer in Utah owes a little to Lewis Shiner's ambition to write what he wants without regard to genre walls.

I know a lot of writers who never want to write anything but science fiction. That is the sum of their ambition. They are inside and content to remain so. That's fine with me; I don't understand them, but I don't disdain them, either; some of them are among our best. But for those of us who have a lot of different stories to tell, for whom the boundaries are claustrophobic, I can only hope that we have enough success that the powers that be begin to realize that those walls don't have to be so high or the doorways always locked.

CABRACAN

Lewis Shiner

When Eddie got to the godhouse he still had to wait outside for the old man to notice him. Chan Ma'ax sat and mashed yellow pine gum into *pom* for the incense pots and pretended he hadn't seen. Eddie was sweating and his nerves were bad, but the old man demanded patience.

In their time the Mayans had worked out the cycles of the planets and built stone temples so graceful they made Eddie's eyes burn. And all that survived was a dozen wood poles and a thatched roof, and a wrinkled old man sitting crosslegged on a mat.

A tractor coughed in the distance, then crashed screaming into the underbrush. Behind the godhouse the logging road split the dense green of the jungle, its orange ruts filmed over with standing water. To either side the pale ovals of mahogany stumps stared back like frightened eyes.

The air was thick and smelled of cookfires and diesel. It congealed on Eddie's face and neck; if he tried to rub his hands together they would stick, just from the humidity.

"*Oken,*" the old man said at last. "Come in, Eddie."

Eddie hiked up his tunic and sat on a low mahogany stool. After a couple of minutes the old man said, "Ma'ax Garcia spent two days in the forest, looking for *copal* to burn in the godpots. Nothing." He spread his hands, palm down, then turned them over and pretended to search them for *copal.* He spoke in Maya, but slowly, so Eddie could follow. Eddie smiled and nodded to show he understood.

The Ma'ax Garcia he was talking about was Eddie's age, mid-thirties. He was Chan Ma'ax's oldest son by his second wife. He loved the old man and wore himself out trying to help him.

"They took all the mahogany," Chan Ma'ax said. "So now we can't even make new canoes. I guess now we have to take that one and start using it on the lake." He pointed to the ceremonial canoe full of sugar cane pulp, white bark, and water. It had been fermenting under a covering of palm leaves since the day before. "So what then? No more *balché?* Then it will truly be the end of the world. My sons will all turn into *evangelistas,* no?"

He laughed, showing brown stubs of teeth. His name meant "little monkey" after his clan, and over the years he'd started to look like one: flat nose, hunched back, matted hair. The first time Eddie had been introduced to him as the *t'o'ohil,* the "great one," he'd assumed it was just another joke.

In his more lucid moments Eddie saw himself as a victim of a fashionable malaise, the leading edge of a fin-de-millennium craziness that would peak in another fifteen years. The rest of the time it seemed like some kind of short circuit in his talent that had made him walk out on a career that was just getting started. But it had gotten to the point where everything sounded stale, where he'd go blank on stage and play obvious shit with no energy or heart. And then late at night he'd hear things in his head that were more feeling than music, things he could never find on the neck of a guitar.

He'd bummed around Europe, but the massive, colorless buildings all seemed to crawl on top of him. He'd tried to work up the nerve for Asia or North Africa but when the time came he'd gotten on a plane for Mexico City. And it was there, pissing away the last of his money, that he'd read a book about the Lacondones and gotten on a bus the next day.

He came the last leg in an oil company pickup. The oilmen were lining up right behind the loggers to take their turn in the gang rape of the Mexican rain forest, and Eddie saw he'd made it just in time.

That had been three years ago. He hadn't expected the Lacondones to make him a better guitarist. All he knew was acid and yoga and macrobiotics hadn't done it for him and he was running out of things to try.

And the Lacondones had opened up to let him in and then quietly closed up behind him. They helped him build a hut and gave him black beans and *balché* and their sour hand-rolled cigars and otherwise left him alone. He felt like somebody's retarded brother that they'd agreed to put up with.

In three years he'd lived a couple months with Nuk, one of Chan Ma'ax's daughters, who'd gotten more and more distant every day; he'd had a week or so with an *evangelista* girl from the Christian side of the lake who was having a crisis of faith and had put deep scratches in his back; and in the last year or so he'd had a kind of clinical sex with the English doctor who passed through every couple of months, who'd lived her whole life in Mexico and never listened to rock and roll.

And beyond the sudden widening of the doctor's eyes when she came, the quick "oh" of her indrawn breath, he'd had no effect on any of them.

"Listen," Eddie said to Chan Ma'ax in halting Maya. "Something's up. Not just the *balché*. Something's going on."

The smile died on the old man's face and his eyes went distant and glassy.

Shit, Eddie thought. He's not going to talk about it.

They were like the Japanese. They had a mental curtain they dropped over themselves that cut them off from somebody who offended them. Eddie knew it was no use to go on but couldn't help himself. "Those bags over there are full of clay. That's why you're keeping them wet. They're for new god pots, aren't they? You're going to break the old pots, aren't you? What's happening?"

Chan Ma'ax looked down at the pine sap. Eddie wasn't there anymore.

He'd been through this before. Once, pretty badly smashed on *aguardiente* he'd brought back from San Cristobal, a kid named Chan Zapata had said something about Chan Ma'ax and the *Haawo'*, the Raccoon Clan. Eddie had read about them in Mexico City. They were supposed to be the last ones with a working knowledge of the Mayan calendar and ceremonies, could even, some said, talk to the gods.

As soon as the word was out Chan Zapata had shut up, too embarrassed even to change the subject. After that Eddie had gone to Chan Ma'ax and then to the rest of the village, but even a mention of the *Haawo'* turned him invisible on the spot.

Finally young Ma'ax Garcia had taken him aside and said, "It's bad luck to talk about . . . you know. The thing you were asking about. Okay? It's bad luck even to say the name. I'll probably get bit by a *nauyaca* for even talking to you about it, but I like you. I don't want you to get in trouble."

Eddie could take a hint.

He stood up and said, "Okay, Max. I'm sorry. *No estoy aqui por pendejo.* I'll shut up."

He was walking away when Chan Ma'ax said, "Eddie?"

"Yeah?"

"You will be back for the *balché* later, no?"

"I wouldn't miss it."

"*Groovy,*" Chan Ma'ax said. It was his favorite English word. It meant Eddie's wrist had been slapped and it was over and now they were friends again. In Maya he said, "Bring your guitar. You can sing for us."

For a second Eddie wanted to tell the old man who he was, that he wasn't just some clown who happened to know a lot of songs on the guitar. But the old man wouldn't care. It had no bearing on whether or not Eddie was a *hach winik,* a real person.

He walked out into the center of the clearing and let the heat wash over him. He shut his eyes and concentrated on the pores of his skin and felt his sweat break all at once, on the backs of his knees and between his shoulders. It made him feel cleaner, less poisonous.

When he opened his eyes the mountains were in front of him, pristine, sharp-edged, nearly the same color as the pale sky behind them. A few thin clouds floated over them, motionless.

Fuck it, he thought. Time to move on.

Everything snapped into focus. He tasted the dust in the air, smelled the jungle broiling in the sunlight, heard the high pitched drone of the cicadas like dueling synthesizers and, over them, the faint voices of women on the far side of the clearing.

Nepal, maybe. Why not? He thought about ragged, ice-covered mountains, impossibly green terraces set into the sides of valleys, whitewashed monasteries growing out of cliffs. For a second he saw them superimposed on the drab browns and tans of the village

It would be complicated. He didn't know the politics anymore, didn't know if he could even get into Nepal. He would have to spend a while in the real world, long enough to get his bearings and put some money together

He went on to his hut feeling lightheaded, precarious. The hut was the same general shape as the godhouse, longer than it was wide, rounded on the ends and thatched with sweet palm leaves. Unlike the godhouse it had walls of a sort, vertical strips of yellow bamboo, braided with string and baling wire.

He opened the door and a woman's voice from inside said, *"Tal in wilech."* I have come to see you.

"Nuk?"

"Yes," she said, switching to Spanish. "I need to talk to you."

He made her out in the dimness. She was barrel chested and thick waisted, not even as tall as Eddie's shoulders, but she was a beauty by local standards. His eyes found the red of the tattered plastic anthurium she always wore in her hair.

Eddie shut the door and sat in the hammock. He smelled the dry spicy odor of her skin and thought about the nights they'd spent together. "*Como no?*" he said.

"It's about my father."

"I just saw him. He's getting ready to drink *balché*."

"Yes," she said. "They will drink *balché* and in the morning they will go on a pilgrimage to Na Chan."

"Pilgrimage," Eddie said, stunned. Na Chan was where Chan Ma'ax's gods lived. It was one of maybe hundreds of Classical Maya ceremonial centers still covered by jungle, never excavated, never even seriously looted because no one had enough time or money for it. Chan Ma'ax would never talk about what went on there. It was *hach winik* stuff, for real people only.

"He must not go. He's old, almost eighty. The government has told him to stay away from there. If he goes I don't think he'll come back. You have to talk to him."

"I don't know why you're asking me," Eddie said. He didn't want it to sound bitter, but it came out that way just the same.

"He trusts you. He thinks you are a good man. He listens to you."

"He'd listen better to Ma'ax Garcia."

"Ma'ax Garcia is too much a part of the old ways. He doesn't care about the danger."

The old ways. Nuk was awed by cars and planes and portable stereos. She still talked about the TV she'd seen in San Cristobal five years ago. That's what I am to her, Eddie thought. Just one more new thing.

"If he talks to me," Eddie said. "I'll do what I can. I'll tell him I think it's dangerous. Okay?"

"Thank you, Eddie." She leaned over him, kissed him quickly and ran out the door. Her lips were soft and he felt the kiss a long time after she was gone.

Finally he got up and stood in front of his shaving mirror. He didn't like the way he looked. It made him nervous, impatient. He got out his straight razor and cut his shoulder length hair to within an inch or so of his skull. He had to do the back by feel. When he was finished he washed himself with cool water from the clay jug in the corner and the last of his hard pink shaving soap.

There was a bamboo shelf in one corner and he reached to the back of it and took down his shoulder bag. The zipper was stiff from disuse. He got out a pair of jeans and a T-shirt and put them on. The jeans were loose, but he punched a new hole in the belt.

The longest journey begins with a single step, he thought. Already he felt different, cut off from the heartbeat of the village, his genitals armored in heavy denim.

He rolled the mirror and razor up in the blue and orange strings of the hammock and put them in the bag. There wasn't anything else to pack.

He left the bag sitting in the dust of the floor and picked up his guitar. It was a gut string acoustic he'd bought for twenty dollars in the *mercado* in Mexico City. The action was brutal and the octaves were about a quarter tone off, but he'd been trying to wean himself from material objects and it had seemed like a good idea at the time. He carried it back to the godhouse where Chan Ma'ax was waiting.

Everybody else was back from the *milpa,* the corn field on the far side of the lake. Maybe fifteen men sat or squatted in a loose hierarchy on the floor of the godhouse. Eddie nodded to them and sat next to Ma'ax Garcia. Nobody said anything about his clothes. Ma'ax Garcia handed him a bowl of the deep brown *balché* and Eddie took it in both hands. It tasted a little like weak stout, a little like strong *pulque.* Eddie drank it off and Ma'ax Garcia passed it forward to be filled again. When the bowl came back Eddie set it at his feet and wrapped both hands around the neck of his guitar.

Chan Zapata served the *balché* from a big clay pot at the front of the godhouse. He was only in his twenties but they all knew he would take Chan Ma'ax's place when the time came. He had clean features and penetrating eyes and he worked hard for Chan Ma'ax when he wasn't on a binge in San Cristobal. He made souvenir bows and arrows that he traded for *aguardiente* and whores, and every time he came home his wife had moved out. She would stay gone a week or so and then he'd convince her he'd never do it again.

He would be going to Na Chan if anyone did.

The others sat in twos and threes, drinking, complaining about the Christian converts on the north end of the lake who'd sold off the mahogany and kept all the money for themselves. One old man asked Chan Zapata if he'd saved up enough "arrows" for a trip to San Cristobal and everybody laughed.

If I painted myself purple, Eddie thought, would anybody say anything?

Chan Zapata took the pot back out to the canoe to refill it. The full pot had to weigh close to a hundred pounds and he staggered back with his knees bent and his arms all the way around it. His face was agonized. If he dropped it the gods would never forgive him. Just past the edge of the roof Eddie could see towering black clouds blowing in from the Gulf, erasing Chan Zapata's shadow and turning the jungle behind him into a wall of foggy green.

The rain started just as suddenly, falling in handfuls that cratered the dust outside and filled the air with the rusty smell of ozone. The sky cracked into a web of white lines and the thunder came after it fast and loud enough to make one of the old men jump.

"It's only lightning," Chan Ma'ax said. His monkey face wrinkled with silent laughter. "Nuxi' is afraid Cabracan is waking up." The others laughed and Chan Ma'ax said to Eddie, "Cabracan is what they call in Spanish the *temblór.*"

"*Earthquake,*" Eddie said in English. The old man's smile terrified him. There had been another quake in Vera Cruz just last week, the third in Central America in the last nine months, each one worse than the one before.

"*Urt quack,*" Chan Ma'ax said. "*Urtquack.*" He finished his *balché* and tucked his legs up under him. "You know the story of Hunahpu and Xbalanque and Cabracan?"

"No," Eddie said. The godhouse went quiet.

"Heart of Heaven sends Hunahpu and Xbalanque, the twins, to kill Cabracan. Cabracan, you know, he has been saying, 'I am greater than the sun. I shake the earth and sky and everyone bows down before me.' Heart of Heaven, of course, he can't just let this go.

"Cabracan is walking across the land, shaking the mountains flat, and the work is making him hungry. He sees Hunahpu and Xbalanque and says, 'Who are you?'

"'Nobody,' says Hunahpu. 'We are only hunters.'

"'What do you have to eat, then?' says Cabracan.

"Now Hunahpu and Xbalanque have the idea that they must bind Cabracan to the earth. They shoot *quetzal* birds from the branches with their blowguns and the giant thinks it is really wonderful because they only use air instead of darts. They cook the birds and they smear some of them with white lime from the lime pits and cook them until they are golden brown and dripping with juices.

"The giant eats the birds that have the lime on them and then he starts walking toward the west again, smashing the mountains. But the lime is making him heavy and it is harder and harder for him to lift his arms or his feet.

"He begins to stumble and fall. Soon he can't get up again and he falls asleep under the mountains. Hunahpu and Xbalanque dance on the ground that covers him, but they are so noisy that they anger Heart of Heaven. Heart of Heaven wanted to see a good contest and is disappointed that the twins beat Cabracan by trickery.

"So every year, while Cabracan sleeps, Heart of Heaven lets him get stronger. You can hear him sometimes turning in his sleep, making the mountains shake the way he used to. Making the *urt quack*."

Chan Ma'ax refilled his bowl, drank it all, smacked his lips. No one moved. They knew when there was more coming, like the audience at a symphony that knew when not to clap.

Finally Chan Ma'ax said, "If you go east, toward the old cities of Chichen Itza or Tulum you can see the land where Cabracan knocked the mountains down. Cabracan is very restless now and soon he will wake up and shake these mountains to pieces."

He looked at Eddie. "Wearing the clothes of a *hach winik* will not save you." Eddie thought there was approval in the old man's voice and it caught him off guard. "Hunahpu and Xbalanque will not save you. They are a part of the old ways. After Cabracan wakes up there will be only new ways."

The *balché* made another round. The old man had always told sports stories before, Hunahpu and Xbalanque playing soccer with the king of the underworld. Nothing like this.

And then Eddie remembered the book. According to the Maya calendar a five-thousand-year cycle was just now ending. It was supposed to wind up with some kind of disaster that would wipe everything out. The book figured it to be earthquakes.

Jesus Christ, Eddie thought. He's talking about the end of the world.

"Play something, Eddie," Chan Ma'ax said.

"Yes, for God's sake," Nuxi' said. "Something cheerful."

Eddie picked up the guitar. What they liked best were the *rancheras*, the traditional crap like "Cielito Lindo" that they could sing along with, but they liked old rock and roll too. He tried "Twist and Shout" and then "La Bamba" to the same chords but the lyrics depressed him savagely. He stopped singing and just hammered the chords, hard enough to split his cuticles and to pull the strings out of tune.

They had all been singing along, slapping their hands in the dust to keep time, but now they stopped and stared at him. The chords disintegrated into two and three string grips, and then out of it somehow came a melody line, taking Eddie by surprise.

His fingers ground into the neck, slurring and smearing the notes, the cheap strings rasping skin from his fingertips, the music pouring out of him uncontrolled. He didn't have any idea how long it went on. Finally his hands slowed on their own and the notes trailed off into silence.

He got up. He was breathing hard, like he'd been running. He walked out into the rain and let the cool water run down his face.

After a few seconds he felt the pressure of the *balché* in his bladder. He walked a little further into the jungle and loosed a strong, clear stream into the undergrowth. He was already high, not fuzzily drunk but tight and focused as a laser. It took a long time to piss.

When he turned back he saw Chan Ma'ax with the front of his robe tucked under his chin, using a neighboring bush. He took a breath and let it go. "Listen, Max," he said. "It's over. It's time for me to move on."

"Okay," Chan Ma'ax said, smiling.

A vague guilt nagged at him, like he'd left the water running somewhere. He wondered if he was being an idiot. Too late, he told himself. He took another step toward the godhouse.

"Eddie," the old man said. Eddie stopped. The old man looked over his shoulder and grinned like he was brain damaged. "I have a goodbye song to sing for you." He straightened out his tunic and faced Eddie and started to sing. The words were meaningless warbling noises but they approximated the lyrics and melody to "Whatcha Gonna Do," the only hit Eddie ever had, peaking just under the top forty in 1974.

Eddie's teeth started to chatter. This isn't happening, he thought.

"I have that little radio, you know," Chan Ma'ax said. "I listen to it all the time. I hear crazy things on there sometimes." He waited a few seconds and then he said, "I don't have answers, Eddie. All I have are the old ways, and the old ways are finished. You understand?"

Eddie nodded. He didn't seem to be able to talk.

"We go on a pilgrimage to Na Chan tomorrow. The last time. To say goodbye. You understand?"

Eddie nodded again.

"You want to come?"

"Yes," Eddie said, shaken, scared, suddenly aware of the rain running down his back, soaking his jeans. "Yes, I want to come."

"*Groovy,*" Chan Ma'ax said and walked away.

And then, so gently that afterwards he couldn't be sure it had really happened, he felt the ground tilt and settle under him, like a boat taking a wave. Enough to turn the fear to terror, for just a second. To turn the solid earth to eggshells, to betray everything he'd ever taken for granted.

He wanted to fall down and cling to the rain-soaked grass, but it wasn't the kind of thing a *hach winik* would do. He stood and watched the rain drops cluster on a stalk of bamboo. The last time, he thought. To say goodbye.

Each drop shone with a fierce and crystalline light. For the moment it was enough.

Introduction to "Rockabye Baby"

by S. C. Sykes

What if somebody offered you the chance to be president, and all you had to do in order to have that lofty office was to cease to be yourself, and instead become Bill Clinton?

(Come to think of it, isn't that how Bill Clinton got to be president in the first place?)

When you think about it, you have to realize: What a cheat! Because then I wouldn't be president, Bill Clinton would. And since he already is, nothing would be changed except that I would no longer be me. So, no thanks.

But . . . what if being you has become intolerable? What then?

To what lengths will we go to preserve who we are? When we go to school, don't we spend decades of our lives trying to shape ourselves into what society expects us to be? Are we not, therefore, ceasing to be ourselves and becoming somebody else? But then, would we want to stay five years old? And doesn't it give us far more power over our lives when we have learned the skills of living respectably in our community?

No, no, relax. I'm not going to launch another diatribe here. In fact, I have seriously misled you. Yes, "Rockabye Baby" does deal with precisely these issues of human identity, but I feel no qualms about telling you so in advance, because by the time you're well into this story you will have forgotten all about the philosophical questions. What you'll care about is this person in this situation. That's why philosophy is best presented in fiction if you want to convince people; but worst if you want to teach them, for you can reach the end of the story without even noticing that it was philosophy you were getting.

This is science fiction at its best: human life, mimetically faithful, except for one little change, but that change makes all the difference; it clarifies everything.

ROCKABYE BABY

S. C. Sykes

He could remember hearing his neck snap. In fact, Cody could remember every long minute after the accident, crumpled in a limp ball against the van's roof. He remembered the immediate numbing sensation, as if everything from his Adam's apple down had gone to sleep. He wondered if this was what death was like and felt cheated. Not a thing passed before his eyes, except a fly which had been in the van all afternoon in spite of his swipes at it with the road map. His St. Christopher's medal, a gift from Jenny before he went into the Navy, had fallen across his right nostril and he was having trouble breathing. He decided it was somewhat ironic to be suffocated by the demoted patron saint of travelers. Okay, so he had no business heading down to Tijuana for the deliberate purpose of losing a weekend in hedonistic debauchery—a broken neck, he felt, was rather severe punishment for a sin only in the planning stages. He hadn't even crossed the border yet. The blowout had sent the van through the guard rail and over the edge of the embankment. There wasn't a thing he could do about it except watch the scenery go by sideways, tilt, then spin, just like in the movies. Only somehow the real thing was much more impressive.

The dumbest things occurred to him, and later he wondered how he had managed to have so much time to think about them. Like worrying about the case of beer in the back—if the ice chest would hold. It had. He remembered the letter to Jenny he'd forgotten to mail. It was still on the kitchen counter in his apartment because he couldn't find a stamp. He remembered worrying that he should have gotten stamps. He worried that the paint job on the van was going to get scratched. Scratched. They showed him pictures of the van later. By then he didn't care.

Mac had been luckier, riding in the Death Seat. He had splattered his nose and cheek against the windshield and broken some ribs but he was able to crawl out through the side window, and kept talking to Cody until help came. Cody would rather have gone to sleep.

The VA hospital became his home for a full year, and it would, he slowly realized, be something of an unwanted umbilical cord for the rest of his life. Jenny had come once, from Texas, to visit. He'd had to get nasty before she believed him when he told her to leave. It was one thing to have a nurse feed him. It was another thing entirely to have someone he loved spooning food into his mouth. He couldn't even put his arms around her with any coordinated dexterity.

He gave Mac his weight lifting equipment and his guitar and asked him to sell off or throw away everything else in the apartment.

"What about the fish?" Mac asked.

"Flush 'em down the john."

He'd been singularly proud of that fish tank. It was the central conversation piece in his first attempt at apartment decorating after getting out of the service. Most of his furniture was early Swap Meet but that 40-gallon cylindrical tank perched on a barrel was something to be admired. Mac asked if he could have it.

"Take it. Take whatever you want. I don't care." And he didn't care. He had difficulty trying to decide on the week's menu whenever the nurse read it off to him, checking his choices. Choice implied a preference, as if life could still offer him one deal that was better than another. As far as Cody was concerned his future was a wide arid wasteland and whether he wanted chicken or veal next Wednesday wasn't going to make much difference. Nothing was going to change the landscape.

He watched his hair grow back. They had shaved his head to clamp his skull in something akin to medieval ice tongs, keeping him immobile after miracle surgery that had failed to produce any miracle at all. By then he was bargaining for even semi-miracles—"Let me move my fingers," he thought. He prayed for inches of healing. But the doctors had been blunt with him. Nerves would not regenerate. What was severed was disconnected for good. No long distance calls to the toes. No forwarding address. No telegrams from the groin. He was aware that some bodily functions went on without him, without so much as his permission or a nod. If a dark stain appeared around the crotch of his blue pajamas then he knew the plumbing had sprung a leak. Somebody took care of it. Somebody took care of everything—from brushing his teeth to turning him over in bed.

He watched the hole in his throat close where the tracheotomy had been. It left a deep hollow but all his vanity had long since evaporated, along with modesty, mortification, and muscle tone. His body, at the time of the accident, had been in peak condition from jogging on the beach and carefully calculated weight lifting. He was sculpting himself for Jenny. Had been. Now, if one wanted to be poetic about it, he thought, his body was Christlike, post-crucifixion, pre-resurrection. He even looked rather biblical, letting his dark hair and beard grow. Being shaved by impatient attendants on the spinal injury ward was a frill Cody easily gave up. He felt guilty taking up their time. Most of the quadriplegics, or quads as they called themselves, grew beards. It was just easier. The place was understaffed as it was. And the ward was filled, due to the advancement of medical technology. Now broken necks weren't automatic death sentences. Just life sentences, Cody thought, watching bodies move, wedded to wheels forever for any semblance of mobility.

Paraplegics, sneeringly called "pares" by the quads, garnered not an ounce of sympathy on the ward. Most pares soon learned to temper their self-pity and helped out, feeding quads meals, fetching things, even emptying filled urine bags. Quads learned not to want things. There were too few hands to respond to their wants anyway. Cody learned to stare at flipping TV images, to lie silently in his own excrement until someone could get around to him, to wait until he could catch a visitor before asking for the magazine that had slid off the bed and onto the floor.

Such was life on the ward. Progress was measured in how many minutes he could sit up in a wheelchair before becoming faint. He watched his fingernails grow. Odd little ridges had appeared at the cuticle of each nail and they moved forward as time passed. They reminded Cody of tree rings, telling of drought years. Something had interrupted the body, a trauma before return to normalcy. Well, yes, thought Cody, a broken neck was slightly traumatic. And not a single thing in his life would ever be normal again. Even nail cutting felt funny. It almost nauseated him. The sensation was distorted somehow, as if an echo of feeling had, by the time it got to his brain, become a convoluted nightmare. He could see the nurse working gently with nail clippers, but it felt as if she were cutting off his fingers. There was a lot of that, a lot of the "phantom limb" syndrome, a Daliesque canvas of body signals, S.O.S. messages spilling out of broken wires. What got through was something he would rather not have received. Ghosts he could do without.

After a year of learning to redefine himself in terms unique to those with spinal injuries, Cody left the medical sanctuary. He had been out on short excursions before, but always with other pares and quads. For a year he had been one of the wheeled majority. Now he was a specific minority in a walking world. And he didn't like it. He moved into a group home in Long Beach where several wheelchaired vets had set up housekeeping. Mac helped him get settled and then hung around, awkward, not knowing how to leave gracefully. He stayed for supper. Cody wished he hadn't, for he was still learning to manipulate the swivel spoon gadget in the hand brace, and self-feeding was still a messy business. His range of movement was limited to shoulders and upper arms, and fine-motor coordination was a skill he was still working on.

"You don't have to stick around," Cody said later as they sat in his room, Mac perched on his hospital bed because there was no place else to sit.

"You want me to go?"

"Yeah, I want you to go."

"I guess you're kinda tired—from the move and all . . . I'll be back in the morning to unpack your stuff—"

"No."

"I mean, to sort of get you settled—"

"Adam can do it." Adam was the live-in aide who ran the house and cooked the meals. He was black and well-muscled and used to lifting a man onto a bed, into a tub, off of a toilet.

"I can do it," Mac argued. "I don't mind doing it. I can take off work. It doesn't matter. I want to do it."

"I don't want you . . . around, okay?" Cody knew how it sounded, but he didn't care. Mac had slunk in and out of the hospital, guilty for walking, apologetic for his wholeness. Cody couldn't stand looking at him. The spidery red scar on his face just made Cody want to hate him and he didn't want to start abusing the last friend he had. Better to cut him free and be done with it.

"Don't . . . come around anymore," he said.

"What?"

"Just get out of my life, Mac. You don't owe me. You're not responsible. I absolve you of all blame. Okay?"

"What are you talking about?"

Cody waited for a leg spasm to stop. "I'm tired of your doing time at my expense. You're part of Before. You don't belong here, in my world anymore. And this is my world. You don't fit in. You're not wanted. How else you want me to say it?"

Mac studied his hands. "I don't know how to help. I don't know what to do."

"There's nothing you can do. I don't want your pain anymore, Mac. Just . . . go away."

And he did. Cody got a few phone calls from him at first—strained small talk. There wasn't much use in either one asking how things were going. They had nothing new in common and the past was something Cody didn't want to think about. The phone calls tapered off to occasional letters, then post cards, then nothing.

Time passed. Cody measured his progress in small triumphs of independence—learning how to empty the urine bag strapped to his right leg, doing his own bowel care, learning to open his own mail when there was any, mostly from his mother in Texas. His father was dead. Jenny's letters were returned unopened until they stopped coming. His mother sent him a clipping out of the local paper about the engagement. Jenny still looked pretty, he thought, and he knew he had done the right thing, closing that door. His mother had always been a clipping sender, but now he wished she would stop. He didn't care to hear what his old school buddies were doing these days. They weren't running in the same league, so to speak. He had endured one long tearful visit from his mother while he was still in the VA hospital and he could do without any more of those, too. He'd chosen to settle in California. At least there he was familiar with the nurses and a lot of the faces he'd come to know since entering his new world. California made space for "his kind," he thought. Building laws had been passed that helped make minor matters a bit more convenient, like drinking fountains he could reach, and more curbs with ramps he could use in his electric wheelchair. And too, California weather suited him. To survive Texas summers one needed to be able to sweat and that was something else his body no longer could do.

He started having preferences again. He learned to eat in public, ignoring stares. He decided to go to school. Mostly, however, he listened, and watched, and read. And thought. To escape. He got good at escaping. He could sit in the sun out on the patio and Go Away. That's what he called it for lack of a better term. He wasn't sure exactly where it was he went, but it felt good, and he didn't like coming back.

It was in his second semester at the local community college that he fitted a pencil into his hand brace and started doodling. He had rather enjoyed drawing in high school, but this was his first attempt at it since the accident. He drew a naked woman with fantasy breasts. He liked it. He drew faces. Then went back to bodies. He liked bodies. Female bodies specifically. Sketching wasn't easy. He had to tell shoulder and arm muscles how to compensate for fingers that could no longer so much as pick his nose. Shading was hard because he couldn't feel how much pressure he was putting on the pencil point except by looking.

Bushnell, Fielding, and Sharkey, the three other quads in the house, admired his work. They asked him to draw them some female bodies with fantasy breasts, too. Some preferred bigger fantasies than others. Sharkey wanted his fantasy in chains. He was into chains. He had been into motorcycles before he broke his neck running his Harley into a truck. Now, mostly he was into beer—and chains. Cody couldn't understand why Sharkey preferred his fantasy women bound until he began taking psychology courses. Then he still wasn't sure.

He began to think of life in terms of semesters. He chose courses because they mildly appealed to him, not because he had any particular goals in mind. He was one hundred percent disabled, according to his medical records. If he fell out of his chair he would have to lie there until somebody rescued him. Uncle Sam sheltered him somewhat financially, since he had given the bloom of his youth to scraping paint off of battleships down in San Diego. It was lucky he had gotten his yen for traveling out of his system, he thought. He had seen the world, at least most of the seaports of the world, but as Sharkey had said, that was a little like judging a woman only by her fanny. You couldn't judge the whole world by its sea. You had to go inland to get perspective.

Cody began to notice that his semesters gravitated toward the arts. He had tried a geology course but the field trip was out of the question. He'd had to do a term paper instead and he hated typing—one letter at a time with a typing stick on an electric typewriter. Art was better.

He bought a drafting table and his art supplies started looking professional. He had a multitude of pencils and knew how to use them with finely honed expertise.

Seasons passed with a kind of sameness, but Cody finally had a passion—his art. Sharkey would sit and watch him draw, opening flip-top beer cans with his teeth until he passed out, sliding out of his chair and onto the floor if his seat belt wasn't fastened. Adam would hoist the man over his shoulder and carry him off to bed.

"He needs a woman," Adam said, "but he ain't got a mind big enough. You got a mind big enough," he said to Cody.

Cody understood what he meant. His inner landscapes were busy. And his woman didn't have chains. There were a few real ones who talked to him on campus, and called him once in a while, but Cody let it go at that. There were phone numbers, passed from quad to pare, for women with special qualities, and there had been times he had used the numbers. But his inner universe was infinitely more appealing. The art consumed him. He would surface from hours of deep concentration on a piece of work and know only that he had been content for a little while.

Besides beer and bondage, Sharkey's other main occupation was as a volunteer guinea pig for a medical research laboratory in L.A. Bushnell, who got his diving into a sunken log while on leave, and Fielding, another van roll, both looked upon Sharkey as a madman.

"I got no government sugar daddy," Sharkey belched, blowing a long strand of copper hair off his nose. They were sitting around watching a Lakers game on TV and Adam was filling out forms that Sharkey would need for the next project.

"I still say you're fuckin' nuts," Bushnell said. "You don't even know what they're going to do, and you're signing your name on the dotted line."

"Did you *read* that fine print?" Fielding asked.

"It don't matter," Sharkey smiled. "What the hell can they do to me? It's all been done, right? Ain't nothin' else they can do to make it any worse. Sure can't hurt." He laughed at his own joke. Sharkey had burned his left calf badly the previous winter when he leaned his leg against a wall heater in the bathroom. His first hint that all was not well was the smell of scorched flesh. The result was a curiously graceful brand in the shape of a spiral, for that had been the design on the heater grillwork. Since his arms were already well-tattooed, he was considering ways to brand his right calf with a skull and crossbones before the others talked him out of it. Pain was only a memory. From the neck down anyway.

Cody pulled a No. 2H pencil out of his hand brace with his teeth and inserted a No. 6B. He was working on a large portrait of Stravinsky, using a small black and white photo as a guide. One of the students in his music theory class had commissioned the work and he was pleased with the way it was turning out. Sharkey had been disappointed. He quickly lost interest if Cody's subject was not female, preferably nude and taut in all the right places.

"What's the name of this project?" Cody asked. Sharkey's last experimental undertaking was called PROJECT IRON-FLEX. It had involved intricately-geared hand and finger braces. His left arm—for he had been lefthanded prior to the smash-up—was encased in something that looked like chromed armor. It was designed to create movement through carefully flexed shoulder muscles. It had worked a little too well. Beer cans, once clutched, were crushed before Sharkey could get them to his lips. One night in a bar he had pinched a girl's bottom and almost caused a riot because the bottom was property claimed by a member of a motorcycle gang. The man had bristled and slung a few epithets at Sharkey who in turn flexed a muscle that raised his middle finger. Later, in the hospital, he said, "I never thought he'd hit a guy in a wheelchair, man." PROJECT IRON-FLEX was scrapped soon after. Cody thought it was just as well. He had an aversion to metal gadgets. He was melded to mechanical devices too much as it was. Watching Sharkey in his hardware reminded him of the artist H.R. Giger's biomechanoids, nightmares that were half human, half metallic torture machines. He could never have become a beneficiary of PROJECT IRON-FLEX.

Sharkey cruised over to Cody's drafting table to check on the drawing.

"When are you gonna get back to tits?"

"Soon. So what's the name of the new project?" Cody asked again.

"R.A.B.B."

Fielding, in the kitchen getting another beer, laughed. "Rab? Like in Rabbit Test? Hey, Bushnell," he hooted, "they're gonna kill Sharkey to find out if some lady's pregnant."

"R-A-B-B," Sharkey spelled.

"What's it mean?" Bushnell asked, rolling over. He preferred using a manual chair for the arm exercise. He was impressive for a quad, Cody thought. Bushnell could lift his butt off his chair with his arms for minutes at a time. It helped keep his skin from breaking down. Decubitus ulcers from lack of circulation were a constant worry. Cody had a terrible time with pressure sores and he envied Bushnell's agility.

"I don't remember what it means," Sharkey muttered. "It don't matter what it means. I can't talk about it. It's top secret."

"A regular threat to national security, huh?" said Bushnell. "God forbid the Russians get quads on their feet before we do. Come on, what's R.A.B.B. mean?"

"Rockabye Baby," Adam read, holding up one of Sharkey's forms.

"Hey, that's secret, man!" Sharkey yelled, zipping over to snatch the document away from the aide.

"I knew it was a rabbit test," Fielding said. "Shark, they're gonna cut you open and—"

"No, they're not!"

"Told you to read the fine print, didn't I? Sucker."

"It's somethin' else. No cuttin'. I'm done with cuttin'." Sharkey had reluctantly agreed a year earlier to have the tendons in his legs cut to try to subdue violent leg spasms. The decision had somehow also severed his last hope of any miracle recovery. It was soon after that that he had turned his body over to the researchers.

On Monday a blue van with a hydraulic lift in back came to collect Sharkey, wheelchair and all. He waved goodbye to everyone on the porch as if he were headed for a trip to Disneyland.

"See you turkeys Friday," he said as the lift clanged shut behind him. Cody felt a flicker of nausea. He was reminded of cages. Traps and cages.

Adam picked up the morning paper from the lawn after the van had departed. "I'm not cooking nothing extra on Friday 'til I see his face, I can tell you that. First legal-type paper I ever seen that laid out funeral arrangements, in case."

Fielding and Bushnell looked at each other. "I *told* him he should have read the fine print," said Fielding.

Cody found his thoughts wandering all week and it irritated him. Sharkey's absence was intruding on his work, blocking his escape. Instead of dissolving into his nameless space, he found himself mulling over mental playbacks of episodes with his quirky housemate. Sharkey had come to their small commune more as a charity case than anything else. He'd had no place to go after leaving the hospital, a nurse had told Cody, except a county home. To be twenty-two and parked in a corridor between the elderly senile was Cody's notion of purgatory. So they had voted and sent for him. There were times they had been sorry. Sharkey's maniacal sense of the absurd bordered on true lunacy. Huck Finn with a pinch of strange. There was the time he tried to enter his electric wheelchair in a dirt bike scramble. And the time he had gotten a ticket for tooling around town in rush hour traffic. The officer had been embarrassed but determined after Sharkey ran the red light in his wheelchair.

But the man had brought some humor back into Cody's life. He had made them all laugh. The house was subdued without the stereo blasting country and western. They ate in silence.

"He'll be back Friday. This is stupid," Bushnell said. "It's like he said, it's no big deal."

"*We* shoulda read the fine print," Fielding mumbled.

On Thursday Cody did a pen and ink cartoon of Sharkey crawling up a Mt. Everest-sized breast. He placed it on the man's bed in preparation for his home-coming. Sharkey's room was a hodge-podge of interrupted projects, from his beer can collection to dead marijuana plants in a terrarium that had once housed a garter snake nobody could find. Motorcycle magazines and magazines full of naked beauties were stacked everywhere. A guitar hung on one wall and Cody wondered if Sharkey had been as good on the instrument as he claimed. His voice in the shower wasn't half bad, with a slight Louisiana inflection. Sharkey was always happy in the shower until the water ran cold. "It's never goddamn long enough," he would complain as Adam lifted him from the shower chair, dripping and shivering. It occurred to Cody that maybe that was Sharkey's escape. He reached up and stroked the guitar strings with a thumbnail. The strings were out of tune. He wondered if Mac had ever learned how to play his guitar. He hoped so. He hoped it was the center of smoky parties and good times as it had been once, long ago. He wanted its amber wood saturated with music, layered with melodies, not hung on a wall like a decorative icon.

On Friday the blue van pulled up and opened its metal mouth to disgorge Project R.A.B.B. It wasn't exactly a confetti and ticker tape return. Sharkey looked no different than he had when he left on Monday. He wasn't sporting any new mechanical devices. His wild copper hair was caught in a sloppy ponytail which was the way he always wore it. His Van Dyke beard was the same, the chipped front tooth from an ancient brawl was still there—nothing at all was changed. And yet Cody sensed a difference. Sharkey rolled up the ramp and into the house and asked what was for dinner.

"Missed your cookin'," he told Adam. "Never thought I'd hear me say that."

Bushnell offered him a beer. "So, how was Project Rockabye Baby? You cover any new terrain?"

Sharkey maneuvered his long lifeless fingers through the plastic mug handle and hoisted it to his mouth, spilling beer down the front of his T-shirt. "God, I been cravin' a beer all week," he sighed, belching.

Cody watched him wipe his face on his arm. What was different? Something had changed. Sharkey glanced up at him and then he saw what it was. Fear. His face was rigid with fear.

"So what did they do?" Fielding asked.

"Nothin'. Just ran a bunch of tests."

"All week?"

"All week."

"What kind of tests?"

Sharkey belched again. "You name it, they ran it. Lot of, you know, head tests, I.Q. junk."

"And they found out you didn't have an I.Q." Bushnell said. "Hell, I could have told them that."

"Nutsy tests," Sharkey went on. "What do you call 'em, those ink blot things. And a physical like you wouldn't believe, man. Felt like I was gettin' ready to go to the Moon." He accepted another beer. "They said I passed."

"Is that good or bad?" Cody asked.

"Good. I guess. Anyway, I got 'til next Wednesday to decide if I wanna do it."

"Do what?"

Sharkey wiped at the beer stain on his T-shirt. "Can't talk about it."

Bushnell lifted himself a few inches out of his chair to exercise. "Probably going to graft his head onto another body. If I was the body I'd sue. Nobody deserves a head like that. Total vacuum."

Suddenly Sharkey slung his beer mug at Bushnell, splashing the man and splitting his lip.

Bushnell wiped at his mouth and saw the blood. "You sonova-bitch." In one swift move he rammed Sharkey's chair and swung his arm, clipping him on the cheek before Adam shoved them apart.

"You start poundin' on each other and I'll take your damned chairs away," the man warned.

Bushnell moved out onto the back patio to cool off. Sharkey departed for his room and asked to be put to bed. After he was settled Cody knocked on his open door. None of them ever closed their doors once they were in bed, for if they needed help Adam wouldn't hear them yell.

"This Project Rockabye Baby," said Cody, "is it risky?"

"All the kinks ain't been worked out, so they tell me." He hooked his arm through the bed rail and tried to roll to his side. "But, I swear to God, man, if it works . . ." His eyes were wet. "If it works . . . it could fuckin' turn the world around."

"How?"

"I can't tell you. God, I wanna talk to somebody about it. You'd be the one I'd wanna tell, man . . . Cody . . . it could change everything. But they're a long way off from gettin' it perfect. There would be things . . . I'd have to *forfeit* they said, if I decide to do it. The way I look at it, it ain't givin' up much."

"My God, it's *not* a head transplant is it?"

Sharkey's laugh was without humor, closer to hysteria, Cody thought, and the emptiness of it, the madness in it, chilled him.

"No. I told you—no cuttin'. I just . . . go to sleep sort of, for a little while and . . . when I wake up—"

"Oh shit, not cryogenics. They're not going to freeze you until they figure out a way to regenerate a severed spinal cord in about two hundred years—"

Sharkey stared at him. "No. No cryo . . . stuff. Cody . . . what if I told you . . . it ain't gonna take two hundred years . . . that it's now. They can do it now."

Cody heard himself swallow. It seemed to take a long time to remember how to breathe again. He could hear Adam in the kitchen whistling as he prepared supper.

"I never told you," Sharkey said finally. "I'll call you a damn liar if you ever repeat it."

It took a minute to make his mouth and mind work again. "How . . . do you know it's now? That they can regenerate nerves? There's no way—"

"There's a way. But it ain't all worked out. There's a few . . . drawbacks . . . I can't tell you no more. But if it works—" Sharkey waved an uncoordinated arm at his room, "they can have it all. It don't matter to me, everything that went before . . . it's nothin' to give up . . . for what I could have—"

He refused to elaborate further. Cody wondered if hopeless hope had finally broken him. Of the four of them, only Sharkey had refused to accept his body the way it was. Cody had, during his year in the VA hospital, gone through what the psychiatrist had called a "period of mourning" for his body. He had even contemplated suicide, hoarding the various pills proffered at night until he had a regular pharmaceutical company. But he had never been able to go through with it. Now, in spite of his limitations, there was a sense of peace within him. He savored every breath. He made plans. He . . . accomplished. His existence had meaning. All Sharkey had were memories of Before, and a pathetic collection of empty beer cans.

"Shark, whatever R.A.B.B. is . . . I hope it works for you. I really do."

"Yeah. Me too. Hey . . . thanks for the drawing."

He said goodbye to them while the blue van waited, mouth gaping. The farewell was oddly subdued. He had told them to rent his room to a new quad, not to wait for him to come back. "I don't know how long this is gonna take, man," he said, "so don't keep a light on for me."

"Are you sure you read all the fine print this time?" Fielding said, squinting in the morning sun.

"Yeah. I read it all. Hey, Bushnell, if you ever find my snake, you can keep him. Code, take care of my beer cans, okay?"

"Sure."

Cody spent the afternoon with country and western blaring on the stereo, drawing naked women in chains.

A month went by. They kept his room ready. Fielding's nine-year-old son was planning to visit him during Christmas vacation so Adam tidied up Sharkey's room a bit to use as a guest room. He hauled the men's magazines out to the garage and stored the beer can collection in boxes in the closet. Fielding was nervous about the marijuana terrarium so that, too, went out to the garage. It was his son's first extended visit since the man's divorce, and he was worried about how it would go. Few marriages could survive a broken neck, Cody had come to realize, and not many old friendships endured. He had heard horrible stories from other quads and pares—of being taken for every cent they had as fast as their wives could pack, of aides and housekeepers who stripped their homes of everything, abandoning them in the night. Bushnell had once almost married, post-accident, but when he demanded that his fiancée sign a carefully worded prenuptial contract, she backed out. Had they divorced, she would have relinquished all rights to any of his possessions. Cody felt it was the distrust that had killed the relationship, not the contract.

Fielding's divorce had been amicable and at his request. His ex-wife still talked to him on the phone and he worshiped his son who had been three at the time of the accident.

"What am I going to do with him for five days?" he said. "What do we do after Disneyland, for Chrissake?"

"You'll think of something," Cody assured him.

"What if I embarrass him?"

"If you do, he'll get over it. He'll get used to you—to all of us. Kids adapt."

"Does the house smell okay? I mean, not like pee or anything."

Cody sniffed. "I can't speak for Sharkey's room. It may smell of dead snake, I'm not sure. Right now all I smell is barbecued chicken in the oven."

The visit went smoothly. Cody got a neighbor to come over and take snapshots of the little boy so he could later make sketches to give Fielding for his birthday. He wondered fleetingly if he might have had children of his own by now had his life not been so altered. Would they have looked like Jenny, he mused. He calculated. He was now into his sixth year as a quad. Had he married Jenny he might have had a child ready for kindergarten by now. He began to sketch imaginary children, and traveled into mind territory he'd never thought about before.

When two months had passed without word from Sharkey, Bushnell called the Bio-Med Research Center to find out what was going on. "They said he's not there anymore," Bushnell reported to the others after he hung up.

Cody pulled away from the drafting table. "What do they mean he's not there? He's got to be there."

"Well, he's not there now. They were real closed-mouthed about it—wanted to know what I knew about Project R.A.B.B. You don't think—"

"No," said Fielding. "They would have told us if he was dead. Wouldn't they?" He looked at Cody. "I mean, we've got all his stuff . . . everything."

The next day two men from the research center came to take away Sharkey's personal effects. They seemed uninterested in the beer can collection, selecting only Sharkey's loud Hawaiian shirts, jeans, and other personal things, including his guitar. They were evasive concerning the man's whereabouts. They did say he would not be returning to the house.

"He's dead. He's gotta be dead," Bushnell said. "And they're afraid if word gets out that they wasted a human guinea pig they'll lose all their government funding. That's why they're not talking. They killed Shark. They killed him."

"No," Cody said slowly. "If he were dead they wouldn't have taken his guitar." A sudden coolness spilled down through him as if all the blood in his body had just rushed to his stomach.

"Why would he want his guitar?" Fielding asked.

"To play it," said Cody.

"Sure. Very funny."

Cody nodded. "Yeah."

Sharkey's absence was a little like that of a friendly alley cat that just wasn't around anymore, Cody thought. As a kid he'd always had cats. They came and went and when they disappeared he sort of wanted to believe it was because they'd found someplace better, not that they had met with disaster. That was the way he thought about Sharkey. At least it let him think of other things. Still, sometimes at night when sleep didn't come, he wondered.

They waited two more months for some kind of contact from the man before reluctantly putting word out for another tenant. No one spoke of him, but they kept his beer can collection and other paraphernalia in storage, waiting. His magazine subscriptions mysteriously stopped so they knew somebody, somewhere, had made some address changes. Cody seized on an inspiration one day and typed out a letter to him in care of the research center. It was returned with all kinds of red-stamped cancellations. It seemed as if Sharkey himself had been cancelled out of existence. Cody tried a second letter addressed to the house and laboriously printed PLEASE FORWARD on the envelope. That letter didn't come back. But they still didn't hear from him.

The rainy season tapered off into the dry season—California summer. Cody became totally absorbed in a graphic arts course. He designed a music festival poster for a contest and won first prize. More commissions came in, more than he could handle. He was happy. Wilson, the new quad, introduced Cody to his sister. Wilson had been a copter pilot in the Navy. He had never even had a near miss. He got his falling off a roof while putting up a TV antenna. Wilson's sister was pretty. She asked Cody out to a movie. He invited her to the Sawdust Arts Festival in Laguna Beach. Cody found her easy to be with, for she was used to quads and the idiosyncrasies that were a part of their world. But he didn't think he could love her. The essence of Jenny was still present in all his fantasy women and always would be.

Cody was waiting for Adam to meet him outside the Book Nook on Hollywood Boulevard when he saw Sharkey crossing the street. Walking. Free and easy. Cody stared. It definitely was Sharkey. There was no mistake. His red hair was cropped neatly and only the mustache remained from his Van Dyke. But it was Sharkey. Cody felt his voice leave him as he tried to shout to the man. Sharkey reached Cody's side of the street and started moving down the walk, away from him.

"Shark! Sharkey! Wait!" Cody hit the switch on his chair and moved after him, weaving between pedestrians. "Sharkey!" he bellowed with what little force his lungs could muster.

The man stopped and turned around. Cody gaped at him. It wasn't Sharkey. The face was so similar—even the gray of his eyes and the Roman nose were like Sharkey's. Cody had an eye for detail and every shadow of cheekbone in that man he knew, for he had sketched his friend many times. But Sharkey's skin was pitted. There had been a scar over his left eye from a broken beer bottle in a gang fight when he was fifteen. This man's face was flawless—without so much as a worry line.

"I'm sorry," Cody said. "I . . . thought you were somebody I knew."

"You called me something," the man said. There was no hint of Louisiana in his voice. He didn't sound remotely like Sharkey.

"You look . . . a lot like somebody I used to know . . . an old friend."

The man stared at him. "Am I? Your old friend?"

Cody swallowed. The early evening crowd was out. He didn't like hanging out on the boulevard after dark. "No. My mistake. Sorry." He wished Adam would show up with the van.

"Did you call my name?" the man asked, continuing to stare at Cody.

"Just a mistake." Cody turned around to head back to the book store.

"My name is Sharkey. John Sharkey. Do you know me?"

Cody spun around so fast he almost tripped a woman with his foot rest.

✿   ✿   ✿

They sat in a table in the smoke-filled bar. Cody couldn't get his chair under the table top, so he parked at an angle. The waitress didn't hide her irritation as she took their order, addressing Sharkey only, as if Cody were mentally incapacitated as well as physically handicapped. It was a reaction he was long used to, but it never ceased to anger him. The fact that he was crying didn't help the situation. Sharkey ordered a beer for Cody and Perrier for himself.

"Oh my God—" was all Cody could say for several minutes. "It can't be you. How can it be you? What happened? Oh Christ! They did it! They really did it." Every time he thought he was under control, the tears welled up again. "It's a goddamn miracle! You're a walking miracle. Shark, why didn't you tell us? Why didn't you come back?"

"I'm . . . not supposed to contact anyone from . . . Before. I didn't know anyone *to* contact. I don't know you. You tell me your name is Cody. You tell me we were friends. I must have known you once. But I don't remember. I don't remember any of Before."

Cody watched him pour the Perrier into a glass, grasping the bottle easily with long tapered fingers. He had never realized how tall Sharkey was. "How did they do it? What did they do to you, Sharkey?"

"I can't talk about it. I'm sorry. I'm not allowed."

"Shark, this is *me*. This is Cody. I know about Project R.A.B.B. You told me about it. Remember?"

"No. I don't remember. How much do you know?"

Cody maneuvered the glass beer mug to the edge of the table, but couldn't lift it. "I've got a plastic mug in my backpack. Can you pour this in it?"

Sharkey reached into the cloth pouch tied to the back of the wheelchair, and transferred the beer to the lighter container.

"I know R.A.B.B. stands for Rockabye Baby. That the research dealt with nerve regeneration. That's all you told me. Sharkey, what happened?"

Rock music blared out of a jukebox. "Did I like music like that?" Sharkey asked. "They tell me I was interested in music, but I don't know what kind. I have a guitar. But I don't know how to play it. I've tried, but—"

Cody watched him make wet circles on the table with his glass. "You like country and western. I like R&B and rock. We used to have fights about it."

"We did?"

"Sharkey, look at me. What the hell did they do to you?"

"I don't know. All I know about anything is what they tell me. I'm still . . . learning. I don't remember Before. But I want to. Can you tell me about Before? What was I like?"

"Different."

"How?"

"I'm not sure—beyond the obvious. You're on your feet." Cody frowned. "Your arms . . . roll up your sleeves." The tattoes were still there. It was really Sharkey all right. "But your face is smooth. And . . . your tooth is fixed. And there's no scar over your eye. Did they do plastic surgery, too? Why?"

Sharkey shook his head. "No. It doesn't involve that."

"Raise your left pants leg."

The man look puzzled, but did as he was told. The spiral scar was gone.

"Everything gets regenerated," Sharkey said quietly. "They can't help it. They can't localize the process. They're working on it, though. My tonsils are back, they said, and my appendix. I had to decide for myself about circumcision. Had to start everything over from scratch. Everything. I feel kind of lost. I don't have much to go on. They're working on that, too. How else am I different? I want to know."

Cody gestured to his glass. "You don't drink beer anymore?"

"I haven't developed a taste for it. I liked it before?"

Cody nodded. "You don't sound the way you used to sound."

"The tapes . . . they try to put things back, afterward. They try to make things the same, but they don't put back . . . the original things. They can't. They don't know how."

"What do you mean?"

"The memories—everything that made me whoever I used to be. Everything gets sort of . . . erased. They can put back academic things. They can do that. They tell me I score better in math than before. I know . . . facts. That's all."

Cody felt dizzy, the way he used to feel when he first sat up in a wheelchair. Everything was distorted. He'd not drunk half the beer, but he was sure that if he took one more swallow he would throw up. "This is damned confusing," he said.

"Yes. It is," Sharkey agreed. "I think I've said too much. But I need to know. Tell me who I am. What did I like? What did I hate? Why did I let them take everything from me?" The intensity of the man made Cody uncomfortable. If ever someone looked haunted, Sharkey looked driven to the brink of madness. And yet there was a distant quality in his face, as if he were operating through remote control, trying to remember expressions that corresponded to emotions that were no longer there. Nothing was quite coordinated. He blinked. "I can't remember why I . . . want to be alive," he said.

Little by little Sharkey told him what he understood of Project R.A.B.B. "It's done through a kind of . . . regression technique. I don't understand much of it. They found out that in each of us there's a sort of genetic switch that controls the production and growth of cells. They were looking for the switch that triggers cancer cells, they told me, and they stumbled across the regeneration switch. There's a time—a very brief time, close to birth, when the body can correct some injuries, if the genetic switch is on. So . . . they figured if the brain could be convinced that the body was prenatal—the regeneration could be triggered. The catch is, when they regress a mind back to that stage, all memories are lost. For good. Everything is erased. I was 'born' nine months ago. My womb was a black tank filled with Epsom salts and water heated to body surface temperature. I had to learn to crawl and walk and talk all over. They try to put things back . . . but—" Sharkey's gaze focused elsewhere for a moment. "They brought me clothes they said were mine. And showed me pictures of who I was. It was like reading a book about somebody else. I can't . . . there's nothing to connect any of it to. My earliest memory is of reaching up to touch a stethoscope. And . . . being cold. I can't get warm. I feel so . . . cold all the time."

"So that was what you had to forfeit," Cody murmured. "Just memories."

For a second something broke through Sharkey's tranquil mask. "*Just* memories? You don't know. You can't know what it's like, living like this."

"And you don't remember," Cody said, "what it's like, living like *this*."

"I've been told what it was like."

"*Telling* isn't *living* it!"

"I know."

Someone had punched buttons on the jukebox for a popular country and western song. It was one Sharkey used to sing in the shower, his favorite. There was no flicker of recognition in his eyes now.

"There were three others, before me," he said, breaking the tension. "They're all dead. They . . . killed themselves."

"Why?"

"They don't know. They're working on it."

"Sharkey, I want to volunteer for this."

"No. Don't." There was fear in his eyes, as if he had just contaminated Cody.

"Whom do I contact?"

He hated hospitals. And every memory connected with them. The Calmar Bio-Med Research Center, however, felt more like a medical Pentagon as he followed a white-coated technician through a maze of corridors and doors, his chair humming. Fielding and Bushnell had called him crazy to consider volunteering himself for research. He had not told them of his meeting with Sharkey. He feared, above all, the failure of promised miracles. Better they didn't know, unless it worked, he thought. Wilson, too, had heard tales of medical guinea pigs and scoffed at hope. It was their only defense, Cody knew. He would not let them bleed needlessly. Adam had flatly refused to take him to the research center.

"You won't come outta there," he grumbled.

So it had been Diane, Wilson's sister, who had driven him in the van to L.A. She waved to him as he was escorted into the white building, promising to be back at two.

Dr. Nicholas Meyers placed his fingertips together, studying Cody through thick glasses.

"Frankly, I'm quite disturbed that you've come here, Mr. Cody. John did tell us he talked to you. . . . You must understand he is still under treatment. Project R.A.B.B. is quite confidential. We are years away from any public statement concerning this research. John left the grounds without our knowledge or permission. That he spoke with you—" The man's fingers parted, apparently opening a floodgate of secrets spilled through the breach in security, Cody thought. He wondered if Sharkey was being kept under guard in some underground cell.

"Where is he?"

"John is, at present, being taught life skills to help him toward independent living. When he has completed training—"

"When will that be?"

"Another year perhaps."

"I want to volunteer."

Meyers placed his hands slowly on the mahogany desk, palms down flat. Cody was reminded of his father. The gesture said, "Let's think this through. Let's not be hasty." His father had always been a careful decision-maker, weighing all options before he spoke. Cody thought more like his mother, making his decision on an emotional wave, then riding it out to the end, refusing to concede that his choice might have been the wrong one. This was how he had wound up in the Navy.

"I'm here to volunteer for Project R.A.B.B.," he said again.

"I'm well aware of that. However . . ."

"I know there are risks. Sharkey told me. I don't care."

"But *we* care, Mr. Cody." The man sat back, considering. "In its present stage of development, Project Rockabye Baby is one of the most exciting and most dangerous discoveries we've ever come across. The potential for its misuse is enormous. Brainwashing in the truest sense of the word. We're looking for safeguards against that. We're trying to find a way to trigger the regeneration process so that it focuses only on specific area." He flashed a sudden smile. "Imagine the possibilities—total body rejuvenation—the ultimate eternity elixir. We *can* live forever, rebirthed over and over . . . but we must find a way to keep the . . . tapes, so to speak, from being erased."

"Memories."

"Yes. Exactly." Meyer's brief effervescence was reined back under scientific control. "We are only beginning to understand the ramifications of this kind of loss. Seemingly trivial matters . . . every experience of your life, from birth, no matter how deeply buried in your mind, is still vivid if tapped by the right probe. These experiences constitute the fullness of one's personality. At present we must forfeit the one for the other."

Cody felt a coolness at the back of his neck. "Is that why they commit suicide?"

Meyers reconnected the tips of his fingers, closing floodgates. "We are studying the . . . side effects, the emotional trauma involved. It's much more complex than simple amnesia. Subconscious memories are also erased. Everything must be replaced."

"They trade a mind for a body and forget what living was for," Cody said.

"We're trying to rectify that."

"How?"

"If you qualify for the program you will be told." The man took several papers from a drawer and placed them in front of Cody. "We'll need your permission to obtain your medical records." He pointed to places for Cody's signature.

"There's a hand brace with a pen attached in my backpack," Cody said, reading over the papers. In minutes his quivery scrawl would set him on a path he was not sure he was ready to explore. Still, he was certain of his future as it was now. He adjusted the pen with his teeth and signed.

The testing took almost two weeks. Cody felt physically drained and brainpicked. He was homesick, to his surprise, and became incensed when he was not allowed to call Fielding and Bushnell, just to talk. He asked for some art supplies and began sketching, desperate to escape into his nameless bliss if even for a few minutes.

"If I pass," he asked Meyers one afternoon while the doctor took another blood sample, "I mean, if I qualify for this, and it works, will I lose my art?"

"We can give you art instruction to try to replace what is lost. Beyond that I can't answer. The creative process is a largely unknown area. It tends to be a right brain function. We find that left brain functions are much more easily replaced."

"You mean I might not be able to draw afterwards?"

"We don't know. You may have a genetic predisposition toward art. Emotional inclination is another matter. No one fully understands the need to create—what drives one man to paint, another to compose music, another to break the world record for flagpole sitting. Whether you re-establish your artistic direction is an unknown. Attempting to replace twenty-seven years of life in a year's time is an arduous task."

"Can you do that?"

"No."

Cody thought about not being able to draw. There was irony in the situation, he knew. Had he never lost the use of his body, his body would probably have been the only part of him he would have developed. He might have gone back to the oil fields, doing blue collar labor, the only job he'd ever held prior to becoming gunner's mate in the Navy. He wondered if he would ever have discovered his artistic ability. No. He would have bowled maybe, and gotten a beer belly, and . . . would he have ever attempted college? Where would his ambitions have led, he mused, had life not played such an ultimate joke, making him whole in halving him, separating his mind from his body?

"Why can't I see Sharkey?"

"Security reasons."

"Does he sing in the shower anymore?"

Meyers withdrew the needle from Cody's arm. "Not to my knowledge."

He qualified. He sat at the long table ringed with white-smocked doctors and scientists and listened as they explained the procedure and the risks involved, should he consent to become a part of the project. It sounded magical, he thought—a deep sleep of approximately six weeks, wired up to a multitude of machines designed to serve as his surrogate mother. He would rest in a kind of fetal position in a black box that looked more like a coffin, he thought, when they showed it to him.

They gave him two weeks to make a decision, longer than they had given Sharkey, and sent him home with a tape recorder.

"Should you decide to participate in the project," Meyers told him, "you'll have three weeks to place whatever memories you want to keep, on tape. Anything you wish to preserve." He paused. "A word of advice—you'd best make it a mixed bag."

"What do you mean?"

"Don't select only good memories. The negative also serve a purpose. One more thing . . . your friend—John Sharkey—"

Cody waited for the words that would confirm what he had suspected for the last several days. Meyers looked upset. Guilty.

"He's dead," the man said finally. "He died two days ago."

"How?"

"He took a motorcycle and ran it into a wall. I'm . . . very sorry."

"Not enough memories?"

Meyers looked at him. "Perhaps. Maybe . . . just not the right memories."

At the house Bushnell and Fielding and Wilson watched him as if he were an impostor they were sure to catch in a mistake eventually. He knew he was making everyone feel awkward. He couldn't concentrate on his artwork. Everything seemed out of kilter, as if he had returned from a trip to a distant galaxy and nothing was quite as he had left it, but he couldn't figure out what was changed. He was changed. What he knew had changed him. That had to be it. He didn't want to tell them that Sharkey was dead. That would lead to more questions than he was prepared to answer. Instead, he sat in his room for hours at a time, running memories onto cassette tapes. Adam had to go out and buy more. They didn't ask what he was doing in his room with the door closed, talking to himself. They didn't ask him anything at all.

Cody tried to organize his memories systematically, in chronological order, reaching back to his earliest childhood. He talked about everything he could think of, including his fear of The Thing Under The Bed and how his mother had taught him to give it a name and the fear had gone away. Ralph-Under-the-Bed became a bedtime game. He didn't know if the memory was trivial, but it was his and he wanted to keep it. He remembered how his mother had read to him, the crushed ice and 7-Up when he had the mumps, the blanket tent in the back yard, the . . . it went on and on. The more he thought, the more there was to remember.

He called his mother up to tell her he loved her and she asked him what was wrong. His sudden nostalgia frightened her. Tapes mounted up. He talked until he was hoarse. In the middle of dinner he would think of something that was totally out of chronological order but he was afraid he wouldn't remember it later, so he zipped back to his room to record it while he had it. Memories came in disorganized clumps. He wondered if he should categorize them according to subject matter, rather than by years. He found himself digressing constantly, so wrapped up in a vivid memory he lost his train of thought. Playing back the tapes simply triggered more memories he'd forgotten to mention. And he wanted them as sharply etched as he could get them, filled with smells and sounds and tastes. The words began to remind him of a Bosch or Bruegel panorama, so intricate and crowded with happenings he felt he was drowning in verbal chaos.

Tapes covered his desk. Tapes were stacked on book shelves, in boxes, all over the floor along the walls. He gave up trying to mark them. There were times he worried that he was repeating himself, but decided twice was better than not at all. After much debate he decided he needed to put down the accident, too, so he would remember the why of things when it was all over.

It was during one such recording that he broke down in tears. There were no words, he realized, that could convey the anguish over what he had lost. No one could ever possibly know unless they had lived it. He remembered what Sharkey had said—that it was like reading a book. Cody looked at the roomful of memories. Would that be all they were, once it was over? A lot of words? Vicarious experiences belonging to someone else? Would the words be enough to hold the memory of Jenny's body next to him—the heat of her, the way her hair spilled over his face . . . the scent of her. . . . He closed his eyes. The tape ran, recording his silence.

"I need more time," he said when two weeks were up.

"We need your decision now." Meyers looked apologetic.

"I'll need more than three weeks to finish my life story. It's not enough time."

"It's all we can give you."

"It's not enough. I don't plan to off myself for lack of a past. I want as much as I can collect. I want my art, all the books I've read—I'm on the seventh volume of *The Story of Civilization.* That's eleven volumes when I'm done, each book numbering God knows how many thousands of pages. You have any idea what that means? Can you put that back? I want nursery rhymes, I want . . ." He stopped. "I can't do it. I can't get it all down."

Meyers straightened the ink blotter on his desk. "Does this mean you chose to bow out of Project R.A.B.B.?"

"No."

"Once you've made the commitment—once you've begun the Sleep, there will be no turning back. You understand that?"

"Yes. I just . . . there's not enough time."

"It's all we can offer." He laid the papers out in front of Cody.

Slowly Cody maneuvered the pen in the brace and signed his name.

Three weeks later, as they began to prep him for the Sleep, he was still capturing his past. In the last week he had begun to sketch memories, hoping pictures truly would be more than thousands of words.

He closed his eyes as they wheeled him into the room with the tank, praying he hadn't forgotten anything.

Suddenly a whole flood of memories tumbled across his mind— the summer of the worst dust storm he could remember, when the sky turned solid black in the middle of the day. They'd held wet washcloths over their faces and stuffed towels around windows and doors and still the dust blew in rivulets across the floor . . . going pecan thrashing with his dad, whacking the tree branches with long cane poles until the nuts fell like green-brown hail all around him . . . the blood brother ceremony at scout camp with Robbie Turner—he still had the scar . . . watching the tornado that sucked up half the town when he was nine . . . the drag race out by the lake when Tony Dawson almost flipped his dad's car into the spillway . . . too much . . . too many things. . . . Everything was important. Absolutely all of it. Cody felt his tears trickle back along his scalp and grinned.

"Wait a minute," he said, opening his eyes. Meyers and the others were like a green cloth wall closing in on him, needles primed.

"What?" Meyers did not sound happy. "You can't stop now. We—"

"Yeah, I can stop. I read the fine print."

There was, he thought, too much to say goodbye to. And yet—and yet there was something tantalizing about a blinding white, blank canvas. *Tabula Rasa.* Cody took a deep breath. "Okay," he said. "I'm ready." He hoped he had enough colors . . . it was going to be some kinda masterpiece.

Introduction to "The Pure Product"

by John Kessel

When Bruce Sterling *fired the first salvoes of the movement that eventually was branded as cyberpunk, he included in his gunsights the "boring old farts" of "humanist" science fiction. It was John Kessel who adopted both names, the first with humor and the second with earnestness, issuing a "humanist manifesto" and becoming the spokesman of a movement that didn't know it existed until it was attacked.*

Time has its own irony in the unfolding of events. Though Sterling's ideology was one of invention and reinvention, of scientific rigor and resistance to mindless consensus futures, "cyberpunk" has become a name for one of the least rigorous and most mindlessly consensual groups in science fiction. The "cyberpunks" write their imitation William Gibson stories with exactly the level of originality that one finds in Star Trek *novels. But Sterling's admonitions did not fall entirely on deaf ears. Oddly enough, the writers who show the most evidence of having listened to Sterling are, yes, the boring old farts of "humanist" science fiction. In the wilderness between* Moby-Dick *and* Neuromancer, *they began to blaze new trails. And now there is more in common between John Kessel and Bruce Sterling than between either of them and the "cyberpunks."*

Which does not mean that you will recognize anything in "The Pure Product" as particularly cyberpunkish. (Actually, it can be read as, among other things, a satire on the amorality of elites.) Nor do I think Kessel necessarily reflects at all times the values he proclaimed in his humanist manifesto. It is not humanism that makes this story go so much as humanity: Kessel's own, and the trust he has in ours.

Kessel and I have, from time to time, disagreed about what makes good fiction good; he tends to reject as worthless whole swaths of fiction that I admire, and I get impatient with the excesses of some that he admires most. It may even be that he and I would disagree about why "The Pure Product" is a good story; but such a disagreement would be about what we meant by good, *not about what "The Pure Product"* is *or* means *or* does *to its community of believing readers.*

Nor did I include "The Pure Product" simply because I had to have *something* by one of the most influential short-story writers of the 1980s (though that would have been reason enough). Even if "The Pure Product" had been the only published story by a writer who sent it off to Asimov's and promptly died, I would have been proud to include it here for its own sake. Happily, the writer is still alive and continuing to do important work—and continuing to grow and change.*

THE PURE PRODUCT

John Kessel

I arrived in Kansas City at one o'clock on the afternoon of the thir-
teenth of August. A Tuesday. I was driving the beige 1983 Chevrolet
Citation that I had stolen two days earlier in Pocatello, Idaho. The
Kansas plates on the car I'd taken from a different car in a parking lot
in Salt Lake City. Salt Lake City was founded by the Mormons, whose
god tells them that in the future Jesus Christ will come again.

I drove through Kansas City with the windows open and the sun
beating down through the windshield. The car had no air conditioning, and my shirt was stuck to my back from seven hours behind the
wheel. Finally I found a hardware store, "Hector's" on Wornall. I
pulled into the lot. The Citation's engine dieseled after I turned off the
ignition; I pumped the accelerator once and it coughed and died. The
heat was like syrup. The sun drove shadows deep into corners, left
them flattened at the feet of the people on the sidewalk. It made the
plate glass of the store window into a dark negative of the positive
print that was Wornall Road. August.

The man behind the counter in the hardware store I took to be
Hector himself. He looked like Hector, slain in vengeance beneath the
walls of paintbrushes—the kind of semifriendly, publicly optimistic
man who would tell you about his crazy wife and his ten-penny nails. I
bought a gallon of kerosene and a plastic paint funnel, put them into
the trunk of the Citation, then walked down the block to the Mark
Twain Bank. Mark Twain died at the age of seventy-five with a heart
full of bitter accusations against the Calvinist god and no hope for the
future of humanity. Inside the bank I went to one of the desks, at
which sat a Nice Young Lady. I asked about starting a business checking account. She gave me a form to fill out, then sent me to the office
of Mr. Graves.

Mr. Graves wielded a formidable handshake. "What can I do for
you, Mr. . . . ?"

"Tillotsen, Gerald Tillotsen," I said. Gerald Tillotsen, of Tacoma, Washington, died of diphtheria at the age of four weeks—on September 24, 1938. I have a copy of his birth certificate.

"I'm new to Kansas City. I'd like to open a business account here, and perhaps take out a loan. I trust this is a reputable bank? What's your exposure in Brazil?" I looked around the office as if Graves were hiding a woman behind the hatstand, then flashed him my most ingratiating smile.

Mr. Graves did his best. He tried smiling back, then looked as if he had decided to ignore my little joke. "We're very sound, Mr. Tillotsen."

I continued smiling.

"What kind of business do you own?"

"I'm in insurance. Mutual Assurance of Hartford. Our regional office is in Oklahoma City, and I'm setting up an agency here, at 103rd and State Line." Just off the interstate.

He examined the form. His absorption was too tempting.

"Maybe I can fix you up with a policy? You look like dead meat."

Graves's head snapped up, his mouth half-open. He closed it and watched me guardedly. The dullness of it all! How I tire. He was like some cow, like most of the rest of you in this silly age, unwilling to break the rules in order to take offense. "Did he really say that?" he was thinking. "Was that his idea of a joke? He looks normal enough." I did look normal, exactly like an insurance agent. I was the right kind of person, and I could do anything. If at times I grate, if at times I fall a little short of or go a little beyond convention, there is not one of you who can call me to account.

Graves was coming around. All business.

"Ah—yes, Mr. Tillotsen. If you'll wait a moment, I'm sure we can take care of this checking account. As for the loan—"

"Forget it."

That should have stopped him. He should have asked after my credentials, he should have done a dozen things. He looked at me, and I stared calmly back at him. And I knew that, looking into my honest blue eyes, he could not think of a thing.

"I'll just start the checking account with this money order," I said, reaching into my pocket. "That will be acceptable, won't it?"

"It will be fine," he said. He took the form and the order over to one of the secretaries while I sat at the desk. I lit a cigar and blew some smoke rings. I'd purchased the money order the day before in a post office in Denver. Thirty dollars. I didn't intend to use the account very long. Graves returned with my sample checks, shook hands earnestly, and wished me a good day. Have a *good* day, he said. I *will*, I said.

Outside, the heat was still stifling. I took off my sports coat. I was sweating so much I had to check my hair in the sideview mirror of my car. I walked down the street to a liquor store and bought a bottle of chardonnay and a bottle of Chivas Regal. I got some paper cups from a nearby grocery. One final errand, then I could relax for a few hours.

In the shopping center that I had told Graves would be the location for my nonexistent insurance office, I had noticed a sporting goods store. It was about three o'clock when I parked in the lot and ambled into the shop. I looked at various golf clubs: irons, woods, even one set with fiberglass shafts. Finally I selected a set of eight Spalding irons with matching woods, a large bag, and several boxes of Top-Flites. The salesman, who had been occupied with another customer at the rear of the store, hustled up, his eyes full of commission money. I gave him little time to think. The total cost was $612.32. I paid with a check drawn on my new account, cordially thanked the man, and had him carry all the equipment out to the trunk of the car.

I drove to a park near the bank; Loose Park, they called it. I felt loose. Cut loose, drifting free, like one of the kites people were flying that had broken its string and was ascending into the sun. Beneath the trees it was still hot, though the sunlight was reduced to a shuffling of light and shadow on the brown grass. Kids ran, jumped, swung on playground equipment. I uncorked my bottle of wine, filled one of the paper cups, and lay down beneath a tree, enjoying the children, watching young men and women walking along the footpaths.

A girl approached. She didn't look any older than seventeen. Short, slender, with clean blond hair cut to her shoulders. Her shorts were very tight. I watched her unabashedly; she saw me watching and left the path to come over to me. She stopped a few feet away, hands on her hips. "What are you looking at?" she asked.

"Your legs," I said. "Would you like some wine?"

"No thanks. My mother told me never to accept wine from strangers." She looked right through me.

"I take what I can get from strangers," I said. "Because I'm a stranger, too."

I guess she liked that. She was different. She sat down and we chatted for a while. There was something wrong about her imitation of a seventeen-year-old; I began to wonder whether hookers worked the park. She crossed her legs and her shorts got tighter. "Where are you from?" she asked.

"San Francisco. But I've just moved here to stay. I have a part interest in the sporting goods store at the Eastridge Plaza."

"You live near here?"

"On West Eighty-ninth." I had driven down Eighty-ninth on my way to the bank.

"I live on Eighty-ninth! We're neighbors."

It was exactly what one of my own might have said to test me. I took a drink of wine and changed the subject. "Would you like to visit San Francisco someday?"

She brushed her hair back behind one ear. She pursed her lips, showing off her fine cheekbones. "Have you got something going?" she asked, in queerly accented English.

"Excuse me?"

"I said, have you got something going," she repeated, still with the accent—the accent of my own time.

I took another sip. "A bottle of wine," I replied in good midwestern 1980s.

She wasn't having any of it. "No artwork, please. I don't like artwork."

I had to laugh: my life was devoted to artwork. I had not met anyone real in a long time. At the beginning I hadn't wanted to, and in the ensuing years I had given up expecting it. If there's anything more boring than you people it's us people. But that was an old attitude. When she came to me in K.C. I was lonely and she was something new.

"Okay," I said. "It's not much, but you can come for the ride. Do you want to?"

She smiled and said yes.

As we walked to my car, she brushed her hip against my leg. I switched the bottle to my left hand and put my arm around her shoulders in a fatherly way. We got into the front seat, beneath the trees on a street at the edge of the park. It was quiet. I reached over, grabbed her hair at the nape of her neck, and jerked her face toward me, covering her little mouth with mine. Surprise: she threw her arms around my neck and slid across the seat into my lap. We did not talk. I yanked at the shorts; she thrust her hand into my pants. St. Augustine asked the Lord for chastity, but not right away.

At the end she slipped off me, calmly buttoned her blouse, brushed her hair back from her forehead. "How about a push?" she asked. She had a nail file out and was filing her index fingernail to a point.

I shook my head and looked at her. She resembled my grandmother. I had never run into my grandmother, but she had a hellish reputation. "No thanks. What's your name?"

"Call me Ruth." She scratched the inside of her left elbow with her nail. She leaned back in her seat, sighed deeply. Her eyes became a very bright, very hard blue.

While she was aloft I got out, opened the trunk, emptied the rest of the chardonnay into the gutter, and used the funnel to fill the bottle with kerosene. I plugged it with a kerosene-soaked rag. Afternoon was sliding into evening as I started the car and cruised down one of the residential streets. The houses were like those of any city or town of that era of the Midwest USA: white frame, forty or fifty years old, with large porches and small front yards. Dying elms hung over the street. Shadows stretched across the sidewalks. Ruth's nose wrinkled; she turned her face lazily toward me, saw the kerosene bottle, and smiled.

Ahead on the left-hand sidewalk I saw a man walking leisurely. He was an average sort of man, middle-aged, probably just returning from work, enjoying the quiet pause dusk was bringing to the hot day. It might have been Hector; it might have been Graves. It might have been any one of you. I punched the cigarette lighter, readied the bottle in my right hand, steering with my leg as the car moved slowly forward.

"Let me help," Ruth said. She reached out and steadied the wheel with her slender fingertips. The lighter popped out. I touched it to the rag; it smoldered and caught. Greasy smoke stung my eyes. By now the man had noticed us. I hung my arm, holding the bottle, out the window. As we passed him, I tossed the bottle at the sidewalk like a newsboy tossing a rolled-up newspaper. The rag flamed brighter as it whipped through the air; the bottle landed at his feet and exploded, dousing him with burning kerosene. I floored the accelerator; the motor coughed, then roared, the tires and Ruth both squealing in delight. I could see the flaming man in the rearview mirror as we sped away.

On the Great American Plains, the summer nights are not silent. The fields sing the summer songs of insects—not individual sounds, but a high-pitched drone of locusts, crickets, cicadas, small chirping things for which I have no names. You drive along the superhighway and that sound blends with the sound of wind rushing through your opened windows, hiding the thrum of the automobile, conveying the impression of incredible velocity. Wheels vibrate, tires beat against the pavement, the steering wheel shudders, alive in your hands, droning insects alive in your ears. Reflecting posts at the roadside leap from the darkness with metronomic regularity, glowing amber in the headlights, only to vanish abruptly into the ready night when you pass. You lose track of time, how long you have been on the road, where you are going. The fields scream in your ears like a thousand lost, mechanical souls, and you press your foot to the accelerator, hurrying away.

When we left Kansas City that evening we were indeed hurrying. Our direction was in one sense precise: Interstate 70, more or less due east, through Missouri in a dream. They might remember me in Kansas City, at the same time wondering who and why. Mr. Graves scans the morning paper over his grapefruit: MAN BURNED BY GASOLINE BOMB. The clerk wonders why he ever accepted an unverified counter check, without a name or address printed on it, for six hundred dollars. The check bounces. They discover it was a bottle of chardonnay. The story is pieced together. They would eventually figure out how—I wouldn't lie to myself about that (I never lie to myself)—but the why would always escape them. Organized crime, they would say. A plot that misfired.

Of course, they still might have caught me. The car became more of a liability the longer I held on to it. But Ruth, humming to herself, did not seem to care, and neither did I. You have to improvise those things; that's what gives them whatever interest they have.

Just shy of Columbia, Missouri, Ruth stopped humming and asked me, "Do you know why Helen Keller can't have any children?"

"No."

"Because she's dead."

I rolled up the window so I could hear her better. "That's pretty funny," I said.

"Yes. I overheard it in a restaurant." After a minute she asked, "Who's Helen Keller?"

"A dead woman." An insect splattered itself against the windshield. The lights of the oncoming cars glinted against the smear it left.

"She must be famous," said Ruth. "I like famous people. Have you met any? Was that man you burned famous?"

"Probably not. I don't care about famous people anymore." The last time I had anything to do, even peripherally, with anyone famous was when I changed the direction of the tape over the lock in the Watergate so Frank Wills would see it. Ruth did not look like the kind who would know about that. "I was there for the Kennedy assassination," I said, "but I had nothing to do with it."

"Who was Kennedy?"

That made me smile. "How long have you been here?" I pointed at her tiny purse. "That's all you've got with you?"

She slid across the seat and leaned her head against my shoulder. "I don't need anything else."

"No clothes?"

"I left them in Kansas City. We can get more."

"Sure," I said.

She opened the purse and took out a plastic Bayer aspirin case. From it she selected two blue-and-yellow caps. She shoved her palm up under my nose. "Serometh?"

"No thanks."

She put one of the caps back into the box and popped the other under her nose. She sighed and snuggled tighter against me. We had reached Columbia and I was hungry. When I pulled in at a McDonald's she ran across the lot into the shopping mall before I could stop her. I was a little nervous about the car and sat watching it as I ate (Big Mac, small Dr Pepper). She did not come back. I crossed the lot to the mall, found a drugstore, and bought some cigars. When I strolled back to the car she was waiting for me, hopping from one foot to another and tugging at the door handle. Serometh makes you impatient. She was wearing a pair of shiny black pants, pink- and white-checked sneakers, and a hot pink blouse. "'s go!" she hissed.

I moved even slower. She looked like she was about to wet herself, biting her soft lower lip with a line of perfect white teeth. I dawdled over my keys. A security guard and a young man in a shirt and tie hurried out of the mall entrance and scanned the lot. "Nice outfit," I said. "Must have cost you something."

She looked over her shoulder, saw the security guard, who saw her. "Hey!" he called, running toward us. I slid into the car, opened the passenger door. Ruth had snapped open her purse and pulled out a small gun. I grabbed her arm and yanked her into the car; she squawked and her shot went wide. The guard fell down anyway, scared shitless. For the second time that day I tested the Citation's acceleration; Ruth's door slammed shut and we were gone.

"You scut," she said as we hit the entrance ramp of the interstate.

"You're a scut-pumping Conservative. You made me miss." But she was smiling, running her hand up the inside of my thigh. I could tell she hadn't ever had so much fun in the twentieth century.

For some reason I was shaking. "Give me one of those seromeths," I said.

Around midnight we stopped in St. Louis at a Holiday Inn. We registered as Mr. and Mrs. Gerald Bruno (an old acquaintance) and paid in advance. No one remarked on the apparent difference in our ages. So discreet. I bought a copy of the *Post Dispatch,* and we went to the room. Ruth flopped down on the bed, looking bored, but thanks to her gunplay I had a few more things to take care of. I poured myself a glass of Chivas, went into the bathroom, removed the toupee and flushed it down the toilet, showered, put a new blade in my old razor, and shaved the rest of the hair from my head. The Lex Luthor look. I cut my scalp. That got me laughing, and I could not stop. Ruth peeked through the doorway to find me dabbing the crown of my head with a bloody Kleenex.

"You're a wreck," she said.

I almost fell off the toilet laughing. She was absolutely right. Between giggles I managed to say, "You must not stay anywhere too long, if you're as careless as you were tonight."

She shrugged. "I bet I've been at it longer than you." She stripped and got into the shower. I got into bed.

The room enfolded me in its gold-carpet green-bedspread mediocrity. Sometimes it's hard to remember that things were ever different. In 1596 I rode to court with Essex; I slept in a chamber of supreme garishness (gilt escutcheons in the corners of the ceiling, pink cupids romping on the walls), in a bed warmed by any of the trollops of the city I might want. And there in the Holiday Inn I sat with my drink, in my pastel blue pajama bottoms, reading a late-twentieth-century newspaper, smoking a cigar. An earthquake in Peru estimated to have killed eight thousand in Lima alone. Nope. A steel worker in Gary, Indiana, discovered to be the murderer of six prepubescent children, bodies found buried in his basement. Perhaps. The president refuses to enforce the ruling of his Supreme Court because it "subverts the will of the American people." Probably not.

We are everywhere. But not everywhere.

Ruth came out of the bathroom, saw me, did a double take. "You look—perfect!" she said. She slid in the bed beside me, naked, and sniffed at my glass of Chivas. Her lip curled. She looked over my shoulder at the paper. "You can understand that stuff?"

"Don't kid me. Reading is a survival skill. You couldn't last here without it."

"Wrong."

I drained the scotch. Took a puff on the cigar. Dropped the paper to the floor beside the bed. I looked her over. Even relaxed, the muscles in her arms and along the tops of her thighs were well defined.

"You even smell like one of them," she said.

"How did you get the clothes past their store security? They have those beeper tags clipped to them."

"Easy. I tried on the shoes and walked out when they weren't looking. In the second store I took the pants into a dressing room, cut the alarm tag out of the waistband, and put them on. I held the alarm tag that was clipped to the blouse in my armpit and walked out of that store, too. I put the blouse on in the mall women's room."

"If you can't read, how did you know which was the women's room?"

"There's a picture on the door."

I felt tired and old. Ruth moved close. She rubbed her foot up my leg, drawing the pajama leg up with it. Her thigh slid across my groin. I started to get hard. "Cut it out," I said. She licked my nipple.

I could not stand it. I got off the bed. "I don't like you."

She looked at me with true innocence. "I don't like you, either."

Although he was repulsed by the human body, Jonathan Swift was passionately in love with a woman named Esther Johnson. "What you did at the mall was stupid," I said. "You would have killed that guard."

"Which would have made us even for the day."

"Kansas City was different."

"We should ask the cops there what they think."

"You don't understand. That had some grace to it. But what you did was inelegant. Worst of all it was not gratuitous. You stole those clothes for yourself, and I hate that." I was shaking.

"Who made all these laws?"

"I did."

She looked at me with amazement. "You're not just a Conservative. You're gone native!"

I wanted her so much I ached. "No I haven't," I said, but even to me my voice sounded frightened.

Ruth got out of the bed. She glided over, reached one hand around to the small of my back, pulled herself close. She looked up at me with a face that held nothing but avidity. "You can do whatever you want," she whispered. With a feeling that I was losing everything, I kissed her. You don't need to know what happened then.

I woke when she displaced herself: there was a sound like the sweep of an arm across fabric, a stirring of air to fill the place where she had been. I looked around the still brightly lit room. It was not yet morning. The chain was across the door; her clothes lay on the dresser. She had left the aspirin box beside my bottle of scotch.

She was gone. Good, I thought, now I can go on. But I found that I couldn't sleep, could not keep from thinking. Ruth must be very good at that, or perhaps her thought is a different kind of thought from mine. I got out of the bed, resolved to try again but still fearing the inevitable. I filled the tub with hot water. I got in, breathing heavily. I took the blade from my razor. Holding my arm just beneath the surface of the water, hesitating only a moment, I cut deeply one, two, three times along the veins in my left wrist. The shock was still there, as great as ever. With blood streaming from me I cut the right wrist. Quickly, smoothly. My heart beat fast and light, the blood flowed frighteningly; already the water was stained. I felt faint—yes—it was going to work this time, yes. My vision began to fade—but in the last moments before consciousness fell away I saw, with sick despair, the futile wounds closing themselves once again, as they had so many times before. For in the future the practice of medicine may progress to the point where men need have little fear of death.

The dawn's rosy fingers found me still unconscious. I came to myself about eleven, my head throbbing, so weak I could hardly rise from the cold bloody water. There were no scars. I stumbled into the other room and washed down one of Ruth's megamphetamines with two fingers of scotch. I felt better immediately. It's funny how that works sometimes, isn't it? The maid knocked as I was cleaning the bathroom. I shouted for her to come back later, finished as quickly as possible, and left the hotel immediately. I ate Shredded Wheat with milk and strawberries for breakfast. I was full of ideas. A phone book gave me the location of a likely country club.

The Oak Hill Country Club of Florissant, Missouri, is not a spectacularly wealthy institution, or at least it does not give that impression. I'll bet you that the membership is not as purely white as the stucco clubhouse. That was all right with me. I parked the Citation in the mostly empty parking lot, hauled my new equipment from the trunk, and set off for the locker room, trying hard to look like a dentist. I successfully ran the gauntlet of the pro shop, where the proprietor was telling a bored caddy why the Cardinals would fade in the stretch. I could hear running water from the showers as I shuffled into the locker room and slung the bag into a corner. Someone was singing the "Ode to Joy," abominably.

I began to rifle through the lockers, hoping to find an open one with someone's clothes in it. I would take the keys from my bene-factor's pocket and proceed along my merry way. Ruth would have accused me of self-interest; there was a moment in which I accused myself. Such hesitation is the seed of failure: as I paused before a locker containing a likely set of clothes, another golfer entered the room along with the locker-room attendant. I immediately began un-dressing, lowering my head so that the locker door hid my face. The golfer was soon gone, but the attendant sat down and began to leaf through a worn copy of *Penthouse*. I could come up with no better plan than to strip and enter the showers. Amphetamine daze. Per-haps the kid would develop a hard-on and go to the john to take care of it.

There was only one other man in the shower, the symphonic soloist, a somewhat portly gentleman who mercifully shut up as soon as I entered. He worked hard at ignoring me. I ignored him in return: *alle Menschen werden Brüder.* I waited a long five minutes after he left; two more men came into the showers, and I walked out with what composure I could muster. The locker-room boy was stacking towels on a table. I fished a five from my jacket in the locker and walked up behind him. Casually I took a towel.

"Son, get me a pack of Marlboros, will you?"

He took the money and left.

In the second locker I found a pair of pants that contained the keys to some sort of Audi. I was not choosy. Dressed in record time, I left the new clubs beside the rifled locker. My note read, "The pure prod-ucts of America go crazy." There were three eligible cars in the lot, two 4000s and a Fox. The key would not open the door of the Fox. I was jumpy, but almost home free, coming around the front of a big Chrysler. . . .

"Hey!"

My knee gave way and I ran into the fender of the car. The keys slipped out of my hand and skittered across the hood to the ground, jingling. Grimacing, I hopped toward them, plucked them up, glancing over my shoulder at my pursuer as I stooped. It was the locker-room attendant.

"Your cigarettes." He looked at me the way a sixteen-year-old looks at his father; that is, with bored skepticism. All our gods in the end become pitiful. It was time for me to be abruptly courteous. As it was, he would remember me too well.

"Thanks," I said. I limped over, put the pack into my shirt pocket. He started to go, but I couldn't help myself. "What about my change?"

Oh, such an insolent silence! I wonder what you told them when they asked you about me, boy. He handed over the money. I tipped him a quarter, gave him a piece of Mr. Graves's professional smile. He studied me. I turned and inserted the key into the lock of the Audi. A fifty percent chance. Had I been the praying kind I might have prayed to one of those pitiful gods. They key turned without resistance; the door opened. The kid slouched back toward the clubhouse, pissed at me and his lackey's job. Or perhaps he found it in his heart to smile. Laughter—the Best Medicine.

A bit of a racing shift, then back to Interstate 70. My hip twinged all the way across Illinois.

I had originally intended to work my way east to Buffalo, New York, but after the Oak Hill business I wanted to cut it short. If I stayed on the interstate I was sure to get caught; I had been lucky to get as far as I had. Just outside of Indianapolis I turned onto Route 37 north to Fort Wayne and Detroit.

I was not, however, entirely crowed. Twenty-five years in one time had given me the right instincts, and with the coming of the evening and the friendly insects to sing me along, the boredom of the road became a new recklessness. Hadn't I already been seen by too many people in those twenty-five years? Thousands had looked into my honest face—and where were they? Ruth had reminded me that I was not stuck here. I would soon make an end to this latest adventure one way or another, and once I had done so, there would be no reason in God's green world to suspect me.

And so: north of Fort Wayne, on Highway 6 east, a deserted country road (what was he doing there?), I pulled over to pick up a young hitchhiker. He wore a battered black leather jacket. His hair was short on the sides, stuck up in spikes on top, hung over his collar in back; one side was carrot-orange, the other brown with a white streak. His sign, pinned to a knapsack, said "?" He threw the pack into the back-seat and climbed into the front.

"Thanks for picking me up." He did not sound like he meant it. "Where you going?"

"Flint. How about you?"

"Flint's as good as anywhere."

"Suit yourself." We got up to speed. I was completely calm. "You should fasten your seat belt," I said.

"Why?"

The surly type. "It's not just a good idea. It's the law."

He ignored me. He pulled a crossword puzzle book and a pencil from his jacket pocket. "How about turning on the light."

I flicked on the dome light for him. "I like to see a young man improve himself," I said.

His look was an almost audible sigh. "What's a five-letter word for 'the lowest point'?"

"Nadir," I replied.

"That's right. How about 'widespread'; four letters."

"Rife."

"You're pretty good." He stared at the crossword for a minute, then rolled down his window and threw the book, and the pencil, out of the car. He rolled up the window and stared at his reflection in it. I couldn't let him get off that easily. I turned off the interior light, and the darkness leapt inside.

"What's your name, son? What are you so mad about?"

"Milo. Look are you queer? If you are, it doesn't matter to me but it will cost you . . . if you want to do anything about it."

I smiled and adjusted the rearview mirror so I could watch him—and he could watch me. "No, I'm not queer. The name's Loki." I extended my right hand, keeping my eyes on the road.

He looked at the hand. "Loki?"

As good a name as any. "Yes. Same as the Norse god."

He laughed. "Sure, Loki. Anything you like. Fuck you."

Such a musical voice. "Now there you go. Seems to me, Milo—if you don't mind my giving you my unsolicited opinion—that you have something of an attitude problem." I punched the cigarette lighter, reached back and pulled a cigar from my jacket on the backseat, in the process weaving the car all over Highway 6. I bit the end off the cigar and spat it out the window, stoked it up. My insects wailed. I cannot explain to you how good I felt.

"Take for instance this crossword puzzle book. Why did you throw it out the window?"

I could see Milo watching me in the mirror, wondering whether he should take me seriously. The headlights fanned out ahead of us, the white lines at the center of the road pulsing by like a rapid heartbeat. Take a chance, Milo. What have you got to lose?

"I was pissed," he said. "It's a waste of time. I don't care about stupid games."

"Exactly. It's just a game, a way to pass the time. Nobody ever really learns anything from a crossword puzzle. Corporation lawyers don't get their Porsches by building their word power with crosswords, right?"

"I don't care about Porsches."

"Neither do I, Milo. I drive an Audi."

Milo sighed.

"I know, Milo. That's not the point. The point is that it's all a game, crosswords or corporate law. Some people devote their lives to Jesus; some devote their lives to artwork. It all comes to pretty much the same thing. You get old. You die."

"Tell me something I don't already know."

"Why do you think I picked you up, Milo? I saw your question mark and it spoke to me. You probably think I'm some pervert out to take advantage of you. I have a funny name. I don't talk like your average middle-aged businessman. Forget about that." The old excitement was upon me; I was talking louder and louder, leaning on the accelerator. The car sped along. "I think you're as troubled by the materialism and cant of life in America as I am. Young people like you, with orange hair, are trying to find some values in a world that offers them nothing but crap for ideas. But too many of you are turning to extremes in response. Drugs, violence, religious fanaticism, hedonism. Some, like you I suspect, to suicide. Don't do it, Milo. Your life is too valuable." The speedometer touched eighty, eighty-five. Milo fumbled for his seat belt but couldn't find it.

I waved my hand, holding the cigar, at him. "What's the matter, Milo? Can't find the belt?" Ninety now. A pickup went by us going the other way, the wind of its passing beating at my head and shoulder. Ninety-five.

"Think, Milo! If you're upset with the present, with your parents and the schools, think about the future. What will the future be like if this trend toward valuelessness continues in the next hundred years? Think of the impact of the new technologies! Gene splicing, gerontology, artificial intelligence, space exploration, biological weapons, nuclear proliferation! All accelerating this process! Think of the violent reactionary movements that could arise—are arising already, Milo, as we speak—from people's desire to find something to hold on to. Paint yourself a picture, *Milo,* of the kind of man or woman another hundred years of this process might produce!"

"What are you talking about?" He was terrified.

"I'm talking about the survival of values in America! Simply that." Cigar smoke swirled in front of the dashboard lights, and my voice had reached a shout. Milo was gripping the sides of his seat. The speedometer read 105. "And you, *Milo,* are at the heart of this process! If people continue to think the way you do, *Milo,* throwing their crossword puzzle books out the windows of their Audis all across America, the future will be full of absolutely valueless people! Right, MILO?" I leaned over, taking my eyes off the road, and blew smoke into his face, screaming, "ARE YOU LISTENING, MILO? MARK MY WORDS!"

"Y-yes."

"GOO, GOO, GA-GA-GAA!"

I put my foot all the way to the floor. The wind howled through the window, the gray highway flew beneath us.

"Mark my words, Milo," I whispered. He never heard me. "Twenty-five across. Eight letters. N-i-h-i-l—"

My pulse roared in my ears, there joining the drowned choir of the fields and the roar of the engine. Body slimy with sweat, fingers clenched through the cigar, fists clamped on the wheel, smoke stinging my eyes. I slammed on the brakes, downshifting immediately, sending the transmission into a painful whine as the car slewed and skidded off the pavement, clipping a reflecting marker and throwing Milo against the windshield. The car stopped with a jerk in the gravel at the side of the road, just shy of a sign announcing, WELCOME TO OHIO.

There were no other lights on the road, I shut off my own and sat behind the wheel, trembling, the night air cool on my skin. The insects wailed. The boy was slumped against the dashboard. There was a star fracture in the glass above his head, and warm blood came away on my fingers when I touched his hair. I got out of the car, circled around to the passenger's side, and dragged him from the seat into the field adjoining the road. He was surprisingly light. I left him there, in a field of Ohio soybeans on the evening of a summer's day.

✷   ✷   ✷

The city of Detroit was founded by the French adventurer Antoine de la Mothe, sieur de Cadillac, a supporter of Comte de Pontchartrain, minister of state to the Sun King, Louis XIV. All of these men worshiped the Roman Catholic god, protected their political positions, and let the future go hang. Cadillac, after whom an American automobile was named, was seeking a favorable location to advance his own economic interests. He came ashore on July 24, 1701, with fifty soldiers, an equal number of settlers, and about one hundred friendly Indians near the present site of the Veterans Memorial Building, within easy walking distance of the Greyhound Bus Terminal.

The car did not run well after the accident, developing a reluctance to go into fourth, but I didn't care. The encounter with Milo had gone exactly as such things should go, and was especially pleasing because it had been totally unplanned. An accident—no order, one would guess—but exactly as if I had laid it all out beforehand. I came into Detroit late at night via Route 12, which eventually turned into Michigan Avenue. The air was hot and sticky. I remember driving past the Cadillac plant; multitudes of red, yellow, and green lights glinting off dull masonry and the smell of auto exhaust along the city streets. I found the sort of neighborhood I wanted not far from Tiger Stadium: pawnshops, an all-night deli, laundromats, dimly lit bars with red Stroh's signs in the windows. Men on street corners walked casually from noplace to noplace.

I parked on a side street just around the corner from a 7-Eleven. I left the motor running. In the store I dawdled over a magazine rack until at last I heard the racing of an engine and saw the Audi flash by the window. I bought a copy of *Time* and caught a downtown bus at the corner. At the Greyhound station I purchased a ticket for the next bus to Toronto and sat reading my magazine until departure time.

We got onto the bus. Across the river we stopped at customs and got off again. "Name?" they asked me.

"Gerald Spotsworth."

"Place of birth?"

"Calgary." I gave them my credentials. The passport photo showed me with hair. They looked me over. They let me go.

I work in the library of the University of Toronto. I am well read, a student of history, a solid Canadian citizen. There I lead a sedentary life. The subways are clean, the people are friendly, the restaurants are excellent. The sky is blue. The cat is on the mat.

We got back on the bus. There were few other passengers, and most of them were soon asleep; the only light in the darkened interior was that which shone above my head. I was very tired, but I did not want to sleep. Then I remembered that I had Ruth's pills in my jacket pocket. I smiled, thinking of the customs people. All that was left in the box were a couple of tiny pink tabs. I did not know what they were, but I broke one down the middle with my fingernail and took it anyway. It perked me up immediately. Everything I could see seemed sharply defined. The dark green plastic of the seats. The rubber mat in the aisle. My fingernails. All details were separate and distinct, all interdependent. I must have been focused on the threads in the weave of my pants leg for ten minutes when I was surprised by someone sitting down next to me. It was Ruth. "You're back!" I exclaimed.

"We're all back," she said. I looked around and it was true: on the opposite side of the aisle, two seats ahead, Milo sat watching me over his shoulder, a trickle of blood running down his forehead. One corner of his mouth pulled tighter in a rueful smile. Mr. Graves came back from the front seat and shook my hand. I saw the fat singer from the country club, still naked. The locker-room boy. A flickering light from the back of the bus: when I turned around there stood the burning man, his eye sockets two dark hollows behind the wavering flames. The shopping-mall guard. Hector from the hardware store. They all looked at me.

"What are you doing here?" I asked Ruth.

"We couldn't let you go on thinking like you do. You act like I'm some monster. I'm just a person."

"A rather nice-looking young lady," Graves added.

"People are monsters," I said.

"Like you, huh?" Ruth said. "But they can be saints, too."

That made me laugh. "Don't feed me platitudes. You can't even read."

"You make such a big deal out of reading. Yeah, well, times change. I get along fine, don't I?"

The mall guard broke in. "Actually, miss, the reason we caught on to you is that someone saw you walk into the men's room." He looked embarrassed.

"But you didn't catch me, did you?" Ruth snapped back. She turned to me. "You're afraid of change. No wonder you live back here."

"This is all in my imagination," I said. "It's because of your drugs."

"It is all in your imagination," the burning man repeated. His voice was a whisper. "What you see in the future is what you are able to see. You have no faith in God or your fellow man."

"He's right," said Ruth.

"Bull. Psychobabble."

"Speaking of babble," Milo said, "I figured out where you got that goo-goo-goo stuff. Talk—"

"Never mind that," Ruth broke in. "Here's the truth. The future is just a place. The people there are just people. They live differently. So what? People make what they want of the world. You can't escape human failings by running into the past." She rested her hand on my leg. "I'll tell you what you'll find when you get to Toronto," she said. "Another city full of human beings."

This was crazy. I knew it was crazy. I knew it was all unreal, but somehow I was getting more and more afraid. "So the future is just the present writ large," I said bitterly. "More bull."

"You tell her, pal," the locker-room boy said.

Hector, who had been listening quietly, broke in. "For a man from the future, you talk a lot like a native."

"You're the king of bullshit, man," Milo said. "'Some people devote themselves to artwork'! Jesus!"

I felt dizzy. "Scut down, Milo. That means 'Fuck you too.'" I shook my head to try to make them go away. That was a mistake: the bus began to pitch like a sailboat. I grabbed for Ruth's arm but missed. "Who's driving this thing?" I asked, trying to get out of the seat.

"Don't worry," said Graves. "He knows what he's doing."

"He's brain-dead," Milo said.

"You couldn't do any better," said Ruth, pulling me back down.

"No one is driving," said the burning man.

"We'll crash!" I was so dizzy now that I could hardly keep from being sick. I closed my eyes and swallowed. That seemed to help. A long time passed; eventually I must have fallen asleep.

When I woke it was late morning and we were entering the city, cruising down Eglinton Avenue. The bus had a driver after all—a slender black man with neatly trimmed sideburns who wore his uniform hat at a rakish angle. A sign above the windshield said, YOUR DRIVER—SAFE, COURTEOUS, and below that, on the slide-in nameplate, WILBERT CAUL. I felt like I was coming out of a nightmare. I felt happy. I stretched some of the knots out of my back. A young soldier seated across the aisle from me looked my way; I smiled, and he returned it briefly.

"You were mumbling to yourself in your sleep last night," he said.

"Sorry. Sometimes I have bad dreams."

"It's okay. I do too, sometimes." He had a round open face, an apologetic grin. He was twenty, maybe. Who knew where his dreams came from? We chatted until the bus reached the station; he shook my hand and said he was pleased to meet me. He called me "sir."

I was not due back at the library until Monday, so I walked over to Yonge Street. The stores were busy, the tourists were out in droves, the adult theaters were doing a brisk business. Policemen in sharply creased trousers, white gloves, sauntered along among the pedestrians. It was a bright, cloudless day, but the breeze coming up the street from the lake was cool. I stood on the sidewalk outside one of the strip joints and watched the videotaped come-on over the closed circuit. The Princes Laya. Sondra Nieve, the Human Operator. Technology replaces the traditional barker, but the bodies are more or less the same. The persistence of your faith in sex and machines is evidence of your capacity to hope.

Francis Bacon, in his masterwork *The New Atlantis*, foresaw the utopian world that would arise through the application of experimental science to social problems. Bacon, however, could not solve the problems of his own time and was eventually accused of accepting bribes, fined £40,000, and imprisoned in the Tower of London. He made no appeal to God, but instead applied himself to the development of the virtues of patience and acceptance. Eventually he was freed. Soon after, on a freezing day in late March, we were driving near Highgate when I suggested to him that cold might delay the process of decay. He was excited by the idea. On impulse he stopped the carriage, purchased a hen, wrung its neck, and stuffed it with snow. He eagerly looked forward to the results of his experiment. Unfortunately, in haggling with the street vendor he had exposed himself thoroughly to the cold and was seized by a chill that rapidly led to pneumonia, of which he died on April 9, 1626.

There's no way to predict these things.

When the videotape started repeating itself I got bored, crossed the street, and lost myself in the crowd.

Introduction to "Out of All Them Bright Stars"

by Nancy Kress

Nancy Kress is so nice that if I wrote a character like her, you wouldn't believe she could exist. But she does.

I've taught a class with her; I've been a guest in her home; I've shared hours of conversation with her at writing workshops we both attended. I read her how-to-write column in Writer's Digest *with pleasure (only slightly tinged with envy that she got that gig and I didn't). Above all, I read and love her fiction, and no story more than "Out of All Them Bright Stars," a tale so real and fragile and lovely that to say more about it would be to risk damaging it, like touching a butterfly's wing or the petal of a camellia. It's the Heisenberg principle: you can't analyze this story without moving it to another place, so it's no longer the story that it would have been.*

So let me say just a few words about Nancy Kress herself.

I've seen and read about a lot of talented people, celebrated artists of one kind or another. I've watched as an undeniably brilliant film director humiliated his loyal and creative and hardworking assistant in front of some of the senior people working on his film. The director's attack was completely unjustified; indeed, he was attacking his assistant for something that was obviously entirely the fault of the director himself. And he did it cruelly, sarcastically, on and on. Everyone in the room was squirming. It was a vile thing to see. And, I was told afterward, it was completely normal. It was how this man treated the people he depended on.

When I talked to his assistant afterward, though, he just laughed it off (though I'm not a fool; I could see how deeply hurt he was, how he barely contained his rage and pain). "That's the price of working with a genius," he said.

I reached two important conclusions right then. First, I would never, never let this director touch any project of mine, if I could help it. Such an atmosphere of selfishness and cruelty does not bring the best work from underlings—nor is it designed to. Rather it is designed to make sure that no matter how good a job they do, they take no pride in their work, so that the finished film will belong solely, completely to this selfish "genius," and no one else will even want to claim it. (And the director is completely in control of these outbursts. He never, never directs them toward the famous, powerful stars he deals with. He only acts this way with people who are powerless compared to him. Bravely done!) This director has since done several powerful films, and people constantly ask me, "Wouldn't it be great if you could get him to direct Ender's Game?" And I always answer, "Life is short. I would rather never see it filmed."

The second conclusion I reached was this: genius excuses nothing. A cruel and selfish tyrant who makes great movies is still a cruel and selfish tyrant. A wife-beater who writes great novels is no less a wife-beater. A child molester who is also a beloved comedian is still a child molester. A famous guy who kills his ex-wife . . . but my point is made.

In our society we tolerate vile behavior from our celebrities. We elect and reelect womanizers and sexual harassers, while the press assures us that the moral character of the officeholder is irrelevant. When a princess who was sexually unfaithful to her philandering husband later died in a meaningless car wreck, she was suddenly revered as a saint, even though she died in the same week as a genuinely saintly woman, Mother Teresa—the contrast couldn't have been clearer, but the holiness adhered to the celebrity. Actor after actor, musician after musician is arrested for assault, for vandalism, for drug use, for trafficking with prostitutes, for the sheer stupidity of taking drugs or weapons on an airplane, and somebody is always willing to write some article about how these torments are the "price of genius." The list of talented people dead of drug overdoses gets longer and longer, and in every case there were dozens of friends and employees who knew they were using and did nothing—except, afterward, to talk about how the stresses of celebrity or creativity killed them.

Here's a clue: what killed them was drugs, and if any of their friends and employees had valued the person instead of the "genius," they would have turned him in for his criminal possession of drugs and thereby, quite possibly, have saved his life.

If we expected the same standard of behavior from our artists, our politicians, our celebrities that we expect from our coworkers, our family members, and our neighbors, then yes, some careers would have been cut very short—but some ruined lives might have been saved. Am I the only one who thinks that River Phoenix and Chris Farley might have been better off with the wake-up call of serious jail time than they are right now, dead? Am I the only one that notices that whatever talent they had became unavailable to us the moment they died?

Genius excuses nothing—and genius is better served if we make no excuses. Faulkner did not write better because he was drunk. He wrote less, not more, because of alcohol. No actor or comic or singer ever gave a better performance because of drugs or drink. No politician who could not keep his marriage vow ever proved able to live up to any promises he made to the public, either—when honor is gone in one part of life, only a fool thinks it survives in any other.

And yet, despite these obvious truths, the myth persists that somehow being a drunk or an addict or a philanderer or simply being a jerk to other people somehow goes along with being a genius. In fact, these traits actually seem to enhance the aura of genius, so that the sexual predator or the habitual drug user is regarded as "cool." What nonsense! What destructive, cruel deception!

And my answer to this myth? Let me set before you exhibit A: Nancy Kress.

Oh, please God, no, says Nancy, flushing with embarrassment as she reads this. Card didn't really say that about me, did he? Is he trying to destroy me forever? How can I show my face in public again with this hanging over me?

What have I done that's so embarrassing, I ask you? I merely declared Ms. Kress, in front of everybody, to be a person of unusual kindness, generosity, open-mindedness, decency—who is, nevertheless, gifted with extraordinary talents which she has used to create many powerful, moving works of art.

In other words, it is possible to be possessed of genius, to create beauty and tell the truth about the world, and still be a decent human being. Nancy Kress is not the only one, she's just such an obvious and extreme example that no one can possibly argue with my assessment. She's not a puritan about it, she's not a fanatic about anything, in fact—she's just . . . well, good.

And she wrote "Out of All Them Bright Stars."

So don't tell me any more of those lies about the price of genius. Genius doesn't come from misbehavior, it comes in spite of it; and letting people get away with intolerable behavior because they're "geniuses" ends up destroying the genius, in the long run—and hurting all those who follow their examples or who have to work with them or who love them through the process of disintegration.

If you love the genius of artists, then love the artists, too. Love them as siblings love each other, as parents love children, as friends love friends. Don't let them get away with any crap. And when you're deciding who's cool, give a thought to bestowing your admiration on the artists who actually live by the rules of human decency.

OUT OF ALL THEM BRIGHT STARS

Nancy Kress

So I'm filling the catsup bottles at the end of the night, and I'm listening to the radio Charlie has stuck up on top of a movable panel in the ceiling, when the door opens and one of them walks in. I know right away it's one of them—no chance to make a mistake about *that*— even though it's got on a nice-cut suit and a brim hat like Humphrey Bogart used to wear in *Casablanca*. But there's nobody with it, no professor from the college or government men like on the TV show from the college or even any students. It's all alone. And we're a long way out the highway from the college.

It stands in the doorway, blinking a little, with rain dripping off its hat. Kathy, who's supposed to be cleaning the coffee machine behind the counter, freezes and stares with one hand still holding the used filter up in the air like she's never going to move again. Just then Charlie calls out from the kitchen, "Hey, Kathy, you ask anybody who won the Trifecta?" and she doesn't even answer him. Just goes on staring with her mouth open like she's thinking of screaming but forgot how. And the old couple in the corner booth, the only ones left from the crowd after the movie got out, stop chewing their chocolate cream pie and stare too. Kathy closes her mouth and opens it again and a noise comes out like "Uh—errrgh . . ."

Well, that made me annoyed. Maybe she tried to say "ugh" and maybe she didn't, but here it is standing in the doorway with rain falling around it in little drops and we're staring like it's a clothes dummy and not a customer. So I think that's not right and maybe we're even making it feel a little bad, *I* wouldn't like Kathy staring at me like that, and I dry my hands on my towel and go over.

"Yes, sir, can I help you?" I say.

"Table for one," it says, like Charlie's was some nice steak house in town. But I suppose that's the kind of place the government people mostly take them to. And besides, its voice is polite and easy to understand, with a sort of accent but not as bad as some we get from the college. I can tell what it's saying. I lead him to a booth in the corner opposite the old couple, who come in every Friday night and haven't left a tip yet.

He sits down slowly. I notice he keeps his hands on his lap, but I can't tell if that's because he doesn't know what to do with them or because he thinks I won't want to see them. But I've seen the close-ups on TV—they don't look so weird to me like they do to some. Charlie says they make his stomach turn, but I can't see it. You'd think he'd of seen worse meat in Vietnam. He talks enough like he did, on and on and on, and sometimes we even believe him.

I say, "Coffee, sir?"

He makes a sort of movement with his eyes, I can't tell what the movement means, but he says in that polite voice, "No, thank you. I am unable to drink coffee," and I think that's a good thing because I suddenly remember that Kathy's got the filter out. But then he says, "May I have a green salad, please? With no dressing, please."

The rain is still dripping off his hat. I figure the government people never told him to take off his hat in a restaurant, and for some reason that tickles me and makes me feel real bold. This polite blue guy isn't going to bother anybody, and that fool Charlie was just spouting off his mouth again.

"The salad's not too fresh, sir," I say, experimental-like, just to see what he'll say next. And it's the truth—the salad is left over from yesterday. But the guy answers like I asked something else.

"What is your name?" he says, so polite I know he's really curious and not starting anything. And what could he start anyway, blue and with those hands? Still, you never know.

"Sally," I say. "Sally Gourley."

"I am John," he says, and makes that movement with his eyes again. All of a sudden it tickles me—"John!" For this blue guy! So I laugh, and right away I feel sorry, like I might have hurt his feelings or something. How could you tell?

"Hey, I'm sorry," I say, and he takes off his hat. He does it real slow, like taking off the hat is important and means something, but all there is underneath is a bald blue head. Nothing weird like with the hands.

"Do not apologize," John says. "I have another name, of course, but in my own language."

"What is it?" I say, bold as brass, because all of a sudden I picture myself telling all this to my sister Mary Ellen and her listening real hard.

John makes some noise with his mouth, and I feel my own mouth open because it's not a word he says at all, it's a beautiful sound, like a bird call only sadder. It's just that I wasn't expecting it, that beautiful sound right here in Charlie's diner. It surprised me, coming out of that bald blue head. That's all it was: surprise.

I don't say anything. John looks at me and says, "It has a meaning that can be translated. It means—" but before he can say what it means Charlie comes charging out of the kitchen, Kathy right behind him. He's still got the racing form in one hand, like he's been studying the Trifecta, and he pushes right up against the booth and looks red and furious. Then I see the old couple scuttling out the door, their jackets clutched to their fronts, and the chocolate cream pie not half-eaten on their plates. I see they're going to stiff me for the check, but before I can stop them Charlie grabs my arm and squeezes so hard his nails slice into my skin.

"What the hell do you think you're doing?" he says right to me. Not so much as a look at John, but Kathy can't stop looking and her fist is pushed up to her mouth.

I drag my arm away and rub it. Once I saw Charlie push his wife so hard she went down and hit her head and had to have four stitches. It was me that drove her to the emergency room.

Charlie says again, "What the hell do you think you're doing?"

"I'm serving my table. He wants a salad. Large." I can't remember if John'd said a large or a small salad, but I figure a large order would make Charlie feel better. But Charlie doesn't want to feel better.

"You get him out of here," Charlie hisses. He still doesn't look at John. "You hear me, Sally? You get him *out.* The government says I gotta serve spics and niggers but it don't say I gotta serve him!"

I look at John. He's putting on his hat, ramming it onto his bald head, and half standing in the booth. He can't get out because Charlie and me are both in the way. I expect John to look mad or upset, but except that he's holding the muscles of his face in some different way I can't see any change of expression. But I figure he's got to feel something bad and all of a sudden I'm mad at Charlie, who's a bully and who's got the feelings of a scumbag. I open my mouth to tell him so, plus one or two other little things I been saving up, when the door flies open and in bursts four men, and damn it if they aren't *all* wearing hats like Humphrey Bogart in *Casablanca.* As soon as the first guy sees

John, his walk changes and he comes over slower but more purposeful like, and then he's talking to John and to Charlie in a sincere voice like a TV anchorman giving out the news.

I see the situation now belongs to him, so I go back to the catsup bottles. I'm still plenty burned though, about Charlie man-handling me and about Kathy rushing so stupid into the kitchen to get Charlie. She's a flake and always has been.

Charlie is scowling and nodding. The harder he scowls, the nicer the government guy's voice gets. Pretty soon the government guy is smiling sweet as pie. Charlie slinks back into the kitchen, and the four men move toward the door with John in the middle of them like some high school football huddle. Next to the real men he looks stranger than he did before, and I see how really flat his face is. But then when the huddle's right opposite the table with my catsup bottles John breaks away and comes over to me.

"I am sorry, Sally Gourley," he says. And then, "I seldom have the chance to show our friendliness to an ordinary Earth person. I make so little difference!"

Well, that throws me. His voice sounds so sad, and besides I never thought of myself as an ordinary Earth person. Who would? So I just shrug and wipe off a catsup bottle with my towel. But then John does a weird thing. He just touches my arm where Charlie squeezed it, just touches it with the palm of one of those hands. And the palm's not slimy at all—dry, and sort of cool, and I don't jump or anything. Instead I remember that beautiful noise when he said his other name. Then he goes out with three of the men and the door bangs behind them on a gust of rain because Charlie never fixed the air-stop from when some kids horsing around broke it last spring.

The fourth man stays and questions me: what did the alien say? what did I say? I tell him, but then he starts asking the exact same questions all over again, like he didn't believe me the first time, and that gets me mad. Also he has this snotty voice, and I see how his eyebrows move when I slip once and accidentally say "he don't." I might not know what John's muscles mean but I sure the hell can read those eyebrows. So I get miffed and pretty soon he leaves and the door bangs behind him.

I finish the catsup and mustard bottles and Kathy finishes the coffee machine. The radio in the ceiling plays something instrumental, no words, real sad. Kathy and me start to wash down the booths with disinfectant, and because we're doing the same work together and nobody comes in, I finally say to her, "It's funny."

She says, "What's funny?"

"Charlie called that guy 'him' right off. 'I don't got to serve him,' he said. And I thought of him as 'it' at first, least until I had a name to use. But Charlie's the one who threw him out."

Kathy swipes at the back of her booth. "And Charlie's right. That thing scared me half to death, coming in here like that. And where there's food being served, too." She snorts and sprays on more disinfectant.

Well, she's a flake. Always has been.

"The National Enquirer," Kathy goes on, "told how they have all this firepower up there in the big ship that hasn't landed yet. My husband says they could blow us all to smithereens, they're so powerful. I don't know why they even came here. *We* don't want them. I don't even know why they came, all that way."

"They want to make a difference," I say, but Kathy barrels on ahead, not listening.

"The Pentagon will hold them off, it doesn't matter what weapons they got up there or how much they insist on seeing about our defenses, the Pentagon won't let them get any toeholds on Earth. That's what my husband says. Blue bastards."

I say, "Will you please shut up?"

She gives me a dirty look and flounces off. I don't care. None of it is anything to me. Only, standing there with the disinfectant in my hand, looking at the dark windows and listening to the music wordless and slow on the radio, I remember that touch on my arm, so light and cool. And I think, they didn't come here with any firepower to blow us all to smithereens. I just don't believe it. But then why did they come? Why come all that way from another star to walk into Charlie's diner and order a green salad with no dressing from an ordinary Earth person?

Charlie comes out with his keys to unlock the cash register and go over the tapes. I remember the old couple who stiffed me and I curse to myself. Only pie and coffee, but it still comes off my salary. The radio in the ceiling starts playing something else, not the sad song, but nothing snappy neither. It's a love song, about some guy giving and getting treated like dirt. I don't like it.

"Charlie," I say, "What did those government men say to you?"

He looks up from his tapes and scowls. "What do you care?"

"I just want to know."

"And maybe I don't want you to know," he says, and smiles nasty like. Me asking him has put him in a better mood, the creep. All of a sudden I remember what his wife said when she got the stitches. "The only way to get something from Charlie is to let him smack me around a little, and then ask him when I'm down. He'll give me anything when I'm down. He gives me shit if he thinks I'm on top."

I do the rest of the clean-up without saying anything. Charlie swears at the night's take—I know from my tips that it's not much. Kathy teases her hair in front of the mirror behind doughnuts and pies, and I put down the breakfast menus. But all the time I'm thinking, and I don't much like my thoughts.

Charlie locks up and we all leave. Outside it's stopped raining but it's still misty and soft, real pretty but too cold. I pull my sweater around myself and in the parking lot, after Kathy's gone, I say, "Charlie."

He stops walking towards his truck. "Yeah?"

I lick my lips. They're all of a sudden dry. It's an experiment, like, what I'm going to say. It's an experiment.

"Charlie. What if those government men hadn't come just then and the . . . blue guy hadn't been willing to leave? What would you have done?"

"What do you care?"

I shrug. "I don't care. Just curious. It's *your* place."

"Damn right it's my place!" I could see him scowl, through the mist. "I'd of squashed him flat!"

"And then what? After you squashed him flat, what if the men came then and made a stink?"

"Too bad. It'd be too late then, huh?" He laughs and I can see how he's seeing it: the blue guy bleeding on the linoleum and Charlie standing over him, dusting his hands together.

Charlie laughs again and goes off to his truck, whistling. He has a little bounce in his step. He's still seeing it all, almost like it really *had* happened. Over his shoulder he calls to me, "They're built like wimps. Or girls. All bone, no muscle. Even *you* must of seen that," and his voice is cheerful. It doesn't have any anger in it, or hatred, or anything but a sort of friendliness. I hear him whistle some more, until the truck engine starts up and he peels out of the parking lot, laying rubber like a kid.

I unlock my Chevy. But before I get in, I look up at the sky. Which is really stupid because of course I can't see anything, with all the mists and clouds. No stars.

Maybe Kathy's right. Maybe they do want to blow us all to smithereens. I don't think so, but what the hell difference does it ever make what I think? And all at once I'm furious at John, furiously mad, as furious as I've ever been in my life.

Why does he have to come here, with his bird calls and his politeness? Why can't they all go someplace else beside here? There must be lots of other places they can go, out of all them bright stars up there behind the clouds. They don't need to come here, here where I need this job and so that means I need Charlie. He's a bully, but I want to look at him and see nothing else but a bully. Nothing else but that. That's all I want to see in Charlie, in the government men—just small-time bullies, nothing special, not a mirror of anything, not a future of anything. Just Charlie. That's all. I won't see nothing else.

I won't.

"I make so little difference," he says.

Yeah. Sure.

Introduction to "The Fringe"

by Orson Scott Card

My own story? On the one hand, it is a repulsively immodest thing to do, to include a story of my own in an anthology of the "important" sf stories of the 1980s. On the other hand, the publisher told me he wouldn't publish these volumes if a story of mine weren't included. And on the third hand, if somebody else had edited this anthology and didn't include something of mine, I would never have forgiven him. So I'm not going to pretend my publisher had to twist my arm very hard to get me to include a story. I wanted to have something in here, and if that proves me to be vain and ambitious, please remember that it was Nancy Kress, not myself, that I set up as a model of virtue.

So, OK, fine, a story of mine—but which one? Has to be one from the 1980s. That eliminates a huge swath of stories. Has to be short—so my one Hugo-winning novella is out. Has to be science fiction, so the whole Alvin Maker collection is eliminated, and so are my mainstream pieces. Just a handful of survivors, now.

This one: The first story I wrote for a writing workshop of fellow professionals. The first story I wrote when I felt like I actually understood what a short story was, as opposed to a novel. The only story I ever wrote that John Kessel liked. And a story I still care about, a character I still love. It's up to you to decide if this story belongs in this book; if it doesn't, then nothing else of mine does, either.

THE FRINGE

Orson Scott Card

LaVon's book report was drivel, of course. Carpenter knew it would be from the moment he called on the boy. After Carpenter's warning last week, he knew LaVon would have a book report—LaVon's father would never let the boy be suspended. But LaVon was too stubborn, too cocky, too much the leader of the other sixth-graders' constant rebellion against authority to let Carpenter have a complete victory.

"I really, truly loved *Little Men*," said LaVon. "It just gave me goose bumps."

The class laughed. Excellent comic timing, Carpenter said silently. But the only place that comedy is useful here in the New Soil country is with the gypsy pageant wagons. That's what you're preparing yourself for, LaVon, a career as a wandering parasite who lives by sucking laughter out of weary farmers.

"Everybody nice in this book has a name that starts with *D*. Demi is a sweet little boy who never does anything wrong. Daisy is so good that she could have seven children and still be a virgin."

He was pushing the limits now. A lot of people didn't like mention of sexual matters in the school, and if some pinheaded child decided to report this, the story could be twisted into something that could be used against Carpenter. Out here near the fringe, people were desperate for entertainment. A crusade to drive out a teacher for corrupting the morals of youth would be more fun than a traveling show, because everybody could feel righteous and safe when he was gone. Carpenter had seen it before. Not that he was afraid of it, the way most teachers were. *He* had a career no matter what. The university would take him back, eagerly; they thought he was crazy to go out and teach in the low schools. I'm safe, absolutely safe, he thought. They can't wreck my career. And I'm not going to get prissy about a perfectly good word like *virgin*.

"Dan looks like a big bad boy, but he has a heart of gold, even though he does say real bad words like *devil* sometimes." LaVon paused, waiting for Carpenter to react. So Carpenter did not react.

"The saddest thing is poor Nat, the street fiddler's boy. He tries hard to fit in, but he can never amount to anything in the book, because his name doesn't start with *D*."

The end. LaVon put the single paper on Carpenter's desk, then went back to his seat. He walked with the careful elegance of a spider, each long leg moving as if it were unconnected to the rest of his body, so that even walking did not disturb the perfect calm. The boy rides on his body the way I ride in my wheelchair, thought Carpenter. Smooth, unmoved by his own motion. But *he* is graceful and beautiful, fifteen years old and already a master at winning the devotion of the weakhearted children around him. *He* is the enemy, the torturer, the strong and beautiful man who must confirm his beauty by preying on the weak. I am not as weak as you think.

LaVon's book report was arrogant, far too short, and flagrantly rebellious. That much was deliberate, calculated to annoy Carpenter. Therefore Carpenter would not show the slightest trace of annoyance. The book report had also been clever, ironic, and funny. The boy, for all his mask of languor and stupidity, had brains. He was better than this farming town; he could do something that mattered in the world besides driving a tractor in endless contour patterns around the fields. But the way he always had the Fisher girl hanging on him, he'd no doubt have a baby and a wife and stay here forever. Become a big shot like his father, maybe, but never leave a mark in the world to show he'd been here. Tragic, stupid waste.

But don't show the anger. The children will misunderstand, they'll think I'm angry because of LaVon's rebelliousness, and it will only make this boy more of a hero in their eyes. Children choose their heroes with unerring stupidity. Fourteen, fifteen, sixteen years old, all they know of life is cold and bookless classrooms interrupted now and then by a year or two of wrestling with this stony earth, always hating whatever adult it is who keeps them at their work, always adoring whatever fool gives them the illusion of being free. You children have no practice in surviving among the ruins of your own mistakes. We adults who knew the world before it fell, we feel the weight of the rubble on our backs.

They were waiting for Carpenter's answer. He reached out to the computer keyboard attached to his wheelchair. His hands struck like paws at the oversized keys. His fingers were too stupid for him to use them individually. They clenched when he tried to work them, tightened into a fist, a little hammer with which to strike, to break, to attack; he could not use them to grasp or even hold. Half the verbs of the world are impossible to me, he thought as he often thought. I learn them the way the blind learn words of seeing—by rote, with no hope of ever knowing truly what they mean.

The speech synthesizer droned out the words he keyed. "Brilliant essay, Mr. Jensen. The irony was powerful, the savagery was refreshing. Unfortunately, it also revealed the poverty of your soul. Alcott's title was ironic, for she wanted to show that despite their small size, the boys in her book were great-hearted. You, however, despite your large size, are very small of heart indeed."

LaVon looked at him through heavy-lidded eyes. Hatred? Yes, it was there. Do hate me, child. Loathe me enough to show me that you can do anything I ask you to do. Then I'll own you, then I can get something decent out of you, and finally give you back to yourself as a human being who is worthy to be alive.

Carpenter pushed outward on both levers, and his wheelchair backed up. The day was nearly over, and tonight he knew something would change, painfully, in the life of the town of Reefrock. And because in a way the arrests would be his fault, and because the imprisonment of a father would cause upheaval in some of these children's families, he felt it his duty to prepare them as best he could to understand why it had to happen, why, in the larger view, it was good. It was too much to expect that they would actually understand, today; but they might remember, might forgive him someday for what they would soon find out he had done to them.

So he pawed at the keys again. "Economics," said the computer. "Since Mr. Jensen has made an end of literature for the day." A few more keys, and the lecture began. Carpenter entered all his lectures and stored them in memory, so that he could sit still as ice in his chair, making eye contact with each student in turn, daring them to be inattentive. There were advantages in letting a machine speak for him; he had learned many years ago that it frightened people to have a mechanical voice speak his words while his lips were motionless. It was monstrous, it made him seem dangerous and strange. Which he far preferred to the way he looked: weak as a worm, his skinny, twisted, palsied body rigid in his chair; his body looked strange but pathetic. Only when the synthesizer spoke his acid words did he earn respect from the people who always, always looked downward at him.

"Here in the settlements just behind the fringe," his voice went, "we do not have the luxury of a free economy. The rains sweep onto this ancient desert and find nothing here but a few plants growing in the sand. Thirty years ago nothing lived here; even the lizards had to stay where there was something for insects to eat, where there was water to drink. Then the fires we lit put a curtain in the sky, and the ice moved south, and the rains that had always passed north of us now raked and scoured the desert. It was opportunity."

LaVon smirked as Kippie made a great show of dozing off. Carpenter keyed an interruption in the lecture. "Kippie, how well will you sleep if I send you home now for an afternoon nap?"

Kippie sat bolt upright, pretending terrible fear. But the pretense was also a pretense; he *was* afraid, and so to conceal it he pretended to be pretending to be afraid. Very complex, the inner life of children, thought Carpenter.

"Even as the old settlements were slowly drowned under the rising Great Salt Lake, your fathers and mothers began to move out into the desert, to reclaim it. But not alone. We can do nothing alone here. The fringers plant their grass. The grass feeds the herds and puts roots into the sand. The roots become humus, rich in nitrogen. In three years the fringe has a thin lace of soil across it. If at any point a fringer fails to plant, if at any point the soil is broken, then the rains eat channels under it, and tear away the fringe on either side, and eat back into farmland behind it. So every fringer is responsible to every other fringer, and to us. How would you feel about a fringer who failed?"

"The way I feel about a fringer who succeeds," said Pope. He was the youngest of the sixth-graders, only thirteen years old, and he sucked up to LaVon disgracefully.

Carpenter punched four codes. "And how is that?" asked Carpenter's metal voice.

Pope's courage fled. "Sorry."

Carpenter did not let go. "What is it you call fringers?" he asked. He looked from one child to the next, and they would not meet his gaze. Except LaVon.

"What do you call them?" he asked again.

"If I say it, I'll get kicked out of school," said LaVon. "You want me kicked out of school?"

"You accuse them of fornicating with cattle, yes?"

A few giggles.

"Yes, sir," said LaVon. "We call them cow-fornicators, sir."

Carpenter keyed in his response while they laughed. When the room was silent, he played it back. "The bread you eat grows in the soil they created, and the manure of their cattle is the strength of your bodies. Without fringers you would be eking out a miserable life on the shores of the Mormon Sea, eating fish and drinking sage tea, and don't forget it." He set the volume of the synthesizer steadily lower during the speech, so that at the end they were straining to hear.

Then he resumed his lecture. "After the fringers came your mothers and fathers, planting crops in a scientifically planned order: two rows of apple trees, then six meters of wheat, then six meters of corn, then six meters of cucumbers, and so on; year after year, moving six more meters out, following the fringers, making more land, more food. If you didn't plant what you were told, and harvest it on the right day, and work shoulder to shoulder in the fields whenever the need came, then the plants would die, the rain would wash them away. What do you think of the farmer who does not do his labor or take his work turn?"

"Scum," one child said. And another: "He's a wallow, that's what he is."

"If this land is to be truly alive, it must be planted in a careful plan for eighteen years. Only then will your family have the luxury of deciding what crop to plant. Only then will you be able to be lazy if you want to, or work extra hard and profit from it. Then some of you can get rich, and others can become poor. But now, today, we do everything together, equally, and so we share equally in the rewards of our work."

LaVon murmured something.

"Yes, LaVon?" asked Carpenter. He made the computer speak very loudly. It startled the children.

"Nothing," said LaVon.

"You said, 'Except teachers.'"

"What if I did?"

"You are correct," said Carpenter. "Teachers do not plow and plant in the fields with your parents. Teachers are given much more barren soil to work in, and most of the time the few seeds we plant are washed away with the first spring shower. You are living proof of the futility of our labor. But we try, Mr. Jensen, foolish as the effort is. May we continue?"

LaVon nodded. His face was flushed. Carpenter was satisfied. The boy was not hopeless—he could still feel shame at having attacked a man's livelihood.

"There are some among us," said the lecture, "who believe they should benefit more than others from the work of all. These are the ones who steal from the common storehouse and sell the crops that were raised by everyone's labor. The black market pays high prices for the stolen grain, and the thieves get rich. When they get rich enough, they move away from the fringe, back to the cities of the high valleys. Their wives will wear fine clothing, their sons will have watches, their daughters will own land and marry well. And in the meantime, their friends and neighbors, who trusted them, will have nothing, will stay on the fringe, growing the food that feeds the thieves. Tell me, what do you think of a black marketeer?"

He watched their faces. Yes, they knew. He could see how they glanced surreptitiously at Dick's new shoes, at Kippie's wristwatch. At Yutonna's new city-bought blouse. At LaVon's jeans. They knew, but out of fear they had said nothing. Or perhaps it wasn't fear. Perhaps it was the hope that their own fathers would be clever enough to steal from the harvest, so they could move away instead of earning out their eighteen years.

"Some people think these thieves are clever. But I tell you they are exactly like the mobbers of the plains. They are the enemies of civilization."

"*This* is civilization?" asked LaVon.

"Yes." Carpenter keyed an answer. "We live in peace here, and you know that today's work brings tomorrow's bread. Out on the prairie they don't know that. Tomorrow a mobber will be eating their bread, if they haven't been killed. There's no trust in the world, except here. And the black marketeers feed on trust. Their neighbors' trust. When they've eaten it all, children, what will you live on then?"

They didn't understand, of course. When it was story problems about one truck approaching another truck at sixty kleeters and it takes an hour to meet, how far away were they?—the children could handle that, could figure it out laboriously with pencil and paper and prayers and curses. But the questions that mattered sailed past them like little dust devils, noticed but untouched by their feeble, self-centered little minds.

He tormented them with a pop quiz on history and thirty spelling words for their homework, then sent them out the door.

LaVon did not leave. He stood by the door, closed it, spoke. "It was a stupid book," he said.

Carpenter clicked the keyboard. "That explains why you wrote a stupid book report."

"It wasn't stupid. It was funny. I read the damn book, didn't I?"

"And I gave you a B."

LaVon was silent a moment, then said, "Do me no favors."

"I never will."

"And shut up with that goddamn machine voice. You can make a voice yourself. My cousin's got palsy and she howls to the moon."

"You may leave now, Mr. Jensen."

"I'm gonna hear you talk in your natural voice someday, Mr. Machine."

"You had better go home now, Mr. Jensen."

LaVon opened the door to leave, then turned abruptly and strode the dozen steps to the head of the class. His legs now were tight and powerful as horses' legs, and his arms were light and strong. Carpenter watched him and felt the same old fear rise within him. If God was going to let him be born like this, he could at least keep him safe from the torturers.

"What do you want, Mr. Jensen?" But before the computer had finished speaking Carpenter's words, LaVon reached out and took Carpenter's wrists, held them tightly. Carpenter did not try to resist; if he did, he might go tight and twist around on the chair like a slug on a hot shovel. That would be more humiliation than he could bear, to have this boy see him writhe. His hands hung limp from LaVon's powerful fists.

"You just mind your business," LaVon said. "You only been here two years, you don't know nothin', you understand? You don't see nothin', you don't say nothin', you understand?"

So it wasn't the book report at all. LaVon had actually understood the lecture about civilization and the black market. And knew that it was LaVon's own father, more than anyone else in town, who was guilty. Nephi Delos Jensen, big shot foreman of Reefrock Farms. Have the marshals already taken your father? Best get home and see.

"Do you understand me?"

But Carpenter would not speak. Not without his computer. This boy would never hear how Carpenter's own voice sounded, the whining, baying sound, like a dog trying to curl its tongue into human speech. You'll never hear my voice, boy.

"Just try to expel me for this, Mr. Carpenter. I'll say it never happened. I'll say you had it in for me."

Then he let go of Carpenter's hands and stalked from the room. Only then did Carpenter's legs go rigid, lifting him on the chair so that only the computer over his lap kept him from sliding off. His arms pressed outward, his neck twisted, his jaw opened wide. It was what his body did with fear and rage; it was why he did his best never to feel those emotions. Or any others, for that matter. Dispassionate, that's what he was. He lived the life of the mind, since the life of the body was beyond him. He stretched across his wheelchair like a mocking crucifix, hating his body and pretending that he was merely waiting for it to calm, to relax.

And it did, of course. As soon as he had control of his hands again, he took the computer out of speech mode and called up the data he had sent on to Zarahemla yesterday morning—the crop estimates for three years, and the final weight of the harvested wheat and corn, cukes and berries, apples and beans. For the first two years, the estimates were within 2 percent of the final total. The third year the estimates were higher, but the harvest stayed the same. It was suspicious. Then the bishop's accounting records. It was a sick community. When the bishop was also seduced into this sort of thing, it meant the rottenness touched every corner of village life. Reefrock Farms looked no different from the hundred other villages just this side of the fringe, but it was diseased. Did Kippie know that even his father was in on the black-marketeering? If you couldn't trust the bishop, who was left?

The words of his own thoughts tasted sour in his mouth. Diseased. They aren't so sick, Carpenter, he told himself. Civilization has always had its parasites and survived. But it survived because it rooted them out from time to time, cast them away and cleansed the body. Yet they made heroes out of the thieves and despised those who reported them. There's no thanks in what I've done. It isn't love I'm earning. It isn't love I feel. Can I pretend that I'm not just a sick and twisted body taking vengeance on those healthy enough to have families, healthy enough to want to get every possible advantage for them?

He pushed the levers inward, and the chair rolled forward. He skillfully maneuvered between the chairs, but it still took nearly a full minute to get to the door. I'm a snail. A worm living in a metal carapace, a water snail creeping along the edge of the aquarium glass, trying to keep it clean from the filth of the fish. I'm the loathsome one; they're the golden ones that shine in the sparkling water. They're the ones whose death is mourned. But without me they'd die. I'm as responsible for their beauty as they are. More, because I work to sustain it, and they simply—are.

It came out this way whenever he tried to reason out an excuse for his own life. He rolled down the corridor to the front door of the school. He knew, intellectually, that his work in crop rotation and timing had been the key to opening up the vast New Soil Lands here in the eastern Utah desert. Hadn't they invented a civilian medal for him, and then, for good measure, given him the same medal they gave to the freedom riders who went out and brought immigrant trains safely into the mountains? I was a hero, they said, this worm in his wheelchair house. But Governor Monson had looked at him with those distant, pitying eyes. He, too, saw the worm; Carpenter might be a hero, but he was still Carpenter.

They had built a concrete ramp for his chair after the second time the students knocked over the wooden ramp and forced him to summon help through the computer airlink network. He remembered sitting on the lip of the porch, looking out toward the cabins of the village. If anyone saw him, then they consented to his imprisonment, because they didn't come to help him. But Carpenter understood. Fear of the strange, the unknown. It wasn't *comfortable* for them, to be near Mr. Carpenter with the mechanical voice and the electric rolling chair. He understood, he really did, he was human, too, wasn't he? He even agreed with them. Pretend Carpenter isn't there, and maybe he'll go away.

The helicopter came as he rolled out onto the asphalt of the street. It landed in the circle, between the storehouse and the chapel. Four marshals came out of the gash in its side and spread out through the town.

It happened that Carpenter was rolling in front of Bishop Anderson's house when the marshal knocked on the door. He hadn't expected them to make the arrests while he was still going down the street. His first impulse was to speed up, to get away from the arrest. He didn't want to see. He liked Bishop Anderson. Used to, anyway. He didn't wish him ill. If the bishop had kept his hands out of the harvest, if he hadn't betrayed his trust, he wouldn't have been afraid to hear the knock on the door and see the badge in the marshal's hand.

Carpenter could hear Sister Anderson crying as they led her husband away. Was Kippie there, watching? Did he notice Mr. Carpenter passing by on the road? Carpenter knew what it would cost these families. Not just the shame, though it would be intense. Far worse would be the loss of their father for years, the extra labor for the children. To break up a family was a terrible thing to do, for the innocent would pay as great a cost as their guilty father, and it wasn't fair, for they had done no wrong. But it was the stern necessity, if civilization was to survive.

Carpenter slowed down his wheelchair, forcing himself to hear the weeping from the bishop's house, to let them look at him with hatred if they knew what he had done. And they would know: He had specifically refused to be anonymous. If I can inflict stern necessity on them, then I must not run from the consequences of my own actions. I will bear what I must bear, as well—the grief, the resentment, and the rage of the few families I have harmed for the sake of all the rest.

The helicopter had taken off again before Carpenter's chair took him home. It sputtered overhead and disappeared into the low clouds. Rain again tomorrow, of course. Three days dry, three days wet; it had been the weather pattern all spring. The rain would come pounding tonight. Four hours till dark. Maybe the rain wouldn't come until dark.

He looked up from his book. He *had* heard footsteps outside his house. And whispers. He rolled to the window and looked out. The sky was a little darker. The computer said it was 4:30. The wind was coming up. But the sounds he heard hadn't been the wind. It had been 3:30 when the marshals came. Four-thirty now, and footsteps and whispers outside his house. He felt the stiffening in his arms and legs. Wait, he told himself. There's nothing to fear. Relax. Quiet. Yes. His body eased. His heart pounded, but it was slowing down.

The door crashed open. He was rigid at once. He couldn't even bring his hands down to touch the levers so he could turn to see who it was. He just spread there helplessly in his chair as the heavy footfalls came closer.

"There he is." The voice was Kippie's.

Hands seized his arms, pulled on him; the chair rocked as they tugged him to one side. He could not relax. "Son of a bitch is stiff as a statue." Pope's voice. Get out of here, little boy, said Carpenter, you're in something too deep for you. But of course they did not hear him, since his fingers couldn't reach the keyboard where he kept his voice.

"Maybe this is what he does when he isn't at school. Just sits here and makes statues at the window." Kippie laughed.

"He's scared stiff, that's what he is."

"Just bring him out, and fast." LaVon's voice carried authority.

They tried to lift him out of the chair, but his body was too rigid; they hurt him, though, trying, for his thighs pressed up against the computer with cruel force, and they wrung at his arms.

"Just carry the whole chair," said LaVon.

They picked up the chair and pulled him toward the door. His arms smacked against the corners and the door-frame. "It's like he's dead or something," said Kippie. "He don't say nothin'."

He was shouting at them in his mind, however. What are you doing here? Getting some sort of vengeance? Do you think punishing me will bring your fathers back, you fools?

They pulled and pushed the chair into the van they had parked in front. The bishop's van—Kippie wouldn't have the use of *that* much longer. How much of the stolen grain was carried in here?

"He's going to roll around back here," said Kippie.

"Tip him over," said LaVon.

Carpenter felt the chair fly under him; by chance he landed in such a way that his left arm was not caught behind the chair. It would have broken then. As it was, the impact with the floor bent his arm forcibly against the strength of his spasmed muscles; he felt something tear, and his throat made a sound in spite of his effort to bear it silently.

"Did you hear that?" said Pope. "He's got a voice."

"Not for much longer," said LaVon.

For the first time Carpenter realized that it wasn't just pain that he had to fear. Now, only an hour after their fathers had been taken, long before time could cool their rage, these boys had murder in their hearts.

The road was smooth enough in town, but soon it became rough and painful. From that, Carpenter knew they were headed toward the fringe. He could feel the cold metal of the van's corrugated floor against his face; the pain in his arm was settling down to a steady throb. Relax, quiet, calm, he told himself. How many times in your life have you wished to die? Death means nothing to you, fool—you decided that years ago—death is nothing but a release from this corpse. So what are you afraid of? Calm, quiet. His arms bent, his legs relaxed.

"He's getting soft again," reported Pope. From the front of the van, Kippie guffawed. "Little and squirmy. Mr. Bug. We always call you that, you hear me, Mr. Bug? There was always two of you. Mr. Machine and Mr. Bug. Mr. Machine was mean and tough and smart, but Mr. Bug was weak and squishy and gross, with wiggly legs. Made us want to puke, looking at Mr. Bug."

I've been tormented by master torturers in my childhood, Pope Griffith. You are only a pathetic echo of their talent. Carpenter's words were silent, until his hands found the keys. His left hand was almost too weak to use, after the fall, so he coded the words clumsily with his right hand alone. "If I disappear the day of your father's arrest, Mr. Griffith, don't you think they'll guess who took me?"

"Keep his hands away from the keys!" shouted LaVon. "Don't let him touch the computer."

Almost immediately the van lurched and took a savage bounce as it left the roadway. Now it was clattering over rough, unfinished ground. Carpenter's head banged against the metal floor, again and again. The pain of it made him go rigid; fortunately, spasms always carried his head upward to the right, so that his rigidity kept him from having his head beaten to unconsciousness.

Soon the bouncing stopped. The engine died. Carpenter could hear the wind whispering over the open desert land. They were beyond the fields and orchards, out past the grassland of the fringe. The van doors opened. LaVon and Kippie reached in and pulled him out, chair and all. They dragged the chair to the top of a wash. There was no water in it yet.

"Let's just throw him down," said Kippie. "Break his spastic little neck." Carpenter had not guessed that anger could burn so hot in these languid, mocking boys.

But LaVon showed no fire. He was cold and smooth as snow. "I don't want to kill him yet. I want to hear him talk first."

Carpenter reached out to code an answer. LaVon slapped his hands away, gripped the computer, braced a foot on the wheelchair, and tore the computer off its mounting. He threw it across the arroyo; it smacked against the far side and tumbled down into the dry wash. Probably it wasn't damaged, but it wasn't the computer Carpenter was frightened for. Until now Carpenter had been able to cling to a hope that they just meant to frighten him. But it was unthinkable to treat precious electronic equipment that way, not if civilization still had any hold on LaVon.

"With your *voice,* Mr. Carpenter. Not the machine, your own voice."

Not for you, Mr. Jensen. I don't humiliate myself for you.

"Come on," said Pope. "You know what we said. We just take him down into the wash and leave him there."

"We'll send him down the quick way," said Kippie. He shoved at the wheelchair, teetering it toward the brink.

"We'll *take* him down!" shouted Pope. "We aren't going to kill him! You promised!"

"Lot of difference it makes," said Kippie. "As soon as it rains in the mountains, this sucker's gonna fill up with water and give him the swim of his life."

"We don't kill him," insisted Pope.

"Come on," said LaVon. "Let's get him down into the wash."

Carpenter concentrated on not going rigid as they wrestled the chair down the slope. The walls of the wash weren't sheer, but they were steep enough that the climb down wasn't easy. Carpenter tried to concentrate on mathematics problems so he wouldn't panic and writhe for them again. Finally the chair came to rest at the bottom of the wash.

"You think you can come here and decide who's good and who's bad, right?" said LaVon. "You think you can sit on your little throne and decide whose father's going to jail, is that it?"

Carpenter's hands rested on the twisted mountings that used to hold his computer. He felt naked, defenseless without his stinging, frightening voice to whip them into line. LaVon was smart to take away his voice. LaVon knew what Carpenter could do with words.

"Everybody does it," said Kippie. "You're the only one who doesn't black the harvest, and that's only because you can't."

"It's easy to be straight when you can't get anything on the side, anyway," said Pope.

Nothing's easy, Mr. Griffith. Not even virtue.

"My father's a good man!" shouted Kippie. "He's the bishop, for Christ's sake! And you sent him to jail!"

"If he ain't shot," said Pope.

"They don't shoot you for blacking anymore," said LaVon. "That was in the old days."

The old days. Only five years ago. But those were the old days for these children. Children are innocent in the eyes of God, Carpenter reminded himself. He tried to believe that these boys didn't know what they were doing to him.

Kippie and Pope started up the side of the wash. "Come on," said Pope. "Come on, LaVon."

"Minute," said LaVon. He leaned close to Carpenter and spoke softly, intensely, his breath hot and foul, his spittle like sparks from a cookfire on Carpenter's face. "Just ask me," he said. "Just open your mouth and beg me, little man, and I'll carry you back up to the van. They'll let you live if I tell them to, you know that."

He knew it. But he also knew that LaVon would never tell them to spare his life.

"Beg me, Mr. Carpenter. Ask me please to let you live, and you'll live. Look. I'll even save your little talk box for you." He scooped up the computer from the sandy bottom and heaved it up out of the wash. It sailed over Kippie's head just as he was emerging from the arroyo.

"What the hell was that, you trying to kill me?"

LaVon whispered again. "You know how many times you made me crawl? And now I gotta crawl forever; my father's a jailbird thanks to you; I got little brothers and sisters—even if you hate me, what've you got against them, huh?"

A drop of rain struck Carpenter in the face. There were a few more drops.

"Feel that?" said LaVon. "The rain in the mountains makes this wash flood every time. You crawl for me, Carpenter, and I'll take you up."

Carpenter didn't feel particularly brave as he kept his mouth shut and made no sound. If he actually believed LaVon might keep his promise, he would swallow his pride and beg. But LaVon was lying. He couldn't afford to save Carpenter's life now, even if he wanted to. It had gone too far, the consequences would be too great. Carpenter had to die, accidentally drowned, no witnesses, such a sad thing, such a great man, and no one the wiser about the three boys who carried him to his dying place.

If he begged and whined in his hound voice, his cat voice, his bestial monster voice, then LaVon would smirk at him in triumph and whisper, "Sucker." Carpenter knew the boy too well. Tomorrow LaVon would have second thoughts, of course, but right now there'd be no softening. He only wanted his triumph to be complete, that's why he held out a hope. He wanted to watch Carpenter twist like a worm and bay like a hound before he died. It was a victory, then, to keep silence. Let him remember me in his nightmares of guilt, let him remember I had courage enough not to whimper.

LaVon spat at him; the spittle struck him in the chest. "I can't even get it in your ugly little worm face," he said. Then he shoved the wheelchair and scrambled up the bank of the wash.

For a moment the chair hung in the balance; then it tipped over.

This time Carpenter relaxed during the fall and rolled out of the chair without further injury. His back was to the side of the wash they had climbed; he couldn't see if they were watching him or not. So he held still, except for a slight twitching of his hurt left arm. After a while the van drove away.

Only then did he begin to reach out his arms and paw at the sand of the arroyo bottom. His legs were completely useless, dragging behind him. But he was not totally helpless without his chair. He could control his arms, and by reaching them out and then pulling his body onto his elbows, he could make good progress across the sand. How did they think he got from his wheelchair to bed, or to the toilet? Hadn't they seen him use his hands and arms? Of course they saw, but they assumed that because his arms were weak, they were useless.

Then he got to the arroyo wall and realized that they *were* useless. As soon as there was any slope to climb, his left arm began to hurt badly. And the bank was steep. Without being able to use his fingers to clutch at one of the sagebrushes or tree starts, there was no hope he could climb out.

The lightning was flashing in the distance, and he could hear the thunder. The rain here was a steady *plick plick plick* on the sand, a tiny slapping sound on the few leaves. It would already be raining heavily in the mountains. Soon the water would be here.

He dragged himself another meter up the slope despite the pain. The sand scraped his elbows as he dug with them to pull himself along. The rain fell steadily now, many large drops, but still not a downpour. It was little comfort to Carpenter. Water was beginning to dribble down the sides of the wash and form puddles in the streambed.

With bitter humor he imagined himself telling Dean Wintz, "On second thought, I don't want to go out and teach sixth grade. I'll just go right on teaching them here, when they come off the farm. Just the few who want to learn something beyond sixth grade, who want a university education. The ones who love books and numbers and languages, the ones who understand civilization and want to keep it alive. Give me the children who *want* to learn, instead of these poor sand-scrapers who go to school only because the law commands that six years out of their first fifteen years have to be spent as captives in the prison of learning."

Why do the fire-eaters go out searching for the old missile sites and risk their lives disarming them? To preserve civilization. Why do the freedom riders leave their safe homes and go out to bring the frightened, lonely refugees in to the safety of the mountains? To preserve civilization.

And why had Timothy Carpenter informed the marshals about the black-marketeering he had discovered in Reefrock Farms? Was it, truly, to preserve civilization?

Yes, he insisted to himself.

The water was flowing now along the bottom of the wash. His feet were near the flow. He painfully pulled himself up another meter. He had to keep his body pointed straight toward the side of the wash, or he would not be able to stop himself from rolling to one side or the other. He found that by kicking his legs in his spastic, uncontrolled fashion, he could root the toes of his shoes into the sand just enough that he could take some pressure off his arms, just for a moment.

No, he told himself. It was not just to preserve civilization. It was because of the swaggering way their children walked, in their stolen clothing, with their full bellies and healthy skin and hair, cocky as only security can make a child feel. Enough and to spare, that's what they had, while the poor suckers around them worried whether there'd be food enough for the winter, and if their mother was getting enough so the nursing baby wouldn't lack, and whether their shoes could last another summer. The thieves could take a wagon up the long road to Price or even to Zarahemla, the shining city on the Mormon Sea, while the children of honest men never saw anything but the dust and sand and ruddy mountains of the fringe.

Carpenter hated them for that, for all the differences in the world, for the children who had legs and walked nowhere that mattered, for the children who had voices and used them to speak stupidity, who had deft and clever fingers and used them to frighten and compel the weak. For all the inequalities in the world, he hated them and wanted them to pay for it. They couldn't go to jail for having obedient arms and legs and tongues, but they could damn well go for stealing the hard-earned harvest of trusting men and women. Whatever his own motives might be, that was reason enough to call it justice.

The water was rising many centimeters every minute. The current was tugging at his feet now. He released his elbows to reach them up for another, higher purchase on the bank, but no sooner had he reached out his arms than he slid downward and the current pulled harder at him. It took great effort just to return to where he started, and his left arm was on fire with the tearing muscles. Still, it was life, wasn't it? His left elbow rooted him in place while he reached with his right arm and climbed higher still, and again higher. He even tried to use his fingers to cling to the soil, to a branch, to a rock, but his fists stayed closed and hammered uselessly against the ground.

Am I vengeful, bitter, spiteful? Maybe I am. But whatever my motive was, they were thieves, and had no business remaining among the people they had betrayed. It was hard on the children, of course, cruelly hard on them, to have their fathers stripped away from them by the authorities. But how much worse would it be for the fathers to stay, and the children to learn that trust was for the stupid and honor for the weak? What kind of people would we be then, if the children could do their numbers and letters but couldn't hold someone else's plate and leave the food on it untouched?

The water was up to his waist. The current was rocking him slightly, pulling him downstream. His legs were floating behind him now, and water was tricking down the bank, making the earth looser under his elbows. So the children wanted him dead now, in their fury. He would die in a good cause, wouldn't he?

With the water rising faster, the current swifter, he decided that martyrdom was not all it was cracked up to be. Nor was life, when he came right down to it, something to be given up lightly because of a few inconveniences. He managed to squirm up a few more centimeters, but now a shelf of earth blocked him. Someone with hands could have reached over it easily and grabbed hold of the sagebrush just above it.

He clenched his mouth tight and lifted his arm up onto the shelf of dirt. He tried to scrape some purchase for his forearm, but the soil was slick. When he tried to place some weight on the arm, he slid down again.

This was it, this was his death, he could feel it; and in the sudden rush of fear, his body went rigid. Almost at once his feet caught on the rocky bed of the river and stopped him from sliding farther. Spastic, his legs were of some use to him. He swung his right arm up, scraped his fist on the sagebrush stem, trying to pry his clenched fingers open.

And, with agonizing effort, he did it. All but the smallest finger opened enough to hook the stem. Now the clenching was some help to him. He used his left arm mercilessly, ignoring the pain, to pull himself up a little farther, onto the shelf; his feet were still in the water, but his waist wasn't, and the current wasn't strong against him now.

It was a victory, but not much of one. The water wasn't even a meter deep yet, and the current wasn't yet strong enough to have carried away his wheelchair. But it was enough to kill him, if he hadn't come this far. Still, what was he really accomplishing? In storms like this, the water came up near the top; he'd have been dead for an hour before the water began to come down again.

He could hear, in the distance, a vehicle approaching on the road. Had they come back to watch him die? They couldn't be that stupid. How far was this wash from the highway? Not far—they hadn't driven that long on the rough ground to get here. But it meant nothing. No one would see him, or even the computer that lay among the tumbleweeds and sagebrush at the arroyo's edge.

They might hear him. It was possible. If their window was open—in a rainstorm? If their engine was quiet—but loud enough that he could hear them? Impossible, impossible. And it might be the boys again, come to hear him scream and whine for life; I'm not going to cry out now, after so many years of silence—

But the will to live, he discovered, was stronger than shame; his voice came unbidden to his throat. His lips and tongue and teeth that in childhood had so painstakingly practiced words that only his family could ever understand now formed a word again: "Help!" It was a difficult word; it almost closed his mouth, it made him too quiet to hear. So at last he simply howled, saying nothing except the terrible sound of his voice.

The brakes squealed, long and loud, and the vehicle rattled to a stop. The engine died. Carpenter howled again. Car doors slammed. "I tell you it's just a dog somewhere, somebody's old dog—"

Carpenter howled again.

"Dog or not, it's alive, isn't it?"

They ran along the edge of the arroyo, and someone saw him.

"A little kid!"

"What's he doing down there!"

"Come on, kid, you can climb up from there!"

I nearly killed myself climbing this far, you fool, if I *could* climb, don't you think I *would* have? Help me! He cried out again.

"It's not a little boy. He's got a beard—"

"Come on, hold on, we're coming down!"

"There's a wheelchair in the water—"

"He must be a cripple."

There were several voices, some of them women, but it was two strong men who reached him, splashing their feet in the water. They hooked him under the arms and carried him to the top.

"Can you stand up? Are you all right? Can you stand?"

Carpenter strained to squeeze out the word: "No."

The older woman took command. "He's got palsy, as any fool can see. Go back down there and get his wheelchair, Tom, no sense in making him wait till they can get him another one, go on down! It's not that bad down there, the flood isn't here yet!" Her voice was crisp and clear, perfect speech, almost foreign it was so precise. She and the young woman carried him to the truck. It was a big old flatbed truck from the old days, and on its back was a canvas-covered heap of odd shapes. On the canvas Carpenter read the words Sweetwater's Miracle Pageant. Traveling-show people, then, racing for town to get out of the rain, and through some miracle they had heard his call.

"Your poor arms," said the young woman, wiping off grit and sand that had sliced his elbows. "Did you climb that far out of there with just your arms?"

The young men came out of the arroyo muddy and cursing, but they had the wheelchair. They tied it quickly to the back of the truck; one of the men found the computer, too, and took it inside the cab. It was designed to be rugged, and to Carpenter's relief it still worked.

"Thank you," said his mechanical voice.

"I told them I heard something, and they said I was crazy," said the old woman. "You live in Reefrock?"

"Yes," said his voice.

"Amazing what those old machines can still do, even after being dumped there in the rain," said the old woman. "Well, you came close to death, there, but you're all right, it's the best we can ask for. We'll take you to the doctor."

"Just take me home. Please."

So they did, but insisted on helping him bathe and fixing him dinner. The rain was coming down in sheets when they were done. "All I have is a floor," he said, "but you can stay."

"Better than trying to pitch the tents in this." So they stayed the night.

Carpenter's arms ached too badly for him to sleep, even though he was exhausted. He lay awake thinking of the current pulling him, imagining what would have happened to him, how far he might have gone downstream before drowning, where his body might have ended up. Caught in a snag somewhere, dangling on some branch or rock as the water went down and left his slack body to dry in the sun. Far out in the desert somewhere, maybe. Or perhaps the floodwater might have carried him all the way to the Colorado and tumbled him head over heels down the rapids, through the canyons, past the ruins of the old dams, and finally into the Gulf of California. He'd pass through Navaho territory then, and the Hopi Protectorate, and into areas that the Chihuahua claimed and threatened to go to war to keep. He'd see more of the world than he had seen in his life.

I saw more of the world tonight, he thought, than I had ever thought to see. I saw death and how much I feared it.

And he looked into himself, wondering how much he had changed.

Late in the morning, when he finally awoke, the pageant people were gone. They had a show, of course, and had to do some kind of parade to let people know. School would let out early so they could put on the show without having to waste power on lights. There'd be no school this afternoon. But what about his morning classes? There must have been some question when he didn't show up; someone would have called, and if he didn't answer the phone, someone would have come by. Maybe the show people had still been here when they came. The word would have spread through school that he was still alive.

He tried to imagine LaVon and Kippie and Pope hearing that Mr. Machine, Mr. Bug, Mr. Carpenter was still alive. They'd be afraid, of course. Maybe defiant. Maybe they had even confessed. No, not that. LaVon would keep them quiet. Try to think of a way out. Maybe even plan an escape, though finding a place to go that wasn't under Utah authority would be a problem.

What am I doing? Trying to plan how my enemies can escape retribution? I should call the marshals again and tell them what happened. If someone hasn't called them already.

His wheelchair waited by his bed. The show people had shined it up for him, got rid of all the muck. Even straightened the computer mounts and tied the computer on; jury-rigged it, but it would do. Would the motor run, after being under water? He saw that they had even changed batteries and had the old one set aside. They were good people. Not at all what the stories said about show gypsies. Though there was no natural law that people who help cripples can't also seduce all the young girls in the village.

His arms hurt and his left arm was weak and trembly, but he managed to get into the chair. The pain brought back yesterday. I'm alive today, and yet today doesn't feel any different from last week, when I was also alive. Being on the brink of death wasn't enough; the only transformation is to die.

He ate lunch because it was nearly noon. Eldon Finch came by to see him, along with the sheriff. "I'm the new bishop," said Eldon.

"Didn't waste any time," said Carpenter.

"I gotta tell you, Brother Carpenter, things are in a tizzy today. Yesterday, too, of course, what with avenging angels dropping out of the sky and taking away people we all trusted. There's some says you shouldn't've told, and some says you did right, and some ain't sayin' nothin' 'cause they're afraid somethin'll get told on *them*. Ugly times, ugly times, when folks steal from their neighbors."

Sheriff Budd finally spoke up. "Almost as ugly as tryin' to drownd 'em."

The bishop nodded. "'Course you know the reason we come, Sheriff Budd and me, we come to find out who done it."

"Done what?"

"Plunked you down that wash. You aren't gonna tell me you drove that little wheelie chair of yours out there past the fringe. What, was you speedin' so fast you lost control and spun out? Give me peace of heart, Brother Carpenter, give me trust." The bishop and the sheriff both laughed at that. Quite a joke.

Now's the time, thought Carpenter. Name the names. The motive will be clear, justice will be done. They put you through the worst hell of your life, they made you cry out for help, they taught you the taste of death. Now even things up.

But he didn't key their names into the computer. He thought of Kippie's mother crying at the door. When the crying stopped, there'd be years ahead. They were a long way from proving out their land. Kippie was through with school, he'd never go on, never get out. The adult burden was on those boys now, years too young. Should their families suffer even more, with another generation gone to prison? Carpenter had nothing to gain, and many who were guiltless stood to lose too much.

"Brother Carpenter," said Sheriff Budd. "Who was it?"

He keyed in his answer. "I didn't get a look at them."

"Their voices, didn't you know them?"

"No."

The bishop looked steadily at him. "They tried to kill you, Brother Carpenter. That's no joke. You like to died, if those show people hadn't happened by. And I have my own ideas who it was, seein' who had reason to hate you unto death yesterday."

"As you said. A lot of people think an outsider like me should have kept his nose out of Reefrock's business."

The bishop frowned at him. "You scared they'll try again?"

"No."

"Nothin' I can do," said the sheriff. "I think you're a damn fool, Brother Carpenter, but nothin' I can do if you don't even care."

"Thanks for coming by."

He didn't go to church Sunday. But on Monday he went to school, same time as usual. And there were LaVon and Kippie and Pope, right in their places. But not the same as usual. The wisecracks were over. When he called on them, they answered if they could and didn't if they couldn't. When he looked at them, they looked away.

He didn't know if it was shame or fear that he might someday tell; he didn't care. The mark was on them. They would marry someday, go out into even newer lands just behind the ever-advancing fringe, have babies, work until their bodies were exhausted, and then drop into a grave. But they'd remember that one day they had left a cripple to die. He had no idea what it would mean to them, but they would remember.

Within a few weeks LaVon and Kippie were out of school; with their fathers gone, there was too much fieldwork and school was a luxury their families couldn't afford for them. Pope had an older brother still at home, so he stayed out the year.

One time Pope almost talked to him. It was a windy day that spattered sand against the classroom window, and the storm coming out of the south looked to be a nasty one. When class was over, most of the kids ducked their heads and rushed outside, hurrying to get home before the downpour began. A few stayed, though, to talk with Carpenter about this and that. When the last one left, Carpenter saw that Pope was still there. His pencil was hovering over a piece of paper. He looked up at Carpenter, then set the pencil down, picked up his books, started for the door. He paused for a moment with his hand on the doorknob. Carpenter waited for him to speak. But the boy only opened the door and went on out.

Carpenter rolled over to the door and watched him as he walked away. The wind caught at his jacket. Like a kite, thought Carpenter, it's lifting him along.

But it wasn't true. The boy didn't rise and fly. And now Carpenter saw the wind like a current down the village street, sweeping Pope away. All the bodies in the world, caught in that same current, that same wind, blown down the same rivers, the same streets, and finally coming to rest on some snag, through some door, in some grave, God knows where or why.